Caught in the Act

 100% recycled paper

Caught in the Act

GEMMA FOX

ISIS
LARGE PRINT
Oxford

First published in Great Britain 2005
by
HarperCollins*Publishers*

Published in Large Print 2006 by ISIS Publishing Ltd.,
7 Centremead, Osney Mead, Oxford OX2 0ES
by arrangement with
HarperCollins*Publishers* Ltd.

British Library Cataloguing in Publication Data
Fox, Gemma
    Caught in the act.– Large print ed.
    1. First loves – Fiction
    2. Class
    3. Large type books
    I. Title
    8 3.9'2 [F]

ISBN 0–7531–7581–9 (hb)
ISBN 978–0–7531–7582–8 (pb)

Printed and bound in Great Britain by
T. J. International Ltd., Padstow, Cornwall

Dedicated with lots of love and thanks to
my editor, Susan Opie at Harper Collins,
my agent, Maggie Phillips at Ed Victor,
but most of all to my family and friends and the
large wrinkly blonde mongrel who thinks he's
still small enough to get under my desk.

CHAPTER
ONE

Carol Hastings lost her virginity on 7 July to Macbeth, Lord of Glamis, Thane of Cawdor and King thereafter. The photographic evidence was there in the downstairs toilet, alongside her wedding certificate and a bad photocopy of her decree absolute; the original being far too valuable to put on public display.

Even now, after all these years, Carol woke up some dark nights in a cold sweat, dreaming that she was still married and in a flurry of panic would run downstairs to check. Not that Carol had married Macbeth, it was just that sometimes it felt like it.

The photograph of Carol and Macbeth seemed as if it had been taken a very long time ago. It was like looking at another life, someone else's life, maybe a good friend's daughter who had grown up and moved away.

It was years since Carol had really studied the picture, rather than just passed over it in a photographic stock-take of what was hanging on the walls. It was an arty black-and-white eight-by-ten; not that it showed the actual deflowering, obviously, but a kind of giddy post-coital group hug on the last day of the Belvedere High School drama tour.

They had just finished the final matinée performance; Carol peered at Macbeth and smiled. Gareth Howard, for ever eighteen, with broad shoulders, big blue eyes and dark floppy hair, all dressed up in his tinfoil crown and cloak. He stood behind Carol, one large hand resting on her shoulder in a very patriarchal gesture for someone whose voice had barely broken, apparently the master of all he surveyed.

Her smile broadened into a grin; it wasn't that many years ago since her stomach fluttered whenever she thought about him. Skulking behind the fly-blown glass, Gareth still looked smug and self-satisfied.

Carol sighed and straightened up. Her trip down memory lane, taken while sitting on the downstairs toilet, had been prompted by a Sunday morning email:

Hi Carol, how are you? I saw that you'd got your profile posted on Oldschooltie.com and wonder if you remembered me? Once upon a time a long time ago in a land far far away I used to be Diana Brown. And if you *have* forgotten then all those things they said about the chemicals in the drinking water at school were most probably true. I still think about the good old days from time to time, especially now that my own kids are at high school . . . although I don't think in terms of *old* . . . obviously. Here's my mobile number: Use it some time!

Diana Brown — the girl who had taken on Carol's wart and triumphed.

2

In the photograph, Diana was hunched over a cauldron along with her fellow witches, Netty Davies and Jan Smith. While Carol, a.k.a. Lady Macbeth, was centre stage, wearing way too much eyeliner and a big grin totally at odds with the whole crazed suicidal psycho-bitch from hell that had been popular with their director that year. Carol was dressed in a purple wool caftan and old velvet door-curtain ensemble, cunningly crafted with silver braid, half a packet of fruit gums and a bottle of Copydex into the robes of a queen. She smiled; like she knew what a man-hating power-crazed psychopath-bitch from hell was back in those days.

Carol really had set her heart on being one of the hags, working on the premise that a bad hair day and acne could be a real advantage on Shakespeare's blasted heath. She'd even tried the wart on to get a feel for the part of Witch One at the lunchtime read-through. But Miss Haze and Mr Bearman — who organised the group tour — briskly agreed she was more than capable of doing Lady Macbeth justice and that false modesty was an unattractive trait.

There was a subtext, barely concealed: if Carol didn't take the part then Fiona Templeton, whose father was chairman of the school governors and whose mother helped out with needlework, would get it, and everyone knew what that meant. Fiona had snatched the part of Juliet from a very evenly matched field the previous summer.

It had been hell. The pressure, the strain, the responsibility, what with Fiona's nerves and her hayfever and her eczema and allergies and her delicate constitution, she had needed a little liedown before, after and sometimes during every performance. Fiona's mother had had to come on tour with them, obviously, to keep an eye on their fragile starlet, cramping everyone's style. Mrs Templeton prowled the wings like some terrible floral wraith, clutching a damp hanky, various inhalers and smelling salts, whispering words of encouragement, making sure that everyone knew what a brave little kitten Fiona truly was, even as she was elbowing her way to the front for another curtain call.

There was no contest. "OK, I'll do it," said Carol weakly, falling on the sword on behalf of the rest of the troupe, while shuffling the pages of photocopied script back into a heap.

There had been a muted cheer from the less regal of *hoi polloi* at the back of the hall, which just about drowned out Fiona's frantic disappointed wheezing and sobbing.

Some are born great, some have greatness thrust upon them. Miss Haze wrapped the rubber wart in a hankie and handed Carol a plastic dagger.

The reviews had been kind; Carol had still got them in a drawer somewhere. "Carol Hastings as Macbeth's ill-fated queen reached fearlessly for the dramatic high notes" — the *Herald*. "With a maturity far beyond her years Carol Hastings' Lady Macbeth made a gallant effort to sustain the darker phrases of the Scottish play without lapsing into untrammelled melodrama." Praise indeed from a man who, when not the drama critic, covered cattle auctions and the stock car racing.

4

Nostalgia is not what it used to be. Carol hung the photo back on the wall and got to her feet.

It did seem impossible, though, that she had lost touch with Diana. God, they used to be joined at the hip. Last time they'd spoken, Diana had just finished college and was off doing VSO in Africa or — something. Carol felt a horrible twinge of guilt. Where had the time gone?

"Mum, are you OK in there?"

The toilet door was ajar; Carol had been sitting fully clothed on the lavatory in the middle of the day staring blankly at a wall for the best part of fifteen minutes. She could see it might make Jake think maybe something wasn't quite right.

"I'm fine, honey. I was just thinking."

"Right," he said. He didn't sound wholly convinced. "Raf said do you want him to open the wine?" Carol could hear the anxiety in her son's voice. After all, she was heading for forty. Anything might have happened. "And he said are you going to do the salad, and will you marry him?"

Carol turned slowly; there was really no point having those great big blue-green eyes-like-a-cat-on-a-moonlit-night unless you knew how to use them. "He knows the answer to all of those questions."

Jake, coming up for fourteen and just beginning to get a grip on the complicated wiring of adulthood, nodded. "Yes, yes, and no, not over the flayed bodies of myself, my infant children and the family pets?"

Carol nodded proudly. "Well done."

"In which case, Raf said, would you consider giving in gracefully and living in sin instead?"

Carol turned the stare up to stun. "When it comes to sin, Jake, I can think of so many better ways to do it than washing underpants and picking up other people's dirty socks."

"And if you do want to do that kind of thing, you've always got me and Ollie, haven't you?"

She nodded. "Exactly."

"Do you want him to start cooking?"

"Did he happen to mention what time he was going home?"

Rafael O'Connell leaned in around the door to the utility room and handed her a glass of wine. It was German, ice cool and far too sweet to be considered grown up. He was good-looking in a lived-in way, forty-two, and wearing a wipe-down apron with a black bra, stockings and suspenders printed on the front of it, which the boys had given him for his last birthday. He was Irish, ice cool and far too sweet to be considered grown up.

"I was hoping you'd ask me to stay the night," he said, attempting to sound hurt and much put upon while pushing a mop of dark brown wavy hair back off his forehead.

Carol smiled, resisting the effects that his brogue had on her even after three years. "It's Sunday, Raf. You know the rules; on Sundays you go home."

"I could make an exception."

"Well, I can't. You're a weekend thing. You should know that by now. Friday to Sunday and then —" still smiling, she made a dismissive sweeping gesture with her hand — "home."

"You'll miss me when I'm gone," he grumbled, backing off into the kitchen, mugging deep and bitter rejection.

Jake looked at Carol and shook his head. "You're really cruel to him. What sort of example are you setting? I'm at a very impressionable age."

"So's Raf. He knows I don't mean it. And besides, he is the kind of man who enjoys a challenge."

Jake pulled a face. He had started dating and Carol suspected he was using her and Raf as an instructional video.

"You should go and talk to him about it," Carol said, waving the wineglass in the general direction of the kitchen.

"I already have. He said he'd give me twenty quid if I could get you to let him stay tonight."

Carol sighed. "That is not what real grown-ups are supposed to do, Jake — it's probably illegal, and definitely immoral. Pass me that big blue glass bowl, will you?"

Jake did as he was asked.

She pulled a large bag of mixed salad out of the bottom of the fridge. It was a bit of a devil's deal really. Long summer Sundays, Mr O'Connell and the boys knocked themselves out building the world's most bizarre kebabs, stuffing chicken breasts with God alone knows what, and baking bananas and apple slices in tinfoil with brown sugar and brandy while she opened a big tub of potato salad, threw a bag of mixed baby leaves into a bowl and chucked half a bottle of shop-bought dressing over it.

Setting the bowl down for a moment, Carol stepped back into the loo and brought the photo of the drama group out into the sunlight. A younger, altogether-less-cynical Carol stared back up at her, all open-faced enthusiasm and too much makeup. What would she have done if she'd known all the things that were coming her way? Even though she was smiling, Carol felt her eyes prickling with tears. The time had gone so quickly. It didn't seem fair.

She picked up the phone and tapped in Diana's mobile number. Half a dozen rings later a bright breezy voice said, "Hello?"

"Hi, is that Diana Brown?"

There was a split-second pause and then a raucous laugh. "Carol? Is that you?"

"Certainly is. It was great to get your email. I was just looking at a photo of us when we did *Macbeth* and thought that if someone doesn't ring soon we'll all be dead."

Diana groaned. "The way I feel today that would be a blessing. It's so nice to hear your voice. I'm really glad you rang. I daren't think about how long it's been since we last spoke. Was it at someone's wedding?" Diana sounded genuinely pleased. "You sound really grown up."

Carol laughed. "You too, but don't be fooled — it's a very thin disguise."

Through the kitchen window she watched Raf laying out various offerings to the fire gods while the boys unfolded the garden chairs and opened up the parasol.

"I thought I'd give you a quick ring to make contact, really. How are you?" asked Carol, a little self-consciously; what did they talk about now? How long *was* it since they had spoken?

"I'm fine, happy, busy. We're living in the Midlands — I don't know if you knew but I married a vicar."

Carol felt her heart sinking. It was worse than she thought. "Really?" she said. "You married him? God, bloody hell — oh damn, bugger — I'm so sorry. Er . . ."

At which point Diana giggled furiously. Carol would have recognised the sound anywhere and felt the tension in her stomach ease.

"It's not that bad, really," Diana replied. "As long as you don't mind working Christmas and Easter and every weekend. How have you been, anyway? I've often thought about you."

"How long have you got?" Carol said wryly.

"Well, unfortunately at the moment about two minutes — which is a real shame because I'd really like the chance to catch up. I'm helping out at the parish luncheon club today and we're in the eye of the storm between the roast beef and apple crumble. Would you mind if I rang you back later?"

"Not at all; I'm in all day."

"It's so good to hear you. One thing, just quickly — my son is coming down your way to scout camp at half term and, well, maybe we could get together?"

Carol smiled. "Sure. I was just thinking how awful it was that we'd lost touch. So yes, of course. Do you know when it is?"

Out in the garden the first of the kebabs committed ritual suicide, dropping through the grill in a wild flurry of wood ash and much swearing.

"Hang on, I've got to go. The dessert stampede just started," said Diana. "I'll ring you back."

"I'll look forward to it."

Diana rang around nine, when Raf had left and the day was slowing down. Carol took the phone and a glass of wine out into the garden.

"I can't imagine you married to a vicar, Di. Are you happy?"

"What on earth is that supposed to mean?" Diana said, sounding deeply amused. "Of course I'm not happy. I've been married donkeys years — I've forgotten what happy means."

"You don't seem the type, or at least you didn't used to be. What happened? Wouldn't you be better off with a nice chartered accountant, or a plumber? What about the sex, drugs and rock and roll?"

There was a moment's pause and then Diana said, "Hedley and I try not to let them interfere with evensong."

"Oh, clever," laughed Carol. "I always thought you'd end up with Chris Morrison."

She heard Diana catch her breath. "My goodness. You know I'd forgotten all about Chris. Chris

10

Morrison? I wonder what he's doing now. How on earth could I forget Chris?"

"He's on Oldschooltie — there's a photo," said Carol, taking another sip of wine. "He's done really well for himself, and he looks like George Clooney."

"No?" Diana said incredulously.

Carol giggled. "No, actually he looks more like George Formby but he sounds really nice on his profile. He lives in Yorkshire now, I think — I'm amazed you didn't look *him* up."

"I only joined a couple of weeks ago. I see the names and it brings back all sorts of memories. I keep wondering what they're all doing now, what do they look like, who they ended up with."

"Well, you ended up with a vicar called Hedley."

"You make it sound terrible; he's a lovely guy. I met him when we were at university. I told you about him. It's not like I don't know all about his dirty linen. He may be a living saint to our flower ladies but to me he is still the guy who climbed the fire escape into my bedroom in the early hours, hellbent on a legover, and threw up all over my bed instead."

"Whoever said romance was dead?"

"It helps me keep him in perspective. So, how do you feel about a flying visit?"

"It would be great, but does it have to be flying? You could come for lunch, the whole day — stay over if you like. That way we can have a drink and it'll give us plenty of time to catch up. I'm sure the boys wouldn't mind your son bunking down with them."

Diana made a hesitant little noise. "It's very kind but —" she began

Carol smiled. "If you're being polite, don't be — if you don't want to stay that's fine but if you do, it would be lovely. You haven't got to make your mind up now. Think about it."

"I don't want to put you to any trouble."

"You won't be, there's a spare room, and if we haven't got anything to say, or we hate the sight of each other, you can always go home early."

"OK, great. Have you got a diary handy?"

Carol took a quick look round the kitchen. It was tidy, there was food in the oven, salad in the fridge, dessert defrosting on the draining board and Raf had said he'd come round for supper. So far so good. Carol looked in the mirror. Some days it still struck her as odd, seeing a grown-up looking back. She tugged her hair into shape, before taking another look at the clock. Diana had said they would arrive around twelve. It was almost that now. Just how many ways were there to worry?

What had been the state of play when they last met? What if Diana had changed — come out, gone in, gone weird, gone mad, gone sensible. Grown up? Carol was surprised to realise just how nervous she felt. What it boiled down to was, what if their friendship had been a passing thing? What if now they were all grown up they had nothing in common except memories and polite conversation? And how much would that colour their notion of the past?

From outside came the sound of wheels over gravel. Taking a deep breath, Carol opened the back door and headed towards the battered Volvo estate now parked under the lilacs.

"Diana?"

As soon as she saw her, Diana practically leaped out of the car.

Carol would have known her anywhere. "My God, you look amazing," Carol said, holding her at arm's length. "How come you haven't got any wrinkles?"

"What can I tell you? Healthy living and a clean conscience," Diana said, doing a little mock twirl.

"That'll be the day. Did you manage to find us OK?"

"Uh-huh. Your directions were really good — so some things have changed for the better. It's really great to see you." Diana, grinning, pulled her close and hugged her tight, all the while watched over by her son, who was sitting in the back of the car, surrounded by great piles of camping gear.

He looked about twelve, and as he clambered out of the car he appeared to be made entirely of elbows, knees and teeth. Carol guessed he was probably the spitting image of his father, all wild, wiry, hamster-coloured hair and pale creamy skin. Unfortunately she couldn't remember his name.

"This is Dylan," said Diana, waving him closer and digging Carol out of a hole.

The boy solemnly held out his hand. "Pleased to meet you," he said in a high-pitched voice totally at odds with the fact that he had to be at least six foot tall.

"Nice to meet you too. My boys are upstairs. Come on in and I'll introduce you. I hope you're hungry," Carol said. "We've got loads to eat. Do you want to bring your stuff in?"

Dylan considered for a few moments and then said, "Probably not. We got soaked; everything smells disgusting."

Carol nodded. "OK — well, we can find you some things if you're stuck." Although probably not trousers, she thought ruefully.

"So come on then," said Diana, grabbing a huge canvas bag and locking the car. "Let's hear it all. All the goss, all the history, every last bit of juicy scandal . . ."

Carol laughed. "You haven't changed, have you?"

Diana shook her head. "You'd better believe it," she said, following Carol inside.

"I thought you'd be all sweetness and light."

"You've got a very naïve view of life as a vicar's wife. I thought I was bad enough."

"I wouldn't say you've been anywhere near bad enough, by the looks of you," Carol said cheerfully. "I bought champagne — or would you rather have tea?"

Diana lifted an eyebrow. "Both. Oh, while we're on the subject of really bad, I've brought all the old school photos with me. I think my mum bought every single one they ever took." She put the canvas bag down on the table and started ferreting around in it. "Some of them are truly dire —"

"If I see one New Romantics haircut or anything involving spray-on glitter or shoulder pads, you're out of here."

"See, I told you I'm not all good — appearances can be deceptive," said Diana, producing the albums with a triumphant grin, and then she paused and looked around the cosy kitchen. "Gosh, it's lovely in here. I'm so hungry, and that smells wonderful."

Carol looked at her. "Gosh?"

Diana waved the word away. "Sorry, too many years helping with Brownies. Took me God knows how long to wean myself of the f-word — and various b-words once Hedley was ordained — which leaves me with things like, oh gosh and, well goodness me. I only use oh God when I'm out."

"Bloody hell, not much of a choice, is it?"

Diana shrugged as Carol took the champagne out of the fridge. "You have to be philosophical about it. It could be worse — we could be staunch tee-total Methodists."

It felt as if they had never been apart. Carol took Dylan upstairs to meet the mob, and then thumbed the cork out of the bottle of champagne and poured it while Diana sat at the table. Dressed in a cream blouse, smart navy-blue skirt and jacket ensemble, sensible shoes and a haircut that made her look like a cross between a social worker and — well — a vicar's wife, really, Diana looked to Carol as if she was dressing up in her mum's clothes, or maybe an adult version of their old school uniform.

She topped up Diana's glass with champagne and lifted it in a toast. "Here's to old friends."

Diana tapped the side of the glass with her own. "Less of the old," she growled.

"I hadn't realised how much I've missed you."

"I was just thinking the same on the way here. Tell me about you and what you've been up to."

"No, first of all tell me what it's like being married to a vicar — every year I've seen it on the Christmas cards and thought who in God's name called your husband Hedley."

"I was hoping we were going to talk about you first," Diana protested.

"Really?" Carol feigned innocence until Diana shrugged and conceded defeat.

"OK, but it is your turn next. Hedley's a family name — his great-great-granddad or someone started it. It's been passed down from generation to generation to the first-born, which has been a boy since the dawn of time the way Hedley tells it — but fortunately, thank God, our first baby turned out to be a girl."

"Oh, I remember," said Carol, sliding the plates onto the table. "You sent me a card. Pink patchwork flopsy bunnies in a basket."

Diana nodded. "That's right. By the time we got to number four I couldn't afford the bloody stamps, let alone find time to write the cards. Anyway, we called our eldest Abigail and then after that we had Lucy and Harriet. So when Dylan came along, as we had circumnavigated the whole first-born son thing, we agreed to give him Hedley as a second name. Although I think Hedley's dad was a little disappointed."

"Who came up with Dylan, then?"

Diana raised her eyebrows, but before she could reply Carol jumped in, "It had to be Hedley — don't tell me he was a *Magic Roundabout* fan?" almost choking with laughter on her drink.

Diana's expression confirmed what Carol already knew. "Dylan Thomas? — Not Bob Dylan?"

"You are still a complete and utter cow, aren't you?" Diana said after a few seconds. "Yes, of course it was Hedley." She lowered her voice although the boys were upstairs playing on the computer and well out of earshot. "You get used to it after a while — and it could have been worse: his first choice was Ethelred."

"No?" Carol stared at her open-mouthed. "You've got to be joking?"

Diana waved Carol's expression away. "Do I look like the kind of woman who would joke about something like Ethelred? What would you have done?"

"Left him," hissed Carol.

Diana grinned and shook her head.

"Grabbed 'Dylan' with both hands?"

Two hours, a really good lunch and a bottle of champagne later they were still at the table, sitting amongst the debris. The boys had gone back upstairs and Carol had broken out a bottle of Baileys.

". . . And the other thing is I've always wanted to ask a vicar — and you're as close as I'm likely to get — did God call him? You know, like the whole voices in the head, road to Damascus thing."

Diana shrugged as she opened the first of the stack of photo albums. "Oh, bloody hell I don't know."

"I see your swearing is coming on nicely. So, go on then — was Hedley called?"

Diana looked her over. "You know, you haven't changed at all, have you?" she said, helping herself to a handful of After Eight mints. "I've genuinely got no idea. You can ask Hedley, if you like. He's very keen to meet you and the boys."

"If I were married to him I would have had to have asked him by now."

Diana shook her head. "I'm not sure I really want to know. Hedley is so rational about everything else. How would you feel if the man in your life was doing something because the voices in his head had told him to do it?"

Carol considered the idea and then nodded. "Fair point." She turned the conversation. "I can't get over how little you've changed."

"You still look the same too. OK maybe a bit wrinklier, but not much — the good thing about getting older is that your eyesight goes too."

"I don't feel any different," said Carol, topping up their glasses. "We just know more. Did you go into teaching? I feel kind of embarrassed that I don't remember any of this stuff — how did we drift so far apart?"

Diana sighed. "I know exactly what you mean. The time goes so quickly. Other things come and fill the gap. I taught till I had the kids and then I went back part time when Dylan started school. I don't think I could handle full time — now, how about you?"

"How long have you got?" said Carol, taking a pull on her drink — a gesture that would have looked altogether tougher and more hard bitten and worldly if the glass didn't have a cocktail umbrella in it and she wasn't sipping it through an extra thick milkshake straw.

"Well, we've got half a bottle of Baileys left — do you think that is going to be enough?"

Carol, still sucking, shrugged. "Once that's done all I've got left is a bottle of advocaat until Raf shows up. I suppose I could always try and make us a Snowball. Do you remember when Netty Davies made those ones with vodka as well as brandy? God, I don't think I've ever been so drunk in my life. Maybe I should try and make a couple for old times' sake?"

"I told Hedley that you were a bad influence."

"For God's sake, a bottle of champagne and two glasses of Baileys is hardly bad. Now come on, let me have a look at the photos," she said, settling herself down so that they were side by side.

Diana held the album closed, tight to her chest. "No, not yet. I want to hear all about what you've been doing and who you've been doing it with." She gazed around, as if she might be able to encompass the whole of Carol's life with a look. "So tell me what you've been up to? And who's Raf?"

"I haven't been up to anything wildly exciting," said Carol dismissively, trying to make a grab for the album, but Diana was way too quick for her.

"OK, so you're still nosy but defensive. How about we start with the easy questions? What do you do? Do you work?"

"Good God, yes, I've got my own company. We design, build and maintain gardens. They did a double-page spread on us in the *Mail on Sunday* last year."

"See, that didn't hurt, now did it? Garden design? Very trendy," said Diana appreciatively, her speech very slightly slurred now.

"Not when I first started doing it, it wasn't, and we're not really at the trendy end of the market. I've got commercial greenhouses and a team of gardeners who do maintenance for the council now that the work is all out to tender. We do some private gardens, but mostly it's lots of corporate stuff. It's — er . . ."

"Trendy?"

Carol laughed. "I was going to say bloody hard work but I suppose trendy will cover some of it, if you insist. And I love it."

"You're not telling me you do the digging with those fingernails?"

Carol looked at her hands. "I did once upon a time and I still can. I just wear gloves. The practical side isn't exactly rocket science, just good old-fashioned hard work but it's great and I love the creative side of it — seeing the projects come together and get more beautiful over time. I'll show you the garden later — it's my other baby. It wasn't quite where I saw myself ending up, but then again how many of us *do* do what we planned? I wanted to do something creative but I didn't really know what." Carol held up her hands in a gesture of resignation. "Life has a way of taking you out on your blind side."

"Married, are you?

"I'll give you your due, Diana, straight to the heart of the matter, no messing," said Carol, miming an arrow flight.

"Years of practice, a class of twenty-nine under-fives demands nerves of steel and a single-mindedness you can only dream of. So, are you married? You *were* married, weren't you?"

"Once upon a time, in a universe far far away."

Diana's eyes narrowed thoughtfully. "So you're not married to Raf? You know, this is so bad. At one time we used to know what the other one was thinking; can you remember we used to end up buying the same things?"

"Uh-huh," Carol laughed. "Even when we didn't go shopping together."

"Remember when we turned up at the fifth-form school disco —"

"Oh God, yes — in those dresses. The blue ones with ribbons?"

"The same dresses."

"And those awful sandals — the dress I could understand but the shoes . . . Bloody hell."

They laughed and then there was a moment's pause, a second of reflection when Carol sensed how much had happened since the blue dresses with ribbons and how much they had missed of each other's life.

"Weren't you married to — what was his name? I can't remember why I didn't come to your wedding," said Diana.

"Probably because I didn't invite you — or anyone else, come to that. We got the cleaner and a woman working in the office to be witnesses. I was very pregnant and —"

"I kept thinking that I really ought to ring when whatshisname didn't feature on the Christmas cards any more," Diana interrupted, her face folded into a concertina of concentration; but then Diana had always been a world-famous face puller. It was nice to see that marrying a vicar hadn't got in the way of her gurning. "Oh, come on, you're enjoying this," she said crossly. "What the hell *was* his name? I'm trying hard over here; help me out."

"What, when it's so much fun seeing you struggle? Let me have a look at the photos while you're thinking about it."

Diana snatched the album back. "Jack," she said with glee. "I'm right, aren't I?"

"Yes. Very good. Now give them here, like a good girl."

Diana held the photos away from her. She always had had bloody long arms. It was very tempting to jump on her, at which point Carol had to remind herself that they weren't thirteen any more.

"Jack French. I remember now — and he was a gardener too? Right?" said Diana with delight.

Carol slumped back onto the chair, admitting defeat, and nodded. "Occasionally, when he wasn't trying to drink himself to death, screw the YTS girls or lie about how much money we owed. Fortunately, I'm divorced now. By contrast, life since Jack is wonderful, peaceful — pure bliss." Her voice lifted to emphasise the sheer joy of it.

Diana was watching her face. "And did God call you — you know, like the whole voices in the head, road to Damascus thing?"

Carol grinned; Diana was still sharp as glass.

"You still got the wart?"

Diana nodded vigorously. "Of course I've got the wart, it goes without saying. Actually I was thinking about bringing it with me. It's in my earring box, preserved for posterity in cling film and talc."

"Maybe we ought to get something a little more salubrious for it. A reliquary; you should be up on that kind of stuff: an ornate ebony casket for the toenail of St Kevin the Just."

"Wrong mob; we're Low Church, less incense and stained glass, more jumble sales and cheery gatherings around the kitchen table, and besides, my jewellery box *is* salubrious. Hedley gave it to me as a wedding present. It's rosewood, I think. Belonged to his mother." There was a long slow silence and then Diana said, her expression softening, "You know, it's so good to see you again. I thought you might have gone and grown up. It's been hard maintaining the whole born-to-boogie ethos all on your own."

Carol snorted. "Born to boogie? When were either of us ever born to boogie, Di? You're a vicar's wife, for God's sake."

Diana laughed and finally handed Carol the photo album. "But I wasn't always a vicar's wife, was I?"

"No, I suppose not. Do you still play cards?"

Diana reddened. "Not for money. Hedley asked me to stop after I cleaned up at his preordination party."

Carol giggled. "Nine-card brag, poker. It was like going around with the Maverick. I remember you used to cut a deck with one hand."

"Oh, I can still do that," Diana said casually. "I've won enough matches at our annual Christmas whist drive to burn down half Europe."

Carol smiled. "OK, well maybe things aren't as bad as they look." She opened the first album.

The photograph was a long shot of the entire school taken the first year that she and Diana had gone up from primary school, when they had first found each other and Netty and Jan — three witches and Lady Macbeth in waiting. The picture was taken on the neatly manicured lawn outside the main school entrance, by the pond. Unexpectedly Carol found a lump in her throat. Bloody hell, was this what happened when you got old? Neat nostalgia.

She swallowed down hard as Diana said, "I got them out of the loft when I joined Oldschooltie — just for old times' sake. I wonder how everyone is now."

"Look at these," said Carol, peering at the rows of faces. "God, I haven't thought about her — oh, look, Mrs Devine, the PE teacher — and Mr Bailey."

"I was thinking on the drive over here — it would be great to see everyone again. What about if we tried to organise a reunion? I mean how hard can it be? People do it all the time. It would be great."

Carol, halfway through a mouthful of Baileys, spluttered. "Are you sure great's the word you're looking for, Diana? I can understand what you mean but it would be loads of work and not everyone grew up to be a vicar, you know. What about Sandy Lewis? You remember?"

"Who could forget?"

"Potential axe-murdering psychopath if ever I met one. Do you remember when he burned the cricket pavilion down? Caught red-handed, petrol can, matches, swore blind he hadn't done it."

"He probably won't come. I doubt they can get Oldschooltie.com in Broadmoor; and besides, he's an extreme example and you know it."

"How about Harry Longman? Put away for fraud? Kate Lynwood, shoplifting and passing dud cheques . . ." She pointed out the faces in the picture.

"All right — don't be so negative, so not everyone turned out a saint," said Diana, "but they're not all nutters and conmen either. I was thinking school reunion here, not Britain's most wanted. Once I started seeing all those names on the register at Oldschooltie curiosity got the better of me. And then I fished out the photos — and since then I keep wondering what they're all up to, what they look like, how they're all doing."

"You always were so nosy," Carol said. "Don't mind me. Actually, it does sound like a nice idea. What had you got in mind? Invite people from our year?"

Diana pulled a thinking face. "I don't know. I've only really just thought about it. We could start there. Would you pitch in?"

"Pitch in?" said Carol. "I smell an ambush. And what is this 'pitch in', Di, Enid Blyton's Famous Five?"

"It is going to be a lot of work and I don't really fancy doing it on my own. We could both contact people and stuff."

Carol nodded. "OK."

"What about if we tried to get the drama group back together?"

"The drama group?" said Carol in amazement.

"Uh-huh, why not? It's a great idea. The last tour was so good. How about one last time with feeling, do something, maybe a read-through and invite the rest of the class, too. It'll be twenty years ago this July."

"A read-through of what?" Carol asked incredulously.

"Well, *Macbeth* would seem the natural choice."

"You can't be serious. A reunion is going to be tough enough. I was thinking more about where we'd hold it."

Diana looked affronted. "We wouldn't have to learn it or anything, just do a read-through of the highlights. You know, witches, murder, madness, suicide, trees moving, ghost, Macduff, the end — it'd be great. We could invite everyone else who was interested from school to come along and watch us." Diana paused, waiting until Carol looked up. "I'm sure Gareth will be there."

"Sorry?" Carol felt a little rush of heat and then cursed herself for being so silly.

"Gareth."

"What do you mean, *Gareth*?"

"Oh, come on. Don't play the innocent with me. Gareth Howard, boy wonder. *The* Gareth Howard. He's on the website, which really took me by surprise. He always used to be so cool, I couldn't imagine him being on there at all, to be honest. But anyway, I emailed him and he mailed back and he suggested we chat, so I sent him my number and he rang me back more or less straight away." Diana paused for effect. "And the first thing he wanted to know was how you were."

"Oh right," Carol snorted, but even so she felt her jaw drop and her stomach do that odd little flipping thing that stomachs do; twenty years on and the first question on Gareth Howard's lips was, how was Carol? "You're pulling my leg."

"I'm telling you the truth; I'm a vicar's wife, for God's sake. He sounded really disappointed when I said we hadn't seen each other for years."

Carol stared at her. "You're making this up."

Slowly Diana shook her head. "Cross my heart," she mimed.

"It's ridiculous," Carol said, blushing furiously and then she flicked quickly on to the next page of the album, barely registering the pictures as the heat rushed through her, driven by a pulse set to boil. Gareth Howard, of all people. How many times had she and Diana run and rerun and replayed things he'd said, picking over the bones to try to work out what every syllable, every last nuance and gesture had meant. She had spent more time trying to translate Gareth Howard than she spent on the whole of her French O level.

Wasn't it true that Carol had fancied him for years before the tour, that she had fantasised about him long after she got married? Hadn't she loved him just a little;

what if he had loved her a lot? Carol shivered and tried very hard to regain her composure.

"A reunion sounds like a great idea but how the hell are we going to get everyone together? How would we find them all, for a start?" Carol said as evenly as she could manage, also realising that she had just said "we".

"Oldschooltie — I'm sure that everyone on there is probably still in touch with one or two others, and maybe the School will help if I contact them. I think we should try for the drama group first and then if that doesn't work just go for a straight reunion. I don't know if you've looked lately but there are an awful lot of our old class on there."

"It sounds like a brilliant if slightly crazed idea," Carol said cautiously.

"But?" said Diana

"But nothing. I was just wondering how many people would actually want to come. Chances are that they're all spread halfway round the globe by now. Have you thought about where we could hold it? A restaurant or a hotel?"

Diana hesitated for a few moments and then said gleefully, "Actually I've got a brilliant idea. I don't know if it'll come off —"

"I'm so glad you clung to your natural modesty."

Diana pulled another of her famous faces. "What about if we tried for a weekend — as you said, people could have miles to drive."

"And?"

"And there is this fantastic old country house I know in Oxfordshire. It's used as a Christian retreat normally, but I'm sure they could find us some space if we asked nicely and it would be peanuts to hire for a couple of days. They've got loads of room and this really nice hall with a stage and everything."

Carol refilled their glasses and then said with a wry smile, "So, Svengali, what else have you got in mind? World domination? Spit it out; there is just bound to be more."

Diana had the bit between her teeth now. "How about — and this is in an ideal world, if we can get the hall — the drama group arrives Friday, everyone rehearses Saturday and then we put the performance on, on Sunday afternoon followed by — I don't — maybe a traditional English tea for everyone. They could bring their families. This place is in its own grounds; the garden is big enough to lose half Wembley in, and it is a lovely house."

"Bloody hell. We've come a long way from a few school photos and Oldschooltie."

"Oh, come on. If we don't try it we'll never know, will we?" Diana said briskly.

"God, I bet you run a mean jumble sale."

Diana refilled her glass. "You better believe it."

CHAPTER
TWO

"Are you sure that you really don't mind doing this?" Carol stood near the front door. Her suitcase was over by the hall stand, she was just about ready to leave, and was only too aware of what a stupid question it was. What on earth would she do if Raf turned round and said yes?

"I've already told you a dozen times, it's fine. Besides, you're always telling me that I'm a Friday-to-Sunday thing. Today's Friday, I know my place." Raf grinned at her grimace and waved her away. "Relax, go, have a good time and don't look so worried. We'll be all right. I've got the list. I know what to water, who to feed and what to turn off. You're OK about the directions? You know where you're going? You've got everything you need?"

Carol patted her jacket theatrically. "Uh-huh, I think so — let me see: dagger, eyeliner, bad attitude — just about wraps it up. I'm just going to go and say goodbye to the boys and then I'll be off. Oh, and did I ever mention, don't fuss?" she added, acting playfully grumpy, touched that he cared whilst all the while struggling to suppress the feeling that she was sloping off for a dirty weekend.

She glanced in the hall mirror and tugged her hair into shape. She'd had it cut and coloured. It looked great. She looked great.

So, OK, Gareth Howard was going to be at the reunion too. So what? So what did that really add up to in the great scheme of things? Nothing, not a thing. Anyway, he was probably old and bald and . . . Carol stopped herself from conjuring up an image of an older world-weary Gareth Howard, aware that Raf was still talking and that she was still smiling and nodding inanely and not listening to a single word he was saying.

The fantasy Gareth refused to be old and bald; instead he looked more or less exactly the same as when Carol had last seen him, just slightly thicker-set with greying hair, swept back from bold regular features that made him appear distinguished and sexy as hell. Carol sighed; the bastard.

Tucked into the top of her handbag was a battered copy of *Macbeth* — stolen from the English and Drama Department twenty years earlier and autographed by all the people who had been there on that last summer tour. Gareth had signed his name with love to her, love and a single kiss. It looked very classy amongst a sea of bad jokes, slushy sentiment and poorly drawn hearts and flowers. Doggedly Carol dragged her attention away from the book and the memories, but it was like trying to take a steak away from a terrier.

"Have a good drive," Raf was saying, "and don't worry about anything or anybody here. We'll be just fine. I'm considering renting a few of those films you said you don't ever want in this house, and filling up on fast food, pizzas, beer and take-out burgers."

She couldn't think of a smart reply quickly enough, so Carol plumped for looking at Raf all damp-eyed and feeling guilty instead. She'd done nothing at all and yet she felt guilty, horribly guilty. Ridiculous. She took a deep breath and squared her shoulders. Ridiculous.

Raf put his arm round her waist and kissed her, and Carol immediately found herself wondering if Gareth would kiss her when they met. Did he still kiss the same as he had all those years ago? She seemed to remember he was a really good — and then, suddenly horribly aware of Raf's lips on hers, Carol hated herself for thinking about Gareth. What a cow she had grown up to be.

Raf looked her up and down admiringly. "You know, you're gorgeous," he purred. Carol softened. This man adored her; he cared for her, stood up for her, stood up to her and wanted to be with her. Raf wanted to marry her, for God's sake — how crazy was that? Over a glass or two of wine out on the terrace he would look up at the stars and wax lyrical about the house they would buy together, the house they would love and grow old in together. He cooked, he bought her flowers and presents that she liked and wanted. He made her laugh; when she was sad or feeling down he brought her carrot cake with proper cream cheese icing from the baker's on Bridge Street, or lemon drizzle cake with crystallised sugar on the top. Carol looked up into Raf's big brown smiling eyes and tried very hard not to cry.

Carol loved Raf and she knew he loved her and yet
. . . and yet, that thing, that, that little zing wasn't there,
that thing that made something happen in your gut
every time you saw someone. It was the bastard factor
that was lacking, that little edge of unpredictability that
adds a bit of a challenge, a bit of bite. Raf was too nice,
and it worried Carol. What if she got bored; what if,
despite all evidence to the contrary, Raf wasn't *the one*
after all? What if loving him turned out to be a terrible
mistake? What if . . . ? The possibilities haunted her. Raf
was so safe, so kind, so right for her — so why was it
exactly that she was thinking about the might-have-
beens with a man she hadn't seen for twenty years?

Raf drew Carol closer still and kissed the tip of her
nose. He smelled of sunshine and a hint of aftershave
all wrapped around by a warm musky man smell. She
felt safe curled in his arms; it was one of the things that
had made her hang on and try to quell the fear. Maybe,
just maybe that she had got it right this time and she
wasn't making a terrible mistake.

"Now you be careful," teased Raf. "We're expecting
you to phone home every night. Don't go talking to any
strange men and if they offer you sweeties or to show
you their puppies —"

"I'll tell them to bugger off, pull out my plastic
dagger and then get Diana to flash them the wart."

"Good, now have you got a clean hanky?" he
continued in the same jokey paternal tone.

Behind them Jake thundered down the stairs, taking
the last few steps two at a time and then swung round
the newel post so he was standing right in front of her.

"And there'll be no staying up late, no drinking, no drugs and no monkey business," he said, wagging a finger at her.

Carol stared at him. "What?" she spluttered.

"You know exactly what I'm talking about. Just make sure you behave yourself, young lady," he said, all mock-parent and raging acne.

To her horror Carol felt her colour rising furiously as she hugged Jake goodbye. Of course she would behave herself. Wouldn't she?

"Ollie?" Carol called, struggling to regain her composure. She glanced down at her watch to hide her discomfort; it was high time she was gone.

Ollie was in the kitchen, excavating something from the Mesozoic layer in the bottom of the fridge.

"I'm off now, love," she said cheerily.

"So's this yoghurt," he huffed miserably. "I might have got food poisoning or something."

Carol took the offending article out of his deeply disgusted paw and dropped it into the pedal bin. "For God's sake, Ollie, you're a new lad, you're not supposed to read the sell-by dates," Carol growled. "You're meant to eat it and then burp appreciatively, green hairy mould and all."

Ollie's expression of unrelenting disdain did not waver. Carol held up her hands in surrender. "OK, OK, my mistake. You can go and buy more tomorrow. Organic, low fat, no fat — whatever."

He sniffed.

Carol pulled him closer and brushed her lips across the top of Oliver's spiky hard-boy haircut. "And don't worry, I'll be back on Sunday evening to mop up any unused emotional blackmail and residual maternal guilt."

His eyes twinkled but his expression remained steadfastly hard done by. "Just as long as we've got that perfectly clear," he said.

Carol resisted the temptation to scrunch his carefully teased and heavily gelled hairstyle into prepubescent fluffiness. "Have a good time without me."

"Yeah, right, we will. Bye, Mum," Ollie said grudgingly.

At least he helped her to feel slightly better; resentment and grumpiness made Carol feel she had every right to go. After all she did for them, ungrateful buggers. She sighed; who the hell was she trying to kid? Although she did want to go and meet everyone and see what they had been up to — she and Diana had got a brilliant response from their ad on Oldschooltie's message board — Carol knew that the main reason she was going was so that she could take a long hard look at Gareth Howard. Not only to see what the years had done to him but also to see if there was a flame still burning after all.

What if she had met Mr Right all those years ago and had been too blind or too young or too naïve to see it? Maybe it wasn't too late to go back and pick up the pieces.

She'd had a thing for Gareth for years — but it wasn't until they started rehearsing the play that he suddenly seemed aware of her for the first time.

"I was looking for you," he'd said, bounding up to her in the corridor on impossibly long legs. "I was wondering if you'd like to read the script through some time before we start rehearsals?" Carol had been hurrying out of the common room, her arms full of books.

"Sorry, that was the bell — I'm supposed to be in History . . ." Ah, that was it. And she had turned away and Gareth had caught hold of her elbow and turned her back towards him. "When's your next private study? It would be good to go through the play a couple of times — you know, get a feel for it."

Carol could feel her colour rising; wasn't this what she had been daydreaming about for years? Her annoyance at being held up faded to a kind of self-conscious discomfort. Get a grip, she thought, and tried smiling.

"This afternoon, after lunch I've got a double free," Carol had heard herself saying, stumbling over the words, trying to forget the pile of work she had to catch up on.

And then Gareth had grinned and brushed his fringe back off his face; he had been playing cricket and tennis and had a tan that made his eyes seem far too blue. "Great. Me too, any idea where we could go?"

Carol stared at him; where the hell did you go with somebody you had been lusting after since you were fourteen?

"How about the library?"

He pulled a face; so maybe it wasn't the best choice but it was all Carol could come up with under pressure.

"Someone is bound to complain about the noise. We need somewhere quiet where we can read through without being disturbed. How about if we go over to the pavilion; we could sit out on the veranda. At least it will be out of the way."

Carol felt her stomach fluttering. The cricket pavilion was up on a bank overlooking the cricket pitch, sheltered on two sides by huge horse chestnut trees with a view back over the main school. People mostly went there to smoke or snog.

"Sure, sounds like a good idea," Carol said, with a confidence she didn't feel.

"OK," he beamed. "See you there first period after lunch then?"

All these years on and Carol could still feel that intense little flutter in the pit of her stomach that he had made her feel then. Across the kitchen Raf was looking at her quizzically.

"Are you all right?" he asked. "You look a bit pale."

Carol made a real effort to smile. How could she possibly tell him? "I'm fine."

"I love you," Raf said gently. "And I'll be here . . ."

What was that supposed to mean? For an instant Carol wondered if Raf had some inkling of what was going through her mind, some Celtic intuition that told him that she was floundering. She stared at him. Why didn't she want to commit herself to living with Raf? Was that what all this hankering after Gareth was really about? Wasn't she aching for a fantasy, some perfect love that had never really had the chance to blossom, or go wrong or get dull or cruel? Fancying Gareth after all these years was like loving a dead war hero; in her mind he hadn't aged, he didn't fart in bed and his hair hadn't thinned or been combed over.

Raf's expression crinkled up a little. "Are you sure you're all right?"

Carol waved her thoughts and his words away. "Just a bit nervous, that's all. I mean, do I really want to see just how wrinkly everyone else is and know they're thinking the same thing about me?" she said with a grin. "All those old faces, all those old memories."

"And all those old flames?" he added casually.

Carol stared at him. He knew. "Maybe," she hedged, aware of something that Shakespeare had written in another play about what a dead giveaway it was to protest too much. Any heated denials would only make things worse, not better. "There's bound to be one or two but they're probably balding with false teeth and half a dozen kids by now," she joked.

"They?"

Carol felt a great rush of heat. "He," she said uncomfortably, cursing her inability to lie.

Raf nodded. She wondered if for an instant he felt worried or hurt or threatened. If he did, it didn't show. Raf looked at her with his big brown eyes and smiled. "Well, have a good time and give my love to Diana. We'll be fine, assuming we can avoid yoghurt poisoning."

They both looked at Ollie, who made a big point of ignoring them.

"God, I'm so glad that you arrived early," said Diana. "I was beginning to panic. I've got the list — did you receive any more replies or apologies?"

She was standing all alone in the huge vaulted hallway of Burbeck House. Once a great baronial manor, it was set in its own grounds at the far end of an impressive sweeping drive. The interior was now painted a pale and rather morbid shade of November afternoon grey. The enormous entrance hall was dotted with hessian pin boards screwed to walls that would have looked far more at home under rows of stags' heads, axes, spears and suits of armour. A reception desk, dwarfed by stone columns, was set up inside the great double door and beside it Diana was standing, surrounded by various boxes, shopping bags, bits of costume and piles of books.

Carol pulled a sheet of paper out of her handbag. "All present and correct, Capt'n Bligh."

"Sorry," said Diana. "It's just that I've been panicking. You found it all right, then?" she continued, gathering assorted bits and pieces together.

"Eventually," said Carol, bending down to help her. "It's a bit out of the way, but it is such a great place. It was a good idea to hold it here, Di. Do you have any idea who designed the park? It almost looks like it might be Capability Brow —" Glancing up, Carol could see from the anxious expression on Diana's face that architecture and landscape weren't the most pressing things on her mind. "What's the matter?"

"We've got a bit of a problem. Well, I'm not sure it's a problem, exactly," she said, shifting her weight uneasily from foot to foot.

"Spit it out," said Carol, straightening up under a carton full of props. "What's the trouble? I'm good at crisis management."

Diana looked even more uncomfortable, as if struggling to find exactly the right words.

"Don't tell me," said Carol, "you've accidentally booked the wrong weekend and nobody is coming after all. Just you, me and a box full of papier-mâché crowns, plastic swords and a pile of scripts?"

Diana shook her head. "Oh, no, as far as I know everyone is coming. It's just that when I rang up to book the rooms I must have said something about it being a school reunion and the receptionist got hold of the wrong end of the stick and . . ." Diana bit her lip and pulled one of her world-famous faces.

"And?" said Carol, willing the words out of Diana's mouth.

"And they've allocated us the dormitories."

Carol stared at her. "The dormitories?"

"Uh-huh, you know — bunk beds, communal washrooms. They thought we were some sort of school party."

Carol laughed. "You're joking?"

"No. We've been allocated segregated dormitories in the east wing with separate accommodation for the members of staff. I couldn't understand why the weekend was so cheap; I thought that maybe it was their group rate. Now I know why."

Carol put the box down. It wasn't that serious, surely — but then again how long was it since she'd slept a dozen to a room in a bunk bed? Probably the last school drama tour.

"And there's no chance of changing it?"

Diana shook her head miserably. "Apparently not, I've already tried. Unfortunately, they've got some sort of delegation of lay church workers in this weekend and they're all very keen on personal space — not seeing each other in their jarmies and rollers, that sort of thing, and that's just the men. No, I'm afraid we're stuck upstairs in Teddy Towers."

"Teddy Towers?" Carol laughed.

"It's what we call it when we bring the Sunday school kids here. Come on, I'll show you what I mean. I'm just hoping that people won't mind too much." Diana sounded genuinely worried.

"I'm sure it'll be fine," said Carol, in what she hoped would pass for a jolly, "it'll be all right, how bad can it be, after all it's only for a couple of nights" sort of voice.

"Bloody hell . . ." hissed Carol as they crested the stairs up into the east wing.

Along one apparently unending landing were two dormitories. The corridor was lit by a series of bare bulbs that dangled on long flexes from high, hugely ornate ceilings. There were two communal bathrooms, two staff bedrooms and a job lot of six-inch-wide border printed with assorted toy town animals that ran the whole length of the wall — in fact as far as the eye could see — all pasted to the battle-scarred plaster at around six-year-old paw-print height. Above the frieze the walls were painted an unpleasant shade of nursery yellow. The ceilings too. Here and there on the walls were outcrops of teddies glued in bouquets of beardom. While below the frieze everything — radiators, skirting boards, even wall sockets and what looked like oak panelling — was painted the same unrelenting battleship grey that graced the rest of the house.

"Oh, don't worry, it gets worse," said Diana grimly as they headed along the corridor.

She pushed open a heavy door on which someone had Blu-Tacked a laminated sheet of A4 paper which read "Girls/Drama Tour", and then stood aside to let Carol step past her.

"Sweet Jesus . . ." breathed Carol as the door swung open.

The enormous room was grey, with a row of wooden lockers and cupboards built in along one wall. The bottom pane in each of the tall sash windows had been replaced by obscured glass, and the carpets — a lurid mustard yellow and grey with a bitter and twisted orange fleck — were definitely not the kind of thing Laurence Llewelyn-Bowen would have chosen for any kind of make-over. But what struck Carol — what would have struck anyone — were the bears.

Some lunatic evidently in the throes of mental illness had pasted cut-out teddy bears to every flat surface — hundreds of bears: tall bears, thin bears, bears with bows, famous bears, unknown bears, cartoon bears, bears cut from wildlife magazines, bears with fish, bears in hats, bears juggling beach balls. Even the beds —

great sturdy two-storey, iron-framed monstrosities that looked as if they might be army surplus — hadn't escaped. On every upright and cross member someone had lovingly stuck pictures of Pooh and Paddington and every bear and shade of bear between, and then varnished over them so that they were sealed on for ever. The bed linen, by contrast, appeared to be ex-army too: crisp white sheets with heavy itchy grey blankets tucked drum tight around wafer-thin mattresses.

"Oh my God," whispered Carol in horrified awe. "Who the hell did this?"

"I've always thought it must have been psychotic nuns," said Diana, dropping a bag onto one of the bedside cabinets. "It used to be various shades of grey, fawn and bilious yellow like the rest of the place — which was bad enough — and then we came back one summer and, shazam — Teddy Towers."

"What's the boys' room like?"

"Same, although rumour has it that they have the odd goat to relieve the tension."

"Goat?"

Diana shook her head. "Yes, goat. And before you ask, I have no idea."

Carol didn't know what to say. Instead she stared at the décor while trying hard to hold on to her jolly "it'll be all right, how bad can it be, after all it's only for a couple of nights" thing.

It was then that the double doors behind them burst open and in giggled two other women clutching bags and suitcases, talking ferociously. As they realised they were not alone there was a moment's silence, almost instantly followed by a great whoop of recognition.

"Bloody hell, as I live and breathe, if it isn't Mrs Macbeth and her evil sidekick Witch One," said the smaller of the two women, slinging her bag onto the floor.

Carol felt her jaw drop and then grinned. "Oh my God, Netty Davies? Jan Smith? The rest of the coven. Oh, wow — God, you look wonderful, both of you," she shrieked in amazement and delight, as the four of them got caught up in a round of hugs and kisses and more giggles.

Annette Davies — Netty Davies to her friends — was, and had been since she was around thirteen, a small curvy brunette with freckles, a lot of red in her hair and even more in her nature. Jan Smith, on the other hand, had thickened up a bit since sixth form, but then again, as she had once been referred to as, "your mate, the stick insect", she could afford a few extra pounds.

Netty had a healthy tan and was dressed in designer jeans, a little V-necked top that emphasised a pair of unnaturally pert breasts and had a cleavage you could park a Harley-Davidson in. By contrast, Jan was very tall, pale and willowy, dressed in what looked like Mary Quant retro — a black and white A-line dress, with black boots and a lot of eye make-up. She still had her trademark hair — long, dark and as straight as expensive well-weighted curtains, which hung more than halfway down her back and was still remarkably very dark brown for a woman of not far off forty.

"Is this our room?" said Jan, looking round speculatively. They seemed totally unfazed by the teddy bear epidemic or the fact that it was a dormitory.

Diana nodded. "Yes. I'm sorry —" she began.

"Great, well, in that case, bags-I the top bunk," yelled Netty, and, taking a great whooping run up, leaped onto the nearest bunk bed with an amazing agility for someone in such high heels.

"In that case I'll have the one underneath," said Jan with equal enthusiasm, dumping a large holdall on the bed.

Without a word Carol and Diana took the set of bunks next to them, Carol on top, Diana underneath. With Netty and Jan next door it was just like the good old days — the three witches and Mrs Macbeth back under one roof for the first time in God knew how long under the watchful eye of God knew how many teddy bears.

Netty and Jan — slightly calmer now — took one look around the room and burst into great gales of laughter.

"What an amazing place," said Netty. "God, I've so been looking forward to this. It's going to be such a laugh." She pulled a packet of cigarettes out of her handbag. "I presume this place is non-smoking — everywhere is these days. I'll have to go and find the fire escape or stick my head out of a window. It's ridiculous, grown adults having to go and hang around the back of the bike sheds. I did that when I was fifteen. What is the world coming to? Where's the bar?"

"I'm afraid there isn't one," Diana said with a grim smile.

Netty and Jan groaned in unison.

"But," continued Diana hastily, in case it dampened their obvious enthusiasm, "the nearest pub is down in the village. It's not far; it was part of the Burbeck estate, ten minutes, if that. You can walk it from here."

"Good-oh. Do you think they'll still be open, only I'm absolutely famished?" asked Netty, fiddling with an unlit cigarette.

Carol looked round at the faces of her friends; the years might all be there, picked out in a raft of lines, but underneath it didn't feel as if very much had changed at all.

Before Diana could answer, a cultured male voice said, "Knock knock, anyone home?"

The four women turned in unison. Standing in the doorway was a tall, blond, nicely tanned man dressed in cream chinos and a black T-shirt, with shoulders to die for, a leather jacket hooked casually on one finger over his shoulder and wearing a pair of shades that made him look like a male model.

Carol stared; who the hell was that? Her brain stalled for a few seconds and then frantically began rifling through the images in her memory. Maybe he wasn't with the drama group at all; maybe he worked at Burbeck House. Maybe he'd found them by mistake; maybe he was one of the lay Christians who had lost his way; maybe he was someone's partner, come to drop her off. Lucky, lucky girl, thought Carol wistfully; at which point the tall blond guy grinned and whipped off the shades to reveal a pair of enormous blue-grey eyes.

"It *is* you lot. I thought it might be," he said with genuine delight, and Carol gasped as her brain joined up the dots.

"Adrian — Adie Gilbert?" she said in amazement. "It is you, isn't it? Bloody hell, whatever happened to you? You've changed."

"How kind of you to notice," he said, doing a little twirl.

"Jesus," said Netty, a split second behind her. "Adie Gilbert, as I live and breathe. Well, hello there, big boy."

The beautifully even grin widened out to full double-page spread and he dipped his head in acknowledgement. "Well, hello yourself, Netty," he said. "Good to see you too."

"God, you're bloody gorgeous," stuttered Carol, while making an effort to clear her mind and close her mouth. Adrian Gilbert, terminal acne sufferer, last seen on leavers' day when he could barely muster five foot six of pale sinewy flesh, the boy who used to have an underbite, and a chest and shoulders that looked as if they were permanently hunched in anticipation of an unexpected gale. Adrian Gilbert, who made them laugh, could plait hair, dance and play Spanish guitar like an angel, Adrian Gilbert, who played Macduff, and who now looked like a million dollars well spent.

"I've just been next door, along the corridor." He indicated an unspecified somewhere over his broad and very muscular shoulder. "God, what a place. The woman downstairs, the one with the moustache and bat-wing arms, directed me up to bear boy city — but none of the other guys seem to have arrived yet and then I heard giggling and thought I'd take a look. I might have guessed it was you lot."

You lot. Twenty years on and they were still "you lot". Carol felt her heart lift and then wondered if the whole weekend was going to be a messy medley of heart-warming moments and eyes filling up like fountains — and whether she could cope with so much undiluted sentiment.

Diana grimaced. "I'm so sorry, Adrian. You don't mind about the bears, do you?" She sounded horribly apologetic. "I didn't realise that they had given us the dormitories."

Adrian snorted and then raised a hand to disburse any lingering doubt. "Oh, please. It's fine, honey, don't panic. I've slept in places a lot worse than this."

Carol resisted the temptation to ask him where that was exactly.

"Yes, for God's sake, Di, stop apologising and just relax about the bloody bears," snapped Netty, still toying with her cigarette. "No one gives a shit. Now will you excuse me while I retire to a nearby bike shed before I die of nicotine withdrawal?" She glanced round. "I don't suppose anyone else would care to join me?"

"Hang on, don't go. It would be a shame to break up the party before it gets going. I'll open a window," said Adie, going over and unfastening one of the sashes. "There's a fire escape out here," he said cheerfully.

Netty peered outside and then with a hand from Adie clambered out onto the windowledge and lit up.

Once Netty was settled, Adie tipped the sunglasses back onto his head and clapped his hands together. "So —" he began, but Netty was way ahead of him.

"What in God's name happened to you?" she asked, snatching the words clean out of Carol's mouth.

He laughed and shrugged. "You know how it is. I grew up, worked out, got a job. How about you?"

Netty sniffed. "Nothing so interesting."

Carol hugged him. "You look absolutely amazing."

"You too. I just love what you've done with your hair," he said, holding her at arm's length to admire her and then cast an eye round the rest of the gang. "And, Jan, I adore that colour. Was it that colour last time I saw you? Netty, it's nice to see that bitch never went out of fashion. God, it's just so good to see you all again. This was such a brilliant idea." Jan reddened furiously under his undisguised delight at her dye job. Carol hugged him tighter, relishing the smell of something expensive and the feel of his nicely muscled body under her fingertips, Diana grinned with sheer pride and Netty, perched like a grumpy dragon out on the windowsill, laughed, blowing out a great plume of smoke. Adrian Gilbert, home from the hills with fantastically good highlights and fabulous teeth — it was enough to restore anyone's faith in the power of fate, peroxide and cosmetic dentistry.

There was a moment then when they all settled and paused to take stock and in a tiny intense silence Carol thought that maybe it was going to be all right after all.

She felt the tension that she didn't know she had been holding on to, slip away.

And then Jan said, "So who else is coming?" unzipping her holdall and taking out a fluffy white dressing gown and toilet bag.

Carol seemed to remember that Jan — even in her teens — liked to move into a place. Every stop on the drama tour, out would come a big pink throw, clock, photos. True to form the next thing Jan pulled out of the bag was a thin scarlet Indian cotton throw, which she arranged over the miserable grey army blanket. It was like lighting a fire in the huge grey room.

Diana, meanwhile, was extricating a printed list from her bag, together with Carol's sheet, and said, "I've got it all written down on here, somewhere," and began to scan the neatly typed pages. "Us, obviously — and the drama teachers, Mr Bearman and Miss Haze."

"God, they're coming too, are they? How the hell did you pull that off?" said Adie.

Diana looked bemused. "I asked them," she said as if it was perfectly obvious.

"That's great. I wonder how old they are. As kids you just don't think. I mean, Miss Haze could only have been, what — four, five years older than us? I often wondered if those two had a thing going. You know," said Adrian conspiratorially, "all that late night rehearsing, away for weeks on end together every summer. The way they looked at each other sometimes. You must have noticed."

"Of course we did, everyone noticed, and we all thought the same thing," snapped Jan.

"You never said anything."

"That was because everyone already knew," Jan bitched right back. "It was obvious."

"Ouch," whined Adie. "Don't bite."

"Play nicely, you two," hissed Netty.

Carol found herself looking backwards and forwards between them, spectator to their verbal tennis match. She had completely forgotten the little needly thing between Jan and Adrian.

"I don't take any notice, she's always like this," said Adie.

"I'm not."

"Are too. Last Christmas you bit me."

"You were the one feeding people grapes."

"No one else bit me."

"Is there any chance we can carry on fighting over a sandwich and pint?" asked Netty, stubbing out her cigarette on the windowsill. "Only I'm dying upwards from hunger over here."

"Great idea," said Adrian. "Everyone coming? We can always unpack later." He looked pointedly at Jan who was busy arranging two small, embroidered cushions. "It's a shame that I'm not bunked down in here with you lot, really."

"Not a chance," said Diana wearily, although Carol wasn't sure whether she meant Adrian sharing a room with them or heading off down to the pub. "I've got to stay here and meet people as they arrive — but you lot go. It's not far. You go out of the back doors of the hall, follow the path down through the vegetable garden," by this point Diana was pointing and directing with her hands, "out through the gates and there you are. Pub, post office and a Spar shop with an offie." She paused, looking pleased with herself. "Everything a girl could want."

"You live in the country, don't you?" Netty said, eyeing Diana thoughtfully as she attended to her lipstick in a tiny silver mirror. "What about you, Jan, are you coming or are you planning on a complete makeover to the whole place before everyone else gets here?"

Jan, busy fluffing the cushions with care, wasn't at all put out. "I just like to be comfortable, that's all. I'm curious about who is going to show up. What time does this shindig officially kick off?"

"Five o'clock," said Diana, glancing at her watch. "Informal high tea in the dining room and then dinner at eight. I thought I might say a few words. Adie, is there any chance you'd be master of ceremonies? I've got a programme of events and rehearsals printed up for everyone but if you could maybe read it through, say something clever, be funny, whatever."

He groaned theatrically but didn't actually say no as Diana handed him one of her photocopied sheets.

"And I just want to say I'm really glad you all got here early. I was worried — well, you know, it feels like you lot are the vanguard — the inner circle — and it means that everyone else will probably turn up as well, and if you don't mind the bears and the bunk beds then maybe nobody else will either." Diana reddened furiously, eyes all bright. "It's so good to see you again."

Carol could see that the nostalgia virus had infected Diana too.

"For God's sake, stop going on about the bloody bears," snapped Netty. "Unless you glued them up yourself they're not your fault."

"Everyone be here for tea and buns?" asked Adrian, looking down at the paper.

Diana shook her head. "No, not everyone — some people have said they won't be able to get here until later. Sheena Mason, Phillip Hudson — Gareth Howard."

As if on cue, everyone, including Adrian, turned to look in Carol's direction. Carol felt a little flurry of something in her belly but, pretending to be totally unconcerned, she carried on unzipping her suitcase.

"Have we got a cupboard each?" she asked casually, hanging a towel over the rail at the end of the bunk to stake her claim, not that she was fooling anyone. There was a pause; she could feel them all still looking at her. "All right, all right, so it will be great to see Gareth again — is that good enough for you?"

Adrian lifted an eyebrow. "We don't know yet, do we? What else had you got in mind?"

Carol slung a pair of socks at him. "Nothing, nothing at all. Besides, Gareth is probably happily married with half a dozen kids, a fish farm and a bloody Labrador by now. It will just be lovely to see him — to catch up, to catch up with everyone — but come on, a lot of water has flowed under the bridge since . . . since . . ." She couldn't quite find the right words to describe exactly since *what*.

Adrian came to her aid: "Since you and Gareth slipped off to God knows where with a sly grin and a packet of three?" he suggested helpfully.

Carol felt the heat roar through her. "I did no such thing," she protested furiously.

There was another weighty silence and then Carol's composure and outrage deflated. "All right, all right, so maybe I did, but that doesn't mean that anything like that is likely to happen again — not at all. Is that clear?"

"OK, well, as long as we've got that straight," said Adie wryly. "So are you coming down to the pub? Only I'm desperate to get all the gossip and, let's face it, we're going to need all the time we can get if we're going to catch up on twenty years each."

Carol hesitated, unsure whether she ought to stay with Diana. After all, hadn't she made some kind of rash promise to pitch in? Also Carol wasn't sure she could stand up to too much close questioning about her motives when it came to seeing Gareth again.

"Go," said Diana, waving Carol away before she could offer to stay behind. "This lot will need someone to ride shot gun on them."

Carol picked up her handbag. "If you're sure . . ."

"I'm sure," Diana said. "Go."

"Oh, by the way, is Fiona coming?" asked Netty as she got to the door.

There was a fraction of a second's pause. Fiona Templeton, the girl for whom the phrase "drama queen" could well have been invented.

54

Diana nodded. "Yes, well, at least she said she would be here."

"I can't imagine that Fiona would miss it," said Netty. "Any chance for a little limelight and adoration."

"Just as long as she doesn't bring her mother," laughed Adrian.

"That's not funny. That old stoat used to make my life hell. Lights out, fags out, boys out. God, the woman was such a pain in the arse," snapped Netty. "Her and her precious little kitten." She mimicked Fiona's mother with spiteful accuracy for someone whom she hadn't seen for years.

"Oh, come on, Fiona has done well for herself," said Diana pleasantly.

"What do you mean *well*?" said Jan. "First road kill in *Casualty*?"

"I saw her in an ad on telly for Boots last Christmas," said Netty.

"Third bunny on the *Emmerdale* Easter special," laughed Carol.

"And first drownee on the *Titanic*," continued Adrian, topping the lot of them.

"Oh, I didn't know that she was in *Titanic*," said Diana innocently, at which point Netty and Jan keeled over giggling.

"You pair are bloody horrible," growled Diana as the penny dropped, although she did say it with a certain affection, which made them laugh all the harder.

"So Fiona is definitely coming?" asked Carol.

"She said she would, although apparently there was a chance she might be called back for filming, in which case it could make things a bit tight."

"Oh, she was just saying that to impress you. Of course she'll be here," said Adrian. "Understudy to Mrs Macbeth, Lady Macduff — if there was ever a woman who needed stabbing . . ." He hesitated and then said to Carol, "You want to watch yourself on these steep stairs, you know. I don't think she ever forgave you for stealing the lead out from under her retroussé nose. She's probably still out for blood."

Carol smiled grimly. "She was always out for blood."

Netty nodded. "She was really pissed off with you, you know — you getting the leading role and the leading man."

"Come off it, it's a long time ago now. Let's go. I could murder a drink," said Carol uncomfortably.

"Poor choice of words," said Jan. "I remember she was livid when the reviews came out; didn't get so much as a word."

Carol laughed. "That's only because you three stole the show. Madam here," she waved towards Diana, "and her magic wart."

"Anyway, Fiona said she might be delayed," finished Diana, determined to bring the conversation round to something a little less anarchic.

"So that's her *and* Gareth," said Adie archly. "Right, well, let's go and find this pub then."

The gang moseyed out with Adrian in the lead.

As they fell into step Carol let thoughts surface that hadn't come to the fore since she left school: why was it

Gareth hadn't been interested in Fiona instead of her? Perhaps it was that he couldn't stand the idea of sharing the limelight. Two egos that big would probably have sent the place up in smoke.

"And Gareth said he had a few things to sort out before he left," said Diana to their backs.

"And what did you say?" asked Carol, turning back but trying hard not to sound too eager.

"Nothing much — God, you have got it bad, haven't you?"

Carol shook her head, reluctant to commit herself. "Not really, I just wondered . . ."

Diana grinned. "You don't fool me. You'd better head off and catch up. We can talk later."

Carol nodded, while somewhere deep in her heart she felt a sharp little stab of betrayal for Raf.

Meanwhile in a large semi-detached town house in an unfashionable suburb of Hemel Hempstead, Gareth Howard was pulling on his jacket.

"About these . . ." Leonora began, as she and Gareth arrived together at the front door. She held a sheaf of bills in her hand.

Gareth leaned forward and kissed her hard on the lips and then each cheek. "I'll miss you, sweetie," he purred.

"What about th—" she began again, but wasn't anywhere near fast enough.

"My God is that the time?" he said, looking down at his watch. "I really need to be gone, darling." As he stepped through the door Gareth took a small box from his jacket pocket, on top of which was an intricate curl of scarlet ribbon.

Leonora pulled a face, trying very hard to sustain the emotion that had propelled her downstairs after him. "What on earth is this?" she snapped.

He grinned. "Something to remember me by."

"What do you mean, remember you by? I thought you said you would be back on Sunday evening?"

As she lifted the lid Gareth was already stepping out into the street. Inside the box was a pair of black silk stockings, not unlike those he had tied Leonora to the bed with the very first night they had slept together.

"Gareth?" she said, looking up, but he was already gone.

"Mummy?" Patrick tugged at her cardigan. "Where's Daddy gone?"

Leonora shook her head. "I've got no idea," she said, taking his hand and scooping the baby up from the pram just inside the hall door. "No idea at all."

CHAPTER
THREE

"Callista? Callista Haze?"

Callista Haze looked up from a battered copy of *Macbeth* and her thoughts. Although it took her a moment or two to focus on the face she would have known that voice anywhere. George Bearman, former head of Drama and English at Belvedere High School, stood beside the pub table, looking down at her and smiling nervously.

George, it seemed, was not quite so certain that he'd got the right person. "It is you, isn't it?" he asked.

She laughed. "Of course it is, George. Who on earth did you think it was? How many women looking like me do you think there are going to be at this reunion?"

"I just wanted to check. Actually, I was thinking how very little you'd changed," he said quickly, colouring up to crimson.

"Been watching me long, have you?" she asked, raising one perfectly plucked eyebrow.

George's colour deepened. "Good God, no, of course not. Well, all right, maybe a few minutes, if that," he blustered. "I was up at the bar and I couldn't help noticing. You look wonderful, actually. You don't mind if I join you, do you?" He indicated the seat alongside hers. He was cradling a pint of beer, a packet of crisps and a pie on a plate. Tucked into his top pocket were a knife and fork wrapped in a checked napkin.

"No, not at all," said Callista, half-rising to greet him.

George set down his drink and makeshift lunch and then, catching hold of her elbows, pulled her towards him and kissed her clumsily on each cheek. He smelled of pipe smoke and shaving cream, his skin all rough and ruddy against hers.

"Have you been up to the hall yet? I dropped my bags off. They said their dining room and some sort of little café place they run was closed until later and recommended the pub; thought I'd come and grab a pint and a bite before the off." George paused, suddenly all dewy-eyed. "I'm gabbling, aren't I? It's just that it's been so many years. You know, I didn't think that I would ever see you again. Isn't it wonderful? I've been trying to imagine what it would feel like, you know, to meet up again after all this time," he said.

"And how does it feel?" Callista asked, her expression held very firmly in neutral.

George considered for a moment or two, lips pursed, face set and then he said, "Rather odd, actually. I felt quite nervous driving down — but it's good — a little unnerving — but it is wonderful to see you again. I wondered whether you might have changed — I mean, one never knows. But you look really, really . . ."

Callista could see him struggling to find the right word. "Wonderful?" she teased.

"Yes, exactly, wonderful," he said.

As George settled himself into the seat alongside her, Callista prodded the slice of lemon down into her gin and tonic and said nothing. After all, what was there to say? Hadn't they said it all before a long, long time ago? Her silence was a sharp contrast to the sounds of the pub around them.

"So," said George, a little self-consciously, "how's life been with you?"

"Well, come on then, who's going to go first?" asked Adie, unpacking the round of drinks from the tray. "Truth or consequences," he continued, handing Jan a glass of white wine, whilst looking at the bemused faces around the table.

On the way down to the pub they had agreed to try to keep all the catching-up on what had happened to who and when and why until everyone was settled down and could listen properly. It had seemed like a good idea. Everyone had found it hard not to break into spontaneous reminiscing during the walk, but now they were all settled and ready, it seemed that no one wanted to be the first to start.

"Oh, come on, for God's sake, we're all ears. Netty, come on — 'fess up," Adie said, taking a pull on his pint.

Netty shook her head. "Good God, no, not me. At least not until I've eaten. Let somebody else go first. I can only cope with my sordid past after a couple of stiff drinks and on a full stomach. How about our leading lady?" Everyone turned to look at Carol. "Come on, off you go, petal. You've got as long as you need on your

61

specialist subject, Carol Hastings," said Netty, doing a very passable impression of John Humphrys. "What I did with the last twenty years of my life, starting now."

"Oh no, not me," Carol protested, waving the words away, but Adie and Netty were insistent.

"Stop being so bloody coy. Someone's got to go first or we'll be here all day."

"Why me?"

"Why not?" said Adie. "C'mon."

Carol sighed. "What do you want to know?"

"Everything. All the usual stuff. What you do, if you're married. And if so, how many times. Are you happy?" offered Netty.

"Where you live." Jan.

"Whether you've got kids, a dog, a cat, a goldfish." Adie.

"And any strange personal habits, peculiar hobbies or bizarre sexual practices." Netty.

"Oh, yes," said Adie, enthusiastically. "C'mon."

"The trouble is it's all surface. I can tell you what I've done but that doesn't tell you anything about who I am or what I feel or what I'm like," said Carol, wriggling uncomfortably under their gaze.

Netty groaned theatrically. "Oh my God, you grew up to be a therapist, didn't you?"

"No, I —" began Carol, but not quite fast enough.

"We know who you are," said Adie encouragingly. "Or at least we knew who you were when we were at Belvedere, and you don't seem to have changed that much. There's a whole leopard-and-spot thing here that I don't plan to go in to."

"No, I think she has changed," said Netty, waving a crisp in her direction. "Counselling, God preserve us — probably reads ink blots and facilitates group hugs with her inner child," she growled angrily.

Jan nodded in agreement as Carol, giggling, inhaled her shandy, and protested, "No, no, look, I'm not a counsellor. I'm a gardener — and before you start on about that, there's no need to go the whole Charlie Dimmock, Netty. Trust me, if I'd have realised that taking my bra off was a good career move I'd have done it years ago."

"You think anyone would have noticed?" asked Jan, deadpan. Netty choked.

"Oh, me-ow," hissed Adie, slapping Jan playfully and indicated to an imaginary waiter. "Saucer of milk, this table, please. The thing is, we need something to go on, Carol. We need the facts, the dirt, the details. The whole enchilada. So, spill it."

"This feels like a job interview," said Carol, pulling a face.

"Not for any job you'd ever want," said Adie.

"You'd never get a job in my place with those shoes or that outfit — Cat boots, a rugby shirt and jeans — what were you thinking?" said Netty.

"What's wrong with them? They're comfortable to drive in," protested Carol, not at all offended.

"You could have made an effort."

"I did," said Carol with a grin.

"Come on, behave," growled Adie. "You look great. So, Carol, after three — two, three — and away."

She paused for an instant, trying to collect her thoughts, painfully aware of how quickly the years had gone by. It didn't seem so very long ago that they had been out buying their first booze together.

Diana, heading up to the counter in an offie near the station, because with her hair up she looked twenty if she was a day, clutching the money from combined Saturday jobs for a bottle of vodka. Adie, arm in arm between Jan and Netty, walking down Bridge Street to catch the train to Cambridge, guitar slung across his narrow back. Everyone smoking, everybody giggling. Getting stoned at the back of the library, getting drunk at the leavers' ball.

Carol smiled; she had loved them all so much and hadn't known it. She took a deep breath, struggling to slow down the frantic slide show of images that filled her head. Maybe if she started to speak, her brain, with something else to think about, would throttle back and slow down the montage of memories, words like weights making the rush of thoughts and recollections into something more manageable.

"Come on, Carol, take no notice of them," said Adie. "So, once upon a time Lady Macbeth left Belvedere High School and then . . .?"

"And then, well, I worked in a bookshop in Cambridge — you remember that, Netty — we used to meet up for lunch? And I worked in a pub at weekends. I was planning on going to teacher training college when I met Jack French. He came into the shop and swept me off my feet, which sounds totally ridiculous now but it was true at the time. He kept coming in and flirting, and I said he would get me the sack. I remember that I was unpacking a whole box of sale books onto a table display when I said it — and so he bought the lot and then took me off to lunch to celebrate in his Mercedes."

"Wow," said Netty. "Bit flash. I don't remember meeting him."

"Unfortunately it was mostly all flash and balls. But I was very impressed, which shows how shallow and how gullible I was back then. To cut a long story short, I moved in with him, we got married — he was a lot older than I was — and we had two kids, two boys called Jake and Oliver.

"He was thirty-six when I met him, and anyone of his own age would have seen straight through him. I think he was rather hoping I'd stay nineteen for ever — he was so very disappointed when I grew up."

At which point Netty cleared her throat as if to say or ask something but Adie raised a hand to silence her. "There will be time for questions at the end," he said officiously, and then nodded for Carol to continue. "Off you go, honey. We're all listening."

"Sad thing was it took me a while to wake up, but by then I'd got Jake. We'd bought a house, Jack had a drink problem, was a financial disaster and had a roving eye that perfectly matched the other parts of his body that were prone to roving. He did about as much for my self-esteem and peace of mind as the *Titanic* did for maritime insurance. But what we did do — against the odds really — was have two really great kids and build up a good business between us, which is mine now. So it's not all bad news. I've been on my own nearly eight years and I'm doing OK, more than OK — I'm doing good."

Adie nodded appreciatively.

"And have you got anyone on the horizon. You know — a man, a dog, a cat, a goldfish?" asked Netty.

Behind them Carol could see two waitresses approaching with late lunches on a tray. She hesitated, hoping that the arrival of their food would break the thread. What could she possibly say that wouldn't make them think she was a perfect cow, keeping a good man on hold while she weighed up Gareth Howard? She suddenly realised it was really important that they didn't think badly of her.

"Yes, I have," Carol said, after what felt like for ever. "His name is Raf — and he's — he's . . ." She could see that she had everyone's undivided attention, "he's really nice."

Netty groaned. "Bugger! Hard luck, kid," she said, taking the plate of steak and chips proffered by the barmaid. "Never mind, it could have been a lot worse."

Adie nodded. "God, yes, he could have had a decent job with a pension."

"Or be sensible." Jan.

"Or reliable." Netty slapped her head and groaned.

"Or no oil painting but good with his hands," said Adie, shaking vinegar over his chips.

There was no answer. Carol looked down at her chicken Caesar salad, wondering how the hell she was going to be able to swallow it down past the great knotted guilty lump in her throat. She looked round the faces. "He really is nice," she said thickly, but there was no way back now.

". . . And how have you been keeping?" George asked, as if there was some real chance that all the years could be condensed into a line or two, as he launched himself gamely into Callista's silence. "I kept meaning to ring — I always think of you on your birthday — but well, you know how it is." He paused, his discomfort increasingly obvious. "There was always Judy to consider and you know how things were, how they still are. I just wanted you to know that I've missed you. Missed you a lot. It wasn't an easy decision at the time, not easy at all."

Callista Haze looked up from her drink, her composure totally unruffled. "George, please, there is really no need to put yourself through all this. It's fine, I'm fine. It was all an awfully long time ago now. Life moves on, people move on, so please just relax and enjoy your lunch."

"I know, I know, it's been so very many years. I'm almost afraid to work out exactly how long it is since I last saw you — and do you know what, Callista?"

"What?" she asked pleasantly. Surely there couldn't be much more. George Bearman looked much the same as she remembered him, except he had a little less hair and what he had left had faded from old gold to a soft grey. He had the florid slightly purple complexion of someone with poor circulation and a bad heart. Poor George.

He took a deep breath. "I regretted ever letting you go," he said. The words spilled out.

Callista stared up at him in astonishment, she felt her heart dropping like a stone. "Sorry?" she began, but George wasn't ready to be halted.

"Please, Callista, hear me out. Every single day since you left Belvedere I have thought what a bloody fool I was to have ever let you go. I'm so sorry, so very sorry, Callista; can you ever forgive me?"

She looked up into his eyes to see if there was some hint of jest, some cruel joke, and found none; instead she saw the bright promise of tears. Callista's expression softened. "Oh, George . . ." she whispered.

But he was in full swing now. "I felt so bad about everything, for betraying you like that, for abandoning you." He shook his head in total despair.

Despite his obvious distress Callista couldn't help laughing. "Oh, come on. George, stop it, people are looking at us, for God's sake. What on earth makes you think that you abandoned me?"

He was surprised. "Well, all those times I told you that I was going to leave my wife for you." He sounded slightly indignant. "All those times I promised you that we would have a life together — a little house, a fresh start, a cocker spaniel, be a real family."

"All those false promises and false hopes you trotted out to keep me hanging on?" she said.

He visibly bristled. "I'm sorry?"

"Oh, don't be so silly, George. I'm not totally stupid. I always knew that you would never leave Judy for me."

68

He looked at her in astonishment. "Really?" he said. He sounded genuinely amazed.

She laughed. "Of course. Don't sound so surprised. Hopeless, impossible, doomed love is a wonderfully dramatic thing — at least for a while. I was young and it all seemed terribly romantic."

"So what happened?"

Callista took a long pull on her drink. "Honestly?"

He nodded.

"I grew up."

"Good God. How terribly pragmatic of you," he said.

Callista stroked his hand. "Yes, that's right. Now eat your pie; you'll feel a lot better."

"But I've pined for you for . . ." George said. "If I'm honest I have pined for you for the last twenty years." He looked pained and sounded quite cross now.

"You silly man," Callista said kindly, pulling the knife and fork from his pocket and shaking out his napkin.

"I've always suspected that Judy knew my heart wasn't altogether in it. All those years —" he shook his head — "all those dreams wasted."

Callista topped up her gin with the last of the tonic, and when it was obvious that she didn't plan to comment, George continued, "And how about you? How has life been with you?"

Callista smiled. "Me? Oh, I'm fine. We've been doing a production of *A Midsummer Night's Dream* this year and our school has been selected for funding from Europe to improve the drama facilities, which is really exciting. We've put a bid in for a drama studio and —"

"That isn't what I meant and you know it," he said, cutting her short. "Didn't you ever miss me?" It was obvious from the tone he was hoping that she had pined for him just a little.

Callista stared at him. How could she possibly tell him that she hadn't thought about him for years? "You really did love me, didn't you?" she said in a low, even voice.

George nodded.

Callista set her hand down over his, wondering what on earth she could say. "George, I am really sorry. If I'd known I might have been more determined to get you, made more of a fuss, fought a little harder, but I thought that you were just toying with me, that I was just a game. I thought maybe — maybe it was something you made a habit of. You know, new female teacher, straight out of college. Easy pickings."

He winced.

Callista sighed. "Then again, if I'd known how you felt it would have been far more painful for both of us, wouldn't it? After I left Belvedere I went up to North Yorkshire, to a lovely school. I married a solicitor called Laurence — I was made head of department five years ago. We've got two daughters, Emma and Charlotte, they're fifteen and seventeen. We've got a nice house, a dog — a little summer place in France. We're very happy. I'm very happy." She paused, seeing the pain on George's face. "Oh, George, I thought that it was just an affair."

He pursed his lips, quite obviously struggling to keep his emotions under control. "You were the love of my life, Callista," he murmured. "I have never forgotten you. Never a day goes past when I don't think about you and how it might have been if I had been brave enough, strong enough, to walk away from my marriage, from Judy." His bottom lip had started to tremble furiously. "Oh, Callista, I'm so terribly sorry," he sniffled.

"George, please don't. How is Judy?"

"Oh, she's well. Well, I assume she is well; we barely speak at all these days. She has her friends, her interests, the choir and the reading group, and I have mine." He paused. "It's been a lot trickier since I retired."

The former Miss Callista Haze stared at George Bearman and wondered what on earth life might have been like if they had ended up together. How odd it was that she had had no idea how George felt about her, or was it that over the years she had become a fantasy that he had clung to, to keep him going inside a failing marriage? A magic might-have-been that had only just slipped through his fingers and helped him to sleep at nights.

"So," he said with forced joviality, "as you say, all water under the bridge now. Why don't you tell me all about this Laurence chap and your girls?"

Callista took a deep breath wondering how much she could tell George without breaking his already battered heart, when a woman walking past the table caught her eye and as recognition dawned she stopped and turned.

"Miss Haze?"

"Yes," said Callista, grateful for the interruption.

Carol grinned as she realised that Mr Bearman was there too, tucked up alongside Miss Haze, cradling a pint of bitter and the remains of a late lunch.

The two of them were sitting at a quiet table at the back of the Master's Arms, apparently deep in conversation. Miss Haze had a copy of *Macbeth* open in front of her. Even from where she was standing, Carol could see that the margins and every available glimmer of white space had been filled with tiny pencilled annotations around the main script; some appeared to have been overwritten.

"How very nice to see you," said Miss Haze, sounding very slightly uncertain who she was talking to.

"Carol Hastings — well, at least I used to be Carol Hastings." Carol held out a hand in greeting. "I'm here for the reunion as well."

"Oh, of course," said Miss Haze. "It wasn't that I didn't recognise you, Carol, but sometimes these days the names just vanish into the ether. I was trying very hard not to call you Lady Macbeth." She smiled, her handshake strong and warm and confident. "You know I often thought that you could have gone on to a career on the stage if you had wanted to."

Carol grinned. "That's very nice of you to say so, but if I'm honest I think I prefer to eat," Carol said.

"Well, there is that," Miss Haze laughed, while Mr Bearman, a little stiffly, added, "How very pragmatic." His handshake was cool and dry, his skin like old vellum.

Carol smiled. "You're early too." She couldn't help wondering if they had turned up together. Maybe they were a couple, married now; maybe they had got together after all.

Miss Haze nodded. "Actually I haven't been here very long. The woman in reception at Burbeck House suggested I come down here. Apparently their kitchen doesn't open until later." Her smiled broadened. "I did wonder whether she might be on commission." Miss Haze glanced down at her watch. "Actually, I was just about to head back when —" she glanced towards Mr Bearman — "when George here showed up."

Carol smiled; it seemed odd to think of Mr Bearman as having a first name but it had solved the couple question.

Mr Bearman beamed warmly in Miss Haze's direction. "Just like the good old days, back on the road again, eh, Callista?" And catching hold of her hand he lifted it and pressed it to his lips. Miss Haze blushed scarlet.

Diplomatically Carol looked away and said hastily, "There are a few of us in the front bar, if you would like to come and join us?"

Even after all these years it felt very odd talking to the teachers as if they were humans. Carol, who had been on her way to the loo when she spotted the pair of them, made a concerted effort to quell the little ripples of anxiety, which included the almost overwhelming feeling that she had forgotten to hand in a vital piece of homework and that by standing so close to them in a social setting she had broken an invisible inviolable rule about the relationship between teachers and pupils.

Across the table Mr Bearman smiled. "Thank you, Carol, that's very kind, but I think we'll probably stay here and catch up, won't we? We haven't seen each other in . . . how long is it exactly, Callista?"

"Rather more years than I care to remember," she said casually. Carol noticed that Miss Haze had extricated her hand from his. "And besides, I'm sure we'd only cramp your style. You can be a lot more raucous without us there. And, as I said, I'm just going to finish my drink and then be off up."

Mr Bearman nodded. "Excellent idea."

Callista Haze smiled coolly.

"It is really nice to see you both again. Diana's up there meeting and greeting people — presumably she's asked you to direct the read-through?" asked Carol, pointing at Miss Haze's script open on the table.

"Not exactly, although we were invited to. Mind you, Diana did add that we weren't to feel under any pressure," said Mr Bearman.

Miss Haze laughed. "I think what George is trying to say is, try stopping us."

Mr Bearman swung round and beamed at her. "I couldn't have put it better myself."

Alongside him Callista looked heavenwards.

"God, you'll never guess who I've just seen," said Carol, slipping back into her seat. Everyone looked up expectantly from the table, which was now covered with the fallout from their long late lunch. During the course of the meal there had been other people filing into the pub, saying hello and grinning madly as

74

recognition dawned and friendships rekindled; the whole place was buzzing with conversation and half-familiar faces.

Netty pouted before slipping a final chip, haemorrhaging tomato sauce, into her mouth, and said, deadpan, "I thought Diana said that Gareth wasn't getting here until later this evening."

Carol decided to ignore her. "Miss Haze and Mr Bearman, snuggled up over there in the snug." She toyed momentarily with the idea of sharing the hand-kissing incident and then decided to leave it out on the grounds that she was trying to maintain some air of maturity.

"Honestly, I used to have the hots for her something dreadful," said Adie unexpectedly, pulling a lusty face and making smoochy sexy noises. "Double Drama, Friday afternoons — I'd got a permanent hard on. I had to get my mum to buy me a longer jumper. Can you remember she used to wear those little black ski pant things?"

"Capri pants," corrected Netty, picking through the remains of Jan's garlic mushrooms.

"Very Audrey Hepburn. God, it was absolute agony," Adie said in a wistful voice, gazing off unfocused into the middle distance.

"Really?" said Carol in amazement. "*You had the hots for Miss Haze?*"

"Absolutely, yes," he groaned.

She stared at him: apparently the struggle to stop slipping back into the agonies of adolescence was hers and hers alone.

Adie blushed. "Well, just a little bit. Do you remember those black leather trousers she had? They were like a red rag to a bull as well. Little white angora sweater, those trousers, high-heeled boots — you'd have had to have been made of stone or been dead not to have thought the whole outfit was incredibly horny. I thought it was all so cute . . ."

Carol didn't say a word.

"Maybe it was a leather thing, although you didn't know about that then," Netty said.

Jan sniffed. "Lots of things you didn't know then."

Carol looked at her. "What's with you two? Twenty years and you're still bitching? How about we declare a truce this weekend?"

Jan waved her words away. "What, and spoil all our fun? Besides, Adie likes that kind of thing, don't you?"

Adie grinned and then growled playfully.

"I think we should be heading back to the hacienda," said Carol, glancing at her watch; hadn't Miss Haze said that she was going up to the house too? They all looked at her. "Well, Diana *is* there all on her own," she added weakly. "And I'd promised to help — and everyone else should be there soon."

"Yes, sirree, Mother Teresa," said Jan. "And maybe Gareth's showed up already. Don't want you missing him now, do we?"

Carol reddened.

"See," said Adie triumphantly. "I told you that Jan's a cow. I'm not being singled out for any special treatment. It's just that I'm just an easy target. She may still look like butter wouldn't melt — but beneath that serene composed chic exterior beats the heart of Lucretia Borgia. I bet she enjoyed a bit of interior decoration as a way of unwinding between all the poisoning and torturing."

"Did Lucretia Borgia torture people? I always thought she was a straight-down-the-line poisoner — bit of a one-trick pony, really," said Jan conversationally, as if being compared to Lucretia Borgia was something that happened every day of her life.

"I see you more as Cruella de Vil," said Netty. "I watched that film and thought: finally somewhere Jan can put her talents to good use. Although I suppose Adie *is* the closest thing we've got to a poor defenceless animal."

Jan, deadpan, said, "Nah, I've never liked spots. I think I'd prefer something with a little tabby in it, or maybe tortoiseshell."

Everyone winced and without a word got to their feet.

Tongues loosened by alcohol and food and a sense of relief that things hadn't changed so very much after all, the four of them headed slowly back, laughing, teasing, still easy and connected up after all these years, meandering through the village, then in through the gates in Burbeck House's kitchen gardens. Although they could hardly say they'd caught up, Carol thought — it felt more like they had just scratched the surface.

"So what about you, Netty?" asked Carol. They were walking side by side, Carol relishing the sound of their feet crunching over the fine gravel, the afternoon sun warming her face. It was a glorious day. There was a sprinkler set up in one corner of the walled garden and where the water arced, rainbows filled the air as millions of tiny droplets refracted the sunlight. It was one of those perfect moments that would linger in the memory.

Ahead of them Adie and Jan were talking, laughing; Carol laid down the images like good wine. Espaliered fruit trees hung on tight to the old brick walls, creating a rich green backdrop to row after row of beautifully laid out vegetable plots, herb gardens and asparagus beds. Just past an old-style wrought-iron greenhouse, figs and peaches and grapevines settled back against a row of pan-tiled sheds and drank in the heat and light. You didn't have to be any kind of gardener to appreciate the tranquillity or beauty of Burbeck House's kitchen garden.

"What have you been up to?" Adie said, swinging round and walking backwards. "We need to get the history all sorted before we get lost in the mêlée — so far we're not doing very well at all. You either 'fess up faster than that or I'm going to have to come bunk down with you lot after all."

Netty lit up another cigarette and blew out a blast of smoke. "Well, in that case, I'll hurry. I've got four hairdresser's shops and beauty salons — all with nail parlours now." She extended her hands to show off a set of perfectly manicured undoubtedly fake talons. "Two ex-husbands, a daughter called Kirsten, who hates me, and a toy boy called Paul, who thinks the sun shines out of — well, all of me, to hear the way he goes on. Kirsten has a real problem with him."

Jan perked up. "Which is?"

"That he doesn't fancy her."

"That'll do it," said Adie, nodding.

"And how old is he?" asked Carol.

"Twenty-seven next birthday," Netty said, almost defiantly.

"Very nice if you can get it," said Adie, with a grin.

"What about you then, golden boy? You've been very quiet so far," said Jan.

"Only because I couldn't get a bloody word in edgeways," he said, smiling still.

"Well, now's your moment," Jan fired straight back. "I mean, I know all about you but I'm sure your fans want to hear all the sordid details."

He pulled a face. "There's not a lot to tell, really. I was hoping that we'd hear all about you first."

"What, so you're hoping for a big build-up, were you?" laughed Jan.

Adie shook his head. "No, I was being gentlemanly."

"OK," said Jan briskly, as if her words and potted biography would clear the decks for his. "Well, I'm single." She flicked her long hair back over her shoulder as if defying anyone to comment. "I've got a Fine Art degree and an MA in textile design and had planned to teach but changed horses after graduation and now I design fabrics, do some styling for magazines — occasionally get some interior design work — and I lecture as well. I've got a really nice little place in Highgate." She paused. "That's about it, really. I travel a lot, work, love my job — well, jobs. It's a kind of patchwork of things that all tie in."

"It doesn't sound like very much for twenty years," complained Netty, lighting up another cigarette. "Are these the U-certificate edited highlights? What about all the sex, drugs, and rock and roll, broken hearts, mad passions, significant others?"

Jan waved the ideas away, a row of bangles on her wrist tinkling like sleigh bells. "Sometimes, occasionally kind of, but it's been a now-and-then thing. To be honest, I travel so much and am so busy that I don't have the time. I kept thinking some day, one day — but it just hasn't happened."

"So far," said Adie.

Netty pulled a face, her expression matched by Carol's.

Ignoring Adie, Carol said, "How can you say that you don't have the time? I don't understand. How can you not have time for *people*?"

Jan bristled. "I *do* have time for people," she protested. "I just don't have time for the sort you wake up with in the morning. I lived with people and I went out with guys at college. And then about ten years ago I was part of a group that set up workshops in India and more recently in Africa. They're both run co-operatively and they print and export fabric. It has really taken off and that takes up a lot of my time and energy, and to be honest I never seem to have the time for all that, you know, bunny-slippers and kissy-face stuff. I've got two Burmese cats called Lucifer and Diablo, and yes, before you say anything, yes, they are my surrogate children and yes, I do spoil them. And that's about it really."

"Sounds a bit dull," Netty growled. "I like a man in my life. I've always enjoyed the exquisite pain that only a really bad relationship can bring."

Jan grinned. "I've spent a lot of time in India and the Far East, sourcing silk and fabrics, and trust me, when it comes to pain, there's nothing beats amoebic dysentery."

Netty snorted.

"Right," said Jan, with barely a pause for breath, "now then, Mr Can't-get-a-Word-in-Edgeways boy. Your shout. Off you go. Let's have it."

They all looked at Adie, who held up his hands in surrender. "OK, I'm not fighting it, I'll come quietly. I went to uni straight from school. Got a pretty shitty degree and then I didn't really know what I wanted to do so I went travelling and did all sorts of stuff. I went to Australia, Bali; worked in bars, played guitar, grew my hair, smoked a lot of dope." He laughed. "And I suppose I finally grew up. While I was in Thailand I met someone, we travelled together for a couple of years and then when we came back we decided to try and give it a go and we've been together ever since — I suppose that must be nearly fifteen years or so now."

"Someone?" asked Jan pointedly.

Adie nodded. "Yup. We bought a really nice place in Tunbridge Wells. I own a shop — I sell clothes — and . . ."

Carol was aware that they were all hanging on his every word now.

"And you're happy?" said Netty suspiciously.

He grinned. "Blissfully, and before you make any kind of sarky remark about it, no one is more surprised than me."

Jan made a funny little noise in the back of her throat that might have been disbelief but could equally well have been disgust.

"Really?" said Carol.

He nodded. "Yes, really. My partner is a GP and I can feel all sorts of middle-aged angst creeping up on me. I've started writing letters to the broadsheets complaining about young people, falling moral standards and litter in the street."

"Oh my God, you've grown up to be Disgusted of Tunbridge Wells," said Carol with a giggle.

He grinned. "Not exactly. Actually, I've grown up to be Gay of Tunbridge Wells. My partner, Mike, said that if I get any more conservative he's going to buy me driving gloves and an Argyll sweater for Christmas."

Carol looked at him. There was a brief moment when the waves parted, and then the sea closed back over the gap with no great sense of revelation, nor anything unexpected being revealed, just an acceptance of what had — at some level — always been obvious.

"How was it at the pub?" Diana was in the dining room, hunched over a box of what looked like Christmas decorations, her whereabouts signposted from the main hall by a number of cards and home-made banners, that read: "BELVEDERE SCHOOL REUNION — THIS WAY >>>" in a confident bold italic hand that suggested they had been written by

82

someone with a lot of experience at impromptu crowd direction.

"Great, you should have come. We ate, we drank, we were merry, but Carol here had a fit of conscience and decided it was too cruel to leave you with all the work, and actually she is most probably right. Here, give me that bunting," said Adie. Grabbing one end, he clambered up onto a stepladder. "Have you got any drawing pins?"

"Well, of course I have," Diana said, sounding terribly affronted.

Carol laughed; as if Diana would be the kind of event planner who would arrive without every eventuality covered. It felt so good to be back with them all; why had they left it so long before meeting up? So many years . . . too many years.

"Why didn't you ask us to help you with all this? We wouldn't have minded," said Netty, pulling out a huge bag of balloons and a thing that looked like a cardboard bicycle pump from one of the boxes. "Do these things actually work?" she said to no one in particular, as she tipped the balloons out in a heap onto the table and then pumped the tube thing furiously into mid-air.

"No, but they make a great noise if you put your finger over the end," said Adie from the top of the stepladder. "Like a big wet fart."

"Oh well, that's really helpful," growled Netty.

"Here," said Jan, "let me," and started to stretch the balloons vigorously with all the zeal of a woman on a mission.

Diana seemed a bit stunned by their manic activity. "Are you sure you don't mind?"

"Come off it, you can't do it all on your own," Carol snorted. "And besides, you asked me to pitch in, I seem to remember."

But before she could say anything else, Adie said, "Yeah, Di, lighten up. We're all more than happy to muck in, aren't we, folks?"

Everyone looked at him and pulled faces and groaned jokingly. Adie scowled, but unperturbed, unrolled a great string of flags that spelled out welcome in a dozen different languages.

Carol took hold of the cord of the flags and pulled it across the room, wondering how likely it was that she could convince them that any enquiry about who else had arrived since they had been down the pub was purely casual. Just as she was about to speak Jan threw down the balloon she had been torturing and snapped, "You're always so fucking flippant, aren't you, Adie? Mr Quickwit. So sure of yourself."

Everyone looked at her; he hadn't said anything for the best part of two minutes.

Adie was stunned. "What on earth is the matter with you?" he said gently.

Jan flipped a stray hand across her face as if swatting away a fly, her eyes bright with tears. "Nothing," she growled crossly. "Nothing at bloody all. I'm just pissed off with you always assuming you're master of ceremonies, Mr I'm so bloody funny."

Carol stared at her.

"I don't know what you mean," Adie began, looking bemused.

Jan sighed. "Why am I not surprised?"

"Hello, anyone home?" called a loud male voice from out in the hallway, diverting everyone's attention away from Jan. Seconds later a vaguely familiar face appeared round the door and then there was another; two more of the backstage crew appeared in the doorway as Diana headed off to greet the first two, and then there was another and another.

Callista Haze and George Bearman were amongst the flurry of newcomers, and all at once it seemed as if there was a roomful of people, the round of hellos and whoops taking the attention away from Jan, who picked up another balloon.

"You sure you're all right?" Carol said in an undertone. "I mean, we all know how frustrating balloon-blowing can be."

"Yes, I'm fine." Jan sniffed back the tears. "Don't mind me."

"But I do," said Carol. "What's the matter?"

Jan shook her head and pulled a tissue out of her sleeve. "Nothing. I think it's seeing all you lot again. Where did the years go? You keep thinking that there is plenty of time and then all of a sudden there isn't."

Carol nodded and patted Jan on the arm. "I know what you mean," she said softly. Raf and the boys felt a million miles away.

Gareth Howard picked up his mobile and, slotting it into the cradle on the dashboard, switched it back on to check his voice mail. There was Diana, ringing to make sure that he was still coming, three angry outbursts and furious pain-filled silences from Leonora and a call from Fiona. He pressed the recall button as Fiona's message ended.

"Hi, Fiona. How's it going? Where are you?"

She giggled. "Oh, hi. It is so nice to hear from you. Stuck in a traffic jam on the M25. How about you?"

"On the way. I'm really looking forward to catching up at long last," he said. "Make up for lost time."

"Really?" purred Fiona's voice on the end of the phone.

He laughed. Oh yes, Gareth planned to make up for lost time, all right.

The signal crackled and broke up. Gareth switched the phone off, threw it onto the passenger seat and put his foot down. With a bit of luck he'd make it to Burbeck House in time for supper.

CHAPTER
FOUR

In her suburban house a long way from Burbeck House, Leonora settled the baby down in her cot and after checking that Patrick was still listening to his story tape in the nursery, headed across the landing into the main bedroom.

It had been such a quiet day since Gareth left. The children were subdued and slightly fretful, as if they knew something was wrong and were anxiously waiting too. Waiting. She had been waiting all day. No phone calls, no texts, nothing. It felt as if Gareth had stepped out of the door and vanished off the planet. Rapture.

In the dining room at Burbeck House, everyone was coming to the end of supper. Carol handed the coffee-pot down the table to Adie, who grinned his thanks. "Penny for them?" he said.

"I'd save your money if I were you. I'd have thought it was pretty bloody obvious what she was thinking about — or rather who," said Netty, dropping sugar lumps into her cup. "She's been miles away all through supper."

"Looking at the door." Jan.

"And the clock." Diana.

The four of them all turned to look at Carol and then at each other, and then Adie burst into the song "It Must Be Love". Two bars in and all of them were singing.

Carol reddened furiously. It was getting really tough to sustain the illusion of being sociable when so much of her was busy waiting for Gareth Howard to show up. Damn him, it was totally crazy, but however hard Carol tried to deny it the feeling was getting worse and worse, and she was driving herself crazy, let alone the others.

"Relax," hissed Diana, dropping out of the impromptu barbershop quartet. "He did say that he would be here as soon as he could."

Carol stared at her; she had had no idea that it was that obvious.

Diana grinned. "You scrub up well and you're all nicely puffed up too. I'm sure he'll be impressed. We are."

Carol resisted the temptation to pinch her.

Gareth would probably barely remember her; he was probably happily married. Actually, he probably was. The thought wedged firm. God, what if he was with someone else, someone he adored? What if he really didn't remember her? Carol shook her head to try and clear it.

"Do you want that?" said Netty, eyeing up the after-dinner mint on her plate.

"Paws off."

"Oh, come on," she whined. "You won't miss it. You're in love, and we all know love makes you blind."

"Blind maybe, but it doesn't effect my eating habits."

88

"I always lose weight when I'm in love and then comfort-eat when they bugger off. Come on, let me have it, and then when it all ends in tears I'll send you a box of Kit-Kats."

Whining aside, Netty was on top form, Adie too — the jokes, the funnies, the sharp digs and long-forgotten memories had been served and volleyed and smashed around the table all evening. Carol had laughed so much her stomach hurt and her face ached. She'd heard about who had stayed in touch with who, courses and colleges, dogs and cats and kids and houses, lovers, love affairs and jobs that had gone horribly wrong.

From across the room came a great roaring whoop of laughter. Diana's decorations looked lost in the dining room, but even vaulted acres of institutional grey couldn't dampen the atmosphere. The long tables were full of people enjoying themselves, the room full to the rafters with the sound of voices and laughter — half-remembered, half-familiar faces all catching up.

She looked up at the clock again; she really ought to have rung Raf and the boys to tell them she had arrived safe and sound, so why hadn't she?

When Carol looked back not only had the mint gone but so had her glass, her coffee, the remains of her dessert and all the cutlery. She looked at the gang. "It's not big and it's not clever," she said with grudging admiration.

"Oh, for goodness' sake, lighten up. Diana said he'd be here," said Jan. "Let's talk about something more serious, like the severe lack of alcohol."

"We could go down to the off-licence and buy a few more bottles of wine, Di, unless you're up for the water trick — or is that just for weddings and the faithful few?" Netty mimed a magician's pass over the carafe of water on the table. Diana rolled her eyes and looked heavenwards while Netty continued, "It never occurred to me that the place would be dry. The backstage crew have all got the shakes from withdrawal symptoms."

Grateful to be rescued, Carol nodded. "Just tell people if they want to have wine to go and buy some."

Diana nodded and then very earnestly scribbled a note down on the pad beside her plate. Carol smiled. It was Netty's turn to roll her eyes and look heavenwards.

The instructions on the invitation were that although Burbeck House was relaxed about appearance, guests and delegates would be expected to dress smartly for dinner. Netty had taken that as a green light to drag out a sparkly cerise and silver cocktail frock from somewhere dark and dangerous that must lead straight back to the eighties, adding a pair of impossibly strappy killer-heeled sandals and a whole heap of diamanté. Everyone else had gone for smart casual or close to it — not that Netty appeared to mind in the least. She was the kind of person who had enough front to carry off wearing a wetsuit and tiara.

Carol had thought very carefully about the clothes she'd brought with her; she might be nearly forty but she didn't want people to think that she had let herself go. She was wearing a long cotton jersey dress in navy, bias cut, with thin straps and a scooped neck that emphasised her narrow waist, toned body and showed off nicely tanned shoulders. She had added just enough makeup to emphasise those great big blue-green eyes and, with a hint of lipstick, she looked good. Very good.

Earlier, drawing and smudging kohl round her eyes, hunched over the child-sized sink in the communal bathroom next to the girls' dormitory, Carol had had to spend a while persuading herself that all this effort wasn't for Gareth — at least it wasn't *just* for Gareth. No, not just for him. She wanted to look good for herself.

Alongside her, Netty had grinned from behind her makeup box, face contorting so that she could outline her lips with a bright pink pencil.

"Just like the good old days, eh? Us lot getting all dolled up in the girls' loos for a night on the town. Shame we haven't got any panstick, really. You remember the stage makeup Miss Haze used to make us wear for the performances? It was like slapping on magnolia emulsion mixed with margarine."

"I'm sure if you ask, Diana has probably got some somewhere."

Netty laughed. Her makeup kit had lots of lift-out layered trays that were now spread across the sink and adjoining bench; they looked like a cross between a mechanic's tool box and an artist's palette.

Carol, looking down at her own small makeup bag, said, "I see that you've come prepared."

Netty — once she had blotted — sniffed. "Oh, come on, facing forty I need all the help I can get. Polyfilla, glass-fibre, sandpaper . . ." She drew a hand over the trays like a market trader displaying her wares.

"Anything you fancy, you just dive right in. I get a lot as samples from work. How about a teensy weensy bit of glitter? You're looking a bit peaky."

"Uh, no, I'm fine, thanks." Carol turned her attention back to the mirror and the kohl.

"Great to see everyone again, huh?" There were the sounds of giggling coming from the dormitory, although it was hard to work out exactly who it was. Painstakingly Netty filled in her lips with a tiny brush. "It is going to be all right, you know," she said, eyes still firmly fixed on her reflection.

Carol looked up in surprise. "What is?"

Netty's concentration didn't waiver. "This whole weekend, the play — you meeting Gareth again."

Carol stiffened and then attempted to sound casual. "It's no big thing," she lied.

"Yeah, right. You're not fooling anybody, you know. Relax, it'll be OK. Forty-eight hours on a magical mystery tour down memory lane and then nothing. Zilch, zippola. We meet up, we all cry buckets and on Sunday afternoon we'll all go home back to our own lives. And before you say I'm being cynical I'm not — not at all. I just know it's true. I went to a tech reunion last year with the crew I'd learned hairdressing with. Panda-eyes, mascara and big snotty hugs. It's all very lovely but, trust me, it won't make a blind bit of difference to your real life."

Carol felt her colour draining. "What won't?"

"Old passions, old pleasure — old boyfriends. People change. They move on. They grow up. Even if you shag Gareth Howard blind all weekend, chances are that

Monday morning, half-past seven, when you look in the bathroom mirror, nothing will have changed. Trust me, I'm a hairdresser."

Carol felt a lump catch in her throat. "I —" she began.

"You what?" said Netty, gaze swivelling to fix Carol's eyes reflected in the mirror. "You are still carrying a torch for him, aren't you?"

Carol nodded, not trusting herself to speak. How very silly it sounded spoken aloud.

"Trust me, you're way better sticking with the fantasy." Netty glanced over one shoulder in case there was anyone within earshot. "I've never told anyone this, not even Jan, but I had a crush for years on one of the boys in our year. Even after we left I used to fantasise about him and me. Sometimes it was wild sex and lots of snogging, but mostly it was all that happy-ever-after stuff. Two kids, him going off to work with me in a pinny. He worked in the bank in Belvedere for a while after we all left school. I'd volunteer to go and bank the takings from my mum's salon. Twice a week, come rain, come shine, I'd toddle off down to Barclays in full makeup and an outfit to die for, and then after about a year he moved away. I was so gutted, I can't tell you. And you know what? He's going to be here this weekend." She smacked her lips and admired the effects.

"Really?" said Carol incredulously. It hadn't occurred to her that anyone else was dreaming about might-have-beens. "Why on earth didn't you say something? Are you excited about seeing him again? How come you never told anybody? Who is it?"

Netty wound up a lipstick and dibbled the brush over the end to touch up a bald patch. "Peter Fleming."

"No, really? *Really?* Not Peter Fleming?" Carol couldn't quite keep the incredulity out of her voice, despite trying really hard. Peter Fleming was real dyed-in-the-wool ginger, with hair the colour of bright copper and skin the colour of skimmed milk, and enough freckles to keep a dot-to-dot fanatic happy for hours. She had never dared let her mind wander to where exactly the freckles might stop — did freckles fade just below the collar or were they an all-over thing? Netty had them too but in a cute all-over-the-nose way. Carol tried to drag her mind from what might happen if two freckly people had kids. Was there an optimum moment when they just had one big all-over freckle?

"Peter Fleming?" she repeated.

He was nice enough but he had never struck Carol as sex on a stick, and certainly not the kind of man or boy that someone like Netty would be interested in.

Netty nodded. "I know, I know," she said, as if she could read Carol's mind — except perhaps for the freckle thing. "Strange but true. Can you imagine what Adie would have said if he'd known? He would never have let me live it down. It doesn't bear thinking about. Between you, you would have made mincemeat of me, and despite what you think I'm not as tough as I look. So I just admired and lusted after him from a distance."

"*You lusted after Peter Fleming?*" said Carol.

Netty pulled a don't-push-your-luck face.

"OK, OK — so are you excited about seeing him again?" Carol asked struggling to gain some ground.

Netty shook her head. "Nope, not so much as a flutter. You see, unlike you, I've already tried living the dream." She said the last few words in a hideously camp American accent and waved her hand dramatically across the mirror, tracing the arc of a cartoon shooting star.

"Really?" said Carol, aware that her mouth was open, aware that with one eye made up and the other one bare she looked daft, but who cared. "You tried living the dream *with Peter Fleming?*"

"Don't say it like that," growled Netty. "Yes, with Peter Fleming. I did see him again, we did meet up. It was maybe ten years ago, in a supermarket of all places. By coincidence we were both home for a visit, so we had a coffee and — well, we flirted and laughed and reminisced about the good old days and then I'm buggered if he didn't ask me out. He said he had always had this thing about me and that he thought our meeting up again was fate." Netty paused.

Carol waved her on. "For God's sake, don't stop there — what happened?"

Netty pulled out an eye pencil. "Fate has got a very nasty sense of humour. It was a total and utter disaster. We had nothing in common, nothing at all, zilch, zippo, nada. They had all gone, my fantasies, my dreams — his too — just ashes, dust, a mirage."

"Oh, Netty," murmured Carol as she heard the catch in Netty's voice. "I'm so sorry. I'd no idea."

Netty snorted. "Don't look like that. It was fine. Really. Take my advice. Monday morning, take a look in the bathroom mirror, and see if anything has changed."

"Do you think I should say a few words now?"

Carol swung round in surprise, snapped back to the present by Diana's voice. "What?"

Diana, sitting beside her, was clutching a notepad. "I really ought to have said something before supper started, but I would have liked everyone to have been here." She glanced round the room, heaving with the rest of the cast and crew. Miss Haze had taken her place on the top table, alongside Mr Bearman. Only Macbeth and Lady Macduff were now conspicuous by their absence.

"I think you should go for it," said Carol, nodding. "God alone knows what time —" she tripped clumsily over Gareth's name — "the others will be getting here."

"That's true." Diana nodded and, clearing her throat nervously, got to her feet. A little further down the table Adie obliged by banging a spoon against one of the institutional tumblers. The room quietened for an instant, Diana reddened and then beamed at the assembled group. When people realised who it was, there was a lot of good-natured rumbling and whistling and clapping, which swiftly faded into a warm convivial silence.

"Good evening," Diana said hesitantly. "I'm not very good at this kind of thing; I'm much happier behind the scenes but I would like to say how wonderful it is to see everyone again. Thank you for making the effort to drive all this way. I was worried you might not come or that only a few of you would say yes — but it looks at the moment as though we will be having a hundred per cent turn-out. Also I have to apologise for the fact that we're going to be staying in dormitories."

"Enough with the dormitories already," growled Netty, with a heavy New York Jewish accent. "We don't mind, and if we do — well, what can ya do?"

There was a ripple of laughter from the room.

Hitting her stride, Diana flipped the page on her notebook and half reading, half remembering, launched into her spiel. "This evening is quite informal, giving everyone a chance to catch up and renew old friendships — and then tomorrow rehearsals will start in earnest after breakfast at ten in the conference room at the end of the corridor. It will be marked so there is no need to worry about finding it. If everyone could at least come to the first get-together, that would be lovely. This is meant to be fun, but if we're going to pull it off it also includes quite a lot of work. I've drawn up a rehearsal schedule, which everyone should have." She waved a photocopied sheet in the air. "Those people who aren't needed are very welcome to use the grounds, there's an outdoor swimming pool and tennis courts — details of the facilities are on the sheet too — and there's the village, which is particularly attractive." She paused and then laughed. "Sorry, I sound like a bad travel brochure but there is just so much to remember. The plan — as I hope you all know now — is to put on a rehearsed reading of *Macbeth* on Sunday afternoon. I am hoping all your families as well as lots of other old schoolfriends will turn up to share the performance and the strawberry tea afterwards." Diana giggled nervously. "I think that's about it, actually. Oh, except to say that although the hall hasn't got a bar you are very welcome to bring wine or whatever in for supper. And besides that, I just wanted to say how very nice it is to see you all again and I hope you enjoy the weekend." And with this, Diana collapsed into her chair with a grin, to a round of rapturous applause.

Adie got to his feet, lifting a glass of squash in a toast. "Thank you for the itinerary, Judith Chalmers. I think we should give Diana a big hand for arranging this weekend and I imagine we are all agreed that she is totally mad to take this on — so no change there. The teetotal toast is Diana."

The response went around the room like a low rumble of thunder. "Diana."

Diana blushed crimson and seemed about to say something, when at that precise moment Carol caught a movement at the corner of her eye and felt her stomach do that instinctive flippy floppy nippy happy thing. Standing on the other side of the room, framed by the French windows, was Gareth Howard and, worse still, he looked gorgeous, a stray breeze ruffling his dark hair. Merchant Ivory couldn't have staged a better entrance. To her total amazement he scanned the room and, as their eyes met, Gareth grinned, a big warm, pleased-to-see-you grin, and then raised a hand in salute.

Oh my God, Carol thought, blushing furiously, trying very hard not to overreact as she smiled back. Resisting the temptation to wave like a demented chimp, Carol coolly tipped her fingers in his direction before putting her hand over her mouth and huffing noisily, wondering if her breath smelled and whether she had any mints in her handbag. Crazy. Was it worse waiting for him or him showing up? Carol's stomach did another little back flip with a half-pike and twist as he made his way across the dining room towards her.

Away over her shoulder Adie's remarks, despite the peels of laughter from the diners, had become no more than a distant drone. Carol felt hot and then cold and then she gasped as Fiona slipped in through the door behind Gareth and he caught hold of her arm and guided her between the diners towards the top table.

Gareth and Fiona. Oh God, please, please, don't let them be a couple, Carol thought as her heart was holed and sank.

But as he walked up towards the table it was Carol Gareth was looking at; she didn't know whether to feel flattered or intimidated. It was a very close-run thing.

"Would you like to say a few words?" Carol looked up dumbly into Adie's face as he spoke to her.

"What?" she snapped.

Adie smiled and then said more slowly, "Watch my lips — I thought you said, when we were walking back from the pub, that you would like to say something too. A few words, remember?"

Carol shook her head. "No, no — it's fine, you've said everything," she said hurriedly. The last thing she wanted to do now was speak publicly, not while Gareth was watching. She was just bound to say something stupid and make a complete and utter tit of herself.

Adie shrugged and turning back to his audience, lifted his hands in a fair impression of a Roman emperor. "In which case, let the games commence." His words brought another explosive round of applause, not to mention much stamping and a volley of whooping cheers from the assembled cast and crew.

A little way along the table Fiona settled into her chair, helped by Gareth, and then he made his way back along to Carol and said warmly, "Hi, great to see you. How have you been?" His voice was as low and dark and sensual as brown velvet, and hearing him speak again after all these years made Carol's scalp tingle.

She opened her mouth to say something but before Carol could speak Gareth leaned forward and kissed her on the cheek. "I've been thinking a lot about you," he purred. "You look absolutely fantastic."

Carol tried very hard to think of something witty to say, something sharp and clever, but settled for giggling inanely instead and saying, "Do I? Really? Right — OK. Um, you too. Are you and Fiona, you know . . ." she nodded in Fiona's general direction while praying the ground would open up and swallow her whole. "You know . . ."

Gareth pulled a face. "I'm sorry, I'm not with you."

Carol felt as if she was clinging on by her fingertips to any remaining shreds of a decent opening conversation. "You and Fiona, are you — are you a couple?" she stammered. "I mean, you arrived together." It was too big a question too soon.

"I met her in the car park just now. We couldn't find the way in," he said.

Carol was so overcome by relief she felt dizzy.

CHAPTER
FIVE

All day long Leonora had been unable to shake the sensation that she was walking through a dream or maybe an abandoned film set, after the actors had left. The thought made her shiver; perhaps she wasn't so far from the truth.

What heightened the feeling was that the whole house, particularly their bedroom, was deliberately theatrical. In the master bedroom a huge bowed double-fronted walnut wardrobe dominated one wall. It had been there when they bought the house, far too heavy and too expensive to be moved and far too wonderful, far too *The Lion, the Witch and the Wardrobe* to be smashed up and skipped. So as an homage to the wardrobe they had decorated the walls with period flock paper — brothel paper, Gareth called it — in the richest purples and golds, adding matching velvet curtains that hung from floor to ceiling on gothic black poles. There were brass and crystal sconces for light fittings, a great big brass bed with white linen bedclothes and a crushed velvet throw the colour of ripe aubergines. The room was as rich as a jewel box and — it occurred to Leonora, still with the shiver lingering in her blood like ice crystals — almost as cold.

She ran her fingers across the deep sensual nap of the velvet bedcover. How many months was it since she and Gareth had slept in here together? How long since they had touched each other, or snuggled up together amongst the bow wave of white linen pillows or, come to that, talked? Since the new baby had been born Leonora had spent more and more nights across the landing in the nursery, curled up alongside Patrick. He was all soft and golden brown, little-boy sweetness pressed tight up against her like a warm puppy, and of course it meant that when the baby woke she was there and that Gareth wasn't disturbed. But her absence wasn't just about the baby, was it? How could he say something so vulnerable, so beautiful was a mistake? It wasn't her fault, tiny thing.

Leonora straightened the bedspread, aware that she only serviced this room now, she didn't live in it any more. It was an alien space, Gareth's space.

She picked up one of his shirts from the bedroom floor and, without thinking, pressed it to her face. It smelled of him, and the scent of Gareth's body made her let out a soft keening wail. How ridiculous, how crazy. How could she still love him when he had walked out on them? How could her heart be so stupid when her head knew so much better?

Silently Leonora picked her way through the landscape of their shared life; opening each drawer in turn — the tallboy, the bookcase, the little chiffonier they had found together in Camden Market. She had a sense that there *were* things missing but it was so hard to be certain of exactly what. Life since the children

103

arrived was so much less linear, less accountable. Maybe there were things in the wash, or the airing cupboard, or tucked away somewhere . . .

Leonora looked around the room, trying to figure out exactly what it was she was feeling. It was so hard to find the edges. Had Gareth abandoned them or had he just gone off to do something related to work — and how the hell was it that after nearly eight years together she didn't know?

Finally Leonora opened up his side of the huge wardrobe, running a finger and an eye along the hangers — the shirts, the trousers — and then she knew with ice-cold certainty that Gareth really had left them. She sucked in a breath to replace the one that had been squeezed from her chest. Gareth's Armani suit had gone, the gap as obvious and raw as a missing front tooth. It was the first thing she noticed, but she was certain now that there would be others.

And there were: his favourite shoes, soft brown leather brogues handmade by a friend in Jermyn Street, a folio edition of *Robinson Crusoe* bought as a present by some doting godparent. A picture of his mother in a silver frame. Once her eye was in, Leonora began to see the things that weren't there as clearly as the things that were.

When she had finished drawing up a mental manifest, Leonora went across into the little boxroom that Gareth used as an office. It had taken her all day to summon up the courage for this but now she was ready. Glancing back over her shoulder she was aware of every noise, every little creak as she stepped over the threshold, moving deliberately slowly, up on her tiptoes, still nervous of being discovered despite the fact that she knew that there was only her and the children in the house.

The office was his space. It smelled of old dust and paper and the warm scent of machines left on too long, all cut and mixed with a sweet undertow of cigar smoke. Gareth never smoked in the house but the scent of cigars clung to his clothes like burrs.

Leonora paused and, like a detective assessing a crime scene, she took it all in, absorbing every last little detail. There were the lamps still lit, the computers on standby purring behind closed darkened eyes, the mismatch of bookcases stacked with files and papers, and alongside those his novels and collections of poetry, favourite books read and reread again and again in the years that she had known him. She held back from touching anything.

There were mugs on the crowded desk, one on a discarded CD, the others scattered between pens and papers, a stapler, a phone, a remote control for goodness knew what, the detritus of his thoughts and his life, the ghost of Gareth lingering still between the posters and prints and badly stacked shelves.

Leonora took a deep breath, dark eyes working backwards and forwards across the piles, the highs and the lows, the backwaters and the blind alleys. There was nothing there, at least nothing obvious on the surface, that gave Gareth away, nothing revealing or betraying whatever it was that she instinctively felt *was* there. But he couldn't hide from her, not for long.

There *was* something there, she had absolutely no doubt of that — disguised as something innocuous, something innocent that was the key to everything. Leonora also knew that she wouldn't know what it was until she saw it and as soon as she did she would be certain.

Methodically, she opened each of the desk drawers in turn, from top to bottom, right to left, pausing for a few moments to stare down unfocused at the contents, as if she might be able to divine the solution from the mess of envelopes and elastic bands and old biros inside, hoping that something, one thing, would tell her what it was she wanted to know — even though she still wasn't sure exactly what that was.

After Gareth's desk Leonora worked her way through the filing cabinets, drawer by drawer, running her finger along the rows of hanging files, much as she had his shirts and jackets, reading each file label in turn. She thumbed through the bookshelves, stroking each spine like a touchstone, and then worked through a stack of unopened post piled high on an old kitchen chair. It was here somewhere, Leonora could feel it, feel it getting closer, knew she was getting warmer, though it was still elusive, like something deliberately hiding in the undergrowth.

And then all of a sudden she had it, pinned to one of the cork message boards just inside the door. On a sheet of page ripped from a spiral-bound notepad was a number, not a mobile number but a proper phone number, and alongside it, written in Gareth's distinctive handwriting, the words: "Diana get-together/weekend?" and a date.

Leonora stared at it and knew, without understanding exactly why, that this was what she had been looking for. She unpinned the sheet of paper, folded it up and slid it into the pocket of her cardigan. Backing out, she closed the door tight, walked slowly downstairs and, picking up the phone, dialled the number that felt as if it had been seared onto her retina.

"Hello, may I speak to Diana, please?" Leonora said as evenly as she could manage when someone lifted the receiver at the other end of the line.

"I'm most terribly sorry, but she is away for the weekend," said a cultured male voice. "Would you like me to take a message? Or perhaps I might be able to help you?" he added brightly.

Leonora hesitated; the adrenalin that had carried her downstairs was rapidly ebbing away. What was it she wanted to say exactly? Should she hang up and if she did where would that leave her? Had this man's wife run away with Gareth? And how could Leonora possibly ask him or contemplate telling him? What if he had no idea what was going on? It didn't sound as if he had any idea.

Leonora bit her lip, letting her thoughts regroup. Just then Patrick, in his pyjamas, padded out onto the top of the stairs to find her. He had a teddy bear in one hand and a storybook in the other, and for a moment he looked totally lost — and then as their eyes met he smiled with relief at having found her. He had his father's eyes.

Leonora's heart ached for him, for them all.

"I'm not sure. I'm trying to find my husband and I thought Diana might be able to help," she said, moving cautiously around the edge of the conversation in case she plunged into the abyss, dragging this unknown man with her.

"Oh, OK," said the man pleasantly. It struck her as an odd thing to say.

Very slowly Patrick bumped down the steps on his bottom towards her and as he got to the final step he held out his arms for her to pick him up.

"I was wondering if Diana might know where he is?" Leonora continued as Patrick climbed her like a tree.

"Righty-oh. What's his name?" asked the man conversationally, as if his concentration was elsewhere.

"Gareth," she said. "Gareth Howard."

"OK. Wait a minute. I think I have a list here somewhere," he said, now sounding even more preoccupied over the noise of papers rustling. "Perhaps you would like Diana's mobile number. That's here somewhere too," he laughed. "Bit chaotic at the moment, I'm afraid. Oh, hang on, here we are."

"A list?" Leonora was struggling to keep up.

"Yes, of course, didn't you know? Sorry, I assumed you knew all about it. They've all gone to a school reunion this weekend. I've got all the details somewhere — oh, yes, this is it. Have you got a pen handy?"

At Burbeck House Carol tried very hard to ignore the nasty rash of kissy, sucky faces and various lovey-dovey noises coming from further along the top table, not to mention Adie pressing his hand to his chest and fluttering his eyelids like a pantomime dame.

Being the kind of establishment that it was — all Christian charity and fuelled by the milk of human kindness — the kitchen staff had saved the latecomers their supper and now produced meals on trays. Despite various suggestions that everyone else headed off to the pub, no one appeared to be in much of a hurry to move either, so the hall was still full of people totally wrapped up in conversation. It felt almost like Christmas, Carol thought as she looked around the tables.

"I've thought about you a lot over the years," Gareth said to Carol as he attacked his supper. The sound of his voice moved her attention back to him. She felt herself blush and then smiled, wishing that there was some way she could control the fluttery sensation in her stomach and suppress a disturbing inclination to giggle furiously.

"You're wearing a wedding ring," she said conversationally. It was one of the first things Carol had noticed when he sat down beside her, and absolutely the last thing she wanted to say, but helpfully her brain had reversed the order.

He nodded, turning the narrow twisted band of gold thoughtfully around long elegant fingers. "Yes, you're right. Sorry, it's force of habit. I suppose I really ought to take it off, but it seems as if I'm casting her adrift."

Carol looked at him expectantly. He sighed. "It's no great mystery. I left her," he said. "It's a little while ago now but it was all very sad."

His eyes darkened down to a stormy grey. Carol wondered what it would feel like to be married to him. Worse, what would it feel like to be left by him? She shivered, struggling to compose herself, and mumbled, "I'm really sorry."

Gareth shook his head. "There's no need to be sorry; it was just one of those things. I'd just come out of a long-term relationship when I met her. Oddly enough, I was working for a touring theatre company." He smiled reflectively. "I was lonely. We got on quite well, went out a few times. You know how these things go, and then — I suppose I was a bit of a fool, really. We'd been seeing each other a couple of months, maybe three, when she told me she was pregnant. It was a bit of a shock but what could I do?"

Carol stared at him. "What do you mean? Are you saying the baby wasn't yours?" The words were out before she had considered just how big the question was.

He shrugged. "No, I'm not saying that. I'm saying that I really had no way of knowing and, looking back, I ought to have been more careful." He grinned and pushed the fringe back off his face. "And I shouldn't be telling you any of this; it's not exactly the kind of thing I make a habit of talking about — and, don't get me wrong, she is the most beautiful person but a very complicated woman — artistic, creative, highly strung. A little unstable at times." He laughed wryly and took a sip of juice. "Quite a lot unstable at times, actually. When I met her she was in one of her good phases, sharing a house in North London with God knows how many others, mostly artists and musicians and she seemed — well, exciting, Bohemian and she was — she is — truly lovely. I stayed for as long as I could, but it was impossible. I felt my being there was doing more harm than good."

"And what about the child?" said Carol, words out before she could stop them.

"Children now — a boy and a girl. I see them as often as I can — don't get me wrong, she is a great mother — but sometimes my seeing them causes more problems than it solves." He shrugged. "So there we are." His voice dropped a little and softened.

Leonora sat on the bottom step of the stairs and very carefully tapped the mobile number that Diana's husband had given her into the phone. She waited, unconsciously holding her breath, hoping that she had made a mistake first time round and that this time she would get through. But sure enough, after a few seconds a bright cheery voice said, "Hello, I'm terribly sorry but I can't take your call at the moment. If you would like to leave a message after the tone then I'll get back to you as soon as I can. Thank you for ringing." It sounded so affable, so banal, so matter of fact, that locked door that barred her way to Diana and Gareth.

Leonora looked up at the clock; it was too late to go to anywhere, even if she could have got through. The children were tucked up in bed and besides that, Gareth had taken the car. But it would have been good to have made plans, to have known more, to have worked out a way forward. The sense of impotence and frustration made her angry. Leonora's eyes filled with tears — not so much from despair as from pure anger. Bloody man, how dare he leave her without some sort of explanation? What was she supposed to do now, just wait and mope around while he decided their fate? Leonora dropped the phone back into its cradle, incandescent with rage.

"Bastard, bastard, bastard," she growled furiously. How was it that Gareth got to make the decision? How was it that he had ended up with all the power? Leonora pulled a road atlas down from the bookshelves and, wrapping her big baggy purple cardigan around her shoulders, curled up in an armchair and searched for Burbeck. Ba — B — B . . . She ran a finger down the columns, mouthing the alphabet to herself. Be, B . . . It had to be in there somewhere.

In the back of her mind Leonora could hear Gareth's voice. Words fuelled and let loose by a bottle and a half of red wine. It was earlier in the year, in the grey wet days between winter and spring. "It would be nice if you wore something a bit less shapeless once in a while. It's depressing to see you dressed like a bag lady all the time. You just don't bother any more — don't make any sort of effort. Have you thought that you should maybe go and see somebody?"

Leonora stared at him. "Gareth, since Maisie was born, nothing fits properly. It would be a waste of money to buy anything at the moment and besides, it's always cold in here and it's either wear something warm or turn the heating up, and we've already had the row about the size of the heating bills."

112

He sniffed. "For fuck's sake, Leonora, that thing makes you look like you're sleeping rough." Noisy cruel-tongued drunken ghosts filled her head. Well, one particular ghost, anyway.

She could see him by the kitchen door, fingers pushing the fringe back off his face. "I don't think I can do it any more, Leonora, in fact I'm not sure I can do it at all," growled the ghost of Gareth past. He didn't shout or rant — it wasn't his style. Instead he dropped the bills onto the kitchen table.

"But I'm not asking you to do it all. I've never asked you to do it all. I am trying. I'm doing the best I can," Leonora had said, realising as she did that that was not what Gareth meant at all.

"Really?" His voice was so very even, so controlled, so cold. "Whatever happened to, 'As soon as I've finished breast-feeding Patrick I'll find a part-time job'?"

"Oh, Gareth, Maisie —"

"Maisie," he hissed. "Maisie? What sort of name is that, anyway? You knew, didn't you? You knew that breast-feeding didn't mean you couldn't get pregnant again. Just tell me that you knew."

"I thought it was safe," Leonora protested; how many times had they had this conversation? "I truly thought —"

"Oh, yes, you *truly* thought — princess Leonora, earth mother, patron saint of childbirth. Half a dozen self-help books and a natural parentcraft class and you're suddenly the world's expert. Well, you were wrong, weren't you?" The venom she could hear just beneath the surface in his voice made her reel.

How could he talk to her like that? Leonora's vision blurred with tears as she ran a finger down the atlas's index. "Ba, Be, B —" she said aloud, trying to steady her thoughts.

When Gareth was angry and drunk he spoke very slowly, icily enunciating every word in a voice barely above a whisper. The measured tone was so much more disturbing than if he had shouted. Words spoken in anger could be excused or apologised for, but these lingered, glacial and unyielding.

"We've already talked about this, I've already said, I can still work in the evenings — or at the weekend," she'd said.

"Oh yes, that's very good, great idea — I get to do a whole day's work and then come home and have to look after those two all night." He spat the word "two" out as if the taste was as bitter as gall.

"Gareth, they are our children, your children. Other people do it. We'll find a way to sort things out. We will. They didn't ask to be born."

"No, exactly, and you know what, Leonora? No one asked me either. One mistake was bad enough — but two? It's driving me crazy." He looked round the kitchen. "The whole place is a mess, you're a mess."

The words hit her like a body blow. Gasping for breath, Leonora said, "I've been trying to economise, I've cut down —"

114

"Cut down . . ." He had shaken his head in disgust. "We need more money, pure and simple. And with them —"

"It takes two. You wanted to make love. You wanted me," she sobbed. He hadn't moved to comfort her, to touch her; instead he refilled his glass. The hurt hung in her heart like a scar.

She remembered the first time they had made love after Patrick was born. At first it was tentative, like strangers, and then — when he realised she wouldn't break — he had pulled her tight against him and fucked her hard and fast, almost cruelly — and Leonora had gasped, and melted into him, loving it, loving him.

It had felt like he was claiming her back for himself, taking her back from Patrick and motherhood and all the things that had separated them, and she had wept with relief as they lay in the dark, thinking it would be all right, thinking that they could make it work, thinking that at last she was home.

"You're right," he said. "But I didn't know what your little game was then, did I?"

"My game?" she gasped. "What little game?"

He carried on as if she hadn't spoken. "You tricked me — this is what you wanted, isn't it, Leonora? Your nice little house, and your cosy little family. Well, I've got news for you . . ."

"No." She shook her head, covering her ears with her hands, not wanting to hear what he had to say, hurt and anger making her eyes fill with bitter tears. "You were the one who wanted a family, Gareth, that's what you said — all that stuff about having kids and dogs, and

115

rabbits in the garden — please, Gareth — please. Where are you going?"

"Out."

"What time will you be —"

The door slammed tight shut on any answer, not that she thought there would be one.

And now Gareth was gone all over again, the cruel ghost slipping through her fingers just as the real man had, and why was it that it made her feel so pitiful? How was it that he had taken all the power with him?

Once she had found whereabouts the village was, Leonora padded barefoot upstairs and put Burbeck House into a search engine on one of Gareth's precious computers and worked out the best route. She scrolled down and read the directions, heart sinking as she did. Whichever way you looked at it, Burbeck was miles from anywhere. It wasn't going to be easy getting there without a car. It wouldn't have been easy getting there even with one. Bloody man.

"And, anyway, what sort of job do you think you're going to get at night with a degree in Art, for God's sake? No one in the real world gives a shit about what you think about Botticelli. You'll end up filling shelves in a supermarket, working behind a bar in the pub. Cleaning offices . . ."

She blanched; Gareth's voice had followed her upstairs like a wraith.

"I don't mind doing any of those things. Maybe I could find something part time during the day. Other people do it," Leonora said, aware of how defensive she sounded.

He looked her up and down. "So they do, but the trouble is that that little pinko gallery job you had before you had the kids wouldn't keep us in biscuits after the childcare costs had been taken out. Your trouble, Leonora, is that you live in a fantasy world."

"I could paint again," she said.

His expression told her everything; there was no need for a single word.

Leonora bit her lip and stared down at the map, trying to shut his voice out.

A taxi was totally out of the question and the train would be tricky, but not impossible — lots of changes and still a taxi ride at the other end. It would be hard with the kids. There wasn't a coach service that ran within twenty miles of Burbeck and, besides that — once she had seen Gareth, once she had had her say, what would happen then? What would they do? Did she truly expect it would all come out right? That Gareth would want to come home with them?

Trembling, Leonora scanned the notes she had made after talking to Diana's husband, trying to make sense of what she'd written. In a sterling effort to be as helpful as possible he had read everything out and she had made an equal effort to write it all down. Times of arrival, times of departure, things to bring, what to wear, schedules and then further down a scrawled note about the performance for family and friends on Sunday afternoon.

Leonora stared at it: "Family and friends are invited to a rehearsed read-through on Sunday afternoon, followed by tea," and as the words settled an idea

117

formed — maybe there was a way after all. If there was someone else going to Burbeck House from close by, or even not so close by but passing, then maybe they might be prepared to pick her up and take her and the children as well? It had to be worth a shot.

She just needed to talk to Diana. Leonora picked up the phone on Gareth's desk and tapped in the number again.

After a second or two Gareth appeared to remember Carol was there, watching him and he said hastily, "I'm sorry, I'm hogging the spotlight. Why don't you tell me about what you've been up to? Diana tells me that you're a gardener now and have got a fleet of hoary-handed sons of the soil hanging on your every word. Shades of Lady Chatterley?"

"I bet Diana didn't say that at all and besides, the Lady Chatterley thing was the gamekeeper not a gardener," Carol said. "And I'm interested in how life has been treating you since we last met." She wanted to know about him, all about him, but Gareth wasn't going to be so easily swayed.

"God, no, I'm just another geek, nothing special."

"Are you still in the theatre?"

"On the periphery. I'm involved in IT for a couple of art projects, galleries, but how about you? Successful business woman, own company, double-page spread in the Sunday colour supplements — you didn't ought to be so modest, Carol. I'm very impressed." To her astonishment, as he spoke Gareth lifted a hand and drew a finger down over her cheek. "You know you haven't changed a bit."

She stared at him. How could anyone say something like that and it not sound like a really cheesy line? "Don't be silly," Carol said, torn between delight and feeling hideously self-conscious. Further up the table Adie and Netty feigned swooning and added mock vomiting. She could have killed them both. Easily.

Gareth seemed oblivious. "I'm serious. OK, maybe there's a wrinkle here and a line there," he traced them with his eyes, "but you look very much like the Carol I remember."

The Carol he had screwed, she thought ruefully, wishing for the first time that there had been some wine.

It was also very different then, when sex and all the things that surrounded it were mysterious possibilities and rumours, uncharted waters out beyond the shallows of a few embarrassed fumblings and a lot of urges that nobody knew the right name for. Certainly not like married sex, a chore that came between sorting the laundry and cleaning out the guinea pig.

Sex in the sixth form then was part of a whole unknown continent — something and somewhere yet to be explored. Sex and desire were noisy back then too, a bit like a loud hum or the insistent buzz of cicadas, that ran like an undercurrent to lots of encounters.

Sitting out on the veranda of the cricket pavilion, reading through a scene in the play, bathed in sunshine the colour of fresh lemons squeezed through a cloudy sky, Carol remembered it well. It had been very noisy, practically deafening.

She must have read the play through a hundred times since that first time in the pavilion with Gareth. The last time was earlier in the week, just before she had packed to come to Burbeck House, from a book that, like Miss Haze's, was all neatly annotated, numbered and underscored. But even so, no matter how many times she read it, without fail it always took her back to that moment and that place and Gareth Howard. Hard-wired history, half a dozen lines in and she was up there on the playing field in the sunshine.

It was a warm day in early spring. Carol had stretched, and pulled up white socks, which were regulation school uniform whether you were eighteen or not, and looked across at him. Gareth was so close she could see the pulse in his throat and the merest trace of shaving stubble.

"So where shall we go from?" he'd said conversationally, flipping through the script. "How about act one, scene five: From the first time we're together. Macbeth and Mrs Macbeth at home, weighing up the pros and cons of killing the king, because the three witches —"

A.k.a. Netty, Diana and Jan and the wart, thought Carol.

"— told him that he'll be king, and Mrs Macbeth has the perfect plan to help him on his way. So she's not best pleased when Macbeth bottles out, and says so. That's a bit later." He flipped through the script. "Act one, scene seven."

120

Carol nodded and began to read and then hesitated, marking where she had dried with a pencil so she wouldn't lose her place. "The woman is a complete loony. I can't believe Macbeth does what she tells him. Surely he must be able to see that she is nuts."

"Self-seeking and morbidly ambitious is what Mr Bearman told me, rather than barking and drooling," Gareth said, looking up from his own notes.

"Right," Carol said, nodding in what she hoped was an intelligent way. She knew what barking and drooling were; morbidly ambitious wasn't quite so obvious.

Gareth smiled at her. There was a funny uncomfortable little pause and the noise that sex and desire made got louder. Carol reddened, self-conscious at being with him and being so close to him.

"Sorry," he said. "I just thought that it might help. I wasn't saying you didn't know or anything."

Carol managed a smile. "No, no. It's OK — it's not that, it's just I'm finding it hard to get my head round the language. You really have to concentrate to make it make sense."

He nodded. "Mr Bearman suggested we might need a line-by-line session to get the meaning. Most of it's OK, it's odd phrases that I don't get but they throw the whole thing out totally."

"It makes more sense said aloud," Carol said.

Simmering away just below the stilted but apparently normal conversation, attraction and desire crackled and rolled like a summer storm, making the hair on the back of Carol's neck stand up. Her tongue felt as if it was too big for her mouth and everything she said sounded either gibberish or totally inane.

She and Gareth were sitting side by side on a big roll of sisal netting that the school used for the cricket teams to practise in. She could smell him, feel the heat of him. It made her heart beat so loud that she couldn't hear herself think.

"So where did we get to?" he said, glancing back at the script.

Carol could barely hear his voice above the roar of her pulse and the white noise of lust. "Halfway down page forty-two, Lady M, all outrage and fury because it looks as if Macbeth might be bottling out, 'What Beast was't then/That made you break this enterprise to me?'"

Gareth nodded. "She's convinced he won't go through with stabbing Duncan."

Carol sighed. "Who could blame him?" She stared at the page and then began to read, trying to find the tone for a woman hellbent on murder. She read haltingly — and on down the page until she got to, "'I have given suck, and know/How tender 'tis to love the babe that milks me —'" Blushing furiously, Carol looked up and realised with horror that Gareth was looking thoughtfully at the curves in her school blouse. It did nothing at all to help her concentration. She took a deep breath.

"'I would, while it was smiling in my face/Have pluck'd my nipp—'" She stopped dead, totally unable to carry on. Nipple was a word too far. She could feel Gareth's eyes as hot as hands on her body, felt a great rolling wave of desire that almost made her choke, and froze. "Sorry," she mumbled lamely. "It's all a bit much — you know."

"It's fine," said Gareth gently. "It is a big speech," and then, barely looking at the page, recited the line she had stumbled over: " '. . . would, while it was smiling in my face/Have pluck'd my nipple from his boneless gums,' " all the while grinning from ear to ear.

"The woman really was a total cow," snapped Carol, slamming the book shut, but they both knew that it wasn't Lady Macbeth's morals that were making Carol blush.

Sitting there under cover of the pavilion canopy, the air heady with the smell of sisal and sunshine and sex, Carol was horribly aware of the effect Gareth was having on her body and damned if, twenty years later, he wasn't doing it all over again.

Across the table at Burbeck House he was still grinning, the face now much older but the expression almost unchanged. Carol shivered.

He tipped a glass of apple juice in her direction by way of salute and invitation. "I'm not sure I can face my rhubarb crumble. How do you fancy a stroll down to the pub instead?"

Before Carol could answer Adie leaned across and nodded. "Damn good idea, Gareth. I don't know about you but I could murder a pint." As he spoke most of the student contingent on the top table rose as a body. It seemed that they were planning to protect Carol from herself. She got up, more from amazement than anything else, and as she did Diana caught hold of

Carol's arm and said, "Are you coming upstairs with me to get a jacket?"

Carol was about to say no, it was a beautiful evening, when Netty nodded on her behalf and between them they guided Carol — who was too surprised to resist — out of the dining room with all the efficiency of a police escort.

"But it's really warm out there," Gareth protested to their retreating backs, not that it made a blind bit of difference.

"What *is* going on?" Carol hissed furiously as Netty caught hold of her elbow.

Gareth watched their progress with interest and so, she noticed, did Fiona, who, before Carol had even reached the door, made her way back along the table towards where Gareth was sitting and slipped into the seat Carol had so recently vacated.

"What is this about?" asked Carol, finally shaking herself free.

"Well, you can put your tongue back in for a start," growled Netty, handing Carol a tissue as they stepped out of the entrance hall into the warm night air.

"What's that for?"

"To wipe the drool off the front of your dress."

"What do you mean?" said Carol, instinctively looking down.

Netty shook her head. "You should be on a leash. That man makes me so angry. Gareth Howard was always a smooth operator at school. He's got it turned up to boil tonight."

"Meaning what, exactly?" snapped Carol, straightening her clothes.

Diana, busy picking her way along the path in dainty sandals, said, "I don't know, Netty. I've spoken to him quite a lot just recently. He seemed very nice to me."

"In that case why did you help her grab me?" growled Carol, rounding on Diana.

"Because Netty told me to," said Diana lamely. "And anyway, I thought we were just going upstairs to get our jackets?"

Netty snorted and mimed slapping her forehead. "Give me strength. The bloody man was all over you like a rash. He's looking to get laid, Carol; carry on where he left off the summer we left school. How much more explicit do you need this to be? You were like a lamb to the slaughter in there."

"I was not," she said.

"OK," said Netty pulling out a cigarette. "It's just that I've met a lot of guys like Gareth in my time and, trust me, you're not in his league."

Carol glared at her. "And you are?"

"I didn't say that; the man is a wolf."

"Maybe that's what I wanted," Carol growled indignantly.

Netty stared at her and lifted an eyebrow. "Really?"

"We're both grown-ups, Netty. We both know what we're up to." Carol could feel her colour rising. Was she going to spend the whole weekend blushing? OK, so he had been flirting, and so had she. Was it really that important? And also — said a little voice in the back of her head — wasn't that exactly what she had come to find out?

Netty didn't look convinced.

"You've barely spoken to him," Carol said crossly, trying to sound suitably outraged while making every effort to hang on to her dignity.

"Oh, trust me, I didn't need to talk to him. What he wanted was coming over loud and clear. You'd have to have been dead not to notice," said Netty, lighting up. For the first time in heaven knew how many years Carol really wished that she still smoked.

"I don't need a moral compass, Netty — I know what I'm doing. I'm nearly forty, for God's sake. I don't need you to tell me what's right and what's wrong. I can do what I like. You did this before — remember? Radwell High? Last performance of the season? Pulling me off after the show and giving me the lecture about being careful and not getting myself hurt?" Carol could feel tears prickling and was angry with herself. "What was all that about?"

Netty stared at her, expression unchanged. "Because I cared then and I care now."

"What if carrying on where we left off is exactly what I want? What we both want? What if that was exactly what I came here for?" Carol could feel her temper rising, and besides, sometimes the best place to hide the truth is right out there in plain sight. "And you have to admit he is gorgeous."

Netty shook her head. "No, he's not gorgeous Carol. He is a predator. The man is a bastard. OK, so he is a charming, good-looking bastard, but he's a bastard nonetheless. He's got it written all over him; probably runs right through him like a stick of rock. He's obviously on the make or the take or both. Trust me — I know these things."

Carol was too angry and too hurt to speak.

"But," said Netty, dropping an arm around her shoulder, "you're going to do what you want anyway, and you're my friend, and sometimes friends do daft things, and it doesn't change anything, I'll still love you, however stupid you are."

Carol's eyes filled up with tears. "Bitch," she sniffed.

Netty laughed. "You say bitch like it's a bad thing."

"Where are we going?" asked Diana, hurrying to keep pace with them.

"Round the back to the fire escape — Jan and I found a short cut earlier."

"Which reminds me, where exactly is Jan?" said Carol, looking back over her shoulder.

"Talking to Adie, I would have thought," said Netty, taking a long pull on her cigarette. "There are a lot of things those two need to talk about."

Carol stared at her. "Meaning what, exactly?"

"Meaning just that. You're not the only one who came here thinking about carrying on where they left off. We've all got a lot of history to clear up. You and Gareth, Adie and Jan —"

Carol stared at her, feeling she had missed something vital. "What about Adie and Jan?" But it was too late. Netty quickened the pace.

Carol sighed, letting her anger bubble away; this wasn't how she wanted the weekend to go. She hurried to catch up with Netty. "I know that you're telling me all this stuff about Gareth because you think it's the right thing to do — but we were only catching up," she said gently.

"Yeah, right," said Netty, with a grin. "You and Diana really haven't got much in the way of a bullshit detector, have you? Maybe you should be catching on instead of catching up."

Carol clenched her fists, instantly furious again and yet at the same time desperate to say something to clear the air. She didn't want to fall out or fight with any of them. She looked into the face of first Netty and then Diana and then sighed. "All right, OK, so I fancy him."

Netty laughed like a drain. "Really? Good God. You amaze me — I would have never guessed in a million years."

"Don't take the piss," Carol began, but before she could really let rip a voice from behind them called, "Hello. Coooo-eeeeee. Wait for me."

All three women turned at the sound of the not-totally-unfamiliar voice.

"Wait for me," said the voice again, more breathlessly and then, "Diana, I wondered if you could show me where my room is? I've got no idea where to go or anything." Fiona appeared out of the gathering shadows, scuttling unhappily along the gravel path, dragging a large suitcase on wheels behind her. The three of them paused, not so much to wait as to stare.

"Hi — God, it's a bit of a hike, isn't it? I thought I'd get the rest of my luggage taken to my room, freshen up a little bit and then maybe we could all head down the pub, just like the good old days."

"What good old days were those, then?" Carol heard Netty growl under her breath as Fiona drew level with them.

"Hello, Fiona, how are y—" began Diana quickly as nobody else made any effort to speak.

But Fiona was just a fraction too fast for her. "Are we all sticking to our previous roles? I mean, it seems a bit silly really, doesn't it? After all, it's only a read-through. I thought it might be rather nice to explore other options. Perhaps we could shuffle things around a little bit, try some other ideas out. When I was in Stratford —"

Netty rounded on her. "We're not in Stratford, Fiona, and we're all staying exactly as we were," she snapped. "Witches, that's me, Diana and Jan, Lady Macbeth," she nodded towards Carol, "and you, Mrs Macduff." She indicated Fiona with a wave of the hand. Fiona winced. "Isn't that right, Diana?" continued Netty in a tone that dared anyone to say differently.

"How did you get to be so tough?" said Carol conversationally as an aside, while Diana considered the options.

Netty looked surprised. "Who, me? Tough?"

"Yes."

"I'm a complete pussycat," she protested.

Carol stared at her with an expression that she hoped repeated the original question.

129

"OK, so maybe it's self-preservation — in my experience people interpret kindness as weakness. I can't bear bullshit or people railroading over someone else just because they're louder or bigger — or just plain pushier." Netty nodded in Fiona's direction as if to indicate a case in point.

"So about changing roles," growled Fiona. "I can't see any reason —"

But this time it was Diana who got in first. "Well, actually," she began, "I do think Netty is right. I mean the whole point of the reunion is the drama tour. How it was, who we were, who we are now. It would be — be . . ." Carol could see Diana was struggling to come up with some valid argument There was no earthly reason why they should stick to the same roles other than for sentimental reasons, which were probably the most compelling reasons of all.

"Inappropriate," growled Netty. "This is about history, not acting."

Happy to be let off, Diana sighed with relief. "Yes, exactly," she said.

Fiona flicked a long strand of blonde hair over her shoulder. "I was only saying it might be fun. Obviously I take your point; although actually I toured as Lady Macbeth with a super little repertory theatre company. We had the most marvellous reviews, made *Time Out* and the *Evening Standard*."

"Was that before or after you were in *Casualty*?" said Netty.

Carol glared at Netty, but apparently Fiona hadn't caught the barb and said, "Oh, wow, you saw that, did

130

you? Gosh." At which point Fiona did a horrible little mock modest hand gesture that she'd probably learned at drama school to use for award ceremonies. "I mean, it was just a small part but it has opened *so many* doors for me. Pantomime, adverts, voiceovers. Although as they say, there really are no small parts, only small people."

There was a moment then — a pause that no one rushed to fill — and so Fiona sailed on. "Actually the *Macbeth* tour was before *Casualty*, but a part like the dark lady never really leaves you. It is such a powerful role. Very harrowing ..." Her face folded into a theatrical interpretation of harrowing and then snapped back. "Where are we going, by the way?"

"The scenic route," said Netty coolly, as they turned the corner of Burbeck House and started across the lawn, through a sea of shadows . . .

"Teddy Towers," added Carol with a wry grin.

Fiona giggled. "What a sweet name. Isn't there a path? My heels keep sinking into the grass. It's such a shame Mummy couldn't have come as well. She was terribly keen. She would have loved this place but she's a little unsteady on her legs these days. She sends her love, by the way, and she said that she'll be here for the performance on Sunday. You know you lot haven't changed at all, have you?"

No, thought Carol darkly as they started to climb the fire escape up to the bear-infested dormitory, and neither have you.

"She seems nicer than I remember," said Diana quietly to Carol, as they clambered in through the open window. Carol lifted an eyebrow and stared at her; maybe Netty was right about their bullshit detectors, after all.

"Oh my God," Fiona said, once they were in and she had dragged the suitcase in over the sill. "No, no, no. I'm sorry, but no. This really will not do."

"Welcome to Burbeck House drama tour," said Jan, who was already in the dormitory and was busy pulling a soft creamy white pashmina out of one of her bags. "We're all off down the pub, apparently. Where the hell did you lot get to?"

"Netty was taking us on the Cook's tour. When we say 'we' are going down the pub, who do *we* mean exactly?" said Carol, taking a cardigan out of her suitcase.

"Everybody, I think, except one of the technical crew, who apparently grew up to be a born-again Christian and plans to stay here and pray for us."

"Is that Tim Goldman?" said Netty, who was still outside on the fire escape, finishing off her fag.

Jan nodded. "Yes, very tall and thin with glasses and an Adam's apple like a cocktail onion. He came over and introduced himself when you lot buggered off. Here, he gave me one of these for each of you." She took a little pile of pamphlets out of her handbag and read the titles of the first couple. "You can take your pick. We've got something on the evils of demon drink or alternatively a cheery little article on moral decline in the new millennium."

She dropped them onto one of the bedside cabinets. "No pushing now, there's plenty to go round."

"I thought you were going to talk to Adie?" said Netty casually.

Jan sniffed and adjusted her pashmina. "I didn't think now was the moment."

Carol pulled on her cardigan and added a teeny-weeny bit more lipstick, waiting to hear if there was more.

Fiona, meanwhile, was still standing in the centre of the room as if she was waiting for them to fall silent, and as soon as they did she shook her head and put her hands on her hips. "This is absolutely ridiculous. I am *not* sleeping in here. Is this some kind of joke? It is, isn't it? You think this is funny, don't you? That it is some kind of good joke to tease me — well, it's not. It's cruel." There was a perfectly timed catch in Fiona's voice that hinted at tears. Above her a lampshade covered in bright pink cartoon bears swung gently in the breeze from the open window.

Diana appeared to be about to launch into her big bear/dormitory apology speech again when Carol decided enough was enough. "Oh, for heaven's sake, get over it, Fiona. It isn't a joke, it's clean, it's cheap and cheerful and it's only for the weekend. It's not a problem."

"Not for you, maybe. Mummy did warn me." Fiona's nostrils flared. Carol stared at her; God, she had completely forgotten that look, the one that made you think someone had just slid a warm gift-wrapped dog turd under Fiona's nose.

"Oh, no," Fiona said more slowly in case they had missed it first time round. "No, I really don't think so.

I don't do dormitories. I don't do communal and I most definitely do not do bears." She pulled a little silver mobile out of her handbag. "What is the name of the pub in the village?"

"The Master's Arms," Diana said helpfully.

"Did you ever play Violet Elizabeth in *Just William*?" Netty asked helpfully.

Fiona, choosing to ignore her, slipped the earpiece into her ear. Her gaze slipped out of focus as she asked directory enquiries for the number and got them to text it through, and they all watched her as she did — which, Carol thought, was probably exactly what Fiona had in mind. It was just like her big moment in *Casualty* all over again. Fiona rang the pub. Everyone waited to hear the outcome.

"Apparently they don't do accommodation," growled Fiona a few seconds later.

Netty, still out on the fire escape, said, "Well, there we are then — that's that settled. I think those bunks over there are free." She waved her cigarette around vaguely.

Fiona sniffed. "What, the ones near the bathroom? I don't think so, there must be more somewhere else. I'm not sleeping in a room full of other people, and most certainly not next to the bathroom."

Diana opened her mouth again to say something, maybe the apology speech, maybe a suggestion, maybe an offer to swap places, but whatever it was she stopped as soon as she spotted Carol glaring at her. Carol glanced left and right; to see that her expression was mirrored on Netty's face and Jan's.

"This is totally and utterly ridiculous," Fiona hissed.

Netty, Carol and Jan shrugged. Synchronised shrugging. It might never make it as an Olympic event but it was remarkably effective.

Fiona sniffed and straightened up.

While they had been on tour with the school she had always managed to blag her way into better accommodation — mainly because her mother insisted on having a separate room and then suggested, given Fiona's delicate constitution, that it might be easier if they moved an extra bed in so that Mummy could keep an eye on her brave little kitten.

But this time Mummy wasn't here.

There was a moment's intense silence when Carol could almost feel Fiona exerting psychic pressure on them all to try to come up with a better solution. Emotional blackmail is potent stuff when finely tuned; Carol did wonder whether Fiona might break out an emergency asthma attack or palpitations or even hock up a fur ball; whatever it was it would have to be something hugely impressive to move her current audience.

Finally her shoulders dropped a little and she made a noble attempt at a stoic smile. "Well, I suppose that we're all in this together, aren't we? The show must go on and all that. Which bunk did you say was free?"

"Either of those two over there," said Netty, waving towards a set of bunks that stood between the toilet door and the open window and that had no luggage or coats on them. Fiona sighed. It was way out beyond theatrical into something far more cosmic and all-consuming.

"And hurry up," snapped Netty, lighting up another cigarette. "The pub closes at half-ten."

"Yes, exactly," said a male voice. "And I could really use a drink."

Adie appeared behind Netty, and an instant later Gareth joined them. As soon as their eyes met Carol felt a funny little ripple in her belly and then sighed. It was going to be a long weekend.

CHAPTER
SIX

"I wondered if we might talk," said George Bearman, topping up his coffee cup and lifting the pot in Callista's direction by way of an invitation. "Would you care to join me in a refill?"

She declined with a shake of the head. "Not for me, George, thanks. Very kind but I'll be up all night." He grinned and Callista looked away, refusing to be tangled up in some boyish double entendre.

The dining room was almost empty now; they were amongst the last people left seated at the top table, up there under the bunting, surrounded by the debris of crumpled paper napkins, discarded mint wrappers, gravy rings and crumbs.

"Or would you rather that we went down to the pub with the rest of them?" he said, indicating the open French windows. "It's a lovely evening for a walk."

Callista shook her head again. "No, but please don't let me stop you, George. I was actually thinking that I might have an early night. It was a long drive down here. It seems to have been a long day."

George Bearman looked crestfallen. "Ah yes, of course, so sorry. I'd forgotten. Yorkshire, wasn't it?"

Callista nodded and began to gather her things together, her handbag and cardigan and glasses. It was hard not to feel sorry for him.

As George drained his cup he pulled a face and grimaced. "Actually you've not missed much. It's stone cold." And then, in a slightly lower tone he added, "You know, Callista, I've been looking forward to this weekend enormously. I mean, I don't want to sound pathetic or anything but it has meant a great deal to me to see you again."

She didn't like to tell him that he had already told her. Instead she nodded again.

He laughed nervously. "Anyway, as you say, maybe an early night might be a good idea. Who knows what tomorrow's going to bring, and the old grey matter isn't quite what it used to be." He got somewhat unsteadily to his feet. "So — up the wooden hill to Bedfordshire it is then."

Callista looked at him in astonishment. Was he still saying that after all these years? God, she would have killed him by now if they had ended up together. Ah, well. The important thing was that they hadn't ended up together and on Sunday evening she would be heading home to Laurence, a man who loved her and who she loved, while George would be driving home to ice-cold Judy. It was a sobering thought. Maybe she was being too hard on him.

"Then again," said Callista brightly, "I don't suppose another half an hour will make that much difference one way or the other and I was rather hoping that we could get some time to talk about the plans for the weekend." She pulled her bag up onto her lap and took out a ring binder. "I've got a few ideas and some notes. I was wondering exactly how much of the play we should aim to get through. Have you had any thoughts on it?"

She glanced across the table; George looked hurt and slightly put out.

Callista realised her mistake immediately. "Ah — you didn't mean you wanted to talk about the play, did you, George? I thought we had been through all this in the pub earlier."

"No, that's fine, just fine," he said, and pulled his chair a little closer. Too close, if Callista was honest. He smiled with false heartiness. "Righty-ho — now tell me, what have you in mind for the read-through?"

Callista stared into his big ruddy face and wished — not for the first time since she had known him — that George Bearman could read minds. She wanted him to understand that their relationship had been over for so long that she had almost completely forgotten all about it. She wanted him to understand that he had waited all those years for nothing and that it was time for him to move on, to finally leave Judy and try to find something special, something better before it was too late. But then again, George Bearman hadn't been able to guess what she was thinking when they saw each other every day, hadn't been able to read her mind when they were sleeping together, so what possible hope was there now?

Callista stared at her notes and, swallowing back a knot of grief for something long gone, said, "Well let's just recap, shall we? It's been a while since I did *Macbeth*. Act One, first three scenes." She began to read the tidy little notes that she'd made. "There's Macbeth and Banquo meeting the witches on the heath, then the witches welcome Macbeth as Lord of Glamis, even though they've never met him before and tell him he's going to be Thane of Cawdor and the King of Scotland, but that Banquo — his friend — will be the father of a line of kings after Macbeth. Then there's Macbeth contemplating the idea of killing the old king, Duncan, so that he can get the throne as the witches have promised him."

George said nothing so Callista continued, running her finger along the notes. She sighed; it was like pulling teeth. It felt like a pre-exam recap for her GCSE students, but then at least, she thought, if they talked about Macbeth they didn't need to talk about each other.

"I've always thought it is a great opening to a play and we need those first few scenes, because it explains the background for the whole story. It gives us the reason Macbeth later kills Banquo — gives us a handle on his jealousy, and it sets the scene for supernatural goings-on later in the play. I was thinking that we could have a narrator to fill in the bits that we decide to cut. Although obviously we'll need to see tomorrow just who we've got here from the original cast. I didn't actually do a head count but Diana said that everyone has shown up so we could possibly run the whole thing. What do you think?"

George Bearman nodded again and then, leaning forward, patted her on the knee. "It's so good to see you again."

Callista looked up into his eyes and wondered for a moment if he had heard a single word she had said.

Meanwhile, down at the Master's Arms, Carol stepped outside, away from the noise of the public bar into the warm stillness of a summer night and switched on her mobile phone. It rang almost at once with a message on voice mail. It was Raf.

He always sounded deliciously Irish with just a hint of horniness when recorded; a talent that on other occasions would have made her go weak at the knees. Tonight it just made her feel guilty. Carol sighed; what the hell was she doing lusting after Gareth Howard when she had a man like Raf waiting for her at home? Damn . . . She closed her eyes and listened to him, not that that really helped.

"Hi, love, I just rang to make sure you'd arrived safe and sound." There was a slight pause. "I miss you, the bed's going to be very empty tonight. I was thinking maybe I'd ask that woman from next door round — you know, the one with the skimpy little bikini that I pointed out to you on the linen line," he said in that warm dark brown brogue. "I hope that you're having a grand time. We're OK — no major domestic incidents or breakages yet but we're working on it. I'm taking the lads out later to pillage that new pizza place in the High Street. You know how much I hate recorded messages — they feel like a trick — and I can never think of anything wildly funny or amazingly clever to say, but if I do then don't you worry, I'll call you back. And — well, have a really good time and we'll see you Sunday. We're thinking of you, or at least I am."

Raf didn't say that he loved her, he didn't need to, Carol could hear it in every word — not squishy-squidgy emotionally blackmailing pink fluffy love but the real thing — love that was warm and allowing and supportive, and wanted her to have what she wanted for herself, even if it was the chance to meet an old flame, even if that meant losing her. The bastard, she sighed, how could Raf be such a good man without even trying?

Carol felt a fist reach in between her ribs and squeeze her heart. Raf was too nice, too kind, and too good to be treated like this. It took a big man to sit back and leave her free to screw it all up; Carol tried to imagine how the hell she would feel if the situation was reversed — the pain and doubt and hurt seared like fire. But then again, perhaps Raf felt it was better to find out now rather than later. Or did Raf think he had already won, that Gareth was no contest or, worse still, that he had already lost?

He'd still be up, it wasn't that late. Carol tapped away at search and waited while the phone came up with her home number. Raf picked it up on the second burble as if he had been sitting waiting for her to call.

"Hi," Carol said, biting her lip. It seemed like a hundred years since she had left home and even longer still since she had spoken to him.

"Hi," Raf said. In contrast to the easy confidence on the voice mail he now sounded stilted, almost as if they were strangers being introduced at a party. Carol wouldn't have been at all surprised if the next thing he said was, "My name is Raf — I'm an architect. How about you?" But he didn't, he was just quiet, which in some ways was a lot worse.

"Well, I got here OK, the directions were great — spot on," she said as lightly as she could manage. "And it's an amazing house; I think some bits are Elizabethan. You'd adore it." Why did it all sound so forced?

"Good, and how's it going?" he asked.

Carol could almost hear Raf feeling his way round the edges of the conversation, weighing up how much to pry, how much to ask — or was that just her paranoia kicking in? "Fine, good, I've met up with my old gang, which is great — they haven't changed. I'm not sure whether that's a relief or a worry," she said, trying hard to laugh. She hesitated. Where should she go next with the conversation?

On the way down to the pub Carol had made a point of walking with Netty, Adie, Jan and Diana in some kind of strange show of solidarity — and to get Netty off her back. But as they walked Gareth kept trying to catch her eye, engage her in conversation and edge over towards her, trying to break the group up.

It was crazy. They were adults, for God's sake, so how come she didn't know how to play this? Fiona had finally insisted on walking with Gareth, occasionally arm in arm, leaving Carol between the two groups, both of which were caught up with and between other members of the cast and crew. Carol felt the pull and push between them all like magnets, people being repelled and attracted like some sort of walking physics experiment.

"Are you still there?" asked Raf.

"Sorry," said Carol, laughing nervously, "I think maybe the signal is a bit patchy here," lying through her eye-teeth to cover the uncomfortable lull in the conversation.

"So how are things going?"

So far Carol couldn't really call it. She took a deep breath, the kind a person takes before jumping into a swimming pool or over the side of a sinking ship and said, "Oh, not so bad. I think everyone who said they were coming has turned up. It's a bit weird how some people look just the same but older and then there are others I wouldn't have recognised in a million years." Carol stopped speaking, the words drying in her throat; they both knew the things Raf was really talking about, the things that were lurking just below the surface of the conversation.

There was a tiny pause, the silence so intense, so very dense that you could almost see it, and before she could stop him Raf leaped right in.

"And how about your Mr Right?" he asked softly. "How is he? Still as gorgeous as ever?"

Carol laughed again. It sounded utterly false but there was no way to claw it back now. "He's — he's . . ." she fumbled around, desperate for something to say, something acceptable, something neutral, and could find nothing.

Raf laughed too. "He's there, then?"

"Yes." It sounded as if she had dragged the word out from between clenched teeth.

"Not changed at all?"

Carol looked in through the bar door and as fate — the bitch — would have it, just at that very moment Gareth looked up and, lifting a hand, grinned at her. Waving her back inside. No, he hadn't changed at all, not in any of the ways that mattered. Carol's stomach fluttered and she heard the catch in her voice as she said, "Don't be so silly." And then more hastily in case there was some chance that Raf might say something else. "Look, I'm sorry but I've got to go. We've all just got to the pub and everyone is desperate to swap stories and catch up before closing time and I have no idea what time they lock the doors up at the hall. I just wanted to ring and tell you that I got here safe and sound and to check and to make sure that you and the boys are OK — as long as you are OK?" The words came out like machine-gun fire, so fast that even if Raf had wanted to say something there was no gap, no pause for him to get back in.

"I'll ring you tomorrow," Carol said. "This was just a quickie. I really do have to go now, sorry. Talk soon. Love you." And despite everything she really truly did; Carol loved him with all of her heart except that maybe loving him was a mistake, maybe her heart was wrong, maybe he wasn't the one. Maybe it was Gareth after all. The thoughts burned like acid.

And how was it that she didn't know?

Raf barely had a chance to say any kind of farewell before Carol snapped the phone shut and dropped it back into her handbag. The relief was enormous, like slipping the pin back into a live hand grenade. Carol felt hot and sick; how was it that she felt so guilty for doing nothing? It would be so very much simpler if Raf was nasty or angry or made her feel like she was justified in looking elsewhere, but he didn't. How did he make her feel? She bit her lip; he made her feel loved for the first time in her life, truly loved.

They had met when she was asked to quote for landscaping during the modernisation of a local leisure centre. "I hope you're good . . ." he said, unrolling the plans for her at their first meeting.

Carol remembered looking up at him to see if he was being rude, or rather, how rude he was being.

". . . because this is the ugliest bloody building in all Christendom," he'd continued. "When they asked me for design ideas, most of the ones I came up with involved a crane, a wrecking ball and a length of chain."

She held his gaze. "But you got the job?"

He nodded. "What can I tell you? I'm cheap."

She got the job and didn't see him again until the official re-opening, when the nobs were out in force, itching to cut ribbons and shake hands. Raf ambled up to Carol, wearing a crumpled cream linen suit and carrying two glasses of champagne.

"I was hoping you'd consider my idea of putting up corrugated iron sheeting round the bloody thing."

"They wouldn't cough up for the posts," she said, halfway through a plate of nibbles.

He didn't move. Carol nodded towards the second glass he was holding. "Am I keeping you?" she said, imagining a wife or girlfriend tucked away somewhere amongst the big hats and official chain brigade.

He considered for an instant. "No, I think I'd prefer to work after we're married but I might consider going part time."

He handed her the glass.

She was herself with him, totally relaxed and whole and funny and horrible, warts and all. Carol took a deep breath trying to quell the rising tendrils of guilt and nausea. All this and yet it was still Gareth Howard who made her go weak at the knees. Damn, blast and bugger.

Lady Macbeth had had a problem with her conscience too — all that hand-washing to get the old king's blood off her hands, thought Carol, as she painted on a smile, squared her shoulders and strode back into the pub. But then Lady Macbeth had got something real to feel guilty about and Carol hadn't, had she? She tried hard to let herself off the hook. Flirting and a bit of lusting never hurt anyone, said a robust voice at the back of her head, and that was all it was. Just a fancying thing, a little bit of window-shopping, nothing serious, nothing life-changing, nothing important.

As Carol got to the bar Gareth — who appeared to be totally rapt by the conversation between Adie and Netty — moved aside without even apparently looking so that there was just enough room for her to stand alongside him. As she stepped into the space he moved fractionally closer and let his hand rest companionably on the small of her back, his fingers set so that they rested on the curve where her bum began to swell. It was done so casually that it seemed like the most natural thing in the world. His touch was like a lightning strike. Carol shivered while her body purred in anticipation. Move over Lady Macbeth.

"Hello, Hedley?" Diana, standing out in the pub garden, pressed her finger to her ear. "How are you?"

"Diana?" Hedley always sounded terribly surprised when she rang him, and very soon dispensed with the small talk. Yes, the children were fine; yes, he had fed the cat. Yes, he had found the meals in the freezer. They had had lasagne for supper. Hedley had a tendency to shout because he seemed to think that mobiles were unreliable and still slightly revolutionary.

"Can you hear me?" he bellowed. "I've got a bit of a problem here."

Hedley was many things, but he had never had any problems coming straight to the point.

"The instructions are on all the freezer bags and the cooking times are absolutely non-negotiable," Diana said firmly.

"No, no, it's not about the meals, they're fine. I've had Dylan arrange them alphabetically so we know exactly what we're doing. No, I had a phone call earlier this evening which, to be perfectly honest, has left me in a little bit of a dilemma."

148

Diana sighed. "Oh, Hedley. It's not that dreadful woman from the Mothers' Union again. You really must stand up to her; it's your church not hers. And no, she can't use the vestry for committee meetings. How many times do you have to tell her? The woman is a complete menace."

"No, it's not the Mothers' Union. It's about your weekend."

"My weekend? What do you mean, 'my weekend'? I thought you said that you didn't mind, Hedley. We've talked about this."

"Of course I don't mind. No, it's about one of the people on it. Hang on, I've written it down here somewhere. Ah yes, here we are. Have you got someone there called Gareth Howard?"

Diana could imagine Hedley standing in their enormous rectory kitchen reading his spidery handwriting from the back of an old envelope. Diana smiled; she missed him when they were apart.

She glanced across the crowded room. Gareth was standing at the bar with Adie, Netty and Carol. From where she was standing she could see Gareth's hand was around Carol's waist, not that she seemed to mind. As Adie turned to order some more drinks Gareth leaned a little closer and whispered something into Carol's ear. She laughed and reddened, a hand covering her mouth.

"Yes, actually we do. Why?" Diana asked.

"Well, his wife rang here a little while ago."

Diana felt an icy finger track down her spine. "What?"

"His wife rang, she wanted to know if he was there."

"His wife, are you sure?"

"Well, yes, that's who she said she was, although obviously I've no documentary evidence one way or the other." It was the kind of thing Hedley said. Diana let the words replay. Gareth's wife.

Inside at the bar Gareth Howard leaned forward and kissed Carol fleetingly on the neck. She swung round and glared at him but certainly didn't offer any resistance and the look on her face suggested any outrage was purely token.

Diana couldn't look away. Meanwhile Hedley said, "She asked me not to tell him that she had phoned but she sounded in the most dreadful state, Diana. Terribly upset. He has just walked out on them."

A breath lodged in Diana's throat. "Them?" said Diana quietly.

"Yes, she was awfully distressed. They've got two children, apparently. From what I can gather the little one can't be more than a few months old, and I think she said the elder one is about two. She was trying to track him down."

Diana nodded even though she knew he couldn't see her; some things didn't need interruption.

"I believe that she was rather hoping to talk to him," said Hedley. "Come down there — talk face to face, that sort of thing."

"Oh," said Diana, wondering what the right thing to do was, and then wondering whether there *was* a right thing to do.

"I've given her your number."

"Oh," said Diana again, wondering what on earth she would have said or done if Gareth's wife had rung her before Hedley had had the chance to speak to her. Hedley always assumed she could cope.

"Are you thinking?" asked Hedley.

Diana laughed. "Yes, Hedley. I am."

"I knew you would," he said; she could hear the admiration in his voice.

"Oh, Hedley."

"I rely on the fact that you'll know what to do. You always know."

"Um," said Diana with a laugh. If only she had his confidence in her abilities.

"Shall I leave it with you, then?"

Diana smiled. He hadn't really given her much choice. "Yes, Hedley. Give my love to the children. I'll call tomorrow. And —"

He laughed. "And I love you too," he said, and then continued, "I told Gareth's wife about your plans for the weekend and I think she was rather hoping to get down there to see him, but it does rather sound as if it would be an awfully long and difficult journey to Burbeck House with the children on public transport. Her name is Leonora — she sounded terribly sweet and very upset."

Diana shook her head, like that really helped.

After she had rung off Diana wondered if what Gareth and his wife got up to was really any of their business. Perhaps she should just pass the message on to Gareth and let him deal with it. After all, they were his family. But Carol was her business. What the hell was she going to do?

Inside, the landlord was calling last orders. The drinkers, barely settled in after their walk down from the hall, moaned loudly although good-naturedly and pressed closer to the bar for one last round.

Diana tried to make her way back to Carol, Adie and the others. It was slow progress as lots of the troupe wanted to say hello, wanted to thank her and congratulate her on the reunion.

"Diana," said Adie as she finally made her way back to the bar, "what a star." Diana blushed furiously as he handed her a drink and then, banging on a table, called for a toast.

"Stop it," she growled. "We've already done this once."

"Not in alcohol we haven't, and it doesn't count unless it's alcohol," he said, and lifted his glass in salute.

Diana wished the floor would open up and swallow her but nevertheless the toast echoed round the pub, a roaring chorus of approval from everyone — drama group and locals included.

"Right, that's enough now," she said from behind a fixed grin.

Adie laughed. "Don't be so modest. So far it's been a roaring success."

"We've only been here since half-past three," said Jan.

"Well, it's a bloody good start," countered Adie. "No fist fights have broken out, no one has stormed off in a huff and neither of the Drama teachers appear to have gone gaga in the interim. I'd say that we were ahead on points so far."

Diana looked at Carol and Gareth, wondering how long their luck was likely to hold out.

While they got another round of drinks in, Gareth excused himself and headed to the toilet. As he became submerged in the crowd Diana touched Carol's arm. "So how's it going then?"

Carol grinned. "OK. I know what Netty says but he seems nice. I just wish I didn't fancy him so much. I didn't expect to after all these years. It muddies the waters a bit — I keep wondering whether it really is him I fancy or the ghost of Christmas past? Let's face it, a lot of water has gone under the bridge since the last time we met. Silly, isn't it? I mean in real terms Gareth and I are complete strangers." She reddened a little. "Sorry I'm talking too much. We've both had complete other lives, and yet there is this shared history — this little magic thing that it's very hard to get past. We'll see." Carol smiled and downed her drink. "There is a nice little buzz between us. I'm just trying not to read anything into it. Maybe he's just being friendly."

"You let all your friends snuggle up like that, do you?"

Carol laughed. "I know what you're saying. But, trust me, it's not anything important. It's a bit like a holiday romance, something and nothing."

Diana nodded. "I've been thinking about what Netty said," Diana began, picking up her fruit juice from the bar. She needed to go carefully.

Carol nodded. "But Gareth and I are only talking, Di — and as far as I know they haven't banned flirting yet. And I don't care what she says, he still is gorgeous. I can see what she means — he is a bad boy but I promise I'll be careful. Honest. Cross my heart."

Carol might be preaching restraint but her eyes were sparkling and excited. Diana bit her lip; there was no easy way to say what was on her mind, and sometimes when that was the case the best way was just to say it.

"Did you know that he's married?"

There was a split second, a little beat that hung in the air between them and then Carol nodded and said very deliberately, "Yes, he told me."

Diana didn't say a word. After years of being a school teacher she knew that sometimes silence could be the most powerful prompt of all.

"They're separated. He told me that she was unstable, quite difficult." Carol shifted her weight from foot to foot. "I mean, he didn't say that she was mentally ill or anything but he did kind of infer it. It can't be easy for anyone — either of them — in that sort of situation."

Diana nodded but still didn't comment.

Carol took a sip of her drink. "I do realise that I'm only hearing his side of the story and he is bound to paint himself in a good light." Carol looked at Diana as if she was looking for approval, or at least some understanding. "But he did tell me."

"At least he was upfront about it," said Diana softly, praying that Carol wouldn't ask how it was she knew and why she had brought it up now. But it looked as if Carol had other things on her mind.

"Yes."

"He seems keen?" said Diana, looking towards the toilets.

Carol reddened. "There was a time when I used to think about Gareth all the time, for years. He'd bubble up in my head. When I look back it feels like we lost something good just when it was beginning, not like losing something that finished and had run its course. I remember he picked me up from work one day and was talking about going to university. He was really excited and I kind of knew then that that would be the end, he'd be meeting new people, doing good things — you know what I mean. I wasn't totally naïve, once he was gone it would be so hard to hold it together," Carol paused. "So on the way home I told him what I'd been thinking and he kissed me — he seemed relieved — and said he'd been thinking it too but didn't want to say anything because he really liked what we had and he didn't want to hurt me. God, I cried for days — it seemed such a waste."

"Excuse me, miss — I don't like to disturb you but can I have your autograph?" said a voice at Carol's shoulder. "You're that woman off the telly, aren't you?"

Carol and Diana turned and looked into the wide, open smiling face of a complete stranger, a small wiry man in a nylon raincoat and cap, who was clutching a sheet of paper and a pen.

Carol was about to say no when she realised he was actually looking at Fiona, who beamed and said, "Oh, of course, how very sweet," and then, with a shrug of mock regret to Carol, Adie and the rest of the gang who were standing around her, added, "I'm so sorry, this happens to me all the time. Price of fame, I'm afraid." And then giggling she turned her full attention on to the man.

"A walk-on part in *Casualty*, that's fame these days, is it?" hissed Adie under his breath.

"Sssh," said Carol, totally enwrapped in Fiona and the fan moment.

Easing the sheet of paper and the pen out of the man's fingers, Fiona asked, "And who is it for?" Her tone was as sweet as boiled syrup.

Behind Fiona, Diana was busy pulling a truly spectacular face, Adie was dumbstruck, while Netty gazed heavenwards. Carol just looked on in amazement.

"Doreen," said the man enthusiastically, not just to Fiona but to all of them. "That's my wife's name. She loves your show, never misses it. Every Thursday without fail, we're there."

Fiona, without missing a beat, beamed again. "Well, isn't that lovely?" she said. "I'm really pleased."

Carol stared at her; so much unforced fawning was positively nauseating, particularly in view of the fact that this man obviously didn't have a clue who Fiona was.

"Oh yes, we watch you all the time," continued the man in case Fiona had missed it first time round.

"Never miss a show. My wife rang up the production company to see if they were going to put you out on video."

Fiona continued to nod and smile, her handwriting flowing across the page. "Really? That's wonderful," she said.

"Watched every single episode we have, right from the beginning."

Carol looked at Diana; OK, they'd all got it now but the little man wasn't put off so easily. "My wife says it's amazing what some people will put up with." He grinned. "You and them builder boys with their MDF don't half do some weird things to people's houses. Glue and fur fabric? All that glitter and fairy lights. I always wonder where you come up with the ideas. That Chinese room you did in Clacton — I said to my wife they won't be best pleased with that, I said, they're more your pine and magnolia with a nice dado rail, I said. Remember that one? They had to bleep a lot of it out. It got in the papers. I think they were planning to sue."

Fiona tipped her head on one side as if listening to every last word and held the smile so tight that Carol wondered if rigor mortis had set in. It was a pose so polished that Carol suspected Fiona had to have practised it a lot at home in front of the mirror.

The man's smile didn't falter either. "I really wish I'd got my camera with me. My wife is never going to believe you were in here in Burbeck. On a bit of a recce, are you?"

Netty, Diana, Jan, Adie and Carol watched and listened and waited. They didn't believe it either. "No, I'm here on a break with friends," Fiona said through gritted teeth.

The man nodded. "Nice work if you can get it. I thought maybe you was going to give the pub the once-over. It could certainly do with it."

Fiona smiled and, totally unfazed, handed him back the sheet of paper, signed, "To Doreen with lots of love and all best wishes from Indecipherable Squiggle," and underneath a row of very neat little kisses.

The man positively beamed now. "That's champion," he said. "You wait till I tell my missus." And with that he scurried away all pink-faced and excited.

Fiona picked up her drink and took a long pull on the straw, every thing about her demeanour and her body language defying anyone to pass any kind of comment at all. A heartbeat later and Gareth reappeared from the loo, and Fiona beamed at him. Carol decided that to appease Diana she wouldn't make a beeline for him; let Fiona have him a while.

"Carol Smillie, what d'ya reckon?" said Adie, a little the worse for wear as they headed back towards the hall.

"No," said Jan, "Fiona is far too ginger for that and not Scots enough."

"I *am not* ginger, I'm new-penny blonde," snapped Fiona from a little further up the path.

"How about that other blonde one then? What's her name?" said Netty. "The one with freckles who does paint effects on everything that hasn't got a pulse?"

"Is that the one on daytime television, great tits and a fan-tas-tic arse?" said a stray unidentified male voice from somewhere amongst the crowd of stragglers.

Fiona huffed. "No, it is not. Look, could we talk about something else? He was terribly sweet and people do make mistakes. It's easily done when you've got a well-known face."

Netty — who had drunk a lot of Pernod — laughed. "A mistake which you were not exactly quick to rectify. Christ, you've got some neck."

The walk back to the hall was punctuated with several more guesses about who the man in the pub thought Fiona was, which on the whole Fiona chose to ignore. She was also getting increasingly huffy with everybody.

Full of her own thoughts, Carol ambled along. She hadn't deliberately meant to hang back but that was what had happened.

"You OK?" asked Gareth.

Carol smiled and pulled her cardigan tight around her shoulders. "Yes, thanks. I'm fine, just tired, that's all."

"We really haven't had much chance to talk."

"No I suppose not, but it's been so nice to be with everybody and we've got the whole weekend." She tried to sound casual.

He moved closer, and caught hold of her hand and then continued in an undertone, "I realised, seeing you tonight, that I've really missed you. I won't say I've thought about you all the time because that would be a

159

lie but I *have* thought about you over the years and wondered."

"And wondered what?" Carol said softly, looking up into his face.

He laughed and fell into step beside her. "Wondered what might have happened if I hadn't gone off to uni or if we had made more of an effort to keep in touch. I suppose I was afraid to push — well, you know — we both had our plans and when you're eighteen you don't think that you might never see someone again. I think we assume it will be easy to just turn round and pick up the pieces where we left off. If only things were that simple."

He pulled her close and kissed her; it felt so easy, so very very easy. Carol felt a warm soft glow in her heart.

"Um, that feels so good," he purred.

They hadn't really been together for very long when they were at school. A few months, rehearsals, the drama tour and then suddenly school was all over and the groups and the friendships that had seemed unshakable, inviolate, had dissolved as people headed off to college and jobs.

They had written once or twice, promised to stay friends, and met up when he came home for the first holiday but by then everything had changed. School days had ended and all at once their relationship was all done and dusted, and that special thing had gone like autumn leaves, crumpled and dried and scattered by the wind. All that was left were the ghosts and the memories and occasional intense recollections fired by a snatch of a pop song on the radio or a face in a crowd or a stray thought. Carol smiled; and now here she was standing in amongst the ghosts.

She was about to try and put her thoughts into words when she realised that Gareth had drifted away again, back to the main group or back into the shadows, she couldn't be sure which. What was she supposed to do? Follow him? Try to find him or play hard to get? Was this a come-on? Or a put-down? Or was he telling Carol that the things he felt for her were in the past?

Just as they got into the arc of lights around the hall's huge back doors Adie swung round and began to run back down the path.

"Adie?" Carol called after his retreating back. "Are you all right? Where are you going? What's the matter?"

"It's no good," he said over his shoulder, heading back the way they had just come. "I've got to go and find out who the hell that bloke thought Fiona was."

CHAPTER
SEVEN

It was dark when the phone rang. Leonora, curled up sound asleep in the nursery with the children, blinked and rubbed her eyes, wondering who on earth would be ringing at this time of night, and then almost instantly she was wide awake. Easing her arm out from under Patrick, she leaped out of bed, hurried across the landing and snatched up the receiver.

"Gareth?" she said, his name spilling out before she could stop herself. "Hello? Is that you?" There was a pause and for a moment Leonora thought that the line had gone dead but it hadn't, because far far away on the edge of her hearing she could just pick out the sound of someone breathing very softly.

"Hello?" said Leonora, more briskly this time with a confidence she barely felt. The house was all shut up for the night, with just a little lamp glowing in the children's room; everywhere else was wrapped deep and dark in velvet-black shadows. Leonora shivered. She felt very alone.

"Hello?" she said again. "I know that there is someone there. Who is this, please? This isn't funny. Hello. Who's calling?"

"Hello," said a little voice, a little female voice.

"Who is this?" Leonora snapped, maintaining the same curt no-nonsense tone, although whoever it was had sounded far more nervous than she was.

"I'm sorry, I know it's late but I'm trying to contact Gareth Howard?" said the little voice, making it a question in her uncertainty. "He told me not to ring him on this number but I didn't know what else to do. You don't mind, do you?"

Leonora felt an odd clutching sensation low down, deep in her belly. "Who am I speaking to, please?" she asked as evenly as she could manage.

"My name is Jasmine," said the voice.

Jasmine? Jasmine who? Which Jasmine thought it was all right to ring her husband in the middle of the night?

"Oh," said Leonora. "Well, Jasmine, I'm afraid that Gareth isn't here at the moment, and you're right, it is very late. What exactly did you want to talk to him about?"

She could almost hear the girl wriggling with discomfort. She made little noises of uncertainty and then said, "It's a bit hard to know where to start really. Maybe I should ring again when he gets back. Do you know when he's going to be home?"

If only. Leonora looked up at the clock. It was just after midnight. "No, I'm afraid I don't," she said softly. "But I can give him a message if you like, when I see him." She held on tight to the great knot of emotion swirling around and around in her belly. She didn't want to frighten Jasmine away — oh, no — what Leonora needed to do was to find out exactly who

Jasmine was, what she wanted and what the hell was going on.

"The thing is he said that he'd be round to see me tonight; he promised," said the voice at the end of the phone. Jasmine's tone was high and nasal. She sounded young and nervous and full of tears. "So I waited in for him at the flat and then when he didn't come round I nipped round to the pub but he wasn't in there either. Nobody had seen him. I didn't know what else to do. You didn't mind me ringing, did you?"

Leonora decided not to answer that.

"I don't understand how you got this phone number," she said slowly, although she could already hear the voice of instinct telling her all the things she needed to know.

"He rang me a couple of times from there and I did 1471 and I told him I'd got his number and he said — well, he said I wasn't to ring him there."

Leonora felt sick.

"What exactly is your relationship with Gareth?" she asked. Leonora almost said "my husband" but managed to hold the words back.

The girl's tone lightened. "Didn't he tell you? He's my boyfriend."

Leonora felt the breath die in her chest. "Your boyfriend?" she repeated.

"Yes, I thought he would've probably said something to you but then again I suppose he's got to be careful, what with the divorce and everything," said the girl called Jasmine at the far end of the line. She sounded so very sure of what she was saying. "I met him when

164

he came in to the shop. I mean, I know he's a bit older than me, but I don't mind — father figure and all that — and I really need someone to keep me in line." She giggled.

Leonora sat down heavily on the top of the stairs. "Do you know who I am?" she began slowly. It sounded as if the words were coming from a very long way away and took so much effort to say.

"His sister," said little Jasmine brightly. "He told me all about it, don't worry; said that he was living with you until he could get himself sorted out; said it was nice for you to have him about, what with the kids and everything. Give you a hand and stuff. He said they were quite young, bit of a handful. Said you were nice — that's why I didn't think you would mind me ringing you up. I know he told me not to, but I really didn't know what else to do. I know that he's been under a lot of pressure lately. He said you'd been really good to him since his divorce — he told me how his wife had robbed him blind, took him for everything he'd got." She paused for breath and then said, "The thing is, he told me he'd be round tonight so's we could go and look at a flat. I imagine you'll be glad to get him out from under your feet, won't you?"

The girl, oblivious to the effect she was having, appeared relieved to have someone to talk to. Leonora could find nothing she wanted to say, and now that Jasmine had found her voice she seemed reluctant to shut up.

"I know that he's strapped for cash at the moment but I've phoned my dad and he's already said that he'd lend me the deposit to give us a bit of a start, and my mum said she'd help us out with some bits and pieces. You know a pram and that, although I said I thought I should wait until after the scan. I mean, you never know, do you?"

No, you never do, thought Leonora as Jasmine's words hit home, one by one like nails into a coffin lid.

Across the landing Patrick began to stir and almost as soon as he did the baby let out a little keening cry. "Jasmine, I think that you and I need to talk," said Leonora quietly. "Can I ring you back? Or maybe you'd like to pop round for a cup of tea some time?"

"Yeah," said Jasmine. "That would be great. I'm really glad I rang now. Have you got a piece of paper? I'll give you my number."

Leonora pulled her big purple cardigan down off the newel post. In the pocket was the piece of paper she had taken from Gareth's office earlier and a biro she must have taken from his desk. Jasmine gave her a number and she wrote it down.

"When is a good time to ring you?" asked Leonora, wrapping the cardigan around her shoulders, amazed that she sounded so very calm, so very even.

"I'm off this weekend," said Jasmine brightly. "So any time is good for me."

From the nursery the baby began to cry in earnest. Leonora felt her milk come in, Pavlov's dog in reverse, but before she could speak Jasmine said, "Sounds like you're wanted. I'd better let you go, hadn't I?" And then laughing, added, "God, I've got all that to look forward to. All the fretting and sleepless nights."

166

"Yes," said Leonora, "yes, I suppose you have." And then, as if she was walking away from the edge of a bad dream Leonora put down the phone, went back to the nursery, picked up the baby and carefully eased a nipple into the soft hungry little mouth. Maisie began to suck and as she did Leonora felt a great big tear roll down her face, one and then another and another until the flow was seamless. How could Gareth do this to them? To any of them?

Leonora didn't make any attempt to stop the tears. There were so many that she wondered if they would ever stop, even if she wanted them to. One dropped off her chin and splashed on to Maisie's face. For an instant the tiny baby pulled away and opened her eyes in surprise and indignation. Then, squinting Leonora's face into focus, she smiled and, snuggling close, carried on feeding.

Leonora stroked the little crystal smear away. Sweet little thing. Her heart ached so hard she thought it might burst. How could Gareth do this to them?

It was well after lights out in the girls' dormitory at Burbeck House, not that Carol was asleep. Oh, no. Fiona snored — come to that, so did Netty — and periodically Jan snuffled and scratched and expelled a peculiar little hissing breath that sounded as if she might have sprung a leak.

God alone knows what Diana was doing. Carol suspected that she might be awake as well but, sleep deprived and getting colder and more uncomfortable with every passing minute, Carol was far, far too grumpy to ask. She pulled the pillow up over her head, put her fingers in her ears and closed her eyes. The mattress on the bunk bed was so thin that she could feel every spring coiled in the frame, and Adie had managed to sneak in somehow and was stretched out on the bottom bunk near the window, wearing black silk pyjamas and looking like an ad from a Sunday colour supplement. He didn't so much snore as gurgle horribly, like a bath slowly emptying through a blocked plughole.

Between her particular friends and the rest of the room's occupants, they created a nocturnal symphony that Carol could have done without. Worse still, every time Carol did manage to slip into sleep her brain switched on a dream reel that featured Gareth Howard in glorious Technicolor, intercut with various conversations with Raf, up to and including a full white wedding where she was standing at the altar and still had no idea which of them was the groom. It had been a long night so far.

Fiona had taken sleeping pills and a lot of trouble over her presleep preparations. She was now lying on her back with her mouth open, on the top bunk near the window. She was caught in a spotlight of moonlight, wearing an opaque purple satin eye mask that covered almost all of the top half of her face, giant green foam rollers and a thick face cream that looked as if it might eventually dry to a crust. She looked like the classic cartoon of a sleeping woman.

Adie had borrowed some of her face cream.

"Psst." A noise cut through the gloom like a blowtorch through butter.

Carol decided the sound had got nothing to do with her. Ignored, it might go away, and anyway, amongst the rest of the noises it could be anything: mice, a squeaky board, one of the other sleepers — possibly Jan — had upped the ante when it came to leaking noises, or maybe Carol had just imagined it.

"Pssssssssssst." The same noise again, longer and louder this time and followed by sharp rapping. Carol peeled the pillow off her face and opened one eye.

Out on the fire escape stood a figure, hands cupped around his face as he peered into the girls' dormitory. Carol froze for a split second. Was it a peeping Tom or a burglar? Surely they didn't normally attract attention to themselves by tapping and calling. Or did they? Did they want to be seen?

"Carol? Carol? Psst. Are you awake? I know you're in there."

Not many burglars knew her by name.

She would have ignored him but he was getting louder and on the top bunk Fiona was beginning to stir.

Carol slipped out from under the covers, clambered down off the bunk and padded across to the window, wondering just how rough she looked and how Gareth felt about blue and white checked pyjamas. She rummaged through her hair, hoping it would look sexy and tousled rather than just sticking up at the back and flat on one side.

"What do you want?" she said through the closed window. It sounded a lot grumpier than she had intended but it had to be three o'clock in the morning, so what did the man expect?

"Hi," he said with a big grin. "I couldn't get to sleep."

"Ssssh," she said, trying to wave the sound of his voice away. "You'll wake everyone up."

"Open the window," he said, miming as he spoke.

"This is the girls' dormitory."

"Adie's in there."

Carol slid the sash up. "Exactly . . ."

He leaned in and before she could stop him, he kissed her. "I thought maybe we could talk," he said. Gareth was dressed, jeans, a white T-shirt, tan leather jacket. He looked almost edible, even at three o'clock in the morning. He grinned. "Fancy a walk?"

"A walk?" she growled. "Are you nuts?"

"Possibly, come on, why not? It's the most beautiful night. Don't you trust me?"

"I don't really think so . . ." Carol began thinking rapidly. It wasn't him she was worried about. Did she dare trust herself?

He offered her his hand.

"Where are we going?"

He grinned. "Wherever you like. If you're worried about wandering off into the night with strange men we could just sit out here on the fire escape and chat amongst the dog-ends."

Carol looked round the dormitory, wondering how long it would be before someone woke up and heard them. As if reading her mind Gareth said, "*Or* we could go for a proper walk — it's lovely out here. How about we go down to the lake? Look at the moon on the water. Or we could go for a swim. How do you feel about skinny-dipping?"

"No skinny-dipping."

He laughed. "OK, a walk then."

Carol considered for a moment or two. Why not? Who would know? What harm would it do? What could they get up to on a walk? Even as she thought it, Carol's brain came up with about fifty different possibilities — ranging from innocent to positively pornographic and back. Even so, some of them, it had to be said, were far from unattractive.

"Just a minute," she said. "I need to get something." Back at her bunk Carol pulled on a dressing gown and slipped on her shoes.

"And just exactly where do you think you're going?" hissed a little voice.

Carol swung round. "Go back to sleep, Adie, your face cream'll crack," she hissed right back.

At the other end of the corridor Callista Haze was also wide awake and staring up at the ceiling. Institutional staff bedrooms on the whole always had a kind of spartan charm — this one being no exception. There was a single bed along one wall with a cabinet and lamp alongside it. Opposite the bed was a wash basin, an oak bookcase with a selection of religious tracts and a Bible on the top shelf. By the far wall stood a writing table and chair and an armchair set to one side of a fireplace, which had been boarded up with a sheet of plywood and then painted battleship grey to match the rest of the room. In front of the plywood was propped a two-bar electric fire. Someone had added a little posy of silk flowers in a jam jar on the windowsill, which was now picked out in moonlight. At least there were no bears.

Before she had got into bed Callista had taken the precaution of slipping a chair under the handle of her bedroom door, just in case George took to sleepwalking.

Slipping in and out of sleep she had been wondering if it was an overreaction, a foolish thing to think after all these years, let alone to do, when — in the small hours — the doorknob rattled violently. There was a grunt of frustration from outside and then another little push and jiggle before her would-be visitor conceded defeat.

"Good night, George," she called cordially.

"Ah, oh yes, good night, Callista," he said. "Sorry about that, m' dear. Just on my way back from the bathroom. Didn't mean to disturb you. Wrong room. Easy mistake to make. See you in the morning. Sweet dreams."

All alone in the darkness Callista smiled to herself; it was almost convincing, or at least would have been if her name hadn't been tacked to the outside of the door on a large sheet of laminated card.

Callista turned off the lamp, and pulled the bedcovers up over her shoulders; some things never change. It was quite sweet, really. Did George seriously think that after all these years he would bring her back into the fold with a late night little seduction? She smiled as she settled down. Poor George. It had been touch and go when he was in his prime.

"Right," said Mr Bearman the following morning, clapping his hands as he brought the rabble in the main hall to order. "If you would like to take your seats, ladies and gentlemen, then Miss Haze and myself will get this show on the road — again." He laughed at his own attempt at a joke, and as the crew and cast settled down Miss Haze got to her feet and took up a place behind the lectern. With the slightest nod of acknowledgement to Mr Bearman she began to speak.

"Hi and good morning, everyone. First of all I wanted to say how very nice it is to see you all again. I have very fond memories of the Belvedere summer drama tours and of this group in particular. Although at the time I doubt anyone in the cast was aware of it, your production of *Macbeth* was my very first major show at Belvedere High School, and my very first tour, and I was incredibly nervous. I have to say that on the opening night as the curtains came down to a standing ovation I have never felt more proud or more relieved in my entire life.

"I feel a little bit of that same nervous excitement today. We've got an awful lot of work ahead of us so I don't propose to waste too much time on reminiscing but I just want to tell you how very pleased I am to be invited back and to be involved all over again. I am also quite certain that if you are half as good as you were first time round then we'll bring the house down." Miss

Haze smiled, waited for silence and then, opening a file on the lectern, said, "Right, well, given that it's been quite a few years since our last performance I thought we'd begin by taking a look at the play and then we'll talk about what we're going to do over the weekend. We're on a very tight schedule, so I do hope you'll bear with us when we start bullying you."

There were muted cheers and laughter from the cast and crew.

Carol stared up at Miss Haze. She was quite small, maybe five foot two or three at the very most, whip thin and packed full of vitality, her face alight with enthusiasm. The younger Miss Haze, just fresh out of drama school, so sexy, so elegant, so very eloquent and talented, had seemed the height of sophistication, a role model if there ever was one. Carol remembered being hugely impressed by her — and it seemed that she wasn't alone.

Alongside her Adie was staring up at the stage totally entranced. "Leather trousers," he purred. Carol laughed and poked him sharply in the ribs. It didn't seem all that long ago since he'd said it for real.

Twenty years ago it had been just the same: there had been him, Jan, Netty and Diana, all standing in a row surrounded by the rest of the cast and crew. Carol looked over her shoulder. Nothing it seemed had changed that much except for the fact that back then everyone had had all their hair, almost everyone had had a waistline and none of them had been in the slightest bit grey.

It felt to Carol that Miss Haze had said almost exactly the same things then too.

Picking up her notes, Callista Haze walked away from the lectern so that everyone could see her more clearly and then began to talk slowly in a warm, expressive, almost melodic storyteller's voice.

"*Macbeth* is one of the most popular and famous of Shakespeare's plays — and I've always thought it is one of his best pieces of writing. The story is emotive and magical and very powerful, and stands up even after all these years. Macbeth, a Scottish warrior, encouraged by his wife — an ambitious, ruthless and ultimately unstable woman — and by the prophetic words of three witches, murders his king, Duncan, and then seizes the throne for himself."

Carol glanced around the room. Just like all those years before, Miss Callista Haze had the troupe's undivided attention. They were hanging on her every word.

"So . . ." said Miss Haze, her voice dropping to a conspiratorial purr as she continued the story.

"So where did *you* get to last night, then? And when are we going to hear all the sordid details?" whispered Adie, leaning a little closer to Carol. Carol blushed crimson. Adie smirked, lifting his eyebrows to emphasise the question. On the stage Miss Haze was still explaining the story of Macbeth — not that Carol heard a word.

"Well?" pressed Adie.

Carol stared at him. Whatever she said she knew that no one would believe it. Hadn't it been just the same first time around too?

"No comment," she said and turned her attention to the sheets of paper Diana had handed out.

Netty elbowed her.

"Not you too. We were only talking," snapped Carol angrily.

Netty pulled a face. "What?"

"You heard me," hissed Carol. "Nothing happened, zilch — nada — Gareth and I, we were only talking."

"What *are* you on about? Miss Haze just said she wants you and golden boy to go down the front and for us to pick up our props and scripts."

Carol stared at her, bluster gone in an instant. "Oh right, sorry," she said.

"Come on, we haven't got all day," said Netty.

Meanwhile, Adie was also on his feet and scurrying down towards the stage, only too eager to go rootling through the dressing-up boxes. After a few seconds he emerged triumphant, clutching a long grey cloak and a huge plastic sword. Carol made the effort to regain her composure while going down to where Diana and a stagehand whose name Carol couldn't remember were rummaging through another box of oddments.

"I know they're in here somewhere," Diana was saying, turfing out a shield and horned helmet. "I put them in myself."

"What exactly are we looking for?" asked Carol, peering at the growing heap of discarded paraphernalia.

"Ah, here we are. These," Diana said with delight, and pulled out a couple of very convincing rubber daggers and handed them to Carol. From up on the stage Miss Haze beamed.

Carol could sense that Gareth was right behind her but didn't turn round.

"Hi," he said. "Sorry I'm late. I overslept. How are you this morning?"

"Fine," she said, without looking round. "How about you?"

Before he could say anything else Miss Haze clapped her hands and said, "Right, well, I think we really ought to make a start. We've got an awful lot to get through today. I thought we'd just go for a straight read-through from the beginning; see how it goes. So if you'd all like to gather round, pull the chairs into a circle . . ." She waited a few moments for everyone to settle down and then looked up at the three witches, Netty, Diana and Jan, who were sitting in a huddle, cradling a huge plastic cauldron between them.

"Well, ladies and gentlemen, if we're all set?" She waited for any protests and when there were none said, "In that case then here we go." With a broad smile and reading from her script she began, "'Act one, scene one. Thunder and lightning. Enter three Witches.'"

For a moment there was an expectant lull — a strange heady quiet — and then Diana pulled a piece of tissue from her pocket and unpeeled what looked like a rather nasty piece of chewing gum from inside it. The wart. Unhesitatingly Diana pressed it onto her chin. There was a muted cheer and as it died back to silence she began to read. "'When shall we three meet again?/In thunder lightning, or in rain?'"

"'When the hurlyburly's done,/When the battle's lost, and won.'" answered Netty.

" 'That will be ere the set of sun.' " Jan.

" 'Where the place?' " asked Diana, hunched now over the cauldron.

" 'Upon the heath,' " answered Netty.

Carol's eyes filled with tears. Or in some Christian retreat miles from anywhere and twenty years on, she thought wistfully.

As the voices rose and fell, the years seemed to vanish and it was easy to imagine that they were all teenagers again.

Carol could remember the first read-through very clearly. She had really wanted to be a witch and had hung back and stayed with the rest of the gang, much too self-conscious and far too unsure of herself to go and sit anywhere near Gareth Howard, despite having spent the previous lunchtime with him on the veranda of the cricket pavilion.

Miss Haze had looked up as they'd settled themselves down in a loose circle around the stage, blissfully unaware of any nerves of self-doubt.

"Right, Carol, if you'd like to go over there and pair up with Gareth and the rest of the Macbeth household." She had waved her over. Carol had bitten her lip and shuffled forward, although at least now their pairing had some kind of an official sanction. "And Adrian and Fiona?" Miss Haze continued, "I know in the play you don't even speak to each other but I want us to think about characterisation. After all, it is your death, Fiona, that ultimately brings about Macbeth's death. As Lord and Lady Macduff we need to consider the relationship between you."

178

Carol grinned. There was not much chance of a relationship between those two. As they settled down alongside each other, Adie pulled a face that suggested he had some kind of terrible abdominal pain while Fiona picked up the script and, oblivious to what the rest of them were doing, started to read her part aloud. It was a match made in hell.

"So, if you'd all like to get into your groups. Witches down here, please." Netty teetered off on stack heels that only just squeaked in under the suitable footwear rule.

Miss Haze had clapped her hands and everyone changed positions. Carol had watched the witches moving away to go through their parts until she was left alone with Gareth and his household. She shifted uncomfortably from foot to foot feeling — although there was no evidence to back it up — that everyone was looking at the two of them.

Carol came to with a jolt as she realised that the play — the one at Burbeck House in the here and now — was rapidly heading her way and she hadn't got a clue where the hell they were. It was like one of those awful dreams where you are standing there, centre stage, spotlights on, naked except for your slippers and a tiara with no idea what the play is or what your lines are.

Panicking, Carol glanced down at the page open in front of her — no one who was currently speaking now was on it. Damn, damn, damn. She looked up and scanned the room in desperation but everyone else was either listening to the speeches or following the book. Damn, bugger and damn.

Just as she felt the pulse in her ears drop down a gear and race away, a hand appeared on the edge of her vision, flicked through a few pages and pointed to the line they were on. As the panic started to abate Carol looked up. Gareth grinned as he caught her eye.

"Nervous?" he mouthed.

Carol pulled a face that she hoped conveyed something grateful but nevertheless quietly confident. "No, I'm fine," she whispered back.

Across the room, the old king — once the lanky boy who had played Duncan and who now, all grown up and balding nicely, could quite easily pass for an ageing Scottish monarch — had got into his stride. Carol struggled to keep her eye on the script, keeping the place with her finger, while all the while her brain desperately tried to pull her away and back to other places and other times.

"God, I'm never going to be able to learn all this," said the voice of a much younger Carol, tugging nervously at her hair, the memory surfacing as vividly as a scene from a feature film in her imagination. "I don't know half of it yet. We start the tour next week and I'm barely off the book. It's going to be a disaster."

And from beside her on a daisy-strewn bank, long forgotten, a teenage Gareth Howard was busy saying, "Relax. It'll be all right. You'll be fine. It sounds great, you're nearly there, Carol. And no, before you ask me — I'm not just saying that, I mean it. You're good." And then — and then, he had loomed up over her on his elbows, head and shoulders obscuring the sunlight. She thought for one heady, time-stopping instant that he

180

was going to kiss her, and there was that nip, that delicious wobbly sensation in the pit of her stomach and Carol had held her breath.

It passed almost as soon as she felt it. After all, Carol realised, she had thought Gareth was going to kiss her lots of times since they had started rehearsal and he hadn't so far. So she relaxed and closed her eyes and was about to say she was still worried about her lines when he really did kiss her.

She gasped as his lips gently touched hers, and as if the sound was some kind of invitation, Gareth slid his hand under the back of her head and pulled her closer. As his fingers closed in her hair, all sense, all reason bubbled away on a great upward surge of desire that took her breath away, all those years ago on a long-forgotten bank of grass in broad daylight. And the night before, sitting side by side on a dewy lawn looking up at the moon in the grounds of Burbeck House, he had done it all over again.

Carol's finger determinedly tracked the speech of the old king and then finally, at last, it was her turn to speak. Act one, scene five, time to read the letter Lady Macbeth had received from Macbeth about the witches' prophecies and hatch a plan to kill Duncan.

"'Enter Lady Macbeth, reading a letter,'" said Miss Haze in a soft voice.

Carol could feel the eyes of the rest of the cast on her. She licked her lips, took a breath, let the silence settle and then began to read, her voice sounding even and sure, despite the chaos in her head.

"'They met me in the day of success;'"

Once they were down the fire escape he had caught hold of her hand, his fingers warm and strong through hers. Carol didn't know what to say and so had waited for him to speak — and he'd said nothing. She shivered; lust and desire were still as noisy, however old you were.

They had walked in silence through the exquisite sculpted lines of formal gardens, out through a topiary arch towards the wilder more natural parkland beyond. Finally he had led her to a place down by the lake where the moonlight reflected in the ripples like molten silver and she realised that Gareth had brought a blanket, which she had thought a little bit previous of him. They sat there for a while under the low-slung moon and then he turned to her.

"It's easy to be quiet with you."

Carol laughed. "I'm still half asleep, that's why," she said, trying hard to dissolve the intensity that hung between them.

"So tell me about what you've been doing for the last twenty years," he said. Carol stared out over the silver-plated water and then she told him about her boys and her business and being married to the wrong person, and in some ways — once she got going — it almost felt as if she was talking to herself.

When finally she was quiet again, Gareth said, "I know how that feels — all those mistakes and wondering how things might have been if you'd done it all differently. Made different choices." And then he turned and very gently stroked her hair.

She tried hard to suppress a sigh of pleasure.

"I've been thinking a lot about might-have-beens just lately," Gareth said softly and pulled her closer to him, and Carol hadn't resisted, hadn't protested, hadn't thought of anything but how very good it felt to be in his arms again after all these years.

He was warm and strong and yet was still somehow tender, which was, Carol remembered, exactly how he had felt before, back when she had had no idea what men were like. And in the moonlight Carol had looked up into his eyes and wondered where all the years had gone and how very, very easy it would be to just melt into him, melt into his hungry relentless persistent mouth. His hand slid across her back, sliding around under her dressing gown, up under the jacket of her pyjamas, stroking her spine, and all the while, as the touch of his hand registered, Carol watched his progress in her mind's eye almost as if it was happening to someone else.

Gareth moaned softly as his fingers stroked across her warm soft skin, or perhaps it was her, it was so very hard to tell. And the kisses made her breathless and dizzy, and then his hand rose higher and his fingers caressed and then cupped the swell of her breast, fingers on hard tight nipples, and Carol gasped and knew that this time the voice was most definitely hers. And then a bird took off or maybe was disturbed somewhere in the reeds — noisy, messy, anxious — and the sound was enough to make Carol pull away.

"No, no, I'm sorry," she said, breathing hard, pulling her dressing gown tight around her, moving back, putting some breathing space between them.

"Sorry?" he said. He hadn't moved. "What on earth for?"

Carol laughed. "What do you mean, what for? Sorry, I can't do this. We're not teenagers any more, Gareth. We've got lives and families and — and I really think that we ought to be getting back to the hall." She clambered to her feet, feeling the cold and the damp in her body. "And besides, I'm frozen and I'm tired and the grass is wet."

"And you don't trust me?"

Carol swung round to look at him. He still hadn't moved, was still sitting there on a rug in the moonlight. "No, not exactly, Gareth. I don't trust myself," she said, "and that is far, far worse."

He laughed. "So? Let me drive. You just have to lay back," he grinned wolfishly.

"And think of England?" Carol shook her head and laughed. "No, I don't think so," she said. "We ought to go back now. We've got a big day tomorrow."

"Are you sure?"

She shook her head. "No, and that is exactly why I'm going to go back to Teddy Towers with the rest of the snorers and try and grab a few hours' sleep."

He shrugged. "OK — if that's what you want. We've got all the time in the world. It was just that I was hoping that maybe —" He stopped short and shook his head, waving the words away. "It doesn't matter."

Carol decided not to ask what it was he was hoping for, just in case she felt the same.

184

* * *

And in the here and now, Carol was standing in the hall with him reading as Macbeth. The rhythm was coming back now, the words and phrases making perfect sense, tripping off her tongue as if all this while they had been stored somewhere in her memory, all primed and ready for this very moment, but — even so, as Carol read — the vast majority of her thoughts were focused not on the play but on Gareth Howard now and Gareth Howard then.

CHAPTER
EIGHT

After the excitement of the morning's read-through lunch was a total scrum; a running buffet on trestle tables set out under Diana's fluttering welcome banners, for a cast and crew that had — in the course of just a few short hours — regressed into the teenagers they once were. Adulthood was apparently not a very robust veneer. In rehearsal there had been all sorts of swerving round people to avoid premeditated nipping, reversion to nicknames, catcalling and much guffawing. Between scenes there had been lots of laughter, lots of good-natured teasing and some sulking. Now during lunch it was revving up. There was the odd wedgie, a lot of playful arm-punching, some very longing looks and huge amounts of unforced giggling going on in the queue for food.

Carol decided to leave before someone suggested a bread roll fight, took a filled tray and made her way out of the dining room, heading through the French windows into the gardens. It had been a long morning. Fiona had had to go for a little lie-down, and while Netty, Jan and Adie went off to roll joints behind the greenhouse, Diana found a quiet corner to check her phone. Miss Haze, who was delighted with the way the

186

morning had gone, headed upstairs to her room with her lunch so she could read through her notes in peace. Mr Bearman spent most of lunchtime looking for her.

On the lawn the lay Christians were praying in tight V formation.

Leonora Howard's message on Diana's mobile was very simple and to the point. "Hello, you don't know me but your husband said that I could ring you. I wonder if you could call me back when you get the chance?"

Diana took a deep breath, tapped in Leonora's number and waited.

Across a broad expanse of immaculately trimmed grass she could see Carol, sitting under the dappled shade of a horse chestnut tree, relaxing on a circular wooden bench that had been built around the base of the broad trunk. Diana lifted a hand in greeting and Carol immediately grinned and waved her over. Diana pointed to the phone and held up an open hand to indicate she'd be there in five minutes.

Carol nodded.

"Hello," said Diana as Leonora Howard answered. She kept the tone light. "This is Diana; you asked me to call you?"

"Oh, yes," said Leonora. She sounded relieved. "You didn't mind me phoning, did you? Only I didn't know what else to do."

"No, not at all," said Diana cautiously. "Although, to be perfectly honest, I'm not sure that I can do anything to help." She spoke softly and calmly. Hadn't Gareth told Carol that Leonora was unstable?

"Did your husband explain the situation to you?"

"Well, not really. He told me that you're Gareth's wife —"

The woman sighed. "Yes I am. The thing is I was really rather hoping to find a way to get down there to talk to him. He is still there, isn't he?"

Diana bit her lip and considered for a moment. Everything was going so well with the drama group reunion. The last thing she wanted was any kind of scene, so she decided to hedge a little, not wanting to commit herself. "Hedley told me that you were separated, you and Gareth, and that he had left you?" Diana winced; that hadn't come out as tactfully as she had intended it to.

Leonora's voice faltered. "Yes, I suppose that you could say that. Gareth walked out on us on Friday afternoon. Or at least I assume he's walked out on us — that's what it feels like — although he didn't actually say where he was going or if he would be coming back. Actually I'm not one hundred per cent certain what is going on. That's why I need to see him."

"But that was only yesterday," said Diana in astonishment. "Do you mean he left you yesterday?"

"Yes, that's right, yesterday afternoon, and then this girl rang up last night looking for him and told me that she was pregnant." On the far end of the line Leonora laughed darkly. "It's been an interesting weekend so far, I can tell you."

Diana swallowed hard. Leonora didn't sound in the least bit unstable; she sounded hurt and lost and angry, and who could blame her? "Oh," was all Diana could manage. While she was composing her thoughts and a reply, from the corner of her eye Diana spotted Gareth heading across the lawn towards Carol. It was all Diana could do not to call out and warn her; it felt as if she was watching a cheetah bearing down on a grazing gazelle.

"Is there any way that I can help?" said Diana hastily.

Across the grass Gareth was getting closer and closer. Carol looked up and Gareth smiled. In the shadows under the horse chestnut his teeth looked unnaturally white. Diana held her breath as he closed on her friend.

"The thing is," Leonora was saying, "that I need to talk to him, but after Sunday, once your reunion is over, I have no idea where he will go or where he will be. He's taken the car and I've got the children. They're only tiny — so I'm kind of stuck." Leonora paused. "Also, I'm afraid that if Gareth finds out that I know where he is he might just vanish. I really need to speak to him, so I was wondering if perhaps — oh, I don't know, maybe I'm just clutching at straws." Her voice crackled and finally broke. "God, this is so awful. It feels as if I've woken up inside a bad dream."

In the dappled shade Gareth's smile broadened and Diana shuddered.

"I'm so sorry," said Diana slowly, making a decision. "It must be awful for you. I'm still not sure what I can do to help you."

"Actually, there might be something," said Leonora.

"Hi, nice spot you've found yourself here," said Gareth, heading towards Carol, carrying his lunch.

She looked up, gaze momentarily unfocused, and nodded. He was a dark shape blocking out the sunlight. "Ummmm, it is beautiful out here. Seemed a real shame to stay inside, even without the chimps' tea party."

"Is that a professional opinion?" he asked.

"Of the stage crew?"

"No," he laughed, glancing back over his shoulder at the view. "The gardens."

Carol smiled. "No, not at all. Professional gardeners can still recognise beauty when they see it. If they can't then they wouldn't be in business for very long. Anyway, look around — these gardens are wonderful whether you understand planting or not. In fact knowing how the original designer achieved it makes it all the more impressive. Can you imagine laying out a scheme of planting that you would never see come to maturity in your lifetime, trying to imagine the combinations and colours as they grow and develop? It may be your grandchildren who are the ones who finally see the garden as you visualised it."

"Sounds as if you really love your job."

"I do, and it grows on you — sorry, no pun intended. I never thought I'd end up as a gardener but the more I know about gardening the more passionate it makes me about plants and trees and creating great gardens and developing landscapes, places for people to enjoy, places that will grow more interesting as time passes."

She stopped and caught sight of him, and realised that he was watching her intently. "Sorry," Carol said. "I'm getting carried away."

Gareth moved a little closer. "No, no, not at all, don't apologise. I'm impressed. Having so much passion for your work has got to be great." He hesitated and then said, "I was worried that you maybe weren't talking to me today," his voice dropped to something low and more intimate, "after last night."

"What on earth makes you think that?" she said briskly. And what was it that had happened last night? If anything? An embrace, a lot of desire and her coming to her senses? Carol looked up into his face.

"Gareth, I've been thinking, all that desire and those longings are not about you." He looked taken aback, so she added quickly, "What I mean is that that thing, that buzz isn't about who you are now — but for who you were first time round. You may look and sound like the Gareth Howard I knew at school, but realistically you're not him. I don't know you at all."

He nodded. "I know what you're saying."

She felt relieved. "If you mean what you said, then we need to start over, take a step back and go slowly while we sort out the might have beens from the reality."

He smiled. "And do you want to do that?"

Carol sighed; being a grown-up and sensible was not something she had ever really expected to be afflicted with. "I'm not sure — I'm not desperate to rush into anything."

"And was that what was happening last night?"

She laughed. "Could have been, but I just about managed to save myself."

"Shame. So if we're starting over, would you mind if I joined you?" he asked, nodding towards the broad wooden bench.

Carol shook her head. "No — not at all, please do." Before adding, "Diana will be here in a minute."

"If I'm disturbing you . . .?" he asked again, this time looking at the space alongside her.

"No, no, it will be fine."

"I thought that maybe you and Diana had things to talk about — things to catch up on."

"We have, we do — but we can do that either with you here or do it later. I'm sure neither of us would mind you sitting in."

He sat down at a respectful distance away and then said, "So what do you think?"

Carol paused, trying to work out what she wanted to say. What was the point of getting older if you still couldn't say those things that were on your mind without thinking the world would end if you opened your mouth?

"I came here hoping to see you, and yes, I was wondering if all that stuff was still there. I'm not sure what I expected, really. I was worried that I might just be grasping at a fantasy that goes back to our teens; something that has sustained me on stormy days. You know how it is. All that stuff filtered and reinterpreted through memory and time."

"All that stuff?"

Carol felt increasingly uncomfortable. He wasn't making this easy for her. "Yes, you know what I mean — stuff: desire, attraction, love and lust."

"And?" he asked, eyes alight. "Was all the stuff still there?"

She winced. "You have to ask me? You know it is, and it wrong-footed me. I'm not sure that I'm not dealing with a mirage. Am I reacting to you or to the memory of what you were? This stuff — relationships, attraction — the older we get, it seems to me, the more complicated it all gets. It's so simple when you're eighteen."

He stretched cat-like, an arm snaking round behind her shoulders. Carol laughed. "That's a very old move, Gareth. Last time I saw anything like that was on the back row of the Majestic Cinema."

Gareth grinned. "Hey, what can I say? If it ain't broke, don't fix it. And I don't see why it has to be complicated. We don't have to start where we left off — we can't." He paused. "We just have to start again. It could be great fun. Me and you." He leaned in a little closer. "I'm on my own too, you know. What are the odds on two incredibly sexy people like us being unattached at the same time?" The tone was so over the top and corny that they both laughed.

"Oh, for God's sake, Gareth —" she began.

"No, no, I'm serious, hear me out. Maybe we ought to look on this as fate, as karma — chances are if we had stayed together once we left school we would have been divorced by now and have hated the sight of each other. This way we get another bite of the cherry, at a stage in our lives when we can truly value what's on offer."

Carol stared at him. It didn't sound corny at all. His tone had moved effortlessly from humorous to something more serious, and his gaze held hers for longer than was comfortable. She felt a flutter of heat rising inside her and quickly looked away.

"But we've only just met," she protested, aware of some big emotive push just beneath Gareth's words that wasn't apparent on the surface. Carol wanted him but some part of her also wanted to hold him off, so that she could explain to him that she wasn't on her own, that she wasn't needy or desperate or lost, but the words just wouldn't come out.

"Doesn't heading towards forty add something that wasn't there when you're seventeen or eighteen?"

She looked up at him. "What? Oh, please. Don't tell me. If you say anything about desperation, a sense of our own mortality or life beginning, I think I'll probably punch you."

He grinned. "Actually, what I was going to say was how good we both know it could be. We could be fantastic together."

More heat rolled through her, wave after wave. "What?" she said in an undertone, hardly able to believe her ears.

The grin widened. "Oh, come on, Carol, don't tell me you haven't thought about it?" he murmured. "Me and you? You felt it last night and panicked and ran away. I was there as well, remember?"

194

Carol bit her lip and tried very hard to hang on to things like good sense and slow progress. Wasn't this the fantasy that she had had ever since leaving school? That Gareth Howard really wanted her more than anything else? Wasn't this what she had longed for? And yet — and yet — why now? Why here?

Carol looked up into his face; shouldn't there be alarm bells ringing and warning lights going off? Her instincts were on red alert, but nevertheless when Carol stared into his eyes, trying to find the lie, she came up empty-handed. Maybe the problem with getting older was that instinctively you always looked over your shoulder for the catch — but what if this time there wasn't one? What if this was the truth after all?

Gareth was so close now that Carol could feel his breath on her face, and she knew he was moving closer still. Slowly, slowly, she could sense his progress and as he did Carol closed her eyes.

"Carol," he said softly, "I want you to know that I have always lo—"

But before he had a chance to finish the sentence Carol heard Diana say in an unnaturally loud voice, "Well, hello there, you two, you don't mind if I join you, do you? Lunch looks good, I'm absolutely famished, is that the salmon and broccoli quiche? It looks wonderful, doesn't it? The food is always amazingly good here . . ."

Carol's eyes snapped open; Gareth pulled away as if he had been bitten.

Diana smiled. "I was wondering whether to have the bacon flan or that — it smells really nice." Her expression was so tight and bright it looked as if it had been painted on.

"Are you all right?" Carol asked.

Diana nodded. "Uh-huh, yes, of course I am. I'm absolutely fine," she said, settling herself down alongside Carol with much flapping and arranging of her napkin and cutlery in a great show of arriving. "Absolutely fine. What time did Miss Haze say we've got to be back? It's going very well, don't you think? This morning went amazingly well."

Carol stared at her, trying to work out what on earth was going on. Diana, now busily unpacking her tray, was flushed and looked deeply uncomfortable.

"Are you sure you're all right?" she asked again in an undertone.

"Oh, yes, just a bit nervous that's all, a bit rusty — but it's been good so far, don't you think? How about you, Gareth, how are you bearing up? We've barely had a chance to speak since you arrived. How are things with you? How's life?"

Carol watched dumbfounded as Diana turned her full attention on him, so intently, so fiercely that it was like a blowlamp — and the questions and her tone were so barbed and so unlike Diana that Carol knew that she must have missed something.

Gareth, who had backed off a little and turned to start on his lunch, smiled and said, "I'm fine, thank you."

"And what are you up to these days?" Diana's tone didn't soften.

His smile held fast. "This and that. I'm an IT consultant. I'm involved mostly in arts projects. I've got my own company — it keeps me out of mischief."

"Does it? And how about the rest of your life?" Diana growled, cutting his answer short. Carol stared at her; it was the most extraordinary performance.

Gareth's expression closed down to neutral. "You know how it is. Busy, fortunately. I meant to congratulate you, Diana. You've done a great job with the whole setup. It's a great place, great idea. Well done. It couldn't have been easy to get all this together."

But it seemed that Diana hadn't finished with Gareth and elbowed his attempt at polite conversation to one side. "Are you married? Have you got any children?"

Carol was stunned. Turning, she said, "Diana, what's going on?"

Diana shook her head. "Nothing. I'm just curious, that's all."

"It's not like you —" Carol began and then stopped. Hadn't she just been thinking about how dangerous it was to assume that people were the same as she had left them?

Gareth, still smiling, got to his feet. "Don't mind me. I'm sure that you two have got a lot to catch up on. If you'll excuse me, I'm just going to pop inside and get some coffee." And then looking at Carol, he added, "Catch you later."

As soon as he was out of earshot Carol rounded on Diana. "What the hell was all that about? I've never seen you like that before."

Diana held up her hand in exasperation. "Call it a hunch, Carol, he's married — and he's got children." She paused. "There is something about him. I just think you need to be more careful, that's all."

Carol looked at Gareth's retreating form. Wasn't that what her instincts were already telling her? To be careful?

"But that isn't what you said last night."

Diana reddened and then shrugged. "I know."

"And I've already told you, Diana, he *told* me he was married and that he has left her," Carol began in his defence. "It's not like he was trying to hide it from me."

Diana nodded, "I know but it all sounds too neat to me." She paused, watching Carol's face. "You'd say the same thing to me if it was the other way round — it's easy to be misled when you only hear one side of the story."

"I do know that," Carol began and then, more thoughtfully: "Are you saying that Gareth is misleading me?" She was surprised; maybe Diana had picked up something she had missed. "And what's changed? I don't understand where all this is coming from. When Netty was on about Gareth last night you leaped to his defence."

"I know," Diana sighed. "Call it a hunch," she said.

"That's not enough," snapped Carol.

"It's all I've got," Diana lied.

As she spoke Diana watched Gareth heading in through the French windows. This was so difficult. She had promised Leonora faithfully that she wouldn't let Gareth know that Leonora knew where he was, but now that she understood what kind of man Gareth was, it was almost impossible to watch Carol with him. Who was she meant to protect? Diana looked across at the woman who had once been her best friend and wondered how much she could tell her — and decided on balance that it might be better to tell Carol nothing at all, at least not yet. It was a very hard decision to make.

Carol shook her head. "All the years that I knew you I've never seen you like this before. You were really rude to him."

Diana laughed. She *would* tell Carol the truth, but not now, not when Leonora was so vulnerable. Surely Carol would understand? Meanwhile, she had to lighten the mood between them. "Was I? Sorry. Maybe it's the stress of the weekend finally getting to me. Maybe it's my age. Who knows? Anyway, I'm sure he'll survive. He's a big boy."

"Who were you talking to?" asked Carol.

Diana felt a little jolt; surely there was no way Carol could know or guess. "Sorry?" she said, not quite meeting Carol's eye.

Carol nodded in the general direction of the bench where Diana had been sitting earlier to talk to Leonora, as if her ghost still lingered there. "On the phone. Seems to me that you were all right up until then, and then you stormed across here like Medusa on a bad hair day."

"Hedley," Diana lied with barely a second's hesitation, transposing the conversation of the night before with the one she had just had with Leonora. "I thought he had had a run-in with the Chair of the Mother's Union but apparently they are all hunky dory and he's had Dylan put their frozen dinners in alphabetical order to make life easier."

Carol laughed. "Easier?"

Diana, starting on a pile of potato salad, nodded. "That's what he said."

"I'm not sure that would make me that mad, though," said Carol after a second or two's reflection. "Then again I've never been married to a vicar."

Diana smiled and turned her attention back to her lunch.

"So, everybody, just to recap on this morning's efforts, you all did very, very well. Miss Haze's notes covered most points." Mr Bearman bowed appreciatively in her direction. "What I'd really like to do is go again from Act one, scene six, at Macbeth's castle." George Bearman glanced at Miss Haze as if for her approval. She gave a tiny nod and he continued, "Where the king has arrived to stay with Macbeth, and he and his wife have plans to murder the old man while he sleeps. It's a nice contrast too: Lady Macbeth, the perfect society hostess, greeting the old man and taking him in to meet his host, Macbeth, followed in the next scene by Lady Macbeth browbeating her husband into murdering the poor old chap. Then we have Macbeth meeting Banquo and his son on the battlements, and from there we're straight into Macbeth's magnificent speech. 'Is this a dagger which I see before me'." Mr Bearman stepped forward and straight into the role with great gusto.

"Looks like beer belly I see before me from where I'm sitting," hissed Netty.

Carol suppressed a giggle; Adie and Jan snorted while Fiona glowered at them.

"When I was at Stratford —" Fiona began, but Carol had already turned her attention back to the stage. While it might only be a rehearsed reading — and despite occasional outbreaks of late-onset regression — everyone was taking the whole thing remarkably seriously. Diana had said that those people not needed in a scene would be free to wander off in the grounds, but it appeared that nobody wanted to go anywhere — except for Diana, who said she had to go and make a couple of phone calls. Everyone else, the cast and the crew, sat in the hall watching the action intently.

Further along the row of seats Gareth cleared his throat. Carol looked across and caught his eye. He smiled and waggled his fingertips at her in a tiny wave and instantly she felt her whole body tingle in response. Carol would like to have heard what it was he was going to say to her before Diana interrupted them over lunch.

"Carol, I want you to know that I've always lo—" Lo what? Loathed your taste in eyeliner, longed to see you dressed in a wet suit clutching a fresh haddock, or was it simply, I've always loved you?

Was that possible? She shivered and looked away.

Mr Bearman was up on the stage alongside Miss Haze, who was consulting the notes she had made during the morning session. It had to be said that time had not been so generous with Mr Bearman as it had with the sylphlike Miss Haze. Despite her age she still had a real spring in her step and a slim well-toned body buoyed up by a huge amount of natural enthusiasm; George Bearman, by contrast, seemed leaden, plump and terribly old.

"Right, if we can have Macbeth, Lady Macbeth, the king and his entourage, Banquo and the others up here on the stage," he said, waving them up to join him. As the players shuffled along towards the steps, Mr Bearman added, almost as a throwaway line, "You know, I really think we ought to try putting some of the action up on its feet, even if we are still on the book. It makes the whole thing so much more powerful — and if it doesn't work then we've lost nothing by trying."

A little buzz of anticipation went through the hall. Real acting.

Carol groaned, "Do we have to?" to Adie, who grinned.

"You're just jealous that we get swords," he said, taking up a fighting stance. "And, let's face it, it's what we're all here for, hon, the play is the thing, to quote another of Mr Shakespeare's tragedies. Come on. Lighten up, you'll be fine. You used to be really good at this kind of stuff."

Fiona swung round, all smiles and expectation. "It is terribly nerve-racking, isn't it? Obviously if you're not keen, Carol, I'm sure everyone would understand. I really don't mind standing in for . . ." Her voice and smile faded as Carol got to her feet.

"I'll be just fine," Carol growled, winking at Adie, and made her way along the row, arriving at the steps at the same time as Gareth, who very gallantly took her hand and guided her up onto the stage. Carol was aware of the eyes of the whole company on them as they climbed the stairs, and wondered if there was anyone who didn't know their history, and anyone who wasn't waiting to see what would happen this time around.

When they were at school it had been different. The whole drama group had been heaving with raging hormones and budding romances, or what passed for romance back in those days. Carol looked round the faces in the hall, playing join the dots with them and other people from school, wondering if any of them had got married. Some of them must have married childhood sweethearts, surely? And she wondered if they were still together or did they, as Gareth said, now hate the sight of each other?

On stage, with half a dozen stacking chairs, a trestle table and a few chalk marks on the floor, Callista Haze had managed to whip up a fairly passable imaginary Scottish castle. George Bearman walked them all through it, opening imaginary doors as he went. The castle gates, the door to the king's bedchamber, the battlements. Easy as one, two, three.

"Right, places, people, please and can we have a little bit of hush," he said peering out into their makeshift audience.

As Carol took her place in the wings, she looked around and there, before she could stop herself, from somewhere deep in her imagination, clear as day were a whole reel of images from the last final rehearsal, the very last run-through before they had gone on tour all those years ago, filling her mind like some amazing Technicolor double take.

Gareth, eighteen, smiled at her and she sighed. God, then and now it had been so tortuous. "Can we get together when we've finished here?" he whispered, straightening his cloak.

"To talk?" she asked lamely in a tiny voice, trying hard to keep her concentration on the stage.

He nodded. "To talk."

Hadn't they already talked enough? Talking had become a euphemism for him kissing her, touching her, getting bolder and bolder over the days, trying very hard to wear down her reserve and her nervousness and reluctance. Out on the veranda at the cricket pavilion, in quiet corners in empty classrooms, sitting out on the bank shaded by trees. Every time he came near her during rehearsal Carol felt a surge of heat that all these years later she knew was lust but back then made her wonder if she was coming down with flu. And so they had waited in the wings for the play to begin, far too near to each other for either of them to feel truly comfortable.

"Much closer and I'm going to have to throw a bucket of water over the pair of you," one of the crew had hissed as they waited for their respective cues. Gareth had grinned at her and as he did so, Carol felt the desire arc between them like lightning. She shivered.

"Whenever you're ready, off we go . . ." said Miss Haze to the players, then and now. Carol took a deep breath and as she did, the here and now of the drama tour reunion at Burbeck House pushed away the memories of the final school rehearsal. She watched as Duncan made his entrance, waited for her cue and then stepped out onto an open stage for the first time in twenty years and looked out into the auditorium.

For a second Carol faltered as she saw the faces and then as she began to read she found that the words sprung into her mind as if she still knew them. It felt like she was flying. In the wings, in the shadows, Gareth smiled appreciatively and her pulse cranked up a gear.

"Hello, is that Raf O'Connell?" said a cultured female voice.

Raf had been working in the garden when the phone rang. Jake came out carrying the handset with a paw clamped over the earpiece. "It's some woman. Says she needs you."

Raf laughed. "That I should be so lucky."

Jake pulled a face.

"I've got more than enough on my hands with your mother — and on your way back can you pick up another beer?"

Jake lifted an eyebrow; he had his mother's eyes. "I'm doing my homework."

"Very noble. Get yourself one if it helps," and then into the phone he said, "Hi."

"Oh, hello. This is Diana. I'm a friend of Carol's. We met a few weeks ago —"

"Of course. How are you?" Raf said, cutting her short. "And how's it going?"

"You remember me?"

Raf laughed. "I was a wee bit tipsy, I have to admit, but thank God it's not affected me memory. You were her best friend at school. Married to the vicar, chief re-union organiser and card sharp. Is that yourself?"

Diana laughed. "The very woman."

"How can I help?" asked Raf.

Diana's tone subtly changed. "I rang to ask you a favour but I also think I need to talk to you."

Something about her voice made Raf stop what he was doing and sit down. "Not a problem. What's the matter; is everything all right down there?" he asked, with a sense of trepidation.

"Yes and no," said Diana, "and it is difficult to know where to begin."

"Why don't we try the beginning?" said Raf gently.

Diana cleared her throat and then began to speak slowly, as if she was weighing every word. "Well, when this group was on tour before — when we were all at school — Carol was going out with someone called Gareth Howard."

"Ah," said Raf softly, "Golden Boy? She didn't mention him by name but I knew that there was someone special that she was hoping to see again. Is that the problem? Is he the problem?"

Diana sighed. "I'm not sure golden boy is the description I'd use, but the thing is that Gareth is married — and he's just walked out on his wife and children and she wants someone to bring her down so that she can talk to him." Diana paused.

"I'm with you so far; and presumably you're hoping that this someone might be me?" said Raf cautiously.

"Well, yes. I know it's a bit of a cheek and also it's probably going to be messier than it sounds," said Diana.

Jake handed Raf a beer. Raf nodded his thanks. "Is that why I feel all sorts of complications coming on?" he asked, taking a pull on the bottle.

Diana sighed. "Yes and no. It isn't just Gareth's ex-wife I'm concerned about. I think Carol might be getting herself in trouble." She paused, out of words.

"Tell me," said Raf softly.

"Well, I know Carol's a big girl but . . ." Diana began all over again and Raf listened carefully and sipped his beer, not saying another word until she had finished.

"Oh, you've got a really lovely house, haven't you?" said Jasmine, stepping into Leonora's hall and making a great show of wiping her feet. Jasmine was slightly built, with pale waxy skin and dark hair drawn back off her face and dragged into a severe ponytail. She was wearing a short denim skirt and a skimpy little white top that barely covered her midriff or her ample cleavage, and was all wrapped around with a long black fluffy cardigan. Leonora smiled darkly to herself — given time, no doubt Gareth would make his views on comfortable cardigans known to her — or had he abandoned Jasmine as well?

Jasmine looked unwell, large nervous dark-rimmed eyes peering out of too thin a face, but then Leonora remembered only too well the rigours of morning sickness and a system running alive with maverick hormones.

The girl, who looked as if she was barely out of her teens but who was probably in her mid-twenties, bit her lip. "The thing is, he hasn't rung me or texted me or anything since I spoke to you. It's not like him. I know he said not to ring him here but I didn't know what else to do. You didn't mind me coming round, did you?"

It was a question without any answer. "I wouldn't have invited you if I didn't want you to come," said Leonora as evenly as she could manage, waving her into the house.

Maisie was asleep in a pram in the hall; Jasmine peered at her in passing. "She's lovely. She looks just like you, doesn't she?"

Leonora smiled. "Only when she is asleep. She has her daddy's eyes." Leonora didn't add that Maisie bore an uncanny resemblance to Gareth when she was awake. Patrick too. Maybe it was a good thing that both of them were taking a nap.

"She looks so content. How old is she?" said Jasmine, stroking a finger across one tiny downy cheek.

"She's nearly five months and Patrick is two and a bit — and a real handful at the moment. Fortunately he's asleep in his cot at the moment too, so hopefully we can get a little peace and the chance to talk. Do you want to come through into the kitchen?" Leonora indicated the way with an open hand.

Jasmine nodded, following her closely while all the while looking around as if she was in a stately home. "You've got some amazing things in here," she said, looking at the old photos and cut-glass wall lights and the stuffed bear that dominated the space just under the stairs and who was decked with hats and coats and all manner of things hung between his threadbare outspread arms.

"I'm a bit of a hoarder," said Leonora, leading the way. "And I like unusual things."

The girl nodded.

Leonora had wondered exactly how she was going to start this conversation; whichever route she tried there was no easy way in and certainly no way to sugar the pill.

She put the kettle on. Jasmine settled herself down at the table. The room was littered with the fallout of family life: toys on the floor, a baby bouncer with a mobile hanging over it by the washing machine, nappies and baby wipes on the dresser, toy cars and a dummy in amongst the washing-up.

"It's a great house for kids to grow up in," Jasmine said, and then indicated the back door. "You've got a garden too?"

"Yes, although it's not very big. That was why we moved out here. It's not a brilliant area but we got a lot more for our money. Well, my money actually. I bought the house with the money my grandparents left me."

Jasmine looked impressed. "Wow, that's cool, and what about your husband?"

Yes, thought Leonora, the thought as heavy as rock, what about my husband? The kettle clicked off the boil. "How do you take your tea?"

"Milk and two sugars, please."

Leonora concentrated her attention on making the tea and then set a mug in front of Jasmine. It was time to begin. "I'm glad you came round, Jasmine. I was wondering how much you know about Gareth."

The girl reddened, her body language defensive. "Well, not very much, really. I've been thinking about that a lot this week. I don't know anything about him, not who he is, what he actually does for a job or anything, really. I know it sounds daft, but it only struck me when he didn't show up on Friday that there's a whole bit of his life that I've got no idea about. And he's been acting a bit odd for the last few days. He usually rings or texts me every day but I've only heard from him once or twice this week and then he's only talked for a couple of minutes and sounded as if he wasn't quite there. You know what I mean? Like as if he's got something else on his mind — and he's not been round to see me at all."

Leonora nodded but said nothing, encouraging Jasmine to go on, which after a few more seconds she did. "I met him about, I dunno, about five or six months ago, maybe a bit more. He was different to everyone else I hang around with. He's quite a bit older than the kind of guys who usually ask me out. But I quite liked that. He seemed more together, more sophisticated, and he was really keen. He asked me to live with him after about a month — and then he said that maybe we ought to wait for a bit longer. He was a bit worried in case I got caught up in his divorce. He said it might get messy and he didn't want me getting mixed up with it. You know, like it wasn't fair."

210

Leonora tried very hard to hold her expression in neutral. "Did he tell you anything about his wife?" she asked softly.

Jasmine wriggled uncomfortably "A bit. I mean, you must know her, must have met her, so you must know what she's like."

Again Leonora said nothing — it wasn't easy — while behind the silence her heart was screaming. Jasmine, uneasy with the empty air, began to fill it with a flood of words. "He told me he met her while he was working for a theatre company, some computer thing they needed for a show. She's an artist, apparently, and there was a gallery there I think, joined on to the theatre. Anyway, she worked there and they got on quite well, him and her. They went out a few times and then he said he felt a bit of a fool really. They'd been seeing each other a couple of months, maybe three, when she told him she was pregnant and, as he said, he's a decent bloke — what could he do? He's a bit old-fashioned that way, so they got married."

Leonora stared at her. She felt a great rush of pain and raw white heat careering through her like a volley of gunfire. Quietly, struggling to swallow down the bitter taste in her mouth she got to her feet and walked over to the dresser. She could feel Jasmine's wide-eyed gaze following her but Leonora waved her on. "Don't mind me," she said. "Carry on."

"So I says to him, 'Are you saying that the baby wasn't yours?' and he kind of shrugged and said he wasn't saying that. He was saying he really had no way of knowing and then he was kind of embarrassed and

211

said that he shouldn't be telling me any of this, that it's not the kind of thing he made a habit of talking about — and that I wasn't to get him wrong — that his wife is a beautiful, beautiful person but very complicated — artistic, creative, highly strung. You know, a bit unstable at times, and then he laughed and said quite a lot unstable at times. He said he stayed for as long as he could, but it was impossible, like him being there was doing more harm than good — and then I asked him about the kids and he said he sees them as often as he can. Don't get me wrong, he says, she was a great mother, but sometimes him going to pick them up causes more problems than it solves.

"It must have been hard for him. So, I said he needn't worry about me, I was solid as a rock. My mum and dad are real hard-working people and they taught me to be the same. They bought me and my brother the shop as an investment. OK, so it's hard work but at least I've got a future. We do fruit and veg and I do the flowers." She grinned and for the first time Leonora caught a glimpse of what it was that Gareth had seen in her and her heart ached.

"I know I'm not the brightest bulb in the marquee but I came top in my year in Floristry at college and we've got a man to do the books and it's going really well. Anyway, Gareth said when he met his wife she was sharing a house with God knows how many others, mostly artists and musicians and she was well, you know, exciting. Different."

Jasmine stopped as if she had finally run out of steam. "Actually, I've never said this to him but she

212

sounds nice — complicated, I suppose, but interesting. I keep wondering why Gareth would want someone ordinary like me when he can have someone exciting like her."

Leonora came back to the kitchen table, carrying a large green leather-bound book and set it down amongst the mugs and the breakfast dishes.

Jasmine's face visibly brightened. "Oh, what have you got there, baby pictures?" she said, taking a long pull on her tea.

Leonora slid out a chair and sat down. "No, actually it's my wedding album," she said, and opened it up to the first page.

"Oh, brilliant," said Jasmine. "I like a good wedding, me. I cry like a baby. I dunno what me and Gareth will have. I suppose it'll have to be a registry office do once his divorce comes through, only I'd really like a church blessing — you know, for my mum and dad's sake. You know what parents can be like — my mum'll want to wear a big hat."

Jasmine moved closer so that she could see the pictures more clearly, and then Leonora heard the breath catch in her throat, saw a hand fly to the girl's mouth.

"Oh my God," she whispered, voice thick with emotion.

"There was no easy way to tell you," said Leonora gently. "But you had to know. I'm so sorry."

The girl looked at her, her eyes bright with fury but as quickly as it flared it faded, to be replaced with a great wave of panic and then pain. "Oh my God," she said again, tears beginning to trickle down her face. "It's me who should be sorry, isn't it? Oh my God, I didn't know, I'd no idea, no idea at all. Do you mind if I have a cigarette? I've been trying to give up but —"

"It's fine," said Leonora, waving the words away; Leonora, who had never smoked in her life but who at that moment really wished she did. "I'll find you a saucer you can use as an ashtray."

The photo album lay open to the first page and showed a beautiful eight-by-ten shot of the bride and groom, standing hand in hand at the lich-gate of the parish church in the village where Leonora grew up. She was dressed in a wine-coloured crushed velvet, silk and lace dress, designed by one of her friends from the theatre. The corseted outfit was a romantic homage to a medieval maiden, Leonora looking for all the world like something from a Rossetti painting, her long dark red-gold and brown hair topped by a circlet of twisted twigs and orange blossom. Long buttoned sleeves and tiny pleats emphasised her slender body, while alongside her, Gareth Howard — dressed in a dark green frock coat — looked back at the camera with a broad smile and an air of total self-assurance. They made a very handsome couple.

"I think I'm going to be sick," said Jasmine suddenly.

Leonora knew exactly how she felt.

214

CHAPTER
NINE

"God, that was fan-tas-tic," said Adie, emphasising every syllable as he leaped through the French windows, sword in one hand, Eccles cake in the other, and did a great sweeping stroke with the curved plastic blade through the late afternoon air. "Take that and that, you varlet."

They were all taking a break, and he was right — the afternoon had gone incredibly well so far.

Despite finding herself dragged back down memory lane every few minutes, Carol had managed to persuade Macbeth to kill the king and go nicely mad before they broke for refreshments — all that and she hadn't dropped her script once. It was a personal triumph. The cakes were pretty good too.

They were all sitting around on a wall just outside the French windows that led into the dining room, although Adie couldn't keep still because he was far too excited. So, dressed in his cloak and a nifty little crown affair, he was leaping around, swiping and parrying and lunging forward enthusiastically across the neatly clipped lawn. Carol smiled; he had turned out so gorgeous and so golden brown, it was a shame that he hadn't bothered to grow up at the same time.

"Take that, you bounder," Adie snarled at his imaginary aggressor, and then turning to his audience. "God, you know I think I was made for swashing and buckling," he said with genuine delight. Carol laughed. In his efforts to eat and play, Adie, a.k.a. Macduff, had managed to smudge powdered sugar all over his face.

Netty, busy sucking the jam out of a doughnut, laughed. "Boys, eh? What can you say?" she snorted, and looked heavenwards. "Sit down, Adie, and have your tea, for goodness sake; you'll choke."

Jan just rolled her eyes.

Gareth, who had been watching him, pulled the sword out of his belt and said, "If Bearman is going to try and put the play up on its feet, we need the practice." He did a few practice thrusts in Adie's direction, pushing his hair back out of his eyes before leaping forward in a sword fighter's pose, hand up behind him to a round of applause and wild cheering from the lighting crew. He looked wonderful — in fact, they both looked wonderful.

Carol tried hard not to drool. Gareth was a lot thicker-set than Adie, broad-shouldered and taller by a head. He slipped his jacket off and threw it to Carol. As she caught it he did a deep-dipping chivalrous bow and then turned back to face Adie, while the rest of the gang groaned and made vomiting noises.

"Very nice," Adie said, eyeing Gareth up as he adopted a fighting stance opposite him.

Gareth laughed. "Sorry, Adie. You're just not my type."

"Shame," said Adie, eyes alight with mischief.

216

"How about we try and choreograph something for the last scene?" said Gareth as they began to shuffle backwards and forwards, sizing each other up.

Adie nodded and, with a twirl of his sword, said, "Great idea. Lay on, Macbeth," and instantly pressed forward with a great rangy thrust.

Carol's eyes moved from one face to the other in the gang who were watching them. Netty shrugged and lit up another cigarette "Don't look at me. I never did understand men," she said. "You'd think that by our age we'd get it, wouldn't you?"

At the far end of the wall, Fiona — who was in a mood because no one wanted to listen to the story about the time she triumphed in Stratford — wasn't speaking to any of them but was sitting close enough to ensure that nobody missed out on being ignored. Jan was also a little subdued, despite the witches' scenes going like a dream.

Only Diana nodded and said. "It does sound like a really good idea. Rehearsing will keep them both out of mischief." She paused, glancing back at the wild swings and thrusts. "Probably."

A little further along the guys playing Duncan and Banquo, who had been drinking tea up until that point, pulled out their swords and leaped over the wall to join Adie and Gareth. It was stunning to see four middle-aged men playing soldiers, complete with whoops and gasps and a lot of overacting as they parried and thrust and stabbed, every action well larded with sound effects and blood-curdling yells. Five minutes later, and anyone who had a sword, and several who hadn't, had joined in.

Carol laughed, wondering what on earth the lay preachers, who were sharing their weekend at Burbeck — and who at the moment were conspicuous by their absence — must think of the goings-on, at which moment Gareth lunged forward, taking Adie by surprise. Adie, trying to escape, stepped backwards onto the hem of his cloak, staggered, stumbled and then fell over flat on his back in a great ungainly heap on the grass.

"Bugger," he snorted, all embarrassed and self-conscious, red-faced and breathing hard, trying to hold on to some last shred of dignity while Gareth reared up over him and mimed a final nasty mortal thrust.

"Hang on a minute," protested Adie, struggling to get back to his feet. "I'm supposed to kill you, you bastard."

It took Jasmine quite a while to compose herself. Leonora made them both more tea and gave her a box of tissues as the shock sank in and tears ran unchecked down her tiny pale face. Owl-eyed and silent, Jasmine watched while Leonora gave Patrick his tea and then fed Maisie. It was almost as if the girl was too tired, too stunned to move or leave or say anything — not that Leonora made any attempt to send her on her way. After all, give or take a detail or two, they were both in the same boat, and somehow, however strange it might be, Leonora found it comforting to have Jasmine there.

218

"What the hell am I going to do?" Jasmine said at long last, sniffing miserably. Leonora had settled Patrick in front of his favourite video and had Maisie nestled in the crook of her arm. Awake, but happy to be carried, she curled tight against Leonora's body.

Leonora sighed. She felt very old and tired and was already way, way beyond the place where tears would help. "I don't know," she said softly. "But it'll be all right, don't worry." Even as she said it Leonora realised it was a stupid thing to say. It wouldn't be all right at all. What possible way back was there for any of them?

"How can you be so calm? He lied to you too," said Jasmine, in case there was some possibility that Leonora may have missed it. "Aren't you angry?"

Leonora shook her head. Anger wasn't her natural ground; she couldn't sustain it for long. But she did feel hurt that someone who once upon a time had said he loved her could behave so very badly. Perhaps anger would be more productive, more useful. "I'm really hurt that he's betrayed us."

"Bastard," spat Jasmine suddenly. "All those bloody lies he told me. All that crap he told me about you — about everything." Her voice crackled with loss and hurt and fury, and her hand settled protectively onto the little rounded swell of her belly which, if Leonora hadn't known better, could so easily have been puppy fat. "How could he do this to me? How could he do this to either of us — to his kids? What a bastard."

Jasmine's thoughts echoed Leonora's own. "I know, but please try not to get too upset. The baby —" she began, but it was too late.

219

"I can't believe this is happening," Jasmine sobbed. "My mum and dad are so excited about the baby and so pleased for me. They keep talking about being a grandma and granddad for the first time and about me being settled. What am I going to tell them now? What can I say? How can I explain all this?" Jasmine looked around, her eyes working over Leonora, the house, Patrick and Maisie. "It's like some bloody daytime phone-in programme or a soap opera. How could he do this? How could he?" She squared her shoulders, all outrage and indignation, puffing herself up like a kitten taking on a Rottweiler. "We've got to find him; we have got to talk to him."

Leonora nodded. How very quickly the two of them had become "we".

"Have you got a car?" asked Leonora, wondering as she did just how much to tell Jasmine about Gareth's whereabouts.

"Yes. Why?"

"I do know where he is at the moment," Leonora said, each word as heavy as lead. "But after tomorrow he'll leave there and then he could go anywhere."

Jasmine visibly brightened. "Well, we could go and see him then, sort all this out. I've only got a van at the moment — you know, what with the shop and that it's more convenient than a car. But it's not a problem — I could take you and me . . ." and she then looked at Maisie and her voice faded. "There are only two seats."

Leonora hesitated, then said, "There's no one to look after the children and I'm still feeding Maisie."

"I could go on my own," Jasmine said quickly. "We can't just let him get away with this."

There was a little weighty silence while Leonora considered the idea. What possible good would Jasmine do on her own? Leonora needed to be there too. They both needed to be there. And then, as if on cue, the phone rang. The two women looked at each other. It rang again, neither of them moved. Maisie stirred, eyes moving left and right, trying to track down the sound.

"Do you think that's him?" whispered Jasmine, staring at the receiver as if it was a snake.

Leonora shrugged, but she knew that she had to find out. She picked up the receiver and almost immediately a smooth Irish voice, said, "Hello, you don't know me but my name is Raf O'Connell. Diana — the woman who organised the Belvedere High School reunion asked me to ring you. She said that you needed a lift down to Burbeck House."

Leonora felt all the tension ebb out of her shoulders. "Diana phoned you?"

"Yes. That's right. A friend of mine is taking part in the drama reunion this weekend too — she's playing Lady Macbeth — and Diana mentioned that you needed a lift. She said you'd got little ones. I've got a people carrier — so it won't be a problem if you'd like me to come over and pick you up. I'm going anyway."

If he'd been there Leonora would have kissed him. "Are you sure you don't mind?" she said.

"Not at all."

Across the table Jasmine was watching her expectantly. Leonora took a deep breath. Their rescuer needed to know what he was getting himself into.

"Did Diana explain what was going on?" Leonora asked. "I mean, it might not be as simple as a straight lift down there and back." She didn't like to dwell on what else it might be.

Raf O'Connell sighed. "She did tell me a little bit but not much. I can understand that you need to talk to your man. And any help I can be . . ." He paused to let the offer sink in.

"Thank you," whispered Leonora. "I just need to get down to Burbeck House. I can't tell you how grateful I am for this."

"Don't mention it. Now whereabouts do you live? I can pick you up first thing tomorrow morning, if you like."

"That's wonderful," said Leonora. She looked across the kitchen; Jasmine was craning forward, hanging on her every word. "Before I give you the directions I was wondering if you've got room for another passenger," Leonora asked.

"Sure, of course, that's not a problem." She could hear the warmth in his voice. "And I can understand that you're in need of a little moral support. I can't say as I blame you."

"Actually it's my husband's girlfriend," she said, trying hard not to choke on the words.

"Ah . . ." said Raf slowly.

"She's pregnant," added Leonora softly, as she struggled to keep her tone neutral.

222

"Right, well, sounds to me as if you've got enough on your plate without having to worry about the transport side of things," said the voice at the end of the phone. "Don't fret, I'll get you all there safe and sound. It's going to be a rough day for you and her, and an interesting day for your husband, although I can't say I'm overcome with sympathy for your man."

"No, me neither," said Leonora, "but I did think you ought to know what you're letting yourself in for." She waited for him to bale out and when he didn't she continued, "If you've got a pen I'll give you my address, Mr O'Connell."

"Call me Raf," he said.

Back on his feet, all dusted down and with his dignity restored, Adie, followed by Gareth and the rest of the crew, headed back into the hall to continue the last of the day's rehearsal. Carol — whose death would be no more than a nasty scream in act five, scene five, and which had always been done on tour by the boy who worked the curtains, hung back with Diana.

Diana — a woman on a mission — was heading off towards the far end of the hall and when she got there she pulled out yet another enormous cardboard box hidden under a table. Behind the table was a hessian pinboard.

"What on earth have you got in there?" said Carol in astonishment as Diana struggled to move it. "Did you drive down here in a truck?"

Laughing Diana shook her head. "No, just the Volvo. I was planning to do a bit of a display on this wall; lots of people have sent me photos and brought things in from the original production. Although I was wondering if maybe I should wait until tomorrow, you know, until after the disco tonight. I don't want any of the stuff defaced or lost or anything."

"You mean nicked?" said Carol, helping her to lift the box up onto the table.

Diana nodded. "Well, I didn't like to say that, but you know what people can be like after they've had a few beers. The crew were talking about getting a barrel of bitter up from the pub."

"I bet you don't get this with the Brownies," said Carol, lifting out a pile of photos. "How about we get the pictures photocopied — they are bound to have a copier in the office."

"Good plan." Diana started sorting the other things in the box into piles.

Carol picked up a large-scale map and unfolded it.

"I was thinking we could use that as a centre-piece," said Diana. "It shows all the performances from the original flyer and the side trips we did. I've marked them on, and I've got some little glass pins as well."

Carol shook the map out and stared at it. "I'd forgotten all about these places. Look at this. It was one helluva trek, wasn't it? As kids you tend not to realise. Oh, and all the dates are on here too. It seemed liked such a huge adventure — can you remember some of those hostels?"

Diana laughed. "Uh-huh, I most certainly can: damp beds, dodgy loos and dark spooky corridors full of spiders and mice. How could I ever forget? Mind you, at least there were no bears."

"That's true."

Diana handed her a handful of drawing pins. "I'll hold it straight," she said. "You can pin it up."

Carol nodded and once the map was firmly in place ran a finger along their route. They had been gone ten days and yet in some ways it had seemed like a lifetime.

Half-past nine on one sunny Friday morning twenty years ago, and Mr Bearman and Miss Haze having waited for the last of the late-comers, shooed everyone out of their groups and gaggles and up onto the bus.

Carol looked back over her shoulder and waved to her mum and dad. There was a huge fizzy giggly feeling of excitement amongst the drama group. OK, so they might be all sixth formers and top of the school's pecking order, but coolness and confidence ebbed and flowed.

This was the first extended drama tour the school had ever done. Their itinerary was a bizarre mix of performances, cultural trips and sight-seeing. A grand tour with *Macbeth* at its heart.

As they filed aboard, Carol momentarily considered sitting with Gareth. After all, everyone knew that they were an item, but it was up to him to make the move, to ask, for her to smile and decline or slide in alongside him. She was too nervous just to do it. What if he had asked her what the hell she thought she was doing? What if someone else shuffled up and said she was in his seat? It was something that she would never have lived down.

Although Carol had had boyfriends before, this felt different. Being around Gareth was much hotter and far less comfortable than going to the pictures with the boy who worked in the local record shop. More significant than the crush she had had on the guy who had been in the year above her last year and now helped out at the local pub; more disturbing than going to the disco with Diana's cousin, Bill. So Carol followed the others and tried hard not to catch Gareth's eye. It was up to him to catch hers, wasn't it?

Netty, who had been lolling by the wall having a last fag, was fractionally too late to get to the back seat, wrong-footed by a big spotty boy in the stage crew, so, a little crestfallen and annoyed, she found them five seats well towards the back and staked a claim. It amounted to three twos really, with Adie taking turns sitting with each of the girls and the spare seat being piled high with the detritus of travelling: bags and books and a pile of packed lunches.

A few rows forward — though not over the wheels, obviously — Fiona and her mother were busy settling in, sorting out travel sickness tablets, plaid blankets and lavender-scented pillows.

Miss Haze moved amongst them, counting and ticking everyone off on her clipboard, while Mr Bearman stood up and, using his best stage projection to rise above the voices and giggles and general pandemonium, set out the ground rules for the trip.

226

"Right, everyone, let's take it from the top. No smoking, no spitting or swearing, no sex, drugs or rock and roll." A huge groan of complaint went up, Mr Bearman laughed and shrugged theatrically. "Don't blame me, blame the chair of governors." Fiona's mother's face folded into a nasty little pleat that passed for an indulgent smile.

"More immediately, no walking around while the bus is in motion and if anyone feels sick, for God's sake tell someone — preferably before it happens. Is everyone clear on that so far?" There was a murmur of agreement amongst the students. "Right now, is everyone here, Miss Haze?"

She nodded. "All present and correct."

"Righty-ho, well, let's get this show on the road then." Mr Bearman signalled to the driver, and the engine roared into life.

School rules insisted that pupils travel in their school uniform. Rumour had it that it was so they could be easily identified if they tried to make a break for it. As soon as the engine on the coach started, Carol slipped off her blazer and, rolling it into a ball, stuffed it in the overhead rack. Everyone else was busy doing the same thing, sliding off their ties, pulling off sweaters and pushing up their sleeves. The morning was already warm and there was a sense of settling in for the long haul.

By the time they got to the bottom of the school drive Fiona was the only person on the coach still in anything approaching full school uniform.

For a moment Carol had felt odd as she caught sight of her dad waving. It felt as if she was leaving for good, as if things would never be the same.

On the bus there was a sense that the adventure was underway. At first there was singing and then talking and whooping, and then finally, as the miles began to roll by and the countryside grew more and more unfamiliar, the noise settled down to a low rumble of conversation, an expectant hum, the excitement still evident but cooled from a roaring boil to a quiet simmer.

Sitting in the window seat, next to Diana, who was talking to Jan across the aisle, Carol pulled out her script and tried to read it through one more time for luck.

"It's too late. If you don't know your part by now, you never will," said Diana, offering her an Opal Fruit. Sighing, Carol declined and then tried closing her eyes, wondering if she would be able to sleep. From where she was sitting Carol could see the back of Gareth's head. He was sitting by himself. She wondered if that was a good thing or a bad thing. Had she missed a signal, had he assumed that she would just sit next to him without any prompting — and how complicated was all this dating stuff that no one knew the rules? Would it always be this hard? Would she always be this unsure, this uncertain about what the right move was? Sleep didn't look as if it was going to work either.

Meanwhile, alongside her, Diana pulled a pack of cards out of her duffel bag. "Poker, anyone?" she said conversationally. "Or how about a little nine-card brag?" And then, as Carol watched, Diana cut and shuffled the deck with one very practised hand before setting it down in two neatly stacked piles on the little drop-down shelf on the back of the seat.

"We ought to do a play set on a Mississippi paddle-steamer. Something hot and steamy in New Orleans," said Carol, picking up the deck and dealing the five of them in. "You'd be a natural, Di. You could have one of those ringletty wigs and a hooped skirt tucked up into your knickers at one side."

Across the aisle Adie grinned. "God, yes, I love all that cowboy gear, checked shirts, tight jeans and leather chaps." No one said anything, just looked down at their cards. "I'm only saying," protested Adie. "Now can you tell me the rules again? What did you say we were playing . . .?"

Later, when Diana had been persuaded to give them all their spending money back, they ate their packed lunches at some sort of badly maintained nature reserve with nasty toilets and a gift shop that sold biros with bats in them and squirrel keyrings, and then headed on to their first venue.

It was a high school somewhere deep in darkest Lincolnshire, and the students would be staying at a small church-run hostel about seven miles from it.

"Right," said Miss Haze as the bus stuttered to a halt outside the front door of the hostel. "Now the plan is that we take all our things inside. Once we've had a cup of tea and a bun we'll be heading off to the school to get the stage set. Any questions so far?"

Carol looked at Diana and then out at the hostel. "Oh my God," whispered Carol grimly. "Will you look at that?"

"Jesus," said Diana. "It looks like a gothic prison."

Netty snorted. "It looks all very *Scooby-Doo* to me. There's bound to be an evil janitor, who would have got away with it if it wasn't for us pesky kids."

Over their heads and apparently oblivious to the looks of horror on most of the students' faces, Miss Haze was still busy running through the evening's itinerary.

Carol swallowed down a little flurry of nerves.

"Welcome," said an officious-looking woman in a grey serge suit, from the steps of the building, who had announced her presence with a sharp clap of her hands followed by a whistle blast.

"See, what did I tell you?" hissed Netty. "Evil janitor material if I ever saw any."

Hands on hips, the woman peered into the pack to see where the noise was coming from. When the culprits weren't immediately obvious she continued, "My colleague is waiting by the boys' entrance. Girls, if you would like to follow me." There was no question in the sentence — who would dare do otherwise? Humbled in the face of so much overbearing and rugged leadership, Miss Haze led a rag-tag crocodile of girls across the tarmac and up the steps.

They were almost at the door when Carol heard someone call her name. She turned round in surprise and saw Gareth loping over to her with a lazy grin on his face.

230

"Wait up," he said, the grin holding firm. There was no disguising it now, Gareth was most definitely calling her. Everybody turned to look at him, even the woman in the grey serge suit.

Carol reddened until she didn't think she could get any redder.

"Is there something the matter?" he asked.

"No, why? Should there be?" she lied.

"I thought you'd sit with me on the bus," he said, smiling. "I wondered if I had done something — you know — something to upset you."

"Oh, oh right — no, no I, just — I wasn't sure . . ." she blustered. Why the hell was he doing this now? Did he want her to die of embarrassment? Couldn't he have done something less public, less obvious? ". . . and Netty saved me a seat."

The grin didn't falter. "I could save you one tomorrow, if you like." So brazen, so confident, so very, very sure of himself — or possibly Gareth was just acting his socks off. Carol looked into his eyes. No, apparently not — it looked as if it might just be real.

Alongside her, Netty and Jan and Diana stood shoulder to shoulder and stared at him. Carol felt uncomfortable on his behalf; it took some front not to back down in the face of three best friends.

"OK then," said Carol, wishing he would go. But he didn't. Instead they all stood there, uneasy, uncomfortable, looking from face to face, not sure where to go from there. It was Netty who finally set them all free. "Well, I don't know about anyone else but I really need a fag and a wee," she said with a dismissive sniff.

At that Gareth turned and waved and trotted back towards the boys.

"Come along, keep up, we haven't got all day," said Miss Haze, reappearing from inside the hostel — and all at once the moment was gone and they turned and hurried after her.

"Well, well, well," said Netty, throwing her holdall onto the bed when they finally got upstairs to their room. "Ain't love grand?"

Fifteen minutes later they were all hauled out to the bus. Carol sat with the gang but did smile at Gareth. At the host school, once the stage was all set, lit and ready, the cast and crew ate in the dining room — where, for some reason, only the lights above the tables they were using were on, which added to their growing tension, last-minute nerves making the food taste like cardboard.

Carol felt sick and excited by turns as she got into her costume and put on her makeup. Finally she settled the crown on her head and looked into the pitted mirror above a shelf that passed for a dressing table.

She looked as pale and haunted as any mad queen should. It felt as if she was walking through a dream.

"Five minutes, this is your five-minute call," said a voice over the Tannoy.

Netty sighed and nipped outside for one last cigarette while the conversation amongst the rest of them dropped to a low tense hum.

"Get your arses up on stage, the music is about to start," said a stagehand, popping his head round the door and then all at once they were off.

232

"Break a leg," said Diana, adjusting the wart as she elbowed her way past Carol in the wings.

"I planned to break wind," hissed one of the boys from Duncan's army.

"I thought that you already had," growled Netty. She was wearing a pointed hat, lots of worry lines and whiskers; they really suited her.

And then all at once the witches were hunched around the cauldron — and there was total stillness. From beyond the heavy curtains Carol could hear the audience, fidgeting and coughing and gossiping, and then the lights went down and the hall was suddenly quiet and expectant.

Carol struggled to stay calm, taking deep breaths, feeling incredibly alone. Her mind went blank, head throbbing as she waited for her cue. And a moment later the curtain went up and the play began — and then it was time and Carol stepped out onto the stage into a great pool of light and began to speak, and strangely enough, despite her fears, all the words were there in her head.

No more than seconds or perhaps a lifetime later, it was all over and done with and the cast stood at the front of the stage, taking the very first bows of the run.

Gareth caught hold of one of her hands, Adie the other. Carol felt relieved and elated, stopping for an instant to look around, taking it all in, the loud applause and the cheers rolling towards them like a warm and appreciative sea. As she had come up for one more bow Carol caught Gareth's eye, and he winked and then grinned, and she shivered, and this time Carol didn't try to fight the feeling. It felt good and exciting to be so close and she grinned right back at him.

Once the great roar of adrenalin had burned off, the long day finally caught up with everyone. Tired and sleepy, they had had to travel to the hostel, which seemed like miles away, and that was the first time Carol and Gareth sat together. It made it kind of official, and whatever people thought — if they thought anything at all or even noticed — no one said a word as she slipped silently into the seat alongside him. He gave her the window seat. Looking back, Carol wasn't sure if Gareth was being gentlemanly or whether he was worried she might slither off, given half a chance. It felt slightly claustrophobic and at first she found it hard to relax. As the miles unrolled past the dusty glass, Carol finally felt tiredness claim her, and sleepily curled up into Gareth's shoulder, pulling her jacket over her like a blanket, eyes heavy.

She didn't resist as he slipped his arm around her and held her close up against him, nor did she fight or protest when she felt Gareth's other hand slide oh-so-stealthily to rest casually, lightly between her knees. But it did have an effect; Carol was instantly wide awake.

She held her breath, wondering whether to pretend to be asleep or to wake and move away. What would she do if his fingers moved higher? What happened if he moved at all? But as it was, before Carol could make up her mind, the bus lumbered into the hostel car park and, yawning and aching, everyone clambered down and went in search of their beds. Gareth moved, stretched and got to his feet. As they parted by the hostel steps, he pulled her close and brushed his lips across hers.

"Night night," he purred. "Sweet dreams."

There was a lot of whooping from people close by. Carol felt her face colour.

The sensation of Gareth's body so close to hers and that hand setting so easily on her thigh lingered. Even the idea of it made something warm and dark and very ancient quiver in the pit of her stomach.

"Well done, everybody. It's going to be a fantastic tour if you keep this standard up," said Miss Haze, following them up to the dormitory. "I'll go and see if we can rustle up some hot chocolate and biscuits from somewhere."

The door to the dormitory swung open behind them. "Oh, there you are, Miss Haze. I tried to catch you when we got off the coach. I think Fiona may be getting a migraine," said her mother accusingly. She was carrying an empty hot-water bottle and smelling salts. "It's the pressure. I do worry about her; she puts so much of herself into the part. It's a good thing that I came along; I've got no idea how you would have dealt with it without me. It's going to be a long night. I would appreciate it if the rest of you would keep the noise down."

All the girls in the dormitory stared at Fiona's mother, though no one dared to speak.

"Thank you," said Miss Haze icily. She watched Fiona's mother withdraw and then said, "Well done everyone — I'll go and sort out the hot chocolate.

Assuming Fiona makes its through the night, we've got another long day tomorrow."

Carol headed off towards her bunk, the imprint of Gareth's fingers on her leg burning like a stigma.

"Carol?"

Carol looked up in surprise, expecting to see herself surrounded by teenage versions of her friends. Instead Diana was rattling a tin in her direction.

"Do you want to put the others in as well?"

Carol blinked to focus her thoughts as well as her eyes. "What?" She could still feel the heat of Gareth's touch.

Oblivious, Diana handed her the little tin full of glass-headed map pins. "I thought if we did red for performances, green for side trips and cultural visits . . . They're all marked and numbered." She pointed to the map.

Carol nodded. There was a list of the numbers pinned alongside.

"Are you all right?" asked Diana anxiously.

"Yeah, I'm fine. I think I'm just coming down with a nasty case of nostalgia. I keep remembering things about what we did and where we went — and who said what to who, all in wide screen, Dolby sound, full Technicolor."

Diana grinned. "I think we all are. It's contagious. I'll ask Netty to pick us up a bottle of Baileys and some wine from the offie, or how about some brandy and vodka, so she can whip up one of her patent snowballs?"

236

Carol laughed. "Good plan, although this time tell her to remember the advocaat."

"The only answer is anaesthetic," said Diana firmly, picking up a pile of photographs. "And lots of it."

"That's my girl, welcome back," smiled Carol.

Diana sniffed. "I don't know what you mean. I've never been away," she said. "I was just semi-retired."

Carol skewered their journey north with a trail of brightly coloured pins. "Remember the bottle of Scotch we had on the last tour disco? We should have got one for tonight."

"What, and throw up and feel lousy tomorrow during the performance?"

"Well, it worked last time — and we don't have to go mad." Carol thought for a few moments and then grinned. "Actually, maybe we do. Maybe it is just what we all need."

"Who is going mad?" said Netty, heading out towards them, eyeing up the display.

"I was just saying we should really get a bottle of Scotch for tonight."

Netty held her hand out. "Are you paying or are we planning to have a whip-round like last time?"

"Actually," said Diana looking thoughtful, "I think last time we paid for the Scotch with my winnings from thrashing Duncan's lot at poker."

Netty grinned. "Anyone got a pack of cards?"

CHAPTER
TEN

The stagehands from the school reunion helped to carry in the speakers for the guy doing the Saturday evening disco. He arrived to set up just after teatime and well before dinner, and was called Dave. He had a bleached blond mullet, a nasty fake tan, badly capped teeth and said "groovy" a lot. He was wearing a turquoise-blue sequinned dinner jacket and Cuban heels. The entire crew dwarfed him by at least a foot. Some by a foot and a half.

Rehearsals over for the day, Diana and Carol stood by the double doors into the main hall, watching the guys trail through with the disco gear, a string of ants with beer bellies, all wearing tour T-shirts and jeans.

"He is absolutely perfect," hissed Carol under her breath as Dave scuttled by them, carrying what looked suspiciously like a smoke machine. "Adie's going to love this. Do you think he's got a mirror ball?"

"Who, Dave? I can't imagine him travelling anywhere without one, can you? Do you think I should go down and invite the preachers to join us later?" said Diana. "I do appreciate that they've been keeping a low profile until now but it's going to get pretty noisy later on." She nodded towards the corridor opposite the one that led into their wing of Burbeck House. At the entrance was a nicely varnished wooden arrow-shaped sign on a stick that read "All Christian Delegates This Way."

It made it seem like their corridor led to perdition.

"You're the one married to a vicar, Di — how do Christians feel about Black Sabbath?"

Diana glanced at Dave the DJ as he pattered past again, this time bearing a box of vinyl marked, "Golden Oldies — M — R" in thick marker pen.

"Hedley likes everything from Led Zeppelin to Vivaldi — but Dave doesn't look much like a rocker to me — he's more of your Bucks Fizz kind of boy. On the phone he told me that he was middle-of-the-road."

Carol laughed as he waved coyly from behind the mixing desk. "Are we talking sexually or musically?"

Diana pulled her oh-very-funny face, and then went on, "He strikes me as someone keener on Dollar and doing the Time Warp, maybe a bit of Slade mixed in to round the evening off, when everyone gets warmed up."

Carol lifted her eyebrows. "Come on. Get real. That isn't going to happen. The stagehands will never let him get away with that sort of stuff. Look at them — they were head-bangers to a man. Don't you remember the mosh pit down the front at the end-of-tour disco? Battle-hardened roadies. I seem to remember that they were stage diving into the crowd at one point. Well, at least onto each other — well, at least he was." Carol pointed to one of the crew as he lurched past them with a set of disco lights balanced precariously on one shoulder.

Diana stared at them. "Yes, I know that, but they're all grown-ups now. Colin's a chartered accountant, Peter's in IT and Robin runs his own transport company. Alan's gone bald, for God's sake. No, I'm sure it will be fine."

As he slid the last of the speakers onto the stage, one of the crew turned round and, back arched, face contorted into a pained grimace, burst into a great flurry of air guitar while da-da-da-ing Deep Purple's, "Smoke on the Water". His performance was met by a wild, whooping, screeching round of applause from the rest of the gang.

"OK, on second thoughts," said Diana, "I better go and invite the Christians. I'd rather have them here from the start than walking in on us halfway through to complain about the noise."

"And the stage diving," added Carol as Diana headed off down the corridor. "Although, you never know, perhaps they'd like to join in. I'll see you upstairs in a few minutes. I need to get these clothes off."

"Is that an invitation?" said a familiar voice.

Carol swung round and laughed. "Hi, I wondered where you'd got to. Are you following me around, by any chance?"

"No, of course not, I just happened to be walking around looking for you and *voilà*, there you are," said Gareth. He leaned forward and kissed her. "How's it going?"

"You were looking for me?" she said, stepping back.

"Yep, it's a fair cop, I own up." He held up his hands in surrender. "I was. Look, I don't know what's going on in that head of yours but I'm not the enemy. I just wondered if you fancied a walk before dinner?"

Carol tried out a disapproving face to see how it felt. "A walk down by the lake with a blanket?" she said. He grinned. "How come you'd got a blanket? Seems a little bit presumptuous."

"What can I say? I was a Boy Scout: be prepared." The grin held. "But no, not down to the lake, unless of course you particularly want to. I was thinking we could talk some more, maybe grab a quick drink." He glanced down at his watch. "There's three-quarters of an hour or so before we eat."

Carol shook her head. "Sorry, I'd love to but I need to have a shower and get changed."

He looked crestfallen. "There's plenty of time," he said.

Carol hesitated just long enough for Gareth to offer her his hand.

"Ten minutes," she said, as he led her out into the garden, "and then I have to get ready. I need to take a run-up at it these days."

"You look great," he said.

Carol narrowed her eyes. "Ten minutes."

"OK, cross my heart," he said. And then, when they had fallen into step side by side, hand in hand, Gareth said, "So tell me about your life — tell me about what you do, your business. I never really had you down as a gardener. But Diana told me that you're very successful."

"Didn't we have this conversation last night?" Carol said.

He laughed. "Maybe, but I want to know everything about you, all of it — what you think, what you do, what makes you tick."

"We've got ten minutes," Carol growled.

"Talk faster."

She giggled.

"We haven't got time for levity," he said, pretending to be cross. And as they walked Carol began to tell him about herself all over again, and as she did he made her laugh and listened and asked good questions and she remembered what it was that once upon a time had made her love him. Love him? The word reared up unexpectedly and hit her like a body blow, stopping her dead in her tracks. All those years ago it wasn't just lust; Carol realised she had really loved him.

"I have to go and get ready," she said, pulling her hand out of his.

"What's the matter? Are you all right?"

Carol nodded, not trusting herself to meet Gareth's eye. "We've had a lot more than ten minutes, I have to go. I'll see you later."

"Sure," he began, but before he could say anything else Carol had scurried away, feeling like Cinderella running away from the ball. She tried not to think about love, just about having a shower, getting ready, and getting through until Sunday.

Her heart was beating frantically as she got to the top of the stairs that led into the dormitory. Wasn't this exactly what she had come to Burbeck House to find out? That she loved him and that he still loved her?

At the top of the stairs Carol turned back: Gareth was still there in the hall below, watching her, and as their eyes met Carol felt her heart lurch. Damn, damn, damn.

Netty's dress for Saturday evening was a tasteful little number in silver lamé with an ecru feather trim — come to that, so was Adie's, although his was a bomber jacket over black T-shirt and jeans. It struck Carol that there had to have been some collusion — how psychic did you need to be to come up with matching party frocks? Maybe the pair of them were planning on going to the disco as the ugly sisters.

Coming out of the shower, wrapped in a bathrobe, towelling her hair dry, Carol caught the pair of them doing a very impressive synchronised stereo twirl across the nasty yellow carpet. She smiled, remembering that first time around — thanks to Adie's diligent tuition in his mum's front room — they had all learned to jive, which had gone down a storm on tour.

"I didn't know you could still do that or get those," said Carol, running her fingers over glittering fish scales of sequins on the lapels of Adie's jacket.

He tapped his nose conspiratorially. "It's not what you know, it's who you know," he said.

Netty pulled a face. "You are so bloody gullible. He bought it in Barnado's."

Adie pouted. "Spoilsport; come on, let's go down and eat; I'm starving. Where did Jan get to?"

"I think she already went downstairs," said Netty, shimmying across the floor and pulling a carrier bag

243

that clinked cheerily out from under her bed. Adie did the same.

"Is she all right?" asked Carol. "She seemed a bit off with everyone."

Netty shrugged. "Oh come on, she's always a bit off with everybody; it's what Jan does best — although I think we're all knackered. I don't know about you but I can't stand the pace these days. I'll have a word with her when we get downstairs. Just don't be long," she added over her shoulder as they headed back downstairs. "And I hope you've brought something quiet and understated to wear. We don't want her showing us up, do we, Adie?"

At which point Diana burst in. "Bloody Christians," she said, red-faced, hair all awry and cardigan flapping as Adie leaped out of her way. "I couldn't believe it. One sniff of a disco and they were like something possessed. It's dreadful down there. Complete and utter bedlam." Angrily she toed off her shoes and began pulling her cardigan off over her head, grabbing a towel from the bed, as she headed off to the showers.

"What do you mean? Have they complained?" said Carol, as Diana started to unbutton her shirt.

"Complained? Good God, no, there's about a dozen of them in the hall, pawing their way through Dave's record collection, looking for special requests, even as we speak. The Bay City Rollers were the last things I heard being discussed when I left. It's going to be pandemonium tonight," she said grimly.

244

"You're very welcome to stay," said Leonora, clearing away the supper things into the dishwasher.

On the far side of the kitchen table Jasmine shook her head.

"I'd better be getting back home." She started to gather her things together, her handbag and cigarettes, her cardigan.

Watching her, Leonora was torn between longing to be alone and wanting Jasmine to stay. How crazy was that?

"Are you angry with me?" Jasmine said quietly.

Leonora looked at her, eyes bright with tears. "No, oh, I don't know. I don't know what I feel. It's like I've woken up in someone else's life."

Jasmine paled. "I didn't know about you."

"I believe you," said Leonora. "I just don't believe him. How could he?" The control she had been holding tight to was quickly ebbing away.

"You'll be all right, won't you, though?" said Jasmine. "If I go?"

Leonora nodded, sniffing to hold back the tidal wave of tears. "You'll be here tomorrow?" she asked. "To go and see Gareth? You don't have to if you don't want to. I'd quite understand. It's not going to be easy."

Jasmine turned to face her, pale-faced and instantly angry. "What, and let him get away with it? I want to see the look on his face, in his eyes, when he sees the pair of us."

There was an iciness in her voice that Leonora almost envied, and for a few moments Leonora wondered if it

245

would feel better if she wanted retribution or had a need for revenge rather than an explanation. "I just wanted to make sure," she said.

"Yes, I want to be there. I'll see you tomorrow then," said Jasmine, heading for the door. "Thanks for the food . . ." She paused as if unsure what to say, ". . . and everything."

Leonora nodded and the two women looked at each other. There were really no words to express what they felt, nor how big the thing was that they shared. Unsure quite how to end it, Leonora hugged Jasmine awkwardly and when all at once they were done, Jasmine pulled back and looked Leonora up and down as if fixing her in her mind, smiled a bleak little smile and then she turned, opened the front door and was gone.

Leonora stood for a long while in the hall, listening to the house cooling down after the heat of the day, listening to her thoughts, and then went back into the kitchen and made herself a cup of tea. The clock ticked, the tap dripped, the house seemed so very empty.

As if she could sense the tension in the air, Maisie began to mewl softly in her pram. Leonora was relieved. At least now there was something else for her to do and to occupy her mind other than Gareth and Jasmine and the baby they had made and how it was she had never guessed, never known that he was playing away, or how it was that she had never seen any of this coming.

Anger and grief and loss and fear threatened to overwhelm her. Leonora picked Maisie up and carried

246

her through into the sitting room. Outside, beyond the bay window, the sunlight was turning to old gold, the warm light softening the day into evening. Leonora curled herself up in one of the big armchairs by the hearth and snuggled Maisie close. The baby cooed with pleasure and then hungrily brushed up against her, nuzzling for milk.

Leonora settled down to feed her. Whatever Gareth did there was nothing he could say or do that could ever rob her of her joy of this, the smell and soft touch of a baby against her breast and suddenly — in amongst everything else — she felt sad for him. Whatever Gareth said to her, whatever he promised, she would never trust him again. He had lost all the things that they shared and that he had once wanted. There was no way he could ever get them back. He had thrown them all away — her, Jasmine, Patrick and Maisie, and the baby Jasmine was carrying — and Leonora knew then with a peculiar sense of clarity and assurance that whatever else happened she and the children would be fine. It might take a while but they would be all right.

"And now for all you groovy funk-filled rockers out there, that great Status Quo classic 'Rocking all over the World'."

Dave, sweating like a weight lifter, smiled nervously into the microphone, his teeth unnaturally white under the ultraviolet disco lights. He looked like a man with a loaded gun to his head. On one side of the podium two of the stage crew were busy sorting through his record collection, although as Carol peered through the gloom and the smoke from the dry-ice machine, she realised that the second member of the editorial committee appeared to be one of the lay preachers.

Diana handed her a tumbler. "There we are," she said with a smile. "Get that across your chest. You'll feel all the better for it."

Carol sniffed it suspiciously. "I thought Netty was going to get Scotch as a tribute to days and card games past."

"Rum and Coke," Diana said. "Apparently it was on special at the offie and Netty let economy get in the way of sentiment." Diana took a long pull on her own glass. "Mm, good choice, though," she purred. "The first one slipped down a treat."

Carol laughed. "My God, who said you couldn't take the vicarage out of the girl?"

Diana lifted her glass in salute.

Carol took a sip, it tasted sickly sweet, deeply alcoholic — a taste right out of her past — and Diana was right. Mixing subversively with Merlot from supper it would probably do her the power of good. She drank a little more and then a little more and then smiled.

Out in the middle of the dance floor, Duncan and Banquo were busy dancing up a storm, hands on their hips, feet apart, firmly rooted to the spot, they were doing the boy dance known and loved by ageing rockers everywhere. Carol stared — surely something so universal ought to have a name, but if it did it had passed her by. The backstage crew joined them. Hands on hips, they were bending forward from the waist,

248

swinging down diagonally towards the floor and then back up again in time with a driving rock beat, red-faced and sweating hard, surrounded by the rest of the gang. Presumably, thought Carol, taking another pull on her rum and Coke, they could all afford osteopaths these days.

After a few more moments Adie joined in, followed by Netty. Carol glanced around, wondering where Gareth had got to — come to that, Jan and Fiona. Netty and Diana had flanked her at supper, seemingly hellbent on keeping her away from him, and Jan hadn't said a word all through the meal. Fiona hadn't put in an appearance since the end of rehearsals, but then there was nothing new in that. She was probably having a little lie-down somewhere, or possibly a migraine, no doubt having persuaded the ladies in the kitchen to bring her supper and a milky drink up on a tray.

"And now boys and girls —" on the stage Dave paused, looking left and right at his two censors — "how do we feel about Wham!?" he asked apprehensively, sotto voce.

There was a nasty little pause and then the lay preacher very deliberately handed him a single. Dave scanned the label and pulled the mike a little closer. "Next up it's 'Paranoid' by the immortal, all-time kings of metal, Black Sabbath," he said with a forced smile. There was a loud roar from a phalanx of lay preachers who had joined the line of people with hands on their hips and started to dance with remarkable abandon and agility.

Carol, cradling her drink, watched in amazement. "Is Hedley like that?" she asked Diana conversationally.

"Oh God, yes, there's no stopping him," said Diana, poker-faced, as she topped up their glasses. "When he's not out visiting the sick and ministering to the needy we're up in the loft in leather gear re-enacting scenes from Meat Loaf videos."

Carol laughed so hard she inhaled half a glass of Lamb's Navy rum. It occurred to her that in some ways it was a pity Gareth was around at all. It almost spoiled things by adding a layer of intrigue and desire and maturity it would be nice to forget about for a while. How much better to take a leaf out of the Christians' book and just get smashed with your friends and have a fun time without worrying how you looked?

As if reading her mind, Diana pointed out a man in a rather nasty toupee in the dance line, who was putting so much effort in to his particular version of the rocker's revenge that it looked if he may very well spontaneously combust at any second.

"You want to dance?" Diana said. "After all we can't look any dafter than this lot."

Carol took one last glance round the hall. Gareth was still nowhere in sight. "Yeah, OK. Why not?" And with that she stepped out onto the floor.

Meanwhile, up in her bedroom up in the east wing, Callista Haze was retouching her lipstick and tidying her hair. Not that discos were her scene really, but it would be churlish not to at least put in an appearance. George had seemed terribly keen to go when they'd been talking about it over supper, their conversation aided and abetted by a bottle of red wine provided by the students.

"Of course you've got to come," he'd said when she had expressed her doubts. "It'll be wonderful. A little Travolta, *Saturday Night Fever* — you can't stay in your room." He got up and pushed his chair under the table. "I used to be very light on my feet when I was younger, back in the good old days. You must remember."

Callista smiled as he executed a rather unsteady pirouette and struck a classic disco pose. Oh, yes, she remembered all right.

Callista glanced in the mirror. She was wearing a tailored cream shirt and black trousers, and in the lamplight, give or take a few lines, she didn't look so very different from when she and George had first met. Her hair was almost the same colour, courtesy of the local salon, and she was still the same size, although it was increasingly difficult to keep that way. Callista added a dab of perfume behind each ear and smiled at her reflection.

It was flattering that George still carried a torch for her and, after all, what harm would a dance or two do? Tomorrow she would be going home with Laurence and the girls, and she and George would probably never see each other again. The idea made her start. It was a sobering thought. One last dance for old times' sake; Callista sighed; there was no point in dwelling on the past or the things that could not be changed. Life had moved on, she had moved on.

Callista could hear the bass beat coming from downstairs. George had gallantly offered to call for her at eight.

"I'll give a little knock," is what he'd said as they had wandered upstairs after supper.

Callista glanced at the bedside clock, it was almost 8.15 and there was still no sign of him. She wondered fleetingly whether he had finally taken the hint and decided that what had been between them was over. Although as she stepped out onto the landing it struck her, more pragmatically, that after drinking the best part of a bottle of wine he'd probably forgotten he'd said he would call for her or, worst still, had passed out.

Callista closed her door and looked up and down the landing. It was deserted. Maybe George had already gone downstairs. She hesitated; surely he *wouldn't* really have gone without her, would he?

She was about to head down to the disco on her own when some instinct, some sixth sense, made her turn on her heel and head down towards the boys' dormitory and George's bedroom at the far end of the corridor. The door to his room was very slightly ajar, which struck her as odd.

"George?" she called softly, knocking with one knuckle, not really expecting any reply. To her surprise there was a muffled sob from inside. Callista pushed the door open a little wider.

Sitting on the end of the bed, caught in a pallid circle of lamplight, head in his hands, was George Bearman. He was dressed in tight blue jeans, a white silk shirt with the cuffs turned back and, worst of all, he had his

252

shirt undone to reveal a plump hairy chest and a gold medallion. He was crying.

"Oh, George," Callista said anxiously.

It took a moment or two for him to realise she was there and then he looked up, all red-faced and red-eyed, his face a mask of total despair.

"Callista, what on earth am I going to do?" he spluttered. "It's terrible — to be honest I'm not sure that I want to go on any more."

She sat down beside him and patted his knee. "Come along now, George, this really won't do, will it? You have to get a grip. I had no idea that you felt like this about me. I never guessed all those years ago and I certainly can't be held responsible now. You shouldn't have drunk all that wine at supper. Please stop crying." She pulled a tissue out of her bag. "Here, wipe your eyes. It was all such a long time ago now." She made an effort to sound warm while adding something a little more no-nonsense to try and make him pull himself together.

George looked up at her, eyes narrowed. "Sorry?" he said, as if trying to work out what she had just said. "I don't understand. What do you mean? What was a long time ago?"

Callista paused and then began afresh. "Ah, my mistake. What exactly are we talking about?"

George handed her his mobile phone. "It's Judy. She's left me. She's met someone else, apparently. At the church choir. What on earth am I going to do?"

Callista peered down at the tiny screen; it took a very particular sort of person to end what must be at least forty years of marriage with a text message. The last line read, "I've had enough, George. By the time you get back I will be gone."

Callista stared at him. "Oh, I'm so sorry."

He sniffed miserably. "I don't know what I'm going to do. How could she leave me after all these years when I bloody well stayed so long for her?"

Because she always knew that your heart wasn't in it, Callista thought sadly, aware that thinking was one thing but that it most certainly wasn't the right thing to say. "Is there anyone you could ring? How about your friends or family — brothers or sisters?"

"I've got a sister in Hastings."

"There we are then," said Callista briskly. "And you must have some friends locally."

He nodded. "Yes. One or two. People I play golf with."

"People you could talk to? People you could stay with?"

George nodded. "Yes, I suppose so."

Callista painted on a happy face. "Well, there, that's a start. Now go and wash your face and I'll see if I can find another bottle of wine downstairs." She paused mid-stride.

George pulled out a large paisley handkerchief and wiped his face. "I know what you're about to say, Callista. That the show must go on. And of course, I know that you're right. You always were such an inspiration, a real trouper . . ."

That wasn't what Callista had planned to say at all. In fact quite the reverse, she was going to suggest

George ring his sister and think about leaving early to see if he could catch Judy but smiled and bit her tongue.

While George set about washing his face. Callista scrolled back through the text. Judy, it seemed, felt that she was wasting the last few good years of her life rotting away in a loveless lonely marriage and was going to grab what little time she had left, fearlessly, with both hands before it was too late. She was apparently madly and passionately in love with someone called Graham, who sang tenor in the choir and had retired from the civil service. At least she had had the good grace to write four linked texts with proper punctuation.

When George came back from the bathroom he looked pink and shiny and rather tearful but, even so, he smiled and said conspiratorially, "You know I've been thinking. Perhaps it's all for the best, after all. Maybe it's fate, karma." He offered her his arm. "Let's go downstairs. Dance all our troubles away. You know what they say, as one door closes another always opens."

Callista hesitated. She wanted to say not always, and most certainly not this door but she hadn't got the heart.

As they stepped out of George's room they came across Gareth Howard deep in conversation with Fiona Templeton. Callista nodded in acknowledgement as they passed and to her horror as she did, Gareth grinned and then winked at her. Callista felt her colour rising, as it occurred to her how it must look; the two of them coming out of George's room, him all red-faced and flustered.

As they got to the fire doors George dabbed at his face with his handkerchief and beamed at her. "Thank you for that, Callista. In some ways it's a great relief, you know," he said. "You're so good. I'm feeling better already."

Callista was sure she heard Fiona snigger but she didn't look back. Instead she glared at George; she could have killed him.

Carol didn't wait for the next record to end; she was dead on her feet. Dancing the night away was hard work. Dave had played a three-track Status Quo medley, followed by a little Meat Loaf and an awful lot of Cher. Adie and Netty were up on stage with the roadies and the Christians, singing along at the tops of their voices, and there wasn't a person in the room who wasn't dancing.

Carol, breathless and hot and heady from the combination of wine and an awful lot of rum and Coke, broke away from the pack and headed towards the great outdoors to get a breath of air and a glass of water.

As she pushed open the hall doors Carol paused for an instant. Hadn't it been the same before? Dancing, too warm for comfort, giddy from booze and Gareth meeting her at the door, catching hold of her arm and kissing her so hard she could barely breathe or think. She wasn't sure that they'd been drinking rum and Coke first time around but they had certainly been drinking. He had pulled her into his arms, tipped her face towards his and they had kissed again, and an instant later she had melted. Remembering it fuelled an excited kick low down in her belly. She had been as eager as he was to find somewhere quiet away from the others, her ears ringing from the driving bass beat, her heart thumping with expectation and desire as they had headed into the shadows. Carol had longed to complete a circle of desire that she didn't quite understand. The memory made her light-headed.

Gareth had taken her hand and led her along a maze of dark corridors up behind the stage to a storeroom full of props and curtains. There were backdrops that smelled of paint and linseed oil, a chaise longue, rack after rack of costumes and hats, a suit of armour, a street-light made from wood, an Aladdin's cave of treasures. It seemed to Carol that they had been kissing all the way, afraid to stop in case their courage failed them.

Along the back wall of the storeroom were great wicker hampers full of heaven knew what. In the gloom Gareth had led her between them into a hidden space barely bigger than a single bed, lined with a great rolling pleat of black velvet. She had no idea whether he had found it or created it but before she could ask, Gareth pulled her down towards him. Not that she had resisted, or wanted to; not that there had been more than a moment's hesitation. Or was that the patina of memory making it all such a smooth unbroken line?

Carol shivered. It was so long ago now and yet the memory, the feel, the smell, the touch of him there in the storeroom seemed as vivid as if it had happened the day before. Looking back with adult eyes she didn't think it could have been his first time. He had seemed so very sure of himself, so certain. Carol remembered how she had felt as he unbuttoned her shirt, warm insistent kisses covering her embarrassment and uncertainty, feeling so very naked as he unhooked her bra, and then hearing herself making soft noises of pleasure and delight as his lips moved oh so slowly down over her throat, down over her shoulder, to her breasts. Even now Carol could feel that great rush of pleasure, the heat of desire, as he touched her. God, it had felt so very, very good then; how would it feel now when they both knew what they were doing?

Carol stepped out through the double doors, half expecting to find Gareth waiting there for her and realising that she was disappointed when he wasn't. But there was someone in the hall, someone standing in the shadows by the window, looking out over the moonlit gardens.

"Jan?" Carol said, not quite able to keep the surprise out of her voice.

The figure turned slowly as if being pulled back into consciousness.

"What are you doing here? Why aren't you inside with everyone else?" Carol asked, noticing the slight slur in her speech. "Are you OK?"

Jan nodded. "Yes. Don't mind me, I'm fine. I don't like discos very much."

Carol snorted. "Oh, come on. This isn't just any old disco. It's an historical re-enactment. It's our past being played out with a cast of thousands and a heavy metal soundtrack."

"I know," Jan said.

"Then come on, come on in. Everyone is in there." It wasn't strictly true. Gareth still wasn't there and she had no idea where Fiona was but it was close enough.

Jan stood her ground. "That's the trouble. No, I'd rather stay out here. I can't bear it. I was thinking of going down to the pub — do you want to come too?"

"Don't be ridiculous, you can't go down the pub on your own." Carol looked at Jan more closely. Her face was puffy and her eyes were red from crying. "What exactly is going on? I don't understand, you've been a complete cow all weekend — way more than usual. What is the matter?"

Jan shook her head. "I wish I hadn't come. I was going to say I couldn't make it. All these years and it's still there."

Carol stared at her. "I don't understand? *What's* still there?"

Jan sighed. "Oh, come on, don't pretend you don't know; it's Adie."

"Adie? What about Adie?" Carol stared at her, all manner of pennies finally dropping. Carol felt her mouth fall open. "Oh my God, really? You fancy Adie, don't you? But he's — he's —"

"Gay," Jan said flatly. "Yes, I do know, but I didn't know it back then — not when we were at school. It never occurred to me, I was so bloody naïve. I just thought he liked being with us." She paused, words slowing to a crawl, "Crazy, isn't it, when it is so obvious now. I thought that he liked being *with me*. He used to walk me home, come back for tea, take me to the pictures. I think I was probably a role model." She laughed grimly.

"You and Adie?"

"Yes, me and Adie."

"You had a crush on him?"

"No, worse than that, I loved him," Jan said without a moment's hesitation. "And I really thought there was a chance he might love me."

"You loved him?"

Jan nodded miserably. "I've always loved him and the trouble is that I still love him. Twenty years later and he is still the first thing I think about when I wake up in the morning and the last thing I think about at night." She sighed. "Crazy, isn't it? You don't have to tell me it's not normal or obsessional. I know, I kept thinking I'd grow out of it, that it would go away. I thought coming here, seeing him again, might cure it — you know, reality slaps bang up against fantasy — but if anything it's worse. I still love him. I waited for years for him to ask me out properly. I kept thinking if I waited long enough he would come round. I kept in touch for ages after we left school. Years. I invited him to my degree show, my first exhibition, and you know what? He came every time, every single bloody sodding time. Every landmark occasion in my life he showed up, the bastard," she sobbed. "We talk all the time!"

"Oh, Jan, I'm so sorry," Carol said softly, and put an arm round her shoulder — and as she did, saw Gareth trotting down the stairs behind them. She didn't know

260

whether to call out or say anything but, as it was, he looked round and saw her, lifting a hand in recognition. He indicated the door to the disco. Carol nodded.

Jan looked up and caught Carol mapping Gareth's progress. "Why don't you go back inside? Looks like lover boy's arrived."

"It's not important."

Jan sighed again. "Don't be ridiculous, of course it's important. He's your might-have-been, just like Adie was mine. Please go back inside. I want to be on my own. I'm fine, honestly. Go."

Carol shook her head.

"I'm serious," Jan said, far more forcefully this time, at which moment the doors to the hall exploded outwards and a great phalanx of disco dance hounds conga-ed their way out into the main hall led by — as sod's law would have it — Adie and Diana singing "Born to Be Wild" at the top of their voices.

"There you are," said Diana to Carol, and Adie to Jan simultaneously.

Diana caught hold of Carol's arm. "I wondered where you'd got to. I thought you might be busy throwing up somewhere," she said, a little unsteadily. "Come back in. Dave is now going to do another three-in-a-row Quo medley followed by 'Spirit in the Sky' and 'Fire' — and after that?" she mimed a hands-up big explosion gesture. "The sky's the limit."

Carol couldn't help laughing; the vicar's wife had gone feral.

Meanwhile, Adie ran over and scooped Jan up in his arms. "Come on, come in, honey," he said, eyes alight with pure joy. "What the hell are you doing out here moping around all on your own, anyway? I've missed you. It's not the same without you in there."

Jan just stood and stared at him, while Carol felt her eyes fill up with tears.

"Come on," he said, not taking no for an answer. "Come over here and dance with me."

Carol looked at his expression and then Jan's. It seemed that love was reciprocal, different but real nonetheless. How cruel was that? Carol felt her heart lurch.

Diana beckoned Carol back too. "C'mon. I haven't had so much fun for years."

Carol followed them into the hall. The music hit her in the chest like a rhino charge.

"Dance?" shouted Gareth as she stepped into the gloom.

She had to wait a few seconds for her eyes to adjust to the gloom. "I thought I might sit this one out. I'm exhausted," she partly mouthed, partly mimed and partly yelled.

He laughed, fingers closing around hers. "Rubbish, it's way too early to be tired," and led her out onto the dance floor.

It was well after midnight when the smoochy lovers' music started. Carol looked around the room and smiled; lots of people had coupled up — amongst them Jan and Adie, and Netty and the very ginger, very freckly Peter Fleming.

262

As they danced past each other, Carol pointed at Peter, miming a question. Netty shrugged. "Maybe I was wrong after all," she said, with a lazy smile.

The music slowed to a sensual roll. "How about we go and find somewhere a little more private?" said Gareth, as he brushed Carol's neck with kisses. "I don't know about you but I keep getting this terrible sense of *déjà vu*." The warmth of his hand on her back and the insistent pressure of his body against hers was making Carol feel hot in ways too ancient, too old and way too horny to have names.

She closed her eyes, drinking in the closeness of him. Guilt mingled with desire as he pulled her closer. "Time to start over," he purred. "You and me."

Carol felt her heart flip, and her pulse quicken.

"I was a fool to ever let you go," he whispered, and when he led her out of the hall there was nothing Carol wanted more than to go with him. She closed her eyes and let him lead her through the darkness.

Leonora couldn't sleep, even though she was dog-tired. Her eyes ached. Her head was full of thoughts, her brain racing. She had lain awake for hours, got up, tried to read, made tea, fed Maisie and now found herself standing outside Gareth's office, tired right through to the bone. She pushed open the door; the room smelled of him. She took a deep breath and stepped inside. It felt as if she was stepping into the lion's den.

What else was there that she didn't know about Gareth, this man who had shared her life for the last few years? How many other things had he hidden from her? Pulling her dressing gown around her, Leonora sat down at his desk and clicked the mouse on the desk to awaken the sleeping computer. She opened files randomly, and then more systematically. Most were business — quotes for installations and IT projects, design ideas, templates, invoices, letters to clients. There was nothing there that gave him away, nothing that revealed him. Emails all neatly filed and labelled, nothing much to catch the eye. But there were hundreds of files; he could have hidden anything anywhere.

Frustrated, Leonora started to go through the desk and the filing cabinet, the landscape of which was fresh in her mind. At least the things there were more tangible, although it felt like a lifetime since she had found Diana's phone number. Where did she begin?

"Accountant", "Bank", "Cheque Books", her fingers spun back over the manila suspension files as she flicked through the little tabs. Where should she look, and what was it she was looking for? Did she need to go through the whole thing a file at a time, looking for something, some clue that may or may not be there? Or would she be drawn to the things she needed to know by some weird form of divination?

Leonora glanced at the in-tray. It was piled high with all sorts of envelopes, invoices and sheets of paper. Here, maybe, where things were relatively new; maybe that would be a better place to look.

She sorted through the letters, the circulars, the bills and then stopped dead as she scanned casually down one of the letters. It was from their bank.

264

Dear Mr and Mrs Howard,
We are delighted to inform you that your recent application to remortgage your property has been agreed in principle. If you would like to make arrangements to come into the branch and fill in the remaining paper work . . .

Leonora felt something cold stirring in her heart. What mortgage? What arrangements? The house was in her name; there was no mortgage against it because it had been bought with money she had inherited as a cash sale. An investment for their future.

Very slowly Leonora flicked through the stapled sheaf of papers. On the back, scribbled on a junk mail flyer for life insurance was her signature — or rather, more precisely, an attempt to copy her signature. Leonora dropped the paper onto the desk as if it was on fire.

It took her a moment or two to consider the implications of what she had found and then she picked up the papers again and read them through more thoroughly.

. . . In view of the fact that the deeds are in your wife's name we will require her signature to be witnessed on the enclosed documents.

Still stapled to the letter, the loan application hadn't been filled in or signed or witnessed, and obviously hadn't been returned. But did this mean he hadn't borrowed the money? Leonora went back to the computer and clicked on the button that would log her on to the Net. They had Internet banking; she should be able to find out.

It took a moment or two to get on to the website of their bank and as she typed in her password she wondered if maybe Gareth had changed that too — but no — there were their accounts — and no, no loan showed up, but apparently there was no money either, no savings, no ISA, nothing. Every penny in their joint accounts had gone. Leonora stared at the screen. The only good thing was that he hadn't been able to mortgage the house out from under them, but he had taken everything else.

Leonora felt both sick and oddly reassured. However awful it felt, she knew then that she wasn't making a mistake about Gareth; this wasn't some terrible accident or case of mistaken identity, not some crazy moment of passion — it was cool and deliberate. He had taken the money and run.

Leonora picked up the phone and called Jasmine — even though it was late she didn't think that she would be asleep. Jasmine answered on the second ring.

"Hello?" said Jasmine brightly. Leonora wondered if she thought perhaps it was Gareth ringing to make it all right after all.

"I need to ask you something. Did you lend Gareth any money?" she said without any preamble.

There was a slight pause and then Jasmine made a little uncomfortable, caught-out sound and said, "Yeah, he said he needed to clear some bills, and that he'd have money coming in as soon as the house was sold."

266

"How much did you give him?" asked Leonora.

"Three thousand pounds," said Jasmine. "It was the money I'd borrowed for my new car."

Leonora took a deep breath; she felt dirty. The things Gareth had done to Jasmine made her feel tainted, as if she was a party to it rather than a victim of his. "I've just been going through some papers here. He was trying to raise a loan against this house; he was planning to forge my signature."

There was an icy silence at the far end of the phone. "God, I can't believe this. What a bastard. I didn't want to say about the money on top of everything else. What a shit. I can't wait to see his face tomorrow," said Jasmine.

Leonora felt the same.

CHAPTER
ELEVEN

Back at Burbeck House, the last strains of "Lady in Red" were fading away. Diana — who had been singing along with Banquo and a couple of King Duncan's other regal henchmen, while still clutching the remains of a large rum and Coke, peered around the hall. Green and purple disco lights did very little to improve the view; added to a large quantity of rum this had made life a little blurry round the edges. It took her a minute or two to focus but, even so, Diana was sure; there was no sign of Carol. Worse still, there was no sign of Gareth.

She took a few deep breaths and let the idea settle for a moment amongst all the other things she knew. It was time for drastic action. Diana set her glass down on a table and grabbed hold of Adie's arm. "Come with me," she snapped. "I need you."

"My lucky night," he said wryly.

"And don't ask any questions," Diana said, "cos at the moment all the answers are top secret."

Adie glanced at the discarded glass on the side table. "How many of those have you had?"

Diana considered for a few moments; the figures were a bit hazy. She shrugged. "Not a clue. So are you in, then?"

Adie nodded. "Certainly am. If only to keep you from doing something dangerous or watching you make a complete tit of yourself."

Indignantly Diana pulled herself up to her full height. "Don't be ridiculous, I'm a vicar's wife. Just grab a woman and come with me."

Ever biddable, Adie did as he was told.

"You've gone very quiet," Gareth said, as he and Carol finally got to the top of the stairs that led up behind the stage.

She nodded thoughtfully. "I was thinking about what it felt like to be with you again after all these years." That and other things. Things like what the hell she was doing there. Doubt flickered like a candle flame. This was crazy. She wasn't eighteen any more.

"And how does it feel?" he said, turning back to look at her over his shoulder. He was grinning and looked wolfish in the half-light, and as their eyes met she felt an intense flutter of desire. "Does it feel good?"

"Yes, it does. It's just as scary, though."

He laughed. "Scary? Are you serious?"

"Yes, except back then it was because I didn't know what I was doing and now I do."

"And that's scary?"

Carol nodded; there is no way back from where she was heading. Even if she and Gareth had no future together, stepping through that door would change everything. Was that what she really wanted?

"You don't regret doing it, though, do you?" purred Gareth. "It felt right then, didn't it?"

"You know it did," Carol said softly. But did it feel right now? said a voice deep in her head.

Gareth was looking at her.

She hesitated, trying to work out what was wrong. "I had to see if it was still here — the thing we talked about last night."

"The stuff?" he asked with a grin.

"Yes, the stuff. The love," Carol said, not afraid of the words.

He smiled, eyes crinkling up around the edges like tissue paper. "That's a big word. So, do you still love me, Carol?"

She stared up at him, drinking in the details of his face and slowly shook her head. "No, Gareth, I don't, but once upon a time I did and I still feel something — like the ghost of something long gone, it's a warm, wonderful memory."

If he was hurt or shaken or disappointed he didn't show it. "I'm the same. And how do you feel about me — us — now?"

Carol's gaze didn't drop; it was important that she found the truth in amongst the tangle of echoes and desires and might-have-beens. "There isn't any 'us' now. I don't know who you are now," she said, steadily meeting his eyes.

He laughed and tried to wave her doubt away. "You know what I think? I think that you worry too much, sweetie. Just relax. There's no rush. We've got plenty of time. I was hoping that we could start over." As he spoke he pushed open the door at the head of the stairs. "I'm between contracts, so at the moment I've got

270

some time on my hands. I've just moved out of my last place. What I'm saying is, I'm a free agent." He paused. "I'd really like to see you. We can start all over again."

"Again?" she repeated.

He nodded and tipped her face up to his. She bit her lip as he peered into her eyes.

"Come on," he said, and moved aside.

Carol peered past him into the gloom. Inside, was a dimly lit storeroom, so much like the one first time around that it made Carol gasp. She stood at the threshold, heart beating in her chest, knowing full well that if she stepped across into the shadows then everything was lost. Going inside with Gareth was a tacit agreement to whatever else might follow. But did she really want him? Heart racing, she hesitated, suddenly stone-cold sober.

Gareth was close now. "Come on, sweetie. You know that this is what you want. You were so good, so perfect," he whispered, pressing his lips into her hair, hands sliding up under her top. "I've missed you so very much. We've got all the time in the world now. We were meant for each other, you know that, don't you? We've got as much time as we need. It will be so good, so right . . ."

But would it? The words were as smooth as oiled silk; but she could feel the pressure behind them. Her whole body ached for him. What was holding her back? Wasn't this exactly what she had dreamed of? Still Carol didn't move, her body absolutely rooted to the spot, leaden and unwieldy.

"I came here to see you, Carol," Gareth was saying. "That was why I came back — to see if I felt the same about you."

Carol pulled away and stared up at him. "Do you mean that?" she said, her voice low and flat.

He nodded. "Of course I do."

Carol barely dared ask the next question, afraid of what the answer might be, but then again wasn't that why she had come to Burbeck House?

"And the feelings you had for me — *are they still there?*" she said in an undertone.

He grinned. "Surely you must already know that?"

She didn't say a word and so he did. "I feel the same as you do. We don't know each other — but unlike you I do know that we're worth another shot, worth another chance." And as he spoke Carol sensed him trying to steer her across the threshold into the storeroom, every molecule in his body encouraging her inside, encouraging her to surrender, guiding her into the gloom.

She stood so still, desperately aware of her own resistance, aware of her desire, aware of being pulled in different directions; wasn't this what she had dreamed about for years? Wasn't this exactly what she wanted? But as she stood there, there was something else, something that refused to be ignored, something that Carol hadn't known up until now.

Gareth's lips met hers, he pulled her up against him and for an instant Carol felt as if she was drowning and panicking, and pulled away.

"What's the matter?" he said, eyes bright with desire. "What is it? Come on — come inside."

She opened her mouth and began to speak. "No, this is a mistake, Gareth — I —"

But before she could finish there was a great whooping wailing cheer from further down, from around the dogleg in the stairs. And all at once the whole troupe and crew, not to mention a host of wild-eyed Christians — led by Dave the DJ and one of the lay preachers who had been helping with record selection — lurched up onto the landing singing, "We can do the cong-a. We can do the cong-a," at the top of their voices, all bobbing and kicking and giggling like maniacs.

"I want you," Gareth said, but it was too late, the moment had gone. His jaw dropped as he saw the revellers heading towards him, although before Gareth could say anything else or protest he was caught up by a great tidal wave, as the crew swept past and around him. A gap opened in the conga chain and an instant later he was swallowed up and carried away on a bubbling, bobbing crest of dancers. Carol watched in astonishment as he vanished around the next corner, quite unable to get away.

"Jump aboard," yelled Diana as she swung past.

Carol laughed and did as she was told.

The conga line threaded its way backstage, down through the dressing rooms, out through the kitchens via a fire exit, around the front of Burbeck House, down through the formal gardens, up through the vegetable patch, twice round the fish pond and then in through the back doors until, triumphant, muddy, totally exhausted and out of breath, the revellers all collapsed back in the main hall. DJ Dave clambered up on the stage, dropped "We are the Champions" on to one of the decks and wound up the volume, to a roar of approval.

Carol looked round for Gareth but it seemed that he had vanished in the melee, which on balance was probably not a bad thing. As she caught her breath Diana handed her a tumbler full of rum and Coke. Without a word they toasted each other with a chink of glasses and as they did, Carol stopped looking for Gareth. If he wanted her he would find her. She took a long pull on her drink, letting the alcohol roll through her. What was hers would come to her.

Diana, grinning, said, "You know, it's been far too many years since we did this. I've really missed you; how come we've left this so long?"

Carol was thinking much the same thing. "I'll drink to that."

"God, I'm completely knackered," said Diana suddenly.

Carol laughed. "You really can read minds, can't you? I'll drink to that too. I'm totally exhausted." And draining her glass to the dregs, she followed Diana, somewhat unsteadily, across the dance floor.

They made their way between the last stragglers in the conga line, across the hallway and up to bed.

On the far side of the hall Callista Haze was helping George Bearman back up onto his feet. It was, she thought, remarkable how agile and how tenacious he was, although she didn't like to add, for a man of his age — but it was true. He'd hung on in there right to the bitter end.

"Time for Bedfordshire, I think, my dear," he said, hobbling slightly. He looked into her eyes as they climbed the stairs. "I was wondering if you would care to join me for a little nightcap? For old times' sake. I've got a bottle of brandy in my room."

She smiled. "George, you are incorrigible."

He laughed. "How very nice of you to notice." He winced. "Oh, my feet are killing me."

"Mine too. But it is hardly surprising. I can't remember the last time I danced so much. I really need to get to bed."

He looked at her expectantly.

"Alone," she added firmly.

George sighed, his expression hangdog, although this time Callista suspected that at least in part it was a joke.

"Are you all right?" she asked, squeezing his arm in what she hoped was a friendly, non-flirtatious manner.

He nodded. "Actually yes, I think I am. You know, the odd thing is I feel rather excited in a funny kind of way. I have waited all these years for things to come right, for some miracle that would set me free without me having to do anything and now suddenly here it is. I've been thinking this evening that even though it hurts terribly at the moment, I've finally got exactly what I wished for." All at once George's eyes filled with tears. "They do say be careful what you wish for, don't they? All those years wasted. I'm just worried that maybe I've left it too late after all."

"It's never too late," Callista said, gently patting his hand.

"Really?" he said, brightening visibly, but Callista shook her head and this time unpeeled his fingers from her arm. "No, I don't mean me, George, I meant life in general. It's high time you started getting on with what you want to do. Judy's right — you need to grab it with both hands while you still can."

It wasn't a particularly good choice of words; Callista followed his gaze as it travelled very slowly up over her body. As their eyes met she raised her eyebrows into a caricature of disapproval.

George grinned sheepishly. "Sorry. You know me. I always was rather slow on the uptake," he said. "But actually I think you're right. It is time to get on with life. So, come on then — how about that nightcap? Just one won't hurt, and I promise to try and behave."

Carol woke up in the wee small hours with a very dry mouth and a nasty angry, troublesome pain in her head. It had to be flu, she thought, or maybe there had been too much salt in the casserole they had had for supper. With eyes narrowed, she pushed back the bedclothes — even doing that hurt. Flu definitely, or maybe it was a bug, a nasty bug with big teeth and horns; she had the most terrible taste in her mouth. Maybe it was food poisoning.

Gingerly she climbed down out of the bunk and walked very slowly across to the bathroom, although it felt as if with every step a landmine was being detonated somewhere up under her skull.

Her fingers lingered over the light switch in the bathroom just long enough to consider whether she really wanted to see her reflection. More to the point, did she want to see her reflection floodlit by heaven knew how many rows of naked overhead fluorescent tubes? On balance the answer was obvious. Eyes thinned down to slits now, Carol picked her way through the heavy velvety black shadows, cursing the producers of rum and Coke, rock music and red wine everywhere.

As she was coming back, having drunk half a gallon of water to reduce the effects of the highly potent rum bug; Carol glanced round the dormitory. At least a lot of alcohol had rendered her oblivious to the amazing cacophony of sounds coming from the various bunks. People were snorting and wheezing and snuffling like there was no tomorrow.

On the far side of the room the sash window by the fire escape was wide open, curtains blowing on a summer breeze. Close by Adie was on his back snoring like an elephant seal calling for a mate.

Carol did a quick stock-take of her friends: Adie, Netty, Jan, Diana — all present and correct and all curled up and sound asleep, some noisier than others — and then she noticed that one bunk was very obviously empty, the bedclothes neatly rolled back, the bundled sheets glowing white in the darkness.

Odd. Odder still when she realised it was Fiona's bunk. Carol paused. Fiona? The name formed again in the achy tangle of barbed wire behind her eyes. It wasn't like Fiona to break the rules, or curfew and go missing — unless, of course, she was in sick bay or having a nasty attack of something somewhere. Carol smiled; not that she had noticed a sick bay and the bathroom had definitely been empty. It occurred to Carol that she hadn't seen Fiona at the disco and had been too tired and far, far too drunk to notice if Fiona had been there when she and Diana had come upstairs at the end of the evening.

The window rattled in its frame and then rattled again, more violently this time as the wind careened recklessly around the old building.

Before she climbed back into bed Carol padded across and pulled the sash closed to stop the noise and as she did, glanced across into the gardens below. There in the moonlight was Fiona — well, at least it looked like Fiona — picking her way tentatively across the dew-heavy moonlit lawn, all wrapped up in a blanket or maybe it was a robe.

That was very odd. Carol narrowed her eyes, trying hard to focus. Fiona wasn't exactly at home in the great outdoors, being allergic to most of it and terrified of the rest of it. Carol stared, wondering if perhaps Fiona was sleepwalking, or maybe Carol was dreaming. Peering into the gloom, she considered calling out and then she saw that Fiona was not alone, or at least she thought she did. As Fiona reached the shrubbery Carol could have sworn that a man stepped out of the shadows and, to her amazement, took hold of Fiona's hand and pulled her towards him.

Carol stared, not quite believing what she had seen. The lawn was empty now. There was no sign of a movement, the only sound a well-timed Hammer House of Horror movie owl hooting somewhere close by. And a single trail of footprints through the dew.

Carol tried hard to focus, squinting to see into the deep shadows until her headache began to complain. Was Fiona all right? Should she go and investigate? As the thought formed the first heavy raindrops of a summer storm breaking began to pitter-patter down onto the windowsill and fire escape, the noise as raucous as gravel being shaken around in a biscuit tin.

Carol considered the idea for a moment or two more. Who on earth was Fiona with? She paused, trying to replay an image that was a millisecond long and picked out in monochrome against a raft of shadows. Fiona hadn't looked as if she was being threatened or anything. Carol was too tired and too drunk to concentrate any longer and so she turned and clambered back into bed. Strangely, despite the driving rain and the clatter of thunder, she was asleep in seconds.

Fiona looked up into Gareth's eyes.

"So are you feeling better now?" he asked.

She nodded. "Yes, you were right, a sleep did me the world of good. I thought I was getting one of my migraines." She giggled. "Mummy is always saying that

I need someone to take care of me. How was the disco?"

"You didn't miss very much." Gareth stroked the hair back off her face. "Are you warm enough?"

Fiona pointedly curled up against him. "Yes, thank you."

"I've missed you," he said softly. "I didn't realise quite how much until I saw you last night."

"Really?" She pulled back a little to look up at him.

"Really. And I'm so impressed — you've done so well for yourself, when I saw you on TV I couldn't believe my eyes. Mind you, I always knew that you'd got talent."

Fiona preened. "You're just saying that. Was it *Casualty*?"

Gareth nodded. "Yes, yes, it was."

"I was *so* lucky to get that part, although it wasn't my first TV credit. I was in — oh God, it's starting to rain." She peered up angrily at the sky. "I think I really ought to be getting back. I don't want to catch cold and my hair goes frizzy if it gets damp." She pulled her dressing gown up over her head.

"You know what I think?" said Gareth, not letting go. "I think that you worry way too much, sweetie. Relax. We've got plenty of time. I was hoping that we could start over." As he spoke he guided her under the cover of the hedge. "Why don't we go back inside? I've found this wonderfully snug little place — out of the way, very private." He smiled wolfishly. "Very, very private. Just like before. Remember?"

"Really?" said Fiona.

Gareth nodded and, taking her hand, set off back towards the hall. He laughed. "Relax. There's no rush. I've been thinking — once we leave here, I'm between contracts at the moment so I've got some time on my hands. I've just moved out of my last place. I'm a free agent." He paused. "I'd really like to see you; we can start all over again."

"Again?" Fiona repeated.

He nodded and tipped her face up to his. She bit her lip as he peered into her eyes.

"Come on, Fiona. You know that this is what you want. You were so good, so perfect," he whispered, pressing his lips into her hair, hands sliding up under her pyjama top. "And I've missed you so very much. We've got all the time in the world now. And it will be all right this time around. We were meant for each other, you know that, don't you? We've got as much time as we need. It will be so good, so right."

Fiona giggled.

"Carol? Wake up. Come on, come on. We're late."

Reptile-like, Carol slowly opened one eye, very reluctantly, despite the urgency in the voice and the vigorous shoulder-shaking, and licked her lips. She had been dreaming that she and the rest of the cast and crew had been asked to do a read-through in the Sahara Desert and they had forgotten to lay on any catering. It hadn't been that hot but God, she was parched. Outside, in the real world beyond the nice cosy darkness of her eyelids, the daylight was horribly bright. She looked across at her torturer. Diana was peering at her anxiously.

"Come on, get up."

"Bugger off."

"No, I won't bugger off. Did anyone ever tell you, you are incredibly grumpy in the morning? Come on, get your arse in gear. We're late. The alarm clock didn't go off." Diana was wrapped up in a pink dressing gown and winceyette nightie. There were bears on the nightie.

"People brought alarm clocks?" said Carol incredulously, trying to ignore the nasty taste in her mouth and Diana's nasty taste in nightwear.

Diana nodded. "Absolutely. Well, I'm sure there must be some people who did, people who are well organised. I heard at least two yesterday morning."

"People who are anally retentive and much in need of psychiatric help," moaned Carol, pulling the bedclothes up over her head to cut out the sunlight. It was so nice to be back in the dark. She rolled over.

"Very possibly but apparently even the anally retentive couldn't get it together last night because none of them seems to have gone off."

Carol didn't ask whether she meant the people or the clocks.

"Anyway, if you remember, we're late."

"Late?"

"That's right," said Diana. "The alarm clock didn't go off."

"So you said. Exactly how late are we?"

"Ten minutes past breakfast and counting. You have to get up. They do this really big fry-up on a Sunday.

282

It's a traditional thing. It's lovely. All freshly cooked and locally grown."

Carol's stomach did a nasty little lurching two-step fandango of complaint. "I'm not really up to breakfast," she said, swallowing hard.

"Oh, of course you are, don't be so silly. I think you should make the effort. It's going to be a long day and besides, they do great bacon and eggs here."

"Bugger off," Carol growled.

Diana laughed. "Baked beans, big juicy sausage, fried slice, nice black pudding . . ."

"You are a complete and utter cow," said Carol, admitting defeat and throwing the bedcovers back. "How come you aren't all horribly hung over and haggard this morning? I feel like shit."

Diana shrugged. "I don't know why really, maybe it's living a wholesome life and having the constitution of an ox. I feel great, although I have to say you don't look exactly a hundred per cent," she added philosophically.

Carol groaned and crawled to the edge of the bunk. Not looking a hundred per cent was a very loose-knit and benign description for the hangover from hell.

She closed her eyes, lay belly down on the thin mattress and swung her legs over the side. Carol paused, every muscle straining. It was a long drop down to the carpet and one she really needed to brace herself for.

The first thing Carol noticed when she was safely on the floor was that the bedroom window was now wide open and that down the grey beary wall and across the nasty yellow carpet was a trail of muddy footprints, which led rather pointedly to Fiona's bed, alongside which was a pair of grass-covered, earth-spattered slippers. Tucked up in bed, Fiona was still sound asleep under her padded purple blackout mask.

Adie — looking all tousled and lovely in his black silk jim-jams, followed Carol's gaze. "Before you ask, Madam managed to get herself locked out last night somehow, apparently. There she was in the wee small hours wailing like a banshee and banging on the window, all frantic and fussed and damp, said she had one of her heads and couldn't sleep. I'm surprised that you didn't hear her. She made enough bloody row to wake the dead."

Carol made an effort to sift through the rather fragmented memories of the previous night and kept coming up with the same picture. Fiona and a man, meeting in the moonlight. But then again maybe she had imagined it? Maybe she heard Fiona's voice in her sleep and dreamed the whole thing. It occurred to Carol that she genuinely didn't know whether it had been a dream or not.

"Was she on her own?" Carol asked.

Adie nodded. "Well, she was when she was banging on the window, why?"

Carol shook her head and then instantly regretted it. Something that had to be her brain had broken loose and was rolling around inside her skull like a giant spiky stainless-steel marble.

"Do you think we ought to wake her up? It's going to be a long day. It would be a shame for Fiona to miss breakfast, although she looks so lovely and peaceful lying there, doesn't she?" said Diana, without an iota of sarcasm. By the window Fiona was lying on her back, mask on, curlers in, with her mouth open, snoring softly, a thin trail of drool running down over her cheek, tethering her to the pillow. Carol was glad that she was the one who was awake and not the one being watched. Fiona snorted and rolled over.

"Yeah, you're right. I think we should wake her up. It wouldn't be the same without her, would it?" Adie said, in an almost identical tone.

Carol thought about it for a moment or two. What would Snow White be without the evil stepmother, or Cinderella without an ugly sister or two? Grudgingly Carol realised that he was right. Fiona did add a certain indefinable something to the proceedings.

And then Adie grinned. "Mind you, I'm not waking her up. She was a complete cow yesterday when she came to and found no one had laid on a tray with a pot of Earl Grey and hot buttered toast for her. Apparently Mummy would have been horrified." And with that he got up, picked up his wash bag and robe and headed out towards the boys' dormitory.

"Well, thanks a bunch," Diana called after his retreating back, rolling up her sleeves manfully.

He grinned. "You already owe me one." Adie tapped the side of his nose. "Don't ask any questions, just grab a woman and follow me, remember?"

Diana reddened furiously.

Carol stared at her. "What was that about?"

"Nothing important. It's a conga thing," said Diana, sounding huffy.

285

Carol shook her head. "Sorry I asked."

Adie had no sooner gone than Jan appeared from the girls' bathroom, all washed and dressed, her hair brushed, makeup done, all buffed, puffed and ready for the off. She looked great — better than great; she looked stunning.

Carol groaned. "What is it with you lot? Did you take some sort of magic potion first thing or was I the only one drinking last night?"

Jan smiled beatifically. "No, not at all," she said. "I got totally hammered."

Carol stared at her; something had changed. "Are you OK?"

"Yes, of course I'm OK. I just said I was," she snapped. "There's just no pleasing some people. You're awful, Carol. You were horrible to me when I felt down in the dumps and now you're doing the same thing when I'm feeling better."

"No, no, I'm not," Carol protested, and then she hesitated for an instant. "Oh, all right, so maybe I am, but I'm glad that you're happier. You seemed so sad last night." There was no easy way to say this. "I'm just surprised, that's all. It seemed kind of insoluble — you know, the thing we were talking about." She hedged around, waiting to see Jan's reaction.

Jan's happy face didn't falter for an instant. "Well, there's no need to be surprised. Adie and I had a really long talk last night. We sorted lots of things out. It's stuff we've talked about before — but never quite came to any firm decision. Until now." The smile still held. Carol stared at her while trying to figure out what the hell Adie could have said that had cured goodness only knew how many years of pain, rejection and love without hope.

"That's nice, I'm glad," she said cautiously.

Jan carried on smiling. "Yes, me too. And relieved as well, and we've made some concrete plans for the future. Finally."

Carol stared at her. "Finally? The future? Your future?"

Jan nodded enthusiastically. "Yes, that's right."

"But he's gay, Jan," Carol protested in a low voice. "You're not going to convert him."

Jan laughed. "Oh, for goodness' sake, I do know that; I don't need to be told. But I love him very much and I think I always will. And I realised — well, we both realised — that we've always loved each other, it's just not in the usual boy-girl sort of way. The Greeks probably had a word for it."

Carol stared at her, trying not to let her brain go galloping off to try to work out what sort of way that might mean. "Which leaves you and Adie where exactly?"

Jan waved her away. "I'll tell you later. Go and have a shower. You look absolutely terrible."

"How kind of you to notice," Carol growled, dragging on her dressing gown.

She tiptoed past the still sleeping Fiona and headed into the bathroom. Dog-eared and bleary-eyed she stared grimly into the mirror above the sink; Jan was bang on. It was going to take a lot of heavy-duty moisturising and concealer stick to make those bags come good.

When Carol finally got downstairs most of the frying was over; just the smell lingered like a great greasy veil, taking her backwards and forwards between nausea and hunger.

Gareth wasn't at breakfast, which was a blessing. Hopefully her face would have decrinkled after a couple of glasses of water, a few mugs of tea and a slice or two of cold bald bare toast, which was all her stomach was prepared to agree to.

Upstairs Callista Haze woke with a start, wondering where on earth she was. Morning sun was streaming in through the window and she had the most terrible headache. She winced and closed her eyes, trying to think back to the night before. And then Callista heard a noise. It was the noise of someone whistling cheerily, followed by sounds of someone making tea.

Making tea? Callista stiffened; she knew exactly where she was now and what that sound was. It was George Bearman making tea, and he was making it for both of them.

Callista groaned and buried her head in the pillow. It was important that she kept her eyes shut and aped sleep for as long as possible. Maybe George would take the hint, do the gentlemanly thing and head downstairs for breakfast whilst she made a discreet exit.

This was not how things were supposed to have turned out. A little nightcap — that's what George had said as they had climbed the bloody wooden hill to

Bedfordshire. Just a nip or two of brandy, a toast to things past and his glorious untried future, and out there on the landing she had finally agreed, suckered in by his hangdog expression and some last remnants of guilt.

After all, it was their last night together. Had he said that or had she? The likelihood was that they would never ever see each other again. Bloody man. She should have known better.

Once they were in his room, George had switched on the electric fire and the bedside lamp, suggested she would be more comfortable on the narrow bed, sitting with her back against the wall. While she got cosy he had found her a glass and poured them a hefty measure of brandy each.

Callista vaguely recalled George moving a little closer and then closer still, remembered him slipping his arm around her shoulders, and then all of a sudden she had looked up at him and wondered why it was exactly that she was resisting him all weekend.

She screwed her eyes tight shut against the memory. Not that it did much good. It was all there in her mind.

They went back a long way after all — was what he had said. Her and George. Oh God, yes, a long long way — and then he had kissed her. And when she hadn't protested he had kissed her some more and with that her resolve had vanished, not — it had to be said, all at once. But over quite a lot more brandy and considerably more conversation — the gist of which now escaped her — Callista began to remember why it was she had been so attracted to George Bearman in the first place. She winced as the images flooded back in glorious Technicolor. Oh yes, they were all there, not terribly pretty but very graphic.

Damn, damn, damn.

"Here we are, my dear," George said.

She peered at him over the rim of the duvet.

"Tea, milk, no sugar — strong, warm but not bitter. Rather like you, eh?" George said with a wry grin.

Callista smiled weakly at his joke, for once her demeanour at odds with her tea. She sat up, making sure that their eyes didn't quite meet and ensuring that she pulled the bedclothes right up to her neck. He had pale blue paisley pyjama bottoms on and a baggy grey T-shirt that, oddly enough, was quite sexy. Damn him.

"George," Callista began hastily, in case he thought a rematch might be in order. "About last night —"

George waved her into silence. "It's all right, I know," he said, slipping back alongside her in the narrow institutional single bed. Never was a bed more constructed to dissuade a body from lewd thoughts. It was almost perverse in its austerity. Callista tried very hard not to let any part of her sleep-warmed body touch his, but it was impossible.

He handed her a cup of tea. "I'm terribly sorry," he said.

"Sorry?" she said quizzically.

"Yes, sorry. I realise now that I should have listened to you. You were absolutely right. All those years I've clung on to a dream, an unreality. It was quite obviously ridiculous and last night proved it to me."

290

Callista reddened with embarrassment and indignation. "George, that really is the most horrible thing to say," she hissed through gritted teeth.

He shook his head. "Oh, no, no, please don't take offence, my dear. It isn't meant to sound in the least ungallant — quite the reverse, in fact. You truly are an extraordinarily beautiful woman and you always were, but you're not my woman, are you? You were, however, my fantasy. At first, thinking about you and what it might be like if circumstances had turned out differently was something that sustained me in a bad marriage. And then later, as things got worse between Judy and me, that fantasy was what kept me from facing up to what was really going on in my life and the things that were wrong. Thoughts of you kept me sane but they also kept me where I was.

"Last night, being with you made me realise just how very much I have missed. All those years wasted — not just for me but for Judy too. We could both have had half a lifetime with someone who loved us and who we really loved, if only I had been brave enough, bold enough to take that first step. I envy you your wonderful Laurence and your daughters and your dog and your little place in France, Callista, I really, truly do. And what makes it worse is that it could have been me you had it with."

Callista stared up at him, tears in her eyes.

He leaned forward and kissed her very gently on the forehead. "You really are a most extraordinary woman, Callista, and that man of yours should be very proud of you." He smiled. "I was a fool to ever let you go."

Too slow to hold it back, Callista felt a single tear roll down her cheek. "Oh, George," she said gently, "you really must get yourself sorted out and find someone to love."

He nodded. "I know. Now drink your tea before it gets cold. I think we may have already missed breakfast. We've got so much to get through this morning. Would you like the first shower?"

Callista shook her head. "It's very kind but I think it would be far better if I went back to my room."

He nodded. "Would you like me to check that it's all clear?"

She smiled. "Yes, I would, but first of all I'd like you to pass me my clothes."

George smiled. "Of course," he said, "and I promise not to look."

"OK, everybody, that was great. Shall we move on to the final scenes on the battlefield?" said Mr Bearman, clapping his hands to get everyone's attention. "And see if we can work the sword fight in around the dialogue. Gareth, you've come out through the gates of Dunsinane Castle to meet your fate. Remember part of you still believes that you are invincible — even if other things have fallen apart, surely that part of the prophecy cannot be messed with. So if you and Adrian would like to take it from where Macduff comes across Macbeth?" He shifted to the side of the stage to make way for the two of them.

Gareth nodded. Both he and Adie were wearing cloaks and carrying swords, and they truly looked the

292

part. Gareth was all together heavier-set, dark and swarthy. Carol noticed that he hadn't shaved. It suited him. Meanwhile, Adie was all blond and heroic.

At the back of the stage Adie was still practising the routine he and Gareth had worked out on the lawn during tea on the previous day, cutting and thrusting and swinging, counting under his breath as he did so.

"If I could have your attention, Adrian, please . . ." said Mr Bearman. Adie nodded and headed down stage. "Right. If you're ready, can we go from Macduff's speech, 'I have no words — /My voice is in my sword:'?"

There was a nod of consensus and a fraction of a second later Adie lifted his sword for the first great thrust.

"God, this is going to be good," said Netty under her breath.

Carol watched them from the back of the hall, watched the two of them lunge and parry, swords swinging back and forth. It must be hard to fight and read but it seemed as if the words were still all in there, still fresh, still remembered after all these years.

Netty was right. It looked stunning. Adie pressed forward, Gareth defended and then pushed back against him. And then there was the big, big speech. Macbeth believed he was invulnerable because he had been told by the witches that he could not be killed, by anyone born of woman. There was a silent, meaty pause, a fantastic theatrical moment and then Macduff, triumphant, tells Macbeth that he, Macduff — wasn't born but was from his mother's womb untimely ripped.

Even after all these years Carol shivered as Adie began to speak. It was such a powerful speech and Adie was brilliant as the avenging angel. Finally Macbeth, knowing that he faces certain death, strides forward to meet his fate. Magnificent. No one could fail to be moved by the lines, the sentiment of the flawed king or Gareth's bleak but passionate delivery. It looked and sounded amazing. In fact, so good that as the scene ended there was a great surge of spontaneous applause.

"That was wonderful. Although I hate to try and improve the damned good, there are just one or two points. Adrian, just make sure you haven't got your back to the audience and Gareth, if you could make sure you don't step too far across. I want the fight to be centre stage. Let's just run through it one more time," said Mr Bearman, waving them into action.

Carol sighed. Once was maybe enough for such stirring stuff. Adie stepped back to take up his starting position and as he did, stepped back onto the hem of his cloak, and just as he had done on the lawn the previous afternoon, fell over, but this time lurched sideways.

"Shit," grumbled the avenging angel, now down flat on his arse on the stage. Gareth offered him a hand up.

"You OK?" Gareth asked.

Adie nodded, allowing himself to be pulled up, and then resumed his starting position, limping a little. "I think I'll live," he said ruefully, rubbing his leg.

"Right, we'll just get this nailed and then we'll take five for a breather and cup of tea. It's going really well," said Mr Bearman brightly, heading back to his seat.

"It's taken years off him doing this," Diana said under her breath. "He looked bloody terrible when he first showed up on Friday, and now look at him, leaping around like a blue-arsed fly."

Carol lifted an eyebrow. "You're really going to have to clean up your language before you go home to Hedley."

Diana giggled. "Bugger off. Come on, you heard what the man said, let's go take five."

Meanwhile, Leonora, with Raf's help, was busy strapping Patrick and baby Maisie into the back of Raf's car, alongside Jake and Ollie and Jasmine, who looked as though she had had a rough night too.

"So," said Raf, when they were all secure and happy, "have you got everything you need, have you now?" The back of the people carrier was full of bags and nappies and buggies. Amazing how such tiny creatures needed so many things.

Leonora nodded, feeling exhausted before the trip had even begun. "I think so."

Raf smiled, his big brown eyes as warm and soft as toffee. "That's grand. In that case we'll be off then."

Leonora looked at him; he struck her as as kind and good a man as any woman could wish for. If Carol truly thought that Gareth was a better option then she was a fool.

"Now is everybody all right? Is everybody happy?" No one answered. Raf's smiled didn't falter, instead he helped Leonora aboard and handed her her seatbelt. "Maybe not the most appropriate question in the world but my experience is that at times like this, there is only really one answer . . ."

Leonora paused expectantly, waiting for some great outpouring of Celtic wisdom and insight.

Instead Raf pulled a rake of CDs out of a case on his lap. "We'll slap some country and western on the CD player and sing along to Johnny and Willie and Dolly. Let me tell you, no one has it rougher or tougher and there is certainly no one does it better. Now what do you fancy? Bluegrass, some Nashville, or how about a little Cajun country? Name your poison."

Leonora stared at him in amazement and then began to laugh. "You're serious, aren't you?"

"Oh by God, yes. Never more so," said Raf, as if a country-and-western cure was the most normal thing in the world.

In the back Jasmine giggled. "Is he for real?" she said to Jake, who sighed heavily.

"Yes, unfortunately he is, and in my experience it doesn't get any better than this," he said wearily. "He may look like a grown-up on the outside but it's only a very thin outer coating — and he sings as well, which is so embarrassing. He couldn't carry a tune in a bucket."

Raf looked hurt. "How can you possibly say that? I've got a grand voice, me. It's in my blood. It's my heritage." He held up a disc triumphantly. "I've got a new John Lee Hooker album, if you're interested."

Nobody said a word.

In the back Patrick started to sing his own very mangled interpretation of "The Wheels on the Bus".

296

"There we are," said Raf with a great big grin. "There's at least one of you keen on the singing." And with that he fired up the engine and they pulled away.

CHAPTER
TWELVE

It was too nice a day to take five in the hall. Adie limped miserably across the lawn towards Carol and Netty, bearing a mug of tea and a grim expression.

"I don't want you to say anything but I think there's a fair chance I'm not going to be able to do the show," he whispered, gingerly easing himself down alongside them. "Alternatively I may have to do the bloody play sitting in a bath chair with a cane, and a tartan blanket over my knees."

"What is the Macduff tartan anyway?" asked Netty conversationally.

Carol stared at him. "I thought you said you were OK. Does it really hurt that much?"

He looked up, all hangdog and pale. "Sure does, and I'm so bloody annoyed. I've been looking forward to doing this for weeks." He whisked his cloak over his shoulders, pulling it tight round him like a security blanket. "Bloody thing, I should have got a shorter cloak."

"Wouldn't that have affected your super powers?" asked Carol.

"Men," said Netty, looking heavenwards. "They're obsessed with size. Don't panic. We've got plenty of time before kick-off. I'm sure someone can rustle up an ice pack, or maybe we could find someone to strap your ankle up for you. Surely at least one amongst our merry band must have decided nursing was a good career move. And if there's no one in our lot we could always ask the Christians. After last night I'd say they owe us. Big time."

"How bad is it?" asked Carol.

Without a word Adie pulled up the leg of his trousers. Above expensive Italian loafers his ankle had swollen to twice the size it ought to be, while red, purple and blue bruising crept up his leg like angry wisteria.

"Oh, bugger me," said Netty, wincing in sympathy. "OK, so maybe you're not overacting after all."

Carol moved her attention from the bruising to his face. "Do you think there's any chance that it might be broken?"

Adie shrugged. "How would I know? I don't think so — you can't walk on something if it's broken, can you?"

"God knows, it looks terrible. What do you want to do? Shall I go and find Mr Bearman?" said Carol. "That looks absolutely awful."

"Really?" Adie said grimly. "You know what they say, the show must go on. I'm going to find some ice; we've only got another hour or so before we break for lunch. I'll rest it up for a while then and see how it feels afterwards. Bearman says we don't have to do the fight scene again until the performance, so it might be OK."

Nobody else looked that optimistic, having seen the swelling and the bruises.

Netty glared at him. "You know, you men are all the bloody same. One minute you're saying you're dying and the next you're saying it will all be just hunky dory after all. What is that about? Wanting us to admire how big and brave you are? Getting the sympathy vote? Being nominated man of the match? Carol's hangover still has my vote — did you see her first thing this morning? Those bags are going to take some beating."

Carol growled in her general direction.

Adie sighed. "Don't get so stressed. I just wanted a second opinion, that's all. It hurts like hell but I'm going to give it a shot, although I would be grateful if you could discreetly ask around to see if there is a doctor in the house — or a nurse."

"Or a vet?" suggested Netty helpfully.

"That's the kind of thing I'd expect Jan to say," said Carol. "Which reminds me, where exactly is she?"

"On the phone to her mum, telling her the good news, probably," said Adie offhandedly as he adjusted his trousers.

"And exactly what good news is that then?" Carol said.

He blushed but looked pleased. "I think you should talk to Jan about it."

Carol stared at him, but he just shrugged. "Oh, come off it, Adie. We're all mates, for goodness' sake. She was like a bear with a sore butt until last night, and now she's like the cat who got the goldfish."

Still he said nothing.

"Do you know anything about this?" Carol said to Netty, who frowned in a gesture of exasperation. Carol glared at Adie; it was no good, she was going to have to get him on his own and bully him or she might never find out what the hell was going on.

Back in the main hall Diana was busy helping to supervise the setting up of chairs for the afternoon's invited audience.

"One way and another it's been rather an interesting weekend," said Mr Bearman cheerily. He was carrying a tray with two cups of tea and a selection of chocolate biscuits on it.

"I'm glad you're enjoying it," said Diana.

"Wouldn't have missed it for the world. How many are we expecting to come and see the performance this afternoon?" he asked, looking round the hall.

Diana followed his glance; the crew were all beavering away with huge stacks of chairs. "I think most people invited at least one other person, and a lot have invited their whole family. Then there are quite a few people from the school. I'm hoping that we're going to get a full house, but even if we don't it doesn't matter. At least the ones that do turn up will all be on our side."

George Bearman laughed. "Well, there is that. Sounds like a damned good idea to me. We'll just do another hour or so after tea break, and then stop for lunch. If we could have everyone back here by what — shall we say one thirty?"

Diana nodded. "The audience should be here any time after two, performance starts at two thirty — sounds perfect."

"Righty-oh. Is your husband coming?"

Diana shook her head. "I don't know, most probably not. He's a vicar; Sunday is his busy day."

"A great shame that he can't see all your hard work. You know, all in all this was a wonderful idea, Diana."

She smiled up at him. "Thank you, Mr Bearman, although perhaps we should save any congratulations and crowing until after the show."

George laughed as he headed off towards Callista with the tea and biscuits. "How very like a woman," he said.

Diana lifted an eyebrow; she didn't like to tell him it wasn't just the play that was on her mind.

"I really don't understand this at all, Gareth. You were all over me like a rash last night," hissed Fiona, hands on hips, her face reddening to magenta. It didn't take a psychologist to work out that she was all wound up and ready to pounce. "I'm very hurt — terribly, terribly hurt, Gareth. *Do you understand?* I feel like you've used me and now you're just throwing me away like a broken toy. Casting me aside." Her tone was icy and yet at the same time Fiona somehow managed to convey a childlike vulnerability, which was what had probably got her the walk-on part in *Emmerdale* that she had told him about the night before.

"I think that you're overreacting, Fiona," Gareth said, and instantly regretted it as her face got even redder. God, maybe this wasn't such a good idea, after all. The woman was totally crazy. "What I mean is, I'm just saying that we should keep the whole 'us' thing under wraps while we're here. It'll only be for a while longer, a couple of days at the most, that's all," he added, speaking calmly but quickly, trying to stem Fiona's rising emotional tide. This wasn't how he imagined the morning-after meeting with Fiona going at all.

"But you told me that you wanted me, that you had come here to see me, that you had always loved me. Or was that just a game too, Gareth? Some sort of nasty trick to get me into bed? From where I'm standing it looks like you've had what you want and now you're off." Her voice quivered slightly and then broke. "I feel so used, and so very, very cheap," she sniffled, a single crystal tear rolling down her cheek. It was a masterly performance.

"Of course I want you," said Gareth softly, lifting a hand to stroke the tear away, hoping to appease her and also encourage her to keep her voice down. She could project like Pavarotti. They were standing at the back of the stage and he really didn't want anyone else hearing. "I just don't think that this is the place to make it public, that's all. I'd prefer if we kept it to ourselves, at least till we're away from Burbeck House."

"Why?" she wailed. "Why not here? It's crazy. Who on earth cares if we're a couple or not? We're both free, we're both single, we're both adults — or is it that you're ashamed of me?"

"No, no, not at all," he began. God, the woman really was barking mad. Worse still, it sounded for all the world as if she was reading from a script.

Fiona glared at him. "Men are all the same, you know. You just use me, treat me like some sort of sex toy — it's because I'm beautiful, I know that — but no one ever sees past my looks. That is what Mummy says. I know that they just see the face and the body and not the real me. I want someone to love me for what I really truly am, Gareth. I want a man who cares about me, the inner me, and isn't just attracted by my natural beauty," wailed Fiona, all red-faced, with eyes puffed up like jam doughnuts. The irony wasn't lost on Gareth. "I thought you were different," Fiona concluded.

Gareth didn't like to say so, but he had had much the same thought; it seems that they had both been proved wrong. It was such a pity that Carol had run off like that. She might not be as classically pretty as Fiona, but she was nice-looking, great eyes, really nice smile and good body, and hadn't struck him as bunny-boiler material, while Fiona on the other hand . . .

Before he could finish the thought, Fiona sobbed, "All those years, wasted, all those hopes dashed . . ." And then blew her nose into a large white lace-trimmed hankie.

Gareth stared down at her, wondering what the hell Fiona was on about but decided on balance that he didn't want to know and didn't plan to ask.

"Don't leave me," she whined in a voice that would have shattered crystal. "Stay with me, please." She threw her arms around him and hung on tight. "Please stay, I can't bear it."

"Please calm down, Fiona. I'm not planning on going anywhere," he said hastily, trying to extricate himself from her clutches. "I wasn't saying I didn't want you, it's just we ought to keep this —" Gareth lifted his hands to indicate some seminal moment, well aware that he was repeating himself — "to ourselves for a while longer, just until the weekend is over. That's all." He enunciated every word in case there was some possibility of her misunderstanding.

She stepped back. "So you said," she sniffed. Wiping her tears away, Fiona added sulkily. "I just don't understand why."

Gareth sighed. "No, I don't suppose you do." Her skin was so thick that it would probably take a blow torch and hammer to get through to her.

"And what is that supposed to mean?" she snapped.

It was exhausting talking to Fiona. Gareth felt as if he was taking part in a particularly high-octane tennis match. It was a terrible shame that Fiona hadn't put as much effort into the sexual stuff. If she had it might almost be worth the effort. Unfortunately Fiona seemed to think that nice girls still laid back and thought of Queen and Country.

"You think that I'm stupid, don't you — that's it, isn't it?" Fiona whined. She was capable of an extremely wide range of emotions for one so small.

"No, no, that isn't it at all."

"Really?" she growled.

"No, it's not. OK, look, I'll be honest with you." Gareth took a deep breath. "Carol has got a bit of a crush on me. You must have seen her this weekend — it's been so obvious — and I don't want to rub it in. I don't know if you remember but we used to be a bit of an item when we were at school." Gareth paused, watching Fiona's face to see how he was doing. "She took it hard when I finished with her and, to be perfectly honest, I don't think she really ever got over it. She's been all over me since we arrived."

Fiona's jaw dropped. "All over you? Carol, Carol French? Lady Bloody Macbeth?" she spat. "Good God. Really?" She laughed and then shook her head.

Gareth stared at her. He wasn't sure what sort of reaction he'd been expecting but incredulity was not top of the list.

"What do you mean, 'really'?"

Fiona wrinkled up her nose as if she could smell something deeply offensive. "I've always thought that Carol was very ordinary. I've still got no idea why they cast her in the lead instead of me. Not that I'm jealous or anything — that would be ridiculous — but Mummy always used to say she thought it was out of pity. You know, trying to give everyone a chance at the brass ring, although it obviously lowers production values. I'm amazed she had the gall to show up and think she could step straight back into the role. I always thought the reviewers were very kind —" And then Fiona's eyes narrowed. "Oh, wait a minute. Yes, you're right, wasn't she the one chasing you before we met, when we first got together? I remember now. We had to keep it quiet then too, at least until after we left school. I think Mummy was worried about me getting involved with someone when I was so young, you know, in case I lost sight of my career goals."

There was a moment's pause and then Gareth, as if pulling the memory up from the cobweb-strewn depths, nodded. "You know, I think you're right."

Fiona sighed. "So we've still got to keep it quiet because of Carol French, have we? Even after all these years?" She sniffed. "Unbelievable."

Gareth smiled. "It would be cruel to rub it in," he said.

Fiona stared at him as if considering the possibility. Gareth waited for his sentence to be meted out and then, unexpectedly, Fiona smiled and stroked his arm. "You know, you are so thoughtful, Gareth. I'd totally forgotten."

"So you agree then?" he said, trying hard to keep any sense of relief to himself.

Fiona smiled, her expression now totally beatific. "I suppose under the circumstances it is the kindest thing to do, really. We don't want to rub it in, do we? Not when we're so perfect for each other." Fiona purred and began to preen. "Carol's divorced, you know. It must be very hard for a woman in her position. He probably got bored and left her, if you ask me. And I know it's very sexy at the moment but working outside can be so unkind on the skin. So very ageing. I would have thought it must be terribly difficult for someone like her to find anyone else. I mean, if you think about it, gardening is practically manual labour."

Gareth clamped his jaw shut and didn't say a word.

Meanwhile, out on the open road, Raf and little Patrick had hit it off right from the start; the wheels on the bus went round and round and seemed to have been doing so for hours. Safely tucked up in the back in her baby seat, Maisie slept. Jake made cow eyes at Jasmine, and Ollie — headphones jammed firmly on over his ears — played on his Gameboy and listened to Metallica, while the English countryside, all dressed up in its blousy summer best, scrolled past the window of the people carrier.

As the miles sped by, Leonora thought about all the things that she wanted to say to Gareth. It seemed as if several years had passed since Friday afternoon. In her handbag she had Gareth's attempts at forgery, a copy of their bank statements, and, of course, there was Jasmine. Something told her that when the time came for words they would all be there and she had some inkling that actually silence might be just as eloquent.

"We're nearly there," said Raf, peering out at a signpost through the windscreen. "Actually we've made a lot better time than I expected." He turned to the occupants of the car. "Now would you like to go straight up to the hall or shall we stop and have a bite to eat first? Stretch our legs and freshen up a bit? We've got plenty of time before the curtain goes up. There's a nice-looking pub just up there on the right and I don't know about you but I could murder a pie and a pint."

In the back Patrick clapped his hands in agreement. Raf grinned. "I like that child more and more."

"OK, I think that that will do, folks. Well done. If you'd like to break for lunch, I want us all to be back here, backstage at one thirty, fighting fit and raring to go," said George Bearman brightly, at the end of the morning session. "We're as ready as we're ever going to be and I think we're looking good, don't you, Callista?"

Miss Haze, who was sitting on the side of the stage, acting as prompt and stage manager, smiled wanly. Carol couldn't help but wonder if she'd had a heavy night too; certainly the spring had gone out of her step since Saturday's rehearsal.

Adie limped across to where the witches and Carol had camped out.

"So how're you doing?" asked Netty, offering him her hand so that he could ease himself down onto the steps at the side of the stage.

Adie lifted his trouser leg, this time revealing a great mummified limb swathed to the knee in crepe bandages. "It's getting worse. One of the crew — you remember Shortie Laxton, the little weasely guy with a dodgy eye and halitosis? Well, he used to be an army medic, apparently — he told me he thought it was a really bad sprain, that I ought to go and see a doctor and that I should stay off it as much as possible." Adie winced as he adjusted the trouser leg. "The man is wasted in telesales."

"So what do you want to do?" asked Diana anxiously. "Do you want me to have a word with Mr Bearman? Maybe we could get you an understudy. There's still time — it's only a read-through, after all."

309

Adie shook his head. "It seems such a bloody waste to have come all this way and then not go on. I think I'm going to try and wing it. I've taken a load of painkillers."

"We could find someone to go on in your place," said Carol thoughtfully.

"Duh," said Netty, groaning theatrically and slapping her forehead, "that *is* what an understudy is."

"I do know what it means," Carol said. "What I meant was, how about if we just got Adie a stunt double for the fight scene? He could read the script in from the side of the stage." She turned to Adie. "How long would it take for someone to learn the moves you've worked out with Gareth?"

"Swashing and buckling?" said Netty. "It comes naturally to boys, doesn't it?"

Adie's eyes narrowed thoughtfully. "It's not that complicated, half an hour at the most, I would have thought."

Diana nodded. "Sounds like a great idea to me. Most of the crew are desperate to get their hands on a sword, and it means, Adie, that you get to do all the bits you can do and sit out the bits you can't."

Grudgingly Adie agreed.

"I'll go and see who I can rustle up," said Diana, getting to her feet.

"Do you want me to help you?" asked Jan anxiously, as Adie eased himself upright. "Maybe they've got a wheelchair in the sick bay."

"Or a crutch and eye patch," said Netty.

"We're doing *Macbeth* not *Treasure Island*," Adie said wryly. "No, I'll be fine. I just need to take it steady."

"Are you sure?" asked Jan, who had come over all Florence Nightingale.

Carol stared at her; Jan was still positively radiant. "Tell you what," Carol said. "Why don't you go and grab a table in the dining room? I'll hobble along with Long John Silver here, if you like?"

Jan hesitated and then nodded, quite obviously reluctant to leave Adie to Carol's mercies.

"I'm not going to hurt him," said Carol. "I promise. I just want to ask him a few things."

Still Jan hung back, so Carol continued, "Private things, you know."

"And I'm desperate for a smoke. Come on," said Netty, catching hold of Jan's arm. "Leave them to it." Jan finally turned away.

"And see if you can't get back to your normal nasty self. We'll all be very relieved," Carol called after them. "I worry when you're nice."

As if to underline the point Jan giggled and practically skipped off towards the dining hall behind Netty, turning briefly to wave at Adie before vanishing through the double doors on the other side of the room.

"Right, come on, I want to know and I want to know now. What on earth is it with you two?" asked Carol, taking his arm and a lot of his weight.

Adie looked uncomfortable "That's the private thing you want to talk about?"

"I didn't say whose private thing it was. Now tell me."

"You should talk to Jan."

Carol nodded. "Uh-huh, I have. She said she would tell me later but I can't bear the suspense. She told me that you've got plans, the pair of you."

Adie blushed. "We have," he said and then smiled enigmatically, all tight-lipped and secretive.

Carol sighed. "To be perfectly honest, Adie, I haven't got the time or the patience to drag this out of you one word at a time. Do you think you could just cut to the chase and tell me what the hell is going on with you and Jan? Or would you like me to kick your bad leg?"

"You wouldn't."

Carol stared at him. "Try me."

"It's a long story."

"In which case, how about we settle for the edited highlights?"

"I didn't twig for ages —" said Adie — "about the way Jan felt about me, and then one day I was at an exhibition she had invited me to. I've always got on really well with her — and thought she invited all of the old gang and that no one else could make it, so I kind of felt sorry for her. Anyway, I saw her looking in my direction, all love and warmth and expectation. And you know what? I was really envious of whoever it was she was looking at like that. I turned round and glanced back over my shoulder and there was no one there and then I suddenly realised that that look was meant for me, that she loved *me*."

Carol stared at him. "Oh, Adie."

"I know, but I genuinely had no idea up until then. It was such a shock. I didn't know what to say to her, and so for a while I tried keeping away, not taking her calls. But the truth is I really missed seeing her. So then I explained — I told her all about Mike and me, and you know what? None of it did any good because she loved me just the same, just the way I was, and weird though it sounds, I realised that I loved her too. And I always have — crazy, isn't it?" He grinned, trying very hard not to put his weight down on the injured leg. "Anyway, I pulled back because I thought if I wasn't around so much, wasn't in her life, then she would find someone else, fall in love and settle down."

"But she didn't?"

Adie shook his head. "No, no, she didn't and I missed her. She is like family, and so we met up, talked on the phone — and for the first time last night we really talked about it — all those years. All those feelings. And in an odd way I feel I owe it to her."

"I'm not with you, Adie. What do you owe her?"

He smiled. "Jan wants to have a baby. Wants my baby."

Carol stared at him, could feel the surprise registering on her face, could feel her mouth dropping open. "A baby? Are you serious?" she whispered.

He nodded. "Absolutely. Never more so. We'd joked about it before but it makes sense. It's probably her last chance and maybe my only one. I've always wanted kids. Mike and I have talked about it loads of times but we've never seen a practical way to do it before."

"Until now? What are you going to do, set up some kind of weird ménage à trois?"

Adie laughed. "Good God, no. No, nothing so grubbily biological. Jan wants kids, so why not use a donor you know and love? Mike and I would be like favourite uncles. We've already got half a dozen godchildren and a whole scrum of nieces and nephews between us. In an ideal world Jan would like two children and I'd contribute financially, and Mike and I would be actively involved. I think it will be great."

Carol looked at him, wondering if he really had any idea what he was saying. "And how is Mike going to feel about all this?"

"During the time we've been together we've talked about it in principle and it's not like I'm going straight. I love him but it would be nice to have kids too. I know he feels the same, and it's not like I'm thinking of leaving him for Jan."

"Won't he feel threatened?"

Adie smiled. "I don't know. Possibly, but we've been together a long, long time and he shouldn't. I love him more than I thought it was possible to love anyone but I think that this is a good idea and it makes us a family in a funny kind of way."

Carol laughed. "Yeah, in a funny kind of a way is about right."

In the dining room Diana wasn't having a lot of luck with finding a stand-in for Adie. It appeared that most of the crew had buggered off down the pub for one last pint before lunch and those who hadn't didn't want to play. Diana wondered if she dare wait for the rest of them to come back. Really she needed someone who would endure a little rehearsal over lunch, wasn't too drunk and would be able to get the moves fixed in his head.

"Look, why don't we just go down the pub and press somebody there? Ply them with booze and false promises. It used to work for the navy, and besides, I could really do with a drink," said Netty. "Come on, we could kill two birds with one stone, nip down to the pub, grab a swift half, a roadie and be back in time for lunch. It'll only take a few minutes, and besides, this may be the last chance we get."

Diana nodded. "Good idea. Are you going to come with us, Jan?"

On the other side of the dining room Jan was lovingly setting a large table for five.

"No, no, I'm fine. You go ahead. I'll wait here for Adie and Carol, keep the table and let them know where you've gone to."

"Oh, come on," growled Netty. "Come with us, for God's sake. How many times are we all going to be together again? He's not going anywhere, you know."

"Who?" said Jan innocently.

Netty laughed. Grudgingly Jan got to her feet. "All right, but just one drink. I want to be sober for this afternoon. Do you think anyone would mind if I put 'Reserved' on this table?"

"I shouldn't think so. The only thing is we'll need Adie's sword and cloak out of the props box," said Diana. "And I suppose we really ought to try and get

315

Gareth to come along as well, if we can track him down." Gareth was the very last person Diana wanted to have anything to do with, but needs must.

"I'll go and get them, it's not a problem," said Jan, eager to be heading back towards the main hall and Adie.

"OK — well, in that case we'll see you in a little while," said Diana, and then in a lower tone said to Netty, "what the hell's going on with Jan?" The table was set with fancy folded napkins, a bowl of fruit that she had scrounged from somewhere, side plates and glasses with a little vase full of daisies in the centre. It was nesting gone mad.

Netty sighed. "It's all supposed to be private but I suppose I can tell you . . ."

Jan met up with Carol and Adie halfway down the corridor to the dining room. Adie was breathing hard and in obvious pain. "There is no way I can make it down to the pub," he said when Jan explained to them where Diana and Netty had gone and why.

"Poor you," Jan said. "I've got us a table just inside the door. I'll be back in a while. Diana wants me to fetch a cloak and sword, and Gareth if I can find him."

Carol waved her back towards the dining room. "Hang on a minute, why don't you stay with Adie, I'll get the stuff and find Macbeth. It seems to me like you pair have got a lot to talk about."

Jan beamed. "You told her?" she said to Adie.

"I didn't see that I had a lot of choice. You're like the cat who's got the cream, and she won't take no for an answer," he growled, although nothing in his voice made him sound genuinely cross, or unduly worried.

"I'm so excited," Jan told Carol.

Carol laughed. "You surprise me — I'd never of guessed," and then smiled. "I think you're mad but I'm delighted for both of you." She paused. "I think."

Adie grinned. "Fair enough — we'll invite you to the christening."

Jan flushed crimson.

Shaking her head, Carol headed off to find the props and Gareth. There was something she needed to talk to him about and the sooner she did, the better.

The main hall was all set up and ready for the performance, rows of chairs arranged in neat lines, numbered and lettered. Carol stood in the doorway and tingled with anticipation; it wouldn't be long now. Diana's trip down memory lane with maps and posters was set up as a display in one corner. The stage, with the curtains tied back to reveal a cavernous space, was marked up with Mr Bearman's cues and at the back, just in front of the curtains, was a table laid out with various props and bits of costume.

The huge room felt like the *Marie Celeste* compared to the hive of activity it had been during the morning but even so, Carol felt a little buzz of excitement in the air. She climbed the stairs and picked Adie's sword and cloak from amongst the props on the table.

"It's no good you looking for him, he's not here," said a familiar voice.

Carol turned in surprise. Fiona, arms crossed over her chest, was standing alone in the wings.

"Sorry?" said Carol. "I'm not with you."

"Really? You know you don't fool me, Carol. I know exactly what's going on. I know that you're looking for Gareth."

Carol was a little nonplussed. "Well, yes, actually I am," she said.

Fiona smiled triumphantly. "I knew it. I think you ought to know, Carol, that there's no point chasing after Gareth like this. You're only making a fool of yourself, you know. He told me that you'd got a crush on him. I want you to know now that you've lost. It's over, it's me that he wants. It's me he has always wanted."

Carol stared at Fiona in amazement. "I don't know what you're on about," she began.

Fiona's face folded into a nasty tight little sneer. "Oh, please," she said, "you've been crawling all over him since we arrived. Making a complete fool of yourself. He told me that he didn't want to hurt you — I think he felt sorry for you."

It felt as if Fiona had punched her. "Actually I came to ask him if he would help someone else learn Adie's moves for the fight scene. Adie's sprained his ankle and we thought it would be a good idea to get a stand-in." Carol struggled to keep her voice calm and even. She felt sick and hot and angry and betrayed, but most of all she really wished that she had managed to talk to Gareth before she had seen Fiona.

"Oh, come off it. You don't fool me. You never got over him," said Fiona icily. "Has it never occurred to you that he might not be interested?"

The words were like body blows, but then Carol stopped and remembered what it was that she had wanted to say to Gareth, and she said steadily, "Actually, Fiona, you're wrong."

"What do you mean, wrong? Gareth told me —"

"What did Gareth tell you?" Carol felt her anger begin to rise and take hold. "Did he tell you that last night at the disco he couldn't keep his hands off me?"

Fiona's face paled. "Don't be so ridiculous. You're lying, I know you're lying. You're making it up," she blustered, but Carol could see by Fiona's expression that she wasn't wholly convinced. "It's me he wants," Fiona hissed. "He came here just to see me again after all these years."

Carol held up her hands in a gesture of surrender. "OK, but I suggest you have a little chat with Gareth before you call me a liar, Fiona. If it hadn't been for Diana coming to the rescue with a conga line last night I would have been mincemeat by now. Just another notch on the bedpost, I suspect. Gareth is very convincing, I'll give him that. He had me fooled — but there was just something about him — something a little too desperate, too pushy. Too much too soon — and although it's terribly flattering I'm not in that much of a hurry — nor am I that easy. It felt as if he wasn't going to take no for an answer."

"You're just jealous," Fiona spat. "It was the same when we were at school. I'd have thought you'd have learned your lesson by now. It's me that Gareth really wants. It's me he's always wanted. He wanted me back then and he still wants me now."

Carol stared at her in horror and then very slowly comprehension dawned. "Back then? Do you mean at school?"

Fiona nodded. Carol shook her head. "The bastard. Don't you see, he's done all this before? To both of us."

"Don't be ridiculous," snarled Fiona.

"He met you out in the garden last night, didn't he? I thought I saw you out there with someone, but I couldn't make out who it was. It *was* Gareth, wasn't it? Don't you see, he's been fishing — stringing us both along to see who would bite first? Maybe that's what he was doing at school as well. Did you end up getting laid during the drama tour too?"

Fiona's jaw dropped. "How can you be so coarse about something so special?" And then after a second or two, in a voice barely above a whisper: "How on earth did you know?"

Carol shook her head, suddenly feeling relieved and able to see clearly for the first time in days. "Because he did the same to me. What a total and utter bastard," she said to no one in particular and then she laughed and shook her head. "How come we didn't see what he was like?"

"You are such a bitch," snarled Fiona. "You don't fool me, you're making it up."

"You don't really believe that," said Carol. "And you know what? I don't care even if you do. I think that you

320

and Gareth deserve each other. I hope you are very happy together."

"But I thought you said you wanted him," Fiona protested.

"Once upon a time, but I don't now — I was on my way to find him to tell him just that before we had this little chat. I was going to tell him that whatever I felt for him was in the past and that I love someone else now — and that it wasn't until I saw Gareth again that I realised just how much. I'm in love with a really nice guy, Fiona, a man who is loving and honest and funny. He cares about me in a way that Gareth couldn't comprehend. He's a safe pair of hands, who will always be there for me, who will catch me if I fall, and you know what? He loves me back. I hadn't really seen it clearly until last night and then I realised I would never be able to trust Gareth as far as I could throw him. He doesn't care about either of us, Fiona — he only cares about himself. He didn't care whether I wanted to go into the storeroom with him or not. He only cared about what he wanted — Gareth had a plan and he intended to see it through. And my feeling is that it isn't the only plan he has."

"The storeroom?" repeated Fiona.

Carol laughed. "Oh God, not you too? Yes, the storeroom."

"The bastard," Fiona hissed.

"He made it then. Eventually," said Carol.

On the far side of the stage Fiona was now crimson with fury, and for one amazing moment Carol thought that Fiona was going to hurl herself across the room and attack her, but instead she paused, her attention momentarily moving to a spot somewhere above Carol's shoulder.

"Hi, there," said a familiar voice. "How's it going?"

Carol turned very slowly. "Hello. Funnily enough, I was looking for you," she said.

"Ah," said Gareth. "Well, here I am. How can I help?"

"I was hoping you'd be free to come down to the pub and rehearse the sword fight with a stand-in. Adie's hurt his ankle," she said flatly.

"Sure, not a problem."

In the wings on the far side of the stage Fiona was glowing white hot. "Wait," she barked.

Gareth froze. Inwardly Carol smiled; it was almost worth the pain to see the look on his face. "Hi, sweetheart," he purred, fixing on a smile. "I didn't see you there. How're you doing?"

It wasn't bad. He managed to sound almost pleased to see her, only the look of utter panic in his eyes gave him away. But no charm offensive, particularly one cobbled together on the hoof, was going to knock Fiona off track. It was like throwing snowballs at a tank.

"She said that you were trying to get her into the storeroom last night," Fiona spat. "And that you've been chasing her too."

"Ah," said Gareth thickly. "Well, the thing is —" he began.

"I'll leave you to it," said Carol, with a wave of the hand. "I'm sure Adie can talk us through the fight."

"No, no — wait," said Gareth, but it was too late, Fiona had already run across the stage and caught tight hold of his arm. It was like watching a wounded animal being brought down by a bad-tempered hyena.

"I want to know what exactly you think you're up to," Fiona snapped.

Gareth held his hands up in defence. "I don't follow you," he spluttered, still managing to hold tight to a very unconvincing smile.

Whatever lies he was planning to tell, Carol really didn't want to hear them, and without looking back she made her way towards the door.

It was only when she got outside that Carol started to shake and let the tears flow. "The bastard, the total and utter bastard," she whispered over and over again, although in amongst the pain and humiliation there was a real sense of relief and certain joy at being free. It would be so nice to see Raf and the boys — so nice to see Raf and know in her heart that it was all right to love him, and that she had got it right after all.

Through the closed doors of the main hall she could hear Fiona shrieking although Carol didn't try terribly hard to make out exactly what she was saying.

Yes, it would be great to see Raf. She grinned and then felt a little flutter of anxiety. What would it be like when they met up again? Would he be hurt that she had gone to meet Gareth, would he understand? The grin faded. What if finding out what Gareth was really like and what she truly felt about him cost her the real thing?

CHAPTER
THIRTEEN

"Right, so what have we got here then, let me see. That's a pint of bitter shandy and a cheese and pickle ploughman's for you, Jake, and chicken nuggety dinosaurs and chips for you, m'lad." Solicitously Raf unpacked the trays of food and drinks for everyone, then stood back to survey his handiwork. "Now, are we all set? Have you all got what you ordered?"

From the far side of the table, tucked up between Jasmine and Jake, Patrick giggled and held up a beaker of juice in one hand and a deep-fried breadcrumbed diplodocus in the other.

"Good lad," said Raf with a grin.

Leonora looked up at Raf. "Thank you for this, it's really kind. I can't thank you enough."

Raf beamed. "Not at all. Now get stuck into your lunch before it gets cold."

His mobile rang. He put the receiver to his ear with a sense of both relief and trepidation. "Carol. How are you doing?"

"Hello, Raf. I'm fine . . ." For a few seconds she sounded so very unsure and nervous that his heart sank; maybe this was it after all.

"How's it going?"

"Oh, so-so." She spoke as if feeling her way forward. "Whereabouts are you?"

"We're here in Burbeck already, but as we were a bit early I've taken a table in a nice little pub down in the village — it's packed to the gills with drunks and strange men wearing all manner of dressing-up clothes, so I assume we've got the right place. It's either that or we've come across some strange sect of morris dancers out on a day trip."

Carol laughed. "Certainly sounds like our lot. Is the pub called the Master's Arms?"

Raf glanced down at the menu card on the table. "The very same."

There was a long pause and then Carol said softly, "That's good. It's really nice to hear your voice, Raf. I've missed you."

"I've missed you too," he said tenderly. "Are you OK?" There were a thousand questions in three short words.

"I am now." He heard the tension ebbing out of her voice. "I'll walk down to meet you — I'll be there in five minutes." There was a long, warm pause. "And Raf?" she said, pulling him back from the edge.

"Yes?"

"I love you."

Raf beamed with joy. There was no lie, no fear, no lingering doubt in Carol's voice. He hadn't realised until now just how nervous and tense he had been. Relief washed through him. He didn't need to know the details of how Carol had come to that conclusion; they didn't matter. It was enough that she knew with such certainty. "I'm glad, and you know what?" he said.

Carol giggled. The sound made him grin.

"Tell me," she purred.

"I love you too," he said. "And I can't wait to see you. Be here soon."

As he hung up, across the table Ollie groaned and looked heavenwards. "God, do you two really have to do that?" he groaned. "All that kissy, fussy, lovey-dovey stuff?"

Raf slipped the phone into his top pocket and patted it. "Indeed we do," he said. "There's no point getting older if you can't spend a fair portion of your time making young people feel deeply uncomfortable and cringing with embarrassment."

"All that snuggy stuff makes me sick. It's always the same with you pair," said Ollie, pulling a face.

Raf shook his head and smiled; if only that were true, or he was as certain as Ollie.

Diana was sitting at a table having a drink with Netty and a ginger guy who coincidentally happened to be in there too; he was someone she had completely forgotten about called Peter Fleming, who had been in their year and seemed to remember her and Netty very well. Diana peered across the room, recognising Jake and Ollie at a nearby table about the same time as Carol came into the bar.

Diana was up and on her feet and halfway across the room before she had time to reason out what she was doing or why.

Halfway through a sentence Netty's mouth dropped open. "What the hell . . .?" she began, but Diana was long gone.

"Was it something we said?" asked Peter, watching her progress as Diana elbowed her way through the crowd.

Although Diana didn't know Leonora and Jasmine, it wasn't hard to work out who was who. She looked from face to face and considered what to do next; this was possibly not going to be the easiest set of introductions.

As she watched, Raf got to his feet, Carol took one look at him and broke into a huge grin and stepped forward into his arms. In the space between their eyes meeting and their embracing, Diana worked her way level with their table, Netty and Peter on the other side of the bar watching her open-mouthed.

Carol stepped back to look Raf up and down, not even registering Leonora or Jasmine or the boys.

"It's so good to see you," she said to Raf, her eyes alight with joy.

Diana sighed; maybe it was going to be all right after all.

Raf grinned. "You too, darling one," he said. "I was afraid that maybe you weren't going to make it back."

Carol's eyes filled with tears and Raf folded her into his arms.

At which point Patrick threw out his arms and yelled, "And me and me."

Carol turned, saw Diana, Ollie, Jake and then Patrick, Maisie and Leonora and Jasmine. Her expression registered surprise, but before she could speak, Diana stepped a little closer, offered her hand to Raf and said in a firm and warm voice. "Hi, Carol, hello, Raf, how nice to see you again."

Raf nodded and, after shaking her hand, embraced her. While barely pausing for breath, Diana continued, "And you must be Leonora. We spoke on the phone," and held her hand out across the crowded table.

Leonora smiled. "Oh hi, I'm so pleased to meet you. Thank you for sorting all this out. I don't really know what I would have done without you and Raf."

Carol looked even more bemused. Netty, whose expression suggested she had run out of patience, arrived with Peter Fleming in tow and said, "What is going on?"

Diana's smile held firm. "Carol, Netty. This is Gareth's wife, Leonora Howard."

There was a beat, a moment's unfathomable silence and then Carol appeared to regain her composure, straightened up and held out a hand in greeting. "Delighted to meet you," and then she turned to Jasmine and said, "And you are?"

Jasmine made a peculiar little choking noise in the back of her throat. "I'm Jasmine," she said nervously.

And then Leonora added in a far stronger voice, "Gareth's girlfriend."

Diana saw Carol's expression slip just a fraction.

Netty hissed, "Fucking hell," under her breath, while across the table Jasmine reddened and her eyes filled with tears. Peter Fleming looked from face to face; a long way behind, he hadn't a cat's chance in hell of catching up.

"I didn't know," Jasmine said thickly. "I really didn't. I had no idea. I'm not a home-wrecker or anything. Gareth told me that he was getting a divorce. He said he'd left her."

"It's all right," said Leonora, gently stroking her arm. "I do know that and you know I don't blame you."

"I didn't know," Jasmine said again, looking unhappily from face to face.

Carol looked across at Diana and said in an undertone, "But you did, didn't you?"

Diana nodded. "Yes, but only since Saturday. Would you like a drink?"

"I think I could probably do with one."

"What exactly is going on here?" snapped Netty.

Raf was back on his feet. "Let me get them. What do you want?"

"I'll have a JD and Coke," Carol said hastily.

Raf lifted an eyebrow. "Bit early in the day for you, isn't it?"

Carol waved his surprise away. "Dutch courage. I've got a feeling that it's going to be a long afternoon."

In more ways than one, thought Diana as she guided Carol towards the bar. "And I'll get them," she said briskly to Raf. "You eat your lunch while it's hot."

Diana's fingers closed around her arm; Carol needed no further invitation.

"Well?" she said softly.

"I'm sorry but I couldn't tell you," Diana said in a voice so low it was almost inaudible. "I was so afraid that you might say something to Gareth and you must see that Leonora needs to talk to him. You probably hate me." She paused, trying to gauge Carol's reaction. "I didn't feel as if I had a choice."

Carol sighed, feeling the anger draining away, and glanced back over her shoulder. "No, I don't hate you. God, what a shitty position to be in."

"You're not angry?"

Carol shook her head. "I don't know. Yes, no? I suppose I feel hurt that you didn't feel you could trust me, but I can understand why. I probably would have said something. Gareth is so bloody plausible." She looked up, eyes bright with tears. "I nearly lost everything. Those kids are so sweet. You know that I truly thought he'd left her too?"

Diana nodded. "He did. On Friday afternoon."

Carol stared at her, colour draining. "Oh God. What a total and utter shit that man is. I feel as if I've made a total fool of myself. Does anyone else know about all this?"

Netty, elbowing her way between them, growled, "Well, I don't. Is anyone going to tell me what the hell is going on here or have I got to try and make something up?"

Carol narrowed her eyes and looked back across the crowded bar. "Wasn't that Peter Fleming, the freckle king, over there?"

Netty pulled a face. "You want to make something of it?"

Carol shook her head. "No."

Netty got the point, sniffed and made her way round to the other side of the bar. "I need to know, you know."

330

"We'll tell you all about it later," said Diana over her shoulder, and then to Carol: "Nobody else knows at the moment. I thought it would be better if I kept it to myself."

"You are a saint Di — and a complete cow."

Diana braced herself, wondering if Carol might let rip but instead she smiled. "You did the right thing. I believed him; I thought she was mad and that he was the wounded one. And to be honest, I don't know if I would have told him or not. Tough call for you, though."

Diana nodded. "I know. So how did it go with Gareth?"

Carol laughed. "Actually, it is the most perfect timing. I wouldn't go back with him if he was the last man on earth, although it took me a while to sort it all out in my head. I was very nearly taken in. He's very persuasive."

Diana nodded back towards the table. "And what about Raf?"

Carol's expression widened out into a huge beaming smile. "Gareth made me realise just how bloody lucky I am to have him."

Diana smiled. "I'm really glad. Leonora is going to need a lot of moral support when they meet up."

"Seems to me like they all are."

Diana nodded. "You can say that again; Jasmine's pregnant."

Carol felt her jaw drop, at which point Raf reappeared. "Have you two eaten, only if you haven't you'd be welcome to join us? There's plenty to go around."

Carol shook her head. "I'd love to, sweetheart, but actually we ought to be getting back to the hall. We've got a lunch being cooked there — and we still need to try and find a stand-in for Macduff."

At which point Netty turned round with a drink in her hand and growled, "And I'm hoping that if I get this pair on their own then someone will tell me what the fuck is going on."

At bang on half-past two, Mr Bearman stepped out from between the heavy navy-blue velvet curtains of the stage at Burbeck House and shuffled his notes into order. The house lights dimmed slowly until at last a single spotlight picked him out like a tomcat on a moonlit wall. The hubbub in the hall died away to a low hum and the odd cough, and then at last there was complete silence.

Mr Bearman cleared his throat and then in a deeply theatrical voice he said, "Good afternoon, ladies and gentlemen. We would like to welcome you to Burbeck House, and to this most extraordinary production of Shakespeare's tragedy, *Macbeth*. It is a great privilege and an honour to be here with a play and a cast reunited after twenty years. I think we are all agreed that it has proved a most interesting and, in some ways, life-changing weekend for many of us."

He looked fondly towards the wings and continued, "It has been wonderful to see the young people we taught all those years ago grow into such fine men and women. We would all like to thank Diana Brown for bringing this amazing idea to fruition and for the dedication and fortitude in getting us all together in one place at one time with such amazing good-natured enthusiasm. So, once again, thank you all for coming to watch us. Thanks too to the cast and crew for showing up after all these years — and enough of my ramblings, as Mr Shakespeare said himself in another of his works; 'The play's the thing.'"

And with that there was a flurry of applause and Mr Bearman lifted an arm to indicate the stage as he moved out of the spotlight. Very slowly the curtains opened to reveal the three witches, well-loved wart and all, crouched around a large plastic cauldron on the blasted heath, scripts in hand while from somewhere close by came the sounds of the crew making all manner of wild and windy-day noises. Diana, Netty and Jan cackled maniacally and began to stir the pot.

From the shadows behind the tabs, Carol looked out past her friends into the auditorium. The whole hall was packed, with the exception of the centre of the first row where there were three empty seats marked with cards that said "Reserved". The spaces were as obvious as missing front teeth. Next to the empty seats were Raf, Ollie and Jake. Carol smiled. It was so good to see the three of them; it felt like months since they had said goodbye on Friday.

"'When shall we three meet again?'" asked Diana.

The opening words of the play rolled out into the audience, and Carol felt her heart tighten. It had taken them all so long to find each other again, she hoped that now they had, they wouldn't lose touch again.

While Carol watched, Gareth stepped up behind her, sword in hand, all poised and ready to take his cue. He dropped a hand onto her shoulder, making her jump.

"Where did you get to?" he whispered. "I was looking for you all over the place. I wanted to explain —"

Carol sshed him and pointed to the players.

Out on stage the witches were fading back into the shadows while King Duncan and his entourage strode manfully out into the limelight to announce their most glorious victory over the scurrilous Norwegians.

When Carol wouldn't answer him, Gareth moved closer so that he was speaking almost directly into her ear. He was so close that she could feel the heat of his body and smell his aftershave. She closed her eyes, trying hard to shut him out.

"Are you all right?" he said. "You look pale. Don't tell me that you're nervous?"

Carol glanced up at him. What could she possibly say to him? Where would she begin? In the end she decided to settle for silence and, pressing a finger to her lips, hoped to quieten him and make him think that she was wrapped up in the action on stage. He just grinned.

"Relax, it'll be all right," he purred. "Break a leg."

"I hope you do too," she said, not meeting his gaze.

"About Fiona —" he began, still smiling.

"There's really no need to explain," Carol whispered.

334

"I knew that you'd understand." Gareth sounded relieved. "You know that she is completely bloody crazy, don't you?"

Carol didn't trust herself to speak.

"I mean I'm not saying she is making it all up but she has always had this thing for me. It's just a crush. You know how it is, and I'm only human. She practically threw herself at me last night after the disco finished. I think she'd had a bit too much to drink and I was as horny as hell after being with you."

Carol stared up at him in total amazement, wondering if he really believed what he was saying and if he did, if he really thought it was any sort of excuse.

"We could meet up once the play is over. Have a drink, some dinner. Set the record straight. We need to talk, sort this out if we're going to carry on from here. You know that you're important to me. I'd really like to see you again; we've got so much to catch up on. There's no need for you to rush off home, is there?"

Carol, white hot with indignation, opened her mouth to speak just as Miss Haze signalled Gareth's cue, circumstances conspiring to prevent her from having her say. Carol was so angry that she could have screamed; the arrogant bastard — just who the bloody hell did he think he was?

As Gareth stepped out onto the stage to hear his destiny from the three witches, Carol wondered what it was that had ever made her think that they could rekindle the past. Was it a trick of light or perhaps a longing for things past? Was it what Gareth represented rather than who he was? Was the whole thing not about wanting him, but about recapturing what it was like to be seventeen, with your whole life ahead of you? About being young and naïve and just starting out?

As Gareth listened to his fate being meted out, for the first time since arriving at Burbeck House Carol thought she truly saw him for what he was.

Yes, he was still as handsome and as striking as he had ever been, but now she could also see how cruel and thin his mouth was, how self-absorbed, how very greedy Gareth was. He was a user, a cheat and a liar, and she knew now with a horrible sense of certainty that he had been all those things back then too, it was just that she couldn't see them.

As he passed her, making his exit, Carol shivered and the play moved on. The old king, Duncan, came and went and then Miss Haze nodded to Carol and she pulled her cloak tight round her shoulders and stepped out onto the stage with Macbeth's letter in her hand, waiting for him to come home to her — and let the story carry her away.

"'Glamis thou art, and Cawdor; and shalt be/What thou art promis'd. Yet do I fear thy nature;/It is too full o' th' milk of human kindness . . .'" Her voice trembled just a little as Carol looked out into the audience and at the three empty seats, the irony of the lines not lost on her. Gareth wouldn't recognise the milk of human kindness if he was drowning in it.

A few lines later Gareth reappeared, on stage, excited and triumphant and home from the wars. As he embraced her, Carol closed her eyes tight shut. She didn't really want him to touch her at all. She struggled

336

to stop herself from pushing him away. As long as she stayed in character she would be fine, although she tried very hard to avoid looking him in the eye.

She also knew now with total certainty that once the weekend was over she would never see Gareth Howard again, and more than that, she wouldn't want to. It was all over.

The play moved on around her like an unstoppable river, Macbeth had Banquo murdered and his ghost limped, bloodied and beaten, through the grand dinner staged to celebrate Macbeth's coronation.

When his guests had all left, Macbeth announced to Lady Macbeth that he intended to find out why Macduff hadn't shown up — little knowing that Macduff had already deserted and was heading south to join the army of Duncan's sons, who were marching north to fight him.

The curtains closed at the end of the first half just as Macbeth decided he would go back to talk to the witches again and find out what else fate had in store for him.

As Macbeth exited stage left, Carol smiled thinly; if only he knew.

Adie, a pale and limping Macduff, had struggled manfully through his scenes. In the interval Carol hurried over to see how he was faring, part of the reason being because she wanted to avoid Gareth, who was crowing and jubilant.

"God, that went really well, didn't it?" he said, hugging Banquo on the way down the steps at the back of the stage. "Well done. That was great."

Banquo — white-faced and all gore — clapped him on the back. Gareth was right; it was going brilliantly and the audience were with them every step of the way.

On the far side of the stage Carol hunkered down beside Adie, who hadn't made it as far as the dressing room. "Are you all set for the second half?" Carol asked him anxiously; he was crouched on a chair, sweating; his face had gone an interesting shade of grey. "I could go and get Mr Bearman, put your understudy on early."

He grinned. "Bugger off. No chance, and will you stop fretting, between you I've never been so fussed over in all my life. I've taken enough painkillers to sedate a horse and Mike is going to drive me to casualty as soon as the show is over. I'll be just fine."

"Oh, he made it then?" said Carol. "That's great."

Adie nodded. "Even better, he's brought a crate of champagne with him, which should add a little fizz to our post-production strawberry tea."

"Brilliant," Carol said, and then added more quietly, "have you talked to him about you know what?"

"Uh-huh, and I've also been talking to Netty and Diana, and Raf. Complicated, ain't it? Thank God you had the good sense to keep your hand on your ha'penny."

Carol reddened furiously.

Adie touched her arm. "It's all right. Don't fret about Gareth, it's not your fault that the man is a complete shit. You shouldn't feel bad about something you're not responsible for."

Carol sighed. "Well, in this particular case I do. God, you'd think by the time we got to our age we'd have got all this stuff sorted out, wouldn't you? Trouble is, I don't seem to be any better at it now than I was when I was eighteen. I almost made the most stupid mistake of my life."

Adie grinned. "Are there any other kind?"

"I nearly threw away the best man I've ever known for Gareth."

"Yes, but you didn't. Stop beating yourself up; it's not your fault and what's more, you're helping to put it right," said Adie gently.

Carol shook her head. "No, I'm not. None of this can put it right, it won't mend anything at all, will it? We're just trying to make him know how it feels to be cheated and lied to."

Adie smiled. "Raf's livid."

Carol laughed. "Don't be silly. Raf? You're joking. Raf's really easy going. He never gets angry about anything."

Adie shrugged. "If you say so."

The second half of the production began quietly enough; Carol waited in the wings, aware that very soon things would change. The seats at the front of the hall were still empty, still marked as reserved. Before the curtains opened Mr Bearman got up and explained that because Macduff had sprained his ankle in rehearsals the final fight scene would be understudied by a volunteer while Adie read the lines in over the action.

It seemed to Carol that the play, which until then had appeared to zip along, now slowed to a snail's pace, the words and the actions as thick as treacle.

The second half of the story began with the three witches talking to the goddess Hecate and explaining that Macbeth would be coming back to see them and how they planned to show him magic that would mislead and trick him and because of it Macbeth would bring about his own destruction.

How very true, Carol thought. She watched Diana, Netty and Jan and Gareth hunched around the cauldron. She watched the witches tricking him and persuading him that everything was going to be all right. He came off the stage looking triumphant, thinking that he was invincible. Carol daren't even look at him.

Finally Carol had a sense that they were almost there — they were on the home straight now. Once Lady Macbeth had gone nicely mad trying to clean her hands of Duncan's blood at the end of act five, scene one, Carol slipped off from the stage and crept round into the auditorium, knowing that a roadie would have a ball with her death scream. Easing off her cloak and crown, she tiptoed to take up one of the reserved front seats, under cover of a troop of soldiers entering stage left, heading to join the army mustering against Macbeth.

She watched as Macbeth, increasingly distraught, waited to take on Duncan's sons in battle.

It was astonishing; Gareth was giving the most brilliant performance as the crazed, increasingly obsessed king. Carol could feel the tension building in the hall and wondered how much of it was her imagination. The audience were totally absorbed. Safe in her seat, Carol could see other people moving quietly into the aisle and took a deep breath. From off stage came the sounds of the approaching army and then Duncan's sons made their entrance to the sound of a beating drum and the swirl of the pipes. Mr Bearman had staged it so that the main body of the army marched in from the back of the hall, down the aisles, and every man who could be mustered from the crew and cast was there. Amongst the royal party were the limping Macduff and his Gaelic understudy Mr Rafael O'Connell, dressed in matching cloaks and both carrying swords.

Raf looked the part; it had been good of him to volunteer and give up his lunch to come back to the hall and learn Adie's moves. Carol could feel her heart tighten as they moved closer. As they and a rabble of supporters made their way up onto the stage, Leonora and Jasmine, carrying Patrick and baby Maisie, made their way from the aisle into the remaining front seats.

Carol caught hold of Leonora's hand as she passed and gave it a squeeze, and then did the same to Jasmine. Leonora smiled grimly, Jasmine's face was unmoving, tight with tears and tension.

Macbeth's servants raised banners to show their defiance and then, at long last, Macbeth stepped forward, made his way to the edge of the stage and looked out towards his destiny — in theory the woods of Dunsinane — creeping slowly, inexorably towards his castle. There was a dramatic hush.

At first, Gareth's sight line was high, focused on the far horizon as if he was looking at a distant hillside. Deep in character, he didn't even look at the faces of the people in the auditorium. In the front row Carol held her breath and waited, wondering at what point he would notice them, wondering if by some terrible stroke of fate he might not notice them at all.

"Daddy," said a little voice, high and excited and warm with recognition, the sound filling the long and expectant silence. There was a little flurry of laughter from the audience, breaking the tension in the play but adding to the real-life drama that was unfolding. For a split second Carol saw Gareth falter. Falter and grow pale. As part of the performance of a king faced with the fulfilment of a prophecy it was perfect. He looked down very slowly into the faces of those people seated in the front row. Carol, Leonora and Jasmine all in a line, with the children on their laps.

Carol was so close that she could see the shock register on Gareth's features, saw him suck in a breath, saw him stop dead in his tracks as his gaze moved slowly along the row. The three women all looked up at him, defiantly, not one of them afraid to meet his cheating eyes.

Carol did wonder for a moment if Gareth would lose it totally. Instead, he let the words from the play catch in his throat, used the emotion to lift the speech to something incredibly heart-rending and extraordinary, though it was impossible to work out whether the effect was deliberate or purely accidental.

And then he picked up his sword and shield, and, turning his back to the three of them, marched out on to the battlefield, to meet Duncan's sons and Macduff. Over the scene's shifting came the sound of a drum roll; or perhaps, Carol thought, it was the sound of her heart beating.

Outside the castle walls Macbeth strode across the field to kill another of Malcolm's courtiers and as he said the lines Gareth's eyes didn't flicker, didn't lift, didn't for one moment roam back to the front row.

And then at last Adie, dressed as Macduff strode on, flanked not just by Raf, dressed in an identical outfit, conjured up by Diana from the props box, but also, by some stroke of improvised directorial genius, the three witches, Diana, Netty, and Jan, all carrying swords and quarterstaves. It seemed to Carol as if the fates had come out to meet him.

This time Gareth did hesitate, and made as if to step back towards the safety of the wings, his face white with horror. It was clear by his expression that he knew that they all knew exactly what was going on.

Raf lifted his sword and stepped forward from the ranks.

"Who the hell are you?" Gareth hissed, in an undertone that was audible in the rapt silence.

Raf smiled darkly, bracing himself for the fight. "Macduff," he said icily, and then in a voice barely above a whisper added, "Carol's boyfriend and Leonora and Jasmine's chauffeur."

If anyone had noticed the deviation from the script nobody said a single word. In fact, if anything, the tension ratcheted up a notch or two. Gareth paled and tried to move away from Raf, only to find his path blocked by the three witches.

From the side of the stage, in a low voice full of menace, Adie — picked out in a single spotlight, book in hand, read, " 'Turn, hell-hound, turn.' "

Gareth looked from face to face, but if he was expecting compassion or support from any of the people on stage, he was looking in the wrong place.

" 'Of all men else I have avoided thee,' " he began slowly, reading from his script.

Raf smiled thinly, his eyes narrowing as he sized Gareth up, and for the first time Carol realised that Adie might be right, maybe Raf really was livid.

Slowly the two men circled each other, carefully working their way through the moves that Gareth and Adie had rehearsed, but this time it felt very different. There was a real tension to it, a real sense of potential threat. Carol realised with a start that she was sitting on the edge of her seat and was holding her breath.

Raf's eyes were locked on Gareth's. As they reached the lines, "Lay on, Macduff; / And damn'd be him that first cries 'Hold, enough!' " instead of thrusting forward as had been planned, Gareth suddenly swung his sword like a scythe, trying to knock Raf off balance. In the wings Malcolm's army were waiting to come on to mask Macbeth's defeat and beheading but instead Gareth swung again, this time in earnest.

Raf looked at him in surprise and then grinned. "You bastard," he said. "You're really trying to hurt me, aren't you?" There was a hint of amazement and amusement in his voice as if he couldn't quite believe it. Gareth took another vicious swing, which Raf side-stepped, then stepped forward, grabbed tight hold of Gareth's sword blade and, jerking him within range, dropped his own sword, drew back his fist and hit Gareth squarely on the chin. One punch.

For an instant Gareth looked bemused, and then he swayed and then with an ugly gasp crumpled at the knees and fell to the floor, just as Malcolm's triumphant army decided enough was enough and marched on to the stage, accompanied by a great recorded swirl of pipes.

The next few moments, as far as Carol was concerned, were a complete blur. She hurried out of her seat and back onto the stage to take a bow, although the final curtain call was remarkable in that Macbeth, half conscious and bleeding from the nose and mouth, took his bow supported on either side by the two incarnations of a triumphant Macduff. To his left Fiona, a.k.a. Lady Macduff, was trying desperately to find out what the hell was going on and interspersed highly professional bowing and waving with anxious enquiring frowns.

As the applause faded Mr Bearman stepped to the front to say a few final words and Diana was hauled out from between the curtains to be presented with a huge bouquet of flowers, and while all this was happening, Fiona was hissing, "What is going on? Will somebody please tell me?" to anyone who would listen, while centre stage Gareth swayed and bled and tried hard to focus.

The curtains opened one more time; the cast took a final bow and then at last the applause died away, the curtains closed and there was the sound of people getting up and shuffling out of their seats.

A traditional strawberry tea was scheduled to take place in the dining room — a time for family and friends to mingle with the cast and crew and to which everyone was cordially invited, was what it said in the programme.

Carol looked up at Raf; he grinned. "I thought you were magnificent, my lady," he said, with a sweeping bow.

"You too," she replied. "I had no idea you had got it in you."

Raf shrugged, looking a little sheepish and self-effacing.

"Come on, you have to admit that Gareth had it coming," said Netty as she passed by, hand in hand with Peter Fleming.

Carol slipped her arm through Raf's. "I love you," she said.

Raf nodded. "I'm glad. For a while there I thought that I'd lost you. It wasn't a good feeling."

Carol's eyes filled up with tears. "I'm so sorry. I don't deserve you."

He nodded. "No, you're right, you don't — but I've got nothing better planned at the moment," he said, eyes alight with mischief.

CHAPTER
FOURTEEN

Leonora and Jasmine had run Gareth to ground in the dining room, and had got him cornered when Carol and Raf arrived. Still a little confused and bloodied, he stood open-mouthed, his eyes moving backwards and forwards between the two women as if he couldn't quite get his head round how it was that they had found him, or, come to that, found each other, and what the hell he was going to do next now that they had? He blinked over and over again as if there was some possibility that they might be a trick of the light. Over at one of the tables Ollie and Jake were busy playing peeka-boo with Patrick and Maisie.

"We need to talk about all this," said Leonora firmly.

"OK, OK, I can understand that," said Gareth, holding his hands up in a show of surrender. "But surely this isn't really the time or the place." He was still looking very pale and a little unsteady from his encounter with Macduff's alter ego. "Couldn't we go outside?" Carol noticed that he had stemmed his bleeding nose with a pile of paper serviettes but it looked as if he might end up with a black eye. "We don't want to air our dirty linen in public, do we, darling?"

Leonora glared at him; it was painfully obvious that she was in no mood to back down, and a million miles away from being placated by casual terms of endearment.

"Don't we? Why on earth not?" she said in a low menacing voice. "Here seems to be as good as anywhere else, as far as I'm concerned. God alone knows where you'll scuttle off to once today is over. And besides, I haven't done anything that I'm not prepared to talk about in public, Gareth. Let's be straight about this. I'm not the one who walked out on his wife and kids and it's not me that's a total and utter two-timing cheating little arsehole."

Carol nodded; she couldn't have put it better herself.

Gareth winced as if Leonora had hit him and then, struggling to regain his composure, said in a conciliatory tone, "You're upset, I can understand that. And you don't really believe those things, Leonora. I know you don't. I'll come home, and we can talk it through, sort things out. To be perfectly honest, I can't believe you came here at all. It's hardly dignified." He looked around as if to check out who was watching them, although he was careful not to catch Carol's eye. "You know that you're making a spectacle of yourself, don't you?" Leonora's jaw dropped while Gareth continued, "Mind you, I suppose I ought to have guessed you'd pull a stunt like this. It's just like you to want to make a scene; you always did enjoy a sense of the melodramatic." He laughed grimly and looked up, addressing no one in particular in a jokey laddish tone, although Jasmine was hanging on his every word. "I've got no idea what she's told you or why but I'll lay money it's all high-octane stuff, highly emotive stuff." And then to Leonora: "And why on earth did you bring them?" He waved towards Patrick and Maisie, who were busy giggling and cooing with Carol's boys. "It'll scar them, you know, your attitude — is that really what you want your children to think of me — that their father is an arsehole? If it hadn't been for the two of them things could have been so different between us. You know that, don't you? You drove me to this. There was no place for me, nothing left." He paused as if struggling to hold back tears. "I'm depressed. I know it's not very mature but I feel left out. You just don't have any time for me any more, Leonora. No time for us as a couple." He sniffed miserably, swinging between appeal and accusation.

Carol was amazed. Gareth's passionate little speech was a masterly scattergun exercise in blame, fault and excuses.

Leonora's face flared scarlet. "Really?" she said, voice dripping with venom. "So you're saying what, Gareth? That I'm a hysteric and that all this is really my fault? You didn't give me any reason to believe that you would be coming back to discuss anything, in fact quite the reverse — and everything I've found out since you left convinced me that you had gone for good."

He nodded, looking all hangdog and hard done by. "Oh, that's it, pile it on, why don't you? High drama. Make it into a big scene. It's always me, me, me with you, isn't it, Leonora? Can't you see that it's been really difficult for me these last few years? I feel totally marginalised, left out. Pressured. Useless. Depressed."

Close by, Jasmine sniffed; Carol thought she looked as if she was torn between heartbreak and fury, but still she stood her ground, wringing the neck of a napkin held tight between her hands.

Leonora's voice was stony when she spoke. "And how exactly were you planning to deal with all this pressure and depression then, Gareth?"

He looked up at her expectantly. "I was going to go and see the doctor. I need help," he said. He tried out a tiny fragile smile on her but Leonora was not so easily swayed. "I appreciate that it can't have been easy for you either but surely there has to be some way that we can work our way through this."

Leonora leaned a little closer so there was no chance he would miss what she was saying. He followed suit and leaned closer too.

"If any of that were true, Gareth, then you're right, we could probably work it out — but it isn't true, is it? Not one single bloody word of it. There's no way back from this and, whichever way you look at it, that's most definitely down to you."

He looked at her quizzically but she hadn't quite finished.

"And the reason that there is no way back, in case you are in the slightest doubt, is because what you did, when things were supposedly going bad because of the children, was go out and get someone else knocked up." She spoke slowly, enunciating every word. "The same man who blamed me for ruining his entire life by

350

having children that weren't planned or wanted, went out and did the same thing all over again."

Gareth's colour drained away. "You know about that?" he said in amazement, looking from face to face of the two women. He swung round and glared at Jasmine. "You told her? I told you not to say anything to anyone," he said to Jasmine.

Jasmine glared at him. "You are a total shit," she snarled. "I wish I'd never clapped eyes on you."

Meanwhile, Leonora shook her head in disbelief. "You amaze me, Gareth. What on earth do you think we talked about, for God's sake? The weather? The price of bloody fish? Of course I know about the baby. God, you make me totally and utterly sick, you really do. We talked about a lot of things — like how you told Jasmine I was crazy and tried to make it sound as if the children weren't even yours. You're despicable."

Alongside Leonora, Jasmine swallowed back a great flood of tears. "How could you do this?" she said, her high-pitched voice close to breaking and so poignant that Carol was tempted to go over and punch Gareth herself. "You knew exactly what you were doing all along. You tricked me and you tricked Leonora too. I don't know how you can live with yourself. I thought that you really loved me. I can't believe that you lied to me. I hate you," she sobbed, no longer able to hold back the tears. "The special thing I thought we had — it was just all lies, wasn't it?"

Carol's eyes filled with tears too; Leonora looked magnificent, pale and angry, statuesque and totally in control of herself, while Jasmine, in her overstretched crop top and pedal pushers, hair scraped back off her milk-pale face, looked about twelve. Carol's heart ached for the two of them but she also knew without a shadow of a doubt that she had had a lucky escape.

Gareth said nothing, but then again what was there that he could possibly say? Before he had the chance to gather his thoughts or muster any kind of defence, Fiona appeared in the mêlée, elbowing her way in through the crowd of family and friends who were gathered around the tea tables and the urn, all post-performance smiles, warmth and excitement.

"Hello," she purred, waving a hand in greeting. Fiona was still in her cloak and was flanked by an elderly woman in a large pink hat and summer suit, both of which looked a little the worse for wear, and a small grumpy-looking man wearing a flat cap and sports jacket.

"Gareth, darling," she cooed. "You were absolutely wonderful. Everyone's saying we really ought to do another performance. I thought you'd like to see Mummy again. I've told her all about you, and this is Uncle Harry, Mummy's friend. Mummy, you remember Gareth, don't you? We used to be at school together? He came round for tea once." And then as an aside to Gareth, "I've told her that you were very keen on me . . ." Fiona giggled. "You know, Mummy is always saying that it's high time that I found myself a good man and settled down."

Carol stared at Fiona; she sounded like something out of a 1950s Doris Day film, not to mention being way off target in her choice of men.

352

"What about last night, the storeroom —" Carol began, quite unable to stop herself.

Fiona looked down her nose at Carol. "Jealousy is the most dreadful thing, although quite understandable in someone like you, obviously. But we're bigger than that, aren't we, Gareth?" She peered up at him adoringly.

At least Gareth had the decency to blush.

"What?" gasped Carol in astonishment.

"I don't think we need to dwell on the sordid details of your little assignation, do we? We've put all that behind us, haven't we, Gareth?"

Fiona fluttered her eyelashes in what she presumably thought was an appealing way and then, appearing to see the rest of the group for the first time, looked at Leonora and Jasmine in some theatrical show of surprise.

"Hello," she said coolly and then, sliding her arm through his, said to Gareth, "would you like to introduce me to your friends?"

Gareth's face was a picture. There followed a long and painful silence. Finally Carol, smiling, stepped into the breach and with an open hand moved slowly around the group. "Fiona, I don't think you've met Gareth's wife, have you? Leonora, this is Fiona. And this is Gareth's girlfriend, Jasmine — oh, and over there are his children — that's Patrick and baby Maisie."

There was a deathly hush. Fiona's colour drained. "What?" she hissed, rounding on Carol. "What do you mean *Gareth's wife*? You don't give up, do you? You

353

really are a complete bitch. You're making this up, aren't you?"

Carol's smile held firm. "Would you like me to run through them again?"

Fiona frowned and, turning back to Gareth, snapped, "What exactly is going on here? I don't understand. I thought you told me that you were divorced?" She paused for an instant; still Gareth said nothing. "Well?"

The silence thickened, everyone waited. Fiona's eyes narrowed. "Gareth, I really think you owe me some kind of explanation, don't you? You told me that you wanted to start a new life with me — you said you wanted to get a spaniel and everything. You told me that we would be a real family." Her voice was steadily growing louder and louder. "Tell me what all this is about," she demanded. "I want to know *now*."

If Gareth had hoped to keep the situation to himself, Fiona's arrival had blown that possibility right out of the water. As the volume increased people were turning to look at them. "You told me that you had always loved me," Fiona growled, her fists clenched, her face contorted with fury.

Gareth opened his mouth as if to speak but still no words came out.

Leonora took up the baton on his behalf. "It's amazing, isn't it? Is that what he told you?" she said evenly. "You know, you should be very careful what you believe, although it's taken me a little while to realise it. I'd got no idea what Gareth was like. All these years and I genuinely hadn't got a clue. He's treated me like

354

dirt, made me feel guilty, undermined my confidence, bullied me, spent all my money, and left me with a pile of debts, having unsuccessfully, and it has to be said fraudulently, tried to borrow money against my house. Actually —" Leonora paused, took a deep breath and then smiled beatifically — "if you want him then you're more than welcome to him, Fiona. It is Fiona, isn't it?"

And with this Leonora turned on her heel and, trailed by Jasmine, headed out through the French windows into the garden. Gareth watched them go open-mouthed. Fiona was practically magenta with outrage.

"Leonora?" he called after her. "Wait, wait, please come back. We can sort this out. I know we can, sweetheart. There's been a mistake. A dreadful mistake." But it seemed as if Fiona had taken Leonora at her word and, holding tight to Gareth's arm, held fast while her mother and uncle closed in around him like hounds around a wounded animal.

"So, tell me again, Gareth, what it is that you do exactly?" Fiona's mother asked loudly. Beneath her enormous pink hat with an ostrich feather, she wore coral-pink lipstick and had eyebrows that appeared to have been drawn on with a bright orange wax crayon.

Gareth looked down at her with an expression of bemused horror. It was difficult to work out whether she was deaf, drunk, mad or some unsettling combination of all three.

"Fiona was telling me that you do something in computers," snapped Uncle Harry. "Lot of money in that, is there? Don't understand them myself, but my niece has one."

"What did you say that you do?" repeated Fiona's mother.

Gasping for breath, Gareth tried desperately to shake himself loose, but Fiona was having none of it. "Gareth," she snapped petulantly, "Mummy was asking you a question."

Diana, tidying things away in the wings, looked around the empty stage and smiled. The weekend had gone far better than she could have possibly hoped for — and in some ways far worse. One thing, it had made her realise that she didn't want to lose contact with her friends again.

"Well done, old thing," said a familiar voice.

Diana swung round to see Hedley was striding down the aisle towards her. "I'm afraid I didn't catch it all but I didn't want to miss your golden moment."

Diana beamed. "Oh, Hedley, it's so good to see you. But what about evensong?"

"Got Godfrey Fielding in to cover for me. How did it go?"

"Like a dream," she said, clambering down off the stage. Diana didn't add that some parts had been closer to a nightmare.

Hedley leaned forward and kissed her. "Missed you," he said. "The place isn't the same without you about."

Diana laughed. "You mean you couldn't find anything?"

He pulled a face. "I didn't say that but now you come to mention it, do you know where my gardening hat is?"

"Hedley," she said, pretending to be cross.

Hedley shrugged. "I know, I know — is there any chance of a cup of tea, only I'm parched?"

Diana nodded. "There certainly is. Come with me and meet the rest of the gang. Did you bring Dylan with you?"

"No, I thought it would be nice to have some time to ourselves — I've left him in charge of catering and cat control."

Slipping her arm through his, Diana led him off towards the dining room. "So do you know where my gardening hat is?" he said.

On the other side of the dining room George Bearman lovingly refilled Callista Haze's teacup and offered her another chocolate éclair. "Well, my dear, all in all it has been a rather interesting weekend, wouldn't you say?" he asked.

Callista smiled. "It has been good, hasn't it? I thought that the play went really well, although I'm not sure what happened at the end exactly. Who was that Irish chap who punched Gareth Howard?"

George Bearman laughed. "God alone knows. Just a bit of high spirits, I think," he said. "But no harm done. I thought it went down rather well, actually." And then he caught hold of her hand. "You know, I hadn't realised just how much I'd missed you. It's been damned good to see you again, Callista." His fingers tightened a little. "Damned good."

Very gently Callista slipped her hand out of his. "Yes, it has. You will be all right, won't you, George? I mean *you will be, won't you?*" she asked.

George nodded. "Yes, of course. I'll be fine." He paused. "I was wondering; is there any chance that I might see you again?"

Callista smiled, choosing to be a little oblique and deliberately misunderstand. "Who knows? But, George, one thing — whatever else you do, don't waste any more time waiting for me. Grab hold of life, don't pine for any more might-have-beens or fantasies. It's time to get on with whatever you want to do and make use of whatever time you've got left."

He took a bite of a buttered scone. "Sounds a little bit morbid."

Callista laughed. "I don't think so. For me, being aware that we don't live for ever has been the greatest spur of all. It's one of the benefits of getting older. Get on with the things you've dreamed of doing now, before it's too late — better to try and fail than never to have tried at all."

"Very inspirational," George laughed, "but I do know that you're right. I've wasted so many years. There is a rather attractive woman who works in our local building society, who has been giving me the eye for months. Maybe I'll ask if she'd like to join me for a spot of lunch. And I've always fancied travelling more, but Judy was never a very keen flyer — besides, I never wanted to go with her and I doubt now looking back that I would have been ideal company."

"There you are then. Chasing women and travelling. That sounds like a jolly good start to me," Callista said warmly.

George lifted his teacup in a toast. "I'll drink to that."

Outside, away from the babble of voices, under the shade of a chestnut tree, Diana and Hedley, Jan, Adie and his partner Mike, Netty and Peter Fleming, Leonora and Jasmine sat with Carol and Raf, Ollie, Jake, Patrick and Maisie, watching the world go by and eating their strawberries and sipping champagne. No one said anything.

Out on the lake ducks dabbled and paddled and bickered in water that reflected the cerulean sky. No one could wave a magic wand and put things right for Leonora or Jasmine, but at least they had had the satisfaction of seeing Gareth's face when he realised that the game was up. And, of course, there was always Fiona.

The late afternoon air was still and heavy, fragrant with the perfume of hot clipped lawn and warm gravel; it was a perfect summer's day. On the grass Raf lay flat out, eyes closed, with his head in Carol's lap. She stroked his hair, totally at peace with the world.

"You know I've been thinking. This would be a great place for a wedding," said Raf suddenly, rolling over onto his belly. "What do you think? It would be fantastic. Out here in the grounds. Under these trees, down by the lake. Could we book the place for a whole weekend, Diana, or do you have to be something to do with the Church?"

Diana looked up in surprise. "No, I don't think so, do you, Hedley? And I'm sure Hedley wouldn't mind officiating, would you?"

Hedley lifted eyebrows the size of baby walruses. "I'd be delighted," he said.

"I could find out for you, if you like," said Diana. "The food here is wonderful. I'm sure they'd do the reception as well if you wanted them to."

"Well, there we are then," said Raf triumphantly. "What more could a person want?"

Carol didn't ask him what the hell he was on about, but then you didn't have to be a rocket scientist to work it out.

"Can we all come? You could book Teddy Towers for the bridal suite as well, if you like," said Adie. "All those bunk beds to romp about on. I'm going to miss sleeping with this lot."

Raf looked up at Carol with a grin. "So how about it then?"

Carol pulled a face. "So how about what?" she asked, being deliberately obtuse.

"Oh, come off it. Getting married. You and me. How about it?

"Oh right, well, that's very romantic, isn't it? Very Hugh Grant," growled Netty from behind a rising pall of cigarette smoke. "'How about it?' They don't write them like that any more. I thought you Celts were famous for your way with words."

360

Carol looked down at Raf and shrugged, although her eyes were alight with mischief. "Maybe. I don't know. I'll think about it," she said casually.

Raf looked delighted. "Do you really mean it? Will you really?"

Netty slapped her forehead. "Oh please, what are you people like? For fuck's sake, Carol, put us all out of our misery. Say yes or no. What sort of answer is maybe?"

Carol raised her eyebrows but before she could say anything, Raf jumped in. "For God's sake, don't knock it, Netty. At least it's a step in the right direction," he said cheerfully. "The last time I asked her she told me to bugger off."